Let's put
the future
behind us

Also by Jack Womack

Ambient

Terraplane

Heathern

Elvissey

Random Acts of Senseless Violence

Let's put the future behind us

jack womack

grove press
new york

Published simultaneously in Canada
Printed in the United States of America
FIRST PAPERBACK EDITION

The Library of Congress has cataloged the hardcover edition as follows:
Womack, Jack.
      Let's put the future behind us / Jack Womack. — 1st ed.
          p.   cm.
      1. Businessmen—Russia (Federation)—Moscow—Fiction.   I. Title.
PS3573.0575L48   1996
813'.54—dc.20   95-43552
      ISBN 0-8021-3503-X (pbk.)

Grove Press
841 Broadway
New York, NY 10003

10 9 8 7 6 5 4 3 2 1

FOR JANE,
who understands me

The tree of liberty must be refreshed

from time to time with . . . blood.

—Thomas Jefferson

—Thomas Jefferson

I

L et me tell you about life in our new Russia. More to the point, let me tell you about death.

You may not believe that sometimes it is more trouble to die in my country than to live, but that is the situation. On those soul-wrenching occasions when my friends suffer losses and desire that their departed be made one with the ground before crows have time to pick the bones white, they seek my assistance. My friends imagine me to be the master of bureaucrats, and, true, often I can compel those devils into fulfilling my personal plans. But this necessitates descending into their abyss while remaining un-muddied by their touch—not an amateur's task, or even one for those adept at time-honored methods of conniving. That is why in their mourning my friends ask me to tangle with moldy uphold-ers of the state. My twenty-five years' experience in the party does not go for naught.

(Of course most of us with such experience have found, in these late days, that our talents are applicable in an unexpected wealth of fields.)

Some time ago I helped my friend Yury Slavkin bury his father, who in an exuberant mood four days ago attempted to climb atop a bus while it moved down Prospekt Mir. Yury asked if I could help. "Yury Ilyich," I assured him, "I will handle everything."

"Will it be done as I wish?"

"It will be done."

"Thank you, Max."

Ah, yes, my name: Maxim Alexeich Borodin. But please, call me Max. My friends call me Max. I have many friends.

"He is to be buried or cremated?" I asked Yury.

"Which is cheaper?"

"Cremation, certainly."

"That will be fine."

It pleased me to hear this. Both are hard, burial is harder. The first funeral for which I provided assistance was my brother-in-law's.

It took three days and thousands of rubles to get his corpse to the cemetery. Then the gravediggers swore that an enormous stone prevented interment. "A very large boulder, but very dark. Hard to see from here," they told me as we stood peering down from the lip of the grave into blackness. "It can't be moved?" I asked. One lout shook his head. The other announced that perhaps with superhuman effort the rock could be shifted a few essential centimeters. I handed them five hundred rubles—so reasonable now, so outrageous then!—and, remarkably, the boulder disappeared. "Perhaps it sank deeper into the soft ground," they had explained, taking up their shovels and humming sorrowful dirges to themselves, in keeping with the somber mood of the ceremony.

"How much will it cost?" Yury asked that day.

"Let me settle accounts directly. We will work out these minor arrangements later."

"You are my good friend, Max."

I smiled.

The next morning I left my fine apartment off Tverskaya Street and went outside. There I met my young friend Sasha, who lives in my building. For evening deliveries, I entrust my missions to more worldly messengers, but for daytime excursions a boy will do. "How's your mother?" I asked, giving him the twenty-dollar bill he required for his services. He wrapped it around a thick roll of candy wrappers—rubles, that is to say—and hastily shoved his wealth into his already-stuffed pocket.

"Quiet."

"Excellent," I said, handing him the envelope I needed him to deliver. "See Vladislav as always."

He ran to the street. Sasha's mother was once a censor at *Vremya*, but her position has since been eliminated. My wife, Tanya, tells me she now watches Mexican novellas and *Twin Peaks* on TV all day while drinking. I believe his father, who was previously in the Ministry of Defense, is at present traveling between Vienna and Berlin, offering for sale bottles of a substance he professes to be red mercury to agents of countries whose names seem little more than the excreta of a romantic imagination. Sasha has not gone to school for over a year. He is too busy learning the techniques of businessmen. His nine-millimeter Beretta is always clean and freshly oiled. Sasha tells me his young friends call him Rambo, but I prefer not to taint his soul with grandiose notions and so call him Sashenka, as I have always done.

I drove my Mercedes to First City Hospital, where Yury waited, rubbing his hands together to warm them. He stood near a row of kiosks huddled together like thieves. On the side of one kiosk a lover of Bulgakov had copied the statement of Woland: WE'LL OPEN A WOMEN'S SHOP. The proprietors sold all manner of *poshlaia*—that is to say, the lint that collects in society's navel: stale candy bars, flasks of cheap perfume, astrological medallions wrought of metal resembling pewter, stuffed bears with dead eyes, flat beer, Estonian pornography, liquid soap in bottles stickered with Donald Duck labels, and stacks of blank tape. Every stall had customers queueing up to make transactions, though most walked away only with vodka or cigarettes. There were many loiterers close by who would have spent money freely, if they had money, and others, more hard-bitten, who undoubtedly wished for a torch with which to set all capitalists alight. So many ingrates fail to appreciate the buffet of opportunities history has set before them in these miraculous days. If they opened their eyes, they would see that our Russia is the land of opportunity.

After parking and locking my car I removed the windshield wipers, the side-view mirrors, and the hood ornament and stored them in the trunk, out of reach of passing hooligans. I crossed the

street to meet Yury. There was no underpass; it took me many
minutes before I could move safely against the flow of traffic. It
seems everyone in Moscow with a car spends all day driving back
and forth around the Garden Ring so that they cannot stop long
enough to have their car stolen.

Flying faster than the traffic when I finally made my run,
I nearly collided with an old grandmother as I reached the opposite curb. She stood before the kiosks, shouting at their proprietors. "Go sell your Snickers elsewhere!" She raised a knotted fist.
"Wreckers! Malefactors!" Granny wore wrapped around her neck
a length of hairy wool upon which she had pinned a portrait of
Stalin. His demon eyes and cockroach whiskers are everywhere
again, for the faithful never lose hope in their messiahs. I remember
being taken by my parents to see the Great Father, the Generalissimo, the Administrator of Abrupt Truths in his coffin, enjoying
undeserved peace. Even in my small boy's innocence I thought it a
good thing that he was there.

Be assured that I am no idolizer of an idyllic past; yet to
revel in nostalgia while recalling pleasurable moments sometimes
does the most rational heart good. Would that all little Stalins in
our country lie so still.

Yury and I embraced. His face was gray with cold and sorrow. "I'm sorry for my lateness," I told him. "The traffic."

"Corrupters of our people!" the old woman shouted, popping
up behind us as she circled one of the kiosks. "Jews! Americans!"

"Go hang yourself, grandma," the entrepreneur shouted
back. "Feed your dogs!" She tottered off, hunching her shoulders
and muttering.

"Will the funeral be possible?" Yury asked. "Everyone is
ready to go to the cemetery, once I call."

"You have your documents ready?"

He handed me a thick sheaf. I perused them quickly, assuring myself that he had filled in what needed filling and obtained
stamps for what needed stamping. Even today, especially today,
there is nothing so essential in Russia as documents; they are as
precious as dollars, and some are worth even more. Had Yury required papers of a less specialized nature, I could have had my
staff produce what he needed, but the documents that command

the admiration of funerary bureaucrats are not the ones my company is best at turning out.

"Let us go, then, and face the hydra," I said to Yury, and we walked toward the entrance, passing an old man being carried in on a stretcher by two thuggish bearers. Hearing a groan and a thud, we looked behind us. Possibly the attendants had glimpsed something in a kiosk that drew their attention and misstepped. Maybe they were just drunk and lost their grip on the handles. Whatever happened, the old man lay on the concrete, holding his side. They shoved his carcass back onto the stretcher and tried to calm him down.

"It happens," they told him.

To enter First City Hospital is to suspect that one has entered a circle of Dante's hell about which the poet neglected to write, not for the horrors' being so indescribable but for their being so banal. In our world, one expects Satan to be nothing more than a thick-necked oaf overseeing the production of rivets in a distant oblast.

"You've had diphtheria shots?" I asked Yury as we walked by several small, wizened girls sitting on the floor, clutching at our trouser legs as we passed.

"This week my clinic has needles but no vaccine. Last week, no needles."

"Don't worry. I will arrange for you to be taken care of at my clinic."

Hundreds of sufferers sat in the gloomy rooms, sneezing and coughing and spraying their fluids like showers of rain. Some of the afflicted held lengths of sausage, hoping to trade them for medical care. Orderlies carried sheets that were no less gray for having possibly once been washed. Hospital workers pasted up signs proclaiming that warm socks would be given out to those willing to donate blood. People who brought more personal samples in coffee jars and vodka bottles sat waiting to have them tested. Members of the formerly cultivated classes stretched out on the floor, taking their naps on the only bed to which they had access. Nothing about the facility resembled the Kremlin Hospital, certainly, which remains in service to treat our bigwigs when they fall prey to dyspeptic attack, gonorrhea, or discover after long benders that the green snake has entwined itself around them. But who is to argue with that? Without the persistent and devoted efforts of our leaders, how might the medical care of the people one day be made thrice more magnificent than it is at present?

My God! Forgive such outbursts. Rhetoric comes as easily as breathing, still.

We reached our destination. On the door of the Pathology Department was this sign, hastily scrawled in purple marker:

CORPSES AVAILABLE ONLY ON RECEIPT OF
DEATH CERTIFICATE AND RESIDENCE PERMIT

We walked into the grim quarters and I confronted the young woman who lazed behind her desk, perusing an astrological guide. "I wish to see the Director regarding the approval of the burial of my friend's father," I told her. "Where is her office?"

"You're in the wrong place," she said, devoting her full attention once more to the procession of planets through her house.

"This is the Pathology Department?" She nodded, slowly, as if trying to remember. "Then where is the Director of the department?"

"I haven't time to be bothered with your questions," she said. Such stalling by those appointed to assist the people is easily dealt with. I drew my hand from my pocket, and a ten-dollar bill fluttered featherlike onto her desk. Her eyes moistened at the sight.

"If you could answer one question," I said, watching as she quickly cleared the surface of her work space.

"Ask."

"Where may I find the Director of this department?"

"Office Forty-two," she said. "Down the hall and on the right. I wouldn't be surprised if she refused to see you."

"I'll treasure your words," I said, and, grasping Yury's arm, dragged him along with me. We trod unwashed floors carpeted with dust. Lining the corridors were numberless beds upon which the stricken lay, awaiting the attentions of doctors who were busy elsewhere. Some few of the suffering heartened as they noticed us, perhaps in their delirium imagining that we were en route to relieve their misery. Most knew better and watched us walk by.

When we reached Office 42 I knocked, at the same time entering before defenders within could have a chance to lock the door against us. The Director's secretary was nowhere to be seen.

The Director of the Pathology Department, a barrel of a woman who would have resembled Beria, had Beria worn flowered dresses, sat chatting on one of her three telephones. In Russia, as in the Soviet Union—some difference!—a bureaucrat's status can at once be gleaned by the number of telephones on the desk, and so I knew immediately that she was not as important as she wished the world to think. In my long experience, the official who rebuffed me most effectively had been a cadaverous shadow in the Ministry of Agriculture who had fourteen telephones. Fewer than half were connected, but that made no difference.

The Director was relating a series of bad jokes to her communicant. I rapped my ring against her desk so she could no longer pretend to not notice us. On the wall behind her still hung a portrait of Lenin. Inferring therefrom that she might prove difficult, I steeled myself. A rayon banner tacked up beneath the portrait proclaimed that her department had won first prize for Socialist Competition. I hesitated to wonder what the criteria might have been.

At last she finished her conversation. "Why are you here?" she asked us.

"We need you to approve a corpse for burial," I said, handing her Yury's documents. "The funeral is scheduled for this afternoon."

She glanced at the documents and then dropped them onto the desk, as if their touch burned her fingers. "Impossible. If you insist on having your funeral today, it will be held without the deceased."

"What would be the purpose in that?"

"It doesn't concern me," she said. "Correct your documents and then come back. He is not going anywhere in the meantime."

"What's the problem?"

"The death certificate is not filled out properly. You must have it redone."

"Everything is in order as it should be. Read it more carefully."

"I haven't time," she said. Yury appeared terribly upset, but not to the point where he would say anything unforgivable. "Why are you still standing here?"

"Let's discuss this like two rational people. My friend's father must have his funeral, and I am here to see that he gets it. Is it not apparent that we should work something out?"

"There is no way I can possibly help you," she said. Then, allowing herself a moment's distraction, she turned her glare to my winter wraps. "What business of yours enables you to afford such beautiful garments?"

"Successful business."

"Evidently. Is that an Armani coat?" she asked, reaching across the desk and rubbing the fine camel hair. "You are a merchandiser of some sort?"

"I have access," I told her, and her hungry look assured me that eventually I would get my way. "Enough of fashion. Time is short."

"Isn't everyone's?" she asked. "Don't be so sharp with me. Who do you think you are? Go back to Israel and bother your own kind."

"As a Muscovite I am already with my kind, and I request your assistance with my problem. What do you say?"

"Your wealth is driving you mad," she told me, but already I was molding her as if she were clay. "Look, I am very busy with my work. I've given you more time than you deserve."

"A little more is all I ask," I said, and then changed the subject to one that would allow access to a broader avenue of discussion. "My, it's cold in here. You must find it hard to do your work in such conditions."

"They don't care about us. Not anymore." The Director glanced out her window at the enshrouding clouds. "It promises to be a hard winter, I think."

"Very cold," I said. "Every precaution should be taken."

"On my salary there is nothing to be done. My husband likes to put on fat for the winter, and I can barely feed him these days. What can I do? I work for the benefit of the people."

"I can see you are giving your life for the benefit of the people."

Yury said nothing while I conversed with the Director; I had told him to allow me to do the talking and not intrude, and he followed my directions without question.

"Look at my coat hanging there," she said, sneering. "Twenty years old."

"Time for a new one."

"Any coat would do, but the better, the warmer."

For a meaningful moment we looked in each other's eyes as lovers might, though certainly we were not in love. "I understand," I said. "So what about getting approval for the burial? We are supposed to be at the crematorium in less than three hours, and we will still be here next year at this rate."

"Be quiet or I cannot devote to your case the attention it needs," she said, studying the death certificate once again. The Director shook her head as she read the words, and made *tcch*ing sounds with her tongue. "This is a most suspicious death. How did the deceased sustain the fatal injury?"

"Mr. Slavkin was attempting to board a bus, and the door closed before he could get in. He was a temperamental man. It angered him that the driver ignored his pleas. He tried to climb onto the back of the bus. When it pulled away, he lost his balance and fell beneath the wheels. Very sad."

"I suppose alcohol was involved?"

"It might have been."

"He's learned his lesson," the Director said, stamping the certificate. "Where is the burial to be?"

"Nicholas Archangel, in Reutov."

"A lovely site. Very peaceful." She handed me Yury's documents and one of her own, which she speedily stamped and signed. I gave her my card, and she rubbed her fingers over the engraved words.

"Call that number tomorrow," I told her. "My associates will be pleased to assist you with your needs."

"Thank you, comrade," she said, blushing.

"What are friends for?" I replied, and smiled. "Where should we go, then?"

"Ground level, Office Twenty-nine," the Director said. "Present the certificate to obtain release."

"Thank you, madam," I said, and we took our leave. The next morning the worthy Director would call my associates, and they would see that she received a new winter coat. I made a note to myself to ask Arteim to supply her with some sausage as well, or a canned Polish ham, so her husband might more rapidly lay on his own winter padding. It is not difficult to deal with bureaucrats as long as there is something they need, and who doesn't need something? I have plenty, so why should she not share in my bounty? In America I understand this is called trickle-down, that what falls from my chin drops into the mouths of the deserving poor, who are then all the more eager to please me in return. In Russia, perhaps we could call it communism.

Yury embraced me as we made our way to the ground floor. "You had her eating from your hand," he said. "Thank you, Max."

"Your father is not in the crypt yet," I reminded him as we came to the Receiving Department. "But he'll be there before the day is out. Here we are. Do you want to come along?"

"I'll meet you outside. I want to remember him as he was, not as he is now."

As Yury departed I stepped into the Receiving Department's antechamber. A young man sat behind the desk, eyeing photos of naked women in a magazine. He was so entranced by their pink delights that even after I rapped several times against his desk he couldn't bring himself to tear his eyes away. "Excuse me," I said, and said again, but he was deaf to my words. Finally I dropped the documents onto the open pages of his journal, shielding him from the leer of Miss Budapest.

"Are you blinded by breasts?" I asked. "Don't you see me standing here before you?"

"I'm waiting for a call," he told me. "I can't be bothered now."

"You have my documents, which are in order. I wish to inspect the deceased before the hearse arrives. Please take me to him."

"I don't see how I can." Much has changed in our country, but something that hasn't changed is what we call nonobtrusive Russian service. It is not precisely the same as it was; heretofore we called it nonobtrusive Soviet service. It is believed, especially by Westerners, that Russians love to be told what to do, but this is not exactly the case. In truth my countrymen love being told what to do only so that they may then try to do the opposite. Whether this is because we are so spoiled as children, and thus used to acting as badly as we can get away with, or because we secretly relish the beatings we receive once we are caught misbehaving, I cannot say. But if you want something from a Russian, as from your children, come prepared to beat or beg, depending on what you want and how badly you want it.

"You cannot try to see your way to clearing my path?"

"*Nichevo*," he said, untranslatable but here meaning he could try, although of course it would be useless and so what would be the point? I tossed a twenty into his steamy lap.

"Try."

"This way," he said, stamping the form. He led me through a door into a much larger, colder room, where plain wooden containers rested on carts aligned in rows. Several aged attendants, whiling away their own final hours in energetic debate, seemed not at all startled by the sudden appearance of the living in their midst. "Here he is," the young man said, and gestured to a grizzled old gasper to remove the lid of a nearby box for us. With no small effort, he did. Perhaps it would seem appropriate to use emotional phrases, but the bare facts themselves are colorful enough. Looking inside the box, I saw an elderly woman lying in peace.

"There is something not entirely right here," I told the young man of the department.

"What is your problem? We did all for him we could."

"A change of sex was not requested, I assure you."

He looked at me as if I were raving mad and for an instant appeared regretful that he hadn't chosen to arm himself before attending to me. After his initial shock passed he walked to the casket and turned his gaze within. He masterfully contained his surprise. He reexamined the death certificate, closely studying its words before making his pronouncement. "This is not Mr. Slavkin."

"I didn't think so, but I thought I should get confirmation. Where is Mr. Slavkin?"

The young man studied the long lines of identical boxes and threw up his hands. Confronting the ancient Bolshevik, he shouted, "How could such an error be made?"

The veteran shrugged and toyed with the armor of his medals. "*Nichevo*. These weeds do not grow in my garden."

"We are looking for Number Seventy-eight. Find him at once." The old ones and their young master started moving from casket to casket, lifting the lids and examining each inhabitant. It should go without saying that Mr. Slavkin was not uncovered until the penultimate casket was reached, twenty minutes later.

"There we are," the young man said. I looked down, taking satisfaction, seeing Mr. Slavkin where he was supposed to be. He looked no less cheerful in death than he had in life. Knots of black thread held his head in the proper position. I motioned to the fools that they should shut him away and then waited until every nail was driven into the lid anew before leaving, to be sure that at least something would be properly done. I suppose I should have been glad that they hadn't lost Mr. Slavkin, as my son had been lost at this very hospital ten years ago. At the time the attendants agreed that he shouldn't have been able to get up and walk away by himself, but, they suggested, that must have been what he'd done. To this day I know not where my son ultimately wandered. Sometimes when I board the Metro's circle line my thoughts turn to him, and I imagine that perhaps he is on the same train with me, but in a different car, a special one set aside for those compelled to forever miss their stop, those who in their absence are most sorely at hand. *Nichevo.*

First class or rough class, we always reach the boneyard. Yury, in his clanking Laika, drove his mother and sisters to Nicholas Archangel. His brother was sobered up and dropped off at the entrance gate by army companions. Mr. Slavkin's trade union representative was hauled to the crematorium by his driver, whom he had been lucky or willful enough to retain. Some of the other mourners came by public bus; a few even got there in time for the funeral. In our country corpses ride in yellow hearses, and that was how Slavkin arrived. In muddier months, the color of death's perambulator is more reminiscent of manure than of the sun, but that seems most appropriate to the earthy nature of its purpose.

I drove to the cemetery alone, trying to steer around the craters in the pavement but hitting them as regularly as I missed them. Many of our roads were last repaired by the Nazis, and aching tailbones are inevitably suffered on even the shortest trips in the best cars. In the lanes leading back to Moscow I counted dozens of old army trucks commandeering the highway as if in the wake of an invasion. Canny importers striving to ship their bounty to market sometimes purchase but more often borrow—steal is perhaps the most exact word—the trucks, reconverting them for civilian if not necessarily pacific purpose. Beneath each green tarpaulin I could without difficulty visualize a regiment's supply of Kalashnikov rifles, rich furs plundered from eastern shores, copper pipe extracted from government facilities, shiny plastic bags bulging with heroin, all to be traded for whatever their expropriators desired. Smaller vehicles were often run off the road by these caravans of monsters, so great was their speed, but I wasn't concerned.

As I sped along I reveled in the sights of the season, although unlike most of my countrymen I have slight fondness for nature. A birch forest stripped of leaves reminds me only of an aging colonel's bad haircut. Windy, empty plains give my soul shivers, the squawks of ravens haunt my dreams, and a bubbling creek never affects my heart so much as my bladder. Still, there is a peace I draw from the dead dawn of the year that satisfies me beyond understanding. While our enchanted land lies slumbering beneath winter's gray sheet, it is easier to forget how repeatedly she has been bruised and broken at the hands of our glorious and steadfast masters, whose love for her was so blinding that they could not help but rape her.

When I reached the cemetery there was already a long queue of hearses waiting to make their deposits at the crematorium. The establishment had been recently privatized, I'd discovered, and the proprietors wasted no time in putting up advertising. The sign on the encompassing fence assured potential customers that THERE IS NO BURIAL MORE DELIGHTFUL THAN IN A BRIGHT CREMATORIUM. Other signboards pictured happy families made all the happier by the efficacious disposal of their departed. I was not surprised to see a notice that cash, vouchers, and all major credit cards could be applied toward payment. As I got out of my car I breathed in a familiar smell, acrid and sweet, which overpowered the fragrant miasmas that generally perfume our air. My eyes watered, stung by greasy cinders. Black smoke erupted from the Glow of Life Columbarium's tall chimney, smoke much heavier than the atmosphere into which it issued. Near the line of hearses was a line of mourners awaiting entry. Each time the wind shifted and the smoke settled earthward, women fainted, aspiring another's beloved.

At the front of the line I saw Yury, who stood stoic amid his sobbing mother and sisters. His brother slouched against the wall, rubbing his head, as if he more deeply regretted the evening before than he did the loss of his parent. Slavkin's friends, and in particular his trade union representative, a well-upholstered bastard whose neck was broader than the space between his ears, appeared no more disturbed by the wait than if they were queueing up to obtain tubes of Sputnik toothpaste. As I studied the gloomy masks in the midst of the party, I was startled by a familiar smile. Its appearance was not hallucinatory. I was heartened but shocked and thought it best not to rush to her at once.

"Everyone is here?" I asked Yury, brushing ash from my coat.

"Some of these people I don't know. They must have known Father."

"Some of them know me, I think," I said, glancing over my shoulder. The smile lingered. A woman in a gray uniform, who looked to have eaten one too many delicious lemons, emerged from the doorway to call out the names of those newly approved to enter.

"Verlotsky. Slavkin. Osipova. Be quick about it!" she shouted. It is easier to quit smoking cigarettes than it is to quit providing nonobtrusive service.

"After the ceremony, we shall take care of final arrangements," I told Yury. "Take your seats. I will be along shortly. Save two for me."

"Two?"

"I see a friend," I said, pointing toward Sonya's smile. "Come to join us in mourning, I'm sure."

He nodded and passed through the antechamber. Yury had never met her before. Except for my office employees, few of my friends had met Sonya, excepting her husband Dmitry. Before you make uninformed moral judgments, I should state firmly that he was not a friend in the closest sense, but rather a businessman with whom I had not yet found it necessary to work. Entering the building, I paused to examine a shoddy model of a new improved columbarium scheduled to be constructed in coming years. Then she and I drew together, iron to magnet.

"Come, my stalwart," she said.

"*Koshka*, why are you here?" *Cat*, I called her, for the way she stretched and purred and nuzzled against me when she craved milk. She had her own names for me, but I don't think it politic to relate this intimate information. It annoyed me that she had come, for on that afternoon my responsibilities to Yury outweighed all others. But I would be lying if I said I wasn't delighted to see her.

"To pay my respects," she said, pressing against me, thrusting a hand into my coat, standing on tiptoes to kiss me. Her tongue slid through my mouth as if she were licking butter from a knife. Before stepping back she took my lower lip between her teeth, nipping gently but effectively. "Why did you come here without me? You knew I'd want to share your grief."

"Not my grief, the grief of a friend," I told her, pushing away her hand. "I see you're overcome."

At once I regretted my brusqueness, but circumstances demanded that I be severe. Sonya looked at me with the eyes of a motherless calf, assuming correctly that I would melt like ice. The stares of others standing close by were not nearly so endearing. "Why are you so cruel to me?" she asked.

"I'm sorry," I said, holding her hands so that I could know her touch while preventing her from making inappropriate gestures. She smiled. Sonya has perfect white teeth; I think she has more of them than anyone in Russia. As she doffed her fur hat, her hair cascaded to her shoulders in a golden waterfall. "How lusty can you be in a crematorium?"

"You'd be surprised," she said. As I let go of her hands, she reapplied them to my waist and even farther below.

"Not here," I said, stepping back, almost knocking down a feeble old pensioner who'd not yet climbed the chimney. Sonya laughed and winked a green eye at me. Our affair awoke with slow-warming spring and hadn't died with the year; it only burned hotter, as if summer came and neglected to go. Neither my wife, Tanya, nor Sonya's husband, Dmitry, knew of our carousing, and as each week passed it became more essential, in my opinion, that our secret history remain so. "I must be with my friend now. Come with me and behave."

"What are you doing after the funeral?"

"Going home," I said. She unbuttoned her coat so I could take note of her short skirt and long legs. "Perhaps not immediately."

"Perhaps not." Sonya, dear girl, is half my age. Sometimes I fear that when my turn comes to board the yellow wagon, it will carry nothing but a dry, empty husk. Such youthful, energetic girls as Sonya are dangerous, even when they aren't married, and can be the death of old goats such as her husband—a glorious and inspirational death, to be sure. Since she redirected her energies toward me, however, I am sorry to say he recovered almost preternatural health. They'd married when she was fresh from Moscow University and he held a mid-level position in the Ministry of Internal Affairs. Now his business is business, and he does well, I gather, though possibly not as well as I. Sonya realized this at once when we met; she is an intelligent girl. Her marks at school were always high, and there were no studies at which she excelled more naturally than those relating to class structure.

"Come now," I said. "It will not be long."

Arm in arm, we crossed the room. The old woman in charge of the checkroom signaled that we should give her our coats but I ignored her; how could I know I would ever see them again? She eyed us as if desiring that we should be the ones whom our friends came to honor. We entered the room in which Yury's party waited and were greeted by an attendant, a fierce young man with blue tattoos of skulls on his fingers. However appropriate his personal artwork might have been to his present position, I was certain he had been decorated during a stay in one of our nation's commodious prisons and wondered what other masterpieces lay beneath his gray uniform. On the sleeves of his outfit were red and black designs symbolizing flame, and pinned to the front was a metal badge stamped with a similar emblem.

"Need help?" he shouted, giving us a rusty smirk. He must have devoted intense study to codes of etiquette while serving out his state-expropriated time.

"We are here to join our party," I told him, but he remained where he stood, blocking our path. "Will you excuse us?"

"All seats taken," he said, his Yakut accent heavy. "Ceremony soon."

"I see our two seats from here," I said. "Let me by, please."

"Full up. *Nichevo.*" I gave him a ten, and he weakened. I gave him another and he collapsed.

Sonya and I took seats next to Yury, in the front row. No sooner did I sit down than a crack in the chair's wood pinched my skin. Sonya held a hand over her mouth, stifling her laughter, and I shifted the tail of my coat beneath me.

A woman, appearing no less charming than the one who had allowed us entry into the facility, walked to the front of the room. "Ten minutes for final farewells," she bellowed, her expression warm with undying affection for the people, and stomped away.

Mr. Slavkin's trade union representative waddled to the front of the room, standing before the casket and preparing himself to deliver his soul-captivating words. Holding in his hand two pieces of paper, one letter-sized and the other no more than scrap, he started reading from the former.

"Honored friends, relatives, and co-workers of the dearly departed—" He shifted glittering pig's eyes to his bit of toilet tissue and read, "Georgi Mikhailovich Slubkin."

"Slavkin!" many of us in the audience cried out. The representative frowned at having been interrupted and continued to read from the larger page, squinting as he rushed through the hollow phrases.

"Always he exerted persistent efforts in the firm support of his comrades. We salute and admire the spirit, discipline, and organization he unswervingly demonstrated—"

He talked as if to blow down the Kremlin; who knew how much wind he might hold? As he droned on, I studied the room. A mud-brown nylon curtain hung behind the catafalque. On either side of the casket, two plastic baskets of day-old flowers stood atop plaster columns. Posters from the 1980 Olympics and swimwear calendars from Thailand papered the other walls, and so Mischa the Olympic Bear and Bangkok bikini girls could also freely participate in all mourning rituals. Most likely the posters were hiding hammers and sickles, the lingering spoor of previous administrators. A metal pan in a rear corner of the room caught a steady drip from the ceiling.

"—unlimitedly"—*splurp*—"devoted"—*splurp*—"to our Motherland"—*splurp*.

Sonya's attention also wandered. Slipping her hand into my coat pocket, she sought out and located the hole she had previously torn through the skin-soft silk. She eased her hand snakelike through the opening and rested it on my leg. I drew my coat close around me so that her movements might go undetected, aghast at her lascivious burrowings but unable to stop her without attracting attention to what others should best ignore. With subtle if not wholly funereal movements, she discovered her prize. Sonya gazed soulfully at the casket and at the representative as he huffed and puffed, revealing nothing to indicate that her thoughts were anywhere other than with the deceased. Certainly her gentle motions did not prevent me from paying any less attention to the eulogist's poignant phrases than I might have wished.

"His turbulent waters," he concluded, "have been forever checked by concrete. When we are asked what a worker should be, always let us warmheartedly picture in our minds the figure of Georgi Mikhailovich Stumkin!"

His victorious conclusion should have been great cause for rejoicing. But ours was a jaded cadre, and our stillness rose only to a thunderous silence, broken by the growling of stomachs. Sonya withdrew her hand, sighing sadly. When I turned harsh eyes her way, wishing to inspire within her the desire—yes, the compulsion—to repent, she smiled. I have never known Sonya to ask forgiveness for her crimes; she sleeps contentedly with guilt. Yury cursed beneath his breath as he watched the workers' counselor depart. I patted his arm as he stood up. Walking to the casket, taking a suitable stance before it, he closed his eyes and intoned a quick, silent prayer. He lifted his head to look at us before speaking.

"Friends," he began, but almost at the instant he started talking, the frenzied pumpings of an unseen organist drowned out his words. The musician was so fat-fingered that we could not tell if the tune was dirge or disco. Yury's face reddened, and with the rest of us he looked around to see if the offender's physical presence could be detected, to no avail. Raising his voice, he attempted to shout the words he had written for his father over the circus melody. It was useless; we couldn't hear anything he said, and he gave up.

Finally, the noise stopped. Yury took a deep breath before making his long-delayed statement. Without warning, the woman attendant burst into the room, throwing open the doors as if to proclaim that the Czar had fallen. Four underlings trailed her, pushing a cart bearing the next deportee—rather, one pushed and the three others ascertained that he performed his job correctly.

"Final farewells must be concluded at this time," she said, slapping Slavkin's box. "Others are waiting."

"I've not had the chance to speak," Yury said.

"Your time is up," she said, and as she did Slavkin's casket, and the cart upon which it rested, descended through the floor. "You think this is Parliament and you can talk until you are blue in the face? Be gone."

"That devil of an organist played through his eulogy," I said, walking over. "We asked for no music, not that you could call it that."

"According to documents presented, standard threnodies were requested. Others are waiting. Who are you to delay them? Take your party and go."

Had she been alone we might have worked out something between us and wheeled Slavkin back in. But her attendants were so muscular they could not have clasped their hands behind their broad backs, and I knew if Yury lost his temper and struck out (as he appeared ever more willing to do), we would not last a minute against them. Plainly a prison cabal of brigands had, upon release, evidently effected a takeover of this operation to serve their purposes; for these attendants, too, bore tattoos of penal provenance on their knobby hands and scarred faces. Such vipers could give a nasty bite. Were we to protest too loudly they would without hesitation be happy to rifle our wallets at their leisure while delivering us to our own unscheduled appointment with the oven king.

"We'd have brought our own cats to skin if we wanted noise, I can assure you," I said. "This is quite unsatisfactory."

"*Nichevo*. Do we run our business solely for your benefit?" she asked. The hidden elevator in the floor reascended, empty, and her assistants rolled the next cart into place. "Be on your way."

"We may make final arrangements where?" I asked.

"Pick up ashes in Retrieval Room first," she said. "Go there now."

"Ashes?" In traditional cemetery praxis, not until several hours following the ceremony are the ashes picked up and properly deposited. "He just went down."

"Science is invading all spheres of life," she said. "New procedures and improved methods enable us to offer customers prompt and convenient satisfaction. I've wasted more than enough time on you now, so go. Go!"

Yury, Sonya, and I squeezed by the next party of mourners streaming into the room. The woman and her beasts gave the new arrivals frigid stares. "Not even the Soviets were ever so contemptuous," Yury said, safely exploding once removed from their presence. "Is nothing improved once it undergoes privatization?"

"Not immediately," I said. "Do you wish me to handle the final details? It could be a delicate matter."

"Please, Max," Yury said, wiping tears from his eyes. "I'm blind with anger."

I walked with Sonya to the Retrieval Room. Passing other attendants, I saw that each man's visible parts were heavily tattooed. One individual had a dagger engraved on his brow, its tip dripping a stream of red down his face. "Is Yury paying you well for your assistance?" Sonya asked.

"We'll work something out," I told her, making certain that my pockets hadn't been picked. Even so I was glad to have come here carrying much cash, for even before seeing the staff in their full magnificence I'd ruled out the possibility of using my American Express card. Giving these reprobates my charge number would be like offering them the keys to my house or the favors of my wife, such as they are. "He is my good friend, after all."

"No fee in advance?" she asked. I shook my head. She always evinced her avarice in forthright terms; I appreciated that. "Then your friends should love you as much as I do."

"How sentimental," I said. "You enchant me."

"That's obvious." She wriggled in my grasp like an eel. "Do you think they're all former prisoners here?"

"They're clearly rehabilitated."

At the entrance to the Retrieval Room I reached my limit. On the door was a sign that read:

DUE TO LACK OF URNS ASHES WILL BE
DELIVERED IN POLYETHYLENE BAGS

There was a problem, of course.

"You should have brought your own suitable bags," the woman attendant told me as we freely exchanged opinions in spirited debate. She, like the other women who worked for the crematorium, was in her autumnal years and must have practiced her glower in deepest sleep. For many years in our country, *druzhinas* sat on guard in each apartment building to keep watchful eyes on residents' actions with calendar precision. *Druzhinas*, inevitably, had been such women as this one. It pleased me to know that the brutes who ran this establishment were making sure even these redundant old biddies might happily share in the fruits of capitalism.

"This is not a market," I told her. "Why should we come so prepared?"

"Why do you think you should have it easy?"

"You have nothing to hold the ashes?"

She ignored the twenty I threw before her, waiting until I added its twin before applying full attention to this problem. "Possibly there is something," she said, slipping the bills into her uniform's breast pocket. Pulling open a drawer behind her counter, she reached into its recesses and took out a type of bag used often for carrying fruit or vegetables. "Here."

I will always love Russia, but uncountable are the times when I wish to live in any other country. "A net bag," I noted. "And?"

"It has many openings in its sides, yes?" She stared at the bag as if she'd not noticed. "Will the ashes not fall through?"

"The larger pieces will be secure."

"Such as a skull or hipbone?"

"You do not appreciate our initiative and persistence?"

"Not at all."

"It is the only bag we have," she said, taking it and replacing it in the drawer. "I haven't time for your impudence. You can carry the ashes in your pocket for all I care."

It shames me to admit it, but sometimes even I lose my temper dealing with the capricious whims of those who know they cannot be ignored. Sonya stopped me before I could express my feelings too openly. "Here," she said, taking from the confines of her purse a carefully folded carrier bag from Christian Dior. "This will do, I'd think."

A fire lit the woman's eyes, which not even hard currency had succeeded in kindling. With slow gestures she unfolded the bag, delighting at its classic form, paying homage to its beauty as if it were a prized icon or one of the old masters in the Pushkin

Museum. I endlessly marvel at the joy the simplest Western trin-
ket continues to produce in those too long familiar with the standard goods of *Homo sovieticus.* "This will do the job," she said,
and stepped through the doorway to her rear. "One moment."

A male attendant remained behind the counter. Of all the
apparent ex-prisoners who presently devoted their labor to the
Glow of Life Columbarium, this one appeared most sinister. His
dark features bespoke a southern origin, but he was larger than
the average inhabitant of those regions; his uniform strained
against his bulk. He wore a veritable gallery of artistic designs.
Tattooed chains encircled his wrists. Blue spiders ascended the
cords of his neck. In the center of his forehead a third eye stared
onto the world, its look as warm as those of the two with which he
was born. He lacked the forefinger of his left hand. Though I
understood that this signifies some criminal rite of passage, I
thought it more likely that he or one of his compatriots might have
bitten it off in a fit of anger, or hunger.

"They have thousands of bags, probably," I said, whispering into Sonya's ear. The attendant watched us, saying nothing.
"They've left him here to guard them."

"Old bags for old ashes, so what?" she said.

"They leave you without a shred of dignity."

"Does dignity profit?" Sonya asked, smiling. "Is it scientifically measurable?"

The woman attendant returned, holding the bag by its
handles. "Your ashes," she said. Peering inside I saw a smooth
layer within, several centimeters deep. Their blackish-gray color
was unflecked by white. Placing a hand on the bottom I felt not
even the shadow of heat. A wild idea came to me. I perceived
that these ashes were not the leavings of Mr. Slavkin at all
but rather those of wood fires, or *papirosi*, or fine old Havana
cigars.

"A remarkable process," I said to the woman. "He was still
in human form not half an hour ago."

"A new method perfected by our wonder-working staff,"
she said. "The cleansing fire is followed by a deep freeze, and here
he is."

"It barely seems possible."

"The gifts of technology," she said, inscribing her initials on a payment slip.

"How does such a method work?"

"I am no scientist. Details are a mystery to me," she said. "Take this to the cashier for settlement."

Now that our country has opened itself wide to the world, some people say that in a short time we Russians will become homogenized, that our country will become indistinguishable from any other (except indisputably larger and arguably more pathetic). Such doubters underestimate the inextinguishable spirit of their fellows. Where else but Russia could you exchange the corpse of a loved one for a sack of cigar ashes while you wait? My mind reeled with questions. What could these criminals be doing with the bodies they claimed to be cremating? Dissecting them to obtain valuable organs for resale? Constructing their own Frankenstein monsters with the spare limbs? Converting the raw meat into dog food—or *sausage?*

What could I do? I might suggest to my contacts in the security ministries that they should come asking questions—and they would come, and ask, and afterward slip the replies they received into their wallets to buy food for themselves or their families. I could direct my workers in more specialized fields to deliver a stern message to the proprietors—and would then be certain to receive an equally harsh response. Perhaps I should relate the plain facts to fellow businessmen—only to discover that my vicious rumors regarded one of their promising investments.

No, better to leave it be and trust that in time the crematorium keepers would suffer at the hands of the free market. It's hard to deny that in this instance my sensibility outweighed my sentiment, but do not think me a heartless bastard. Had my late father, say, been switched for fireplace sweepings, I might have taken one of those aforementioned approaches—or maybe not; for would he have done the same for me? *Nichevo.*

Russia is sometimes the land of too much opportunity.

I examined the bill the woman handed me. The total cost was in dollars. You'll not find rubles tainting the premises of privatized establishments, excepting in those stores and restaurants where their use is required by law. "Three thousand eight hundred?"

"A fair figure," she said. "For ceremony, use of facilities, threnodies, use of crematorium and attendant services, preparation of ash, and crypt enclosure. Do you know we take all major credit cards?"

"That's good to know," I said. "Thank you."

"Thank *you*." She grimaced, as if confusing the expression with a smile. "Be mindful of us for all your future needs."

Sonya and I paid the cashier. After ringing up the sale on her machine, she checked the addition on her abacus. Concluding our transaction, we walked outside. Yury and his family waited for us, standing in twilight, facing the wind. "Everything is settled?" he asked.

"Absolutely," I said, passing the bag to him as if it were a folded flag. He held it with utmost care, never looking inside. His weeping began anew, but he soon caught himself and dammed his tears. I clasped his shoulder.

"Thank you again, Max."

"We must be going," I said. "Anytime you need help, I will do what I can."

We watched Yury and his family walk down the pathway to make their deposit. They had bottles of vodka with which to toast Slavkin's soul as it set off on its final journey. The bottles clinked together in the bag Yury's mother carried, sounding as sleigh bells.

"How did you get here?" I asked Sonya.

"Hired driver," she said. "A militiaman in our neighborhood happy to provide services in his spare time."

"Trustworthy?"

"As long as I pay him," she said. "Perhaps I can get a ride back with you?"

"Perhaps."

We walked to the parking lot, arm in arm. There were as many hearses as before, and as many mourners. The black smoke clouded the air as it had earlier. The scent still choked; the falling flakes were as greasy. "Who do you think the smoke comes from?" Sonya asked, holding her scarf over her nose and mouth.

"Competitors?" I said; someone was burning, no question. "Who knows?"

It was good to see my car where I'd left it, and better to see it untouched. I was surprised that the proprietors hadn't yet begun stealing their clients' cars. After I replaced the detachable elements, we climbed in and drove away. Not far from the entrance a group of small boys, as yet untattooed, hurled mudballs at the windshields of cars stopped at the light. After effectively blinding the drivers the little bastards dashed up, waving filthy sponges, shouting, "Need clean?" I avoided them by not bothering to stop, instead pulling quickly onto the main highway that leads back to Moscow and falling into line with the great trucks of contraband.

Sonya unbuttoned her coat. Reaching down and opening her purse, she extracted a cassette player. "What would you like to hear?" No radio stays long in a Moscow car, and I'd had none installed. I hate listening to music while driving, but what did my koshka care?

"Vysotsky."

"Such tired old drunken protests," she said, laughing. "Soviets bad, people good, drinking best of all. Who cares? Here is a much better selection." She dredged up several tapes. "Madonna. Nirvana. Vanilla Ice."

"It's all the same to me."

Though the light was fading quickly in the car now that the sun had set, I saw her spread her legs. The briefest glimpse of her sheltered gate shook me, as she knew it would. I turned my eyes toward the road, toward the city. In early evening, from beyond the Outer Ring, the rosy glow in the sky above Moscow can make the neurasthenic fear that our great metropolis has been stormed and set aflame, but this will never be the case; we are uninvadable from without. Moscow's residents burned down the city so that Napoleon could loot only cinders; at the height of his power they stopped Hitler in his tracks. But the most dangerous invasions are from within, and as the citizens once prostrated themselves before Stalin so they now give fealty to Madonna. Tomorrow, who knows? Who could imagine that one day our future would be as unpredictable as our past?

My koshka inserted a tape into the player. Baleful caterwauling reverberated through the car. At least Sonya is no partisan of disco, which presently is heard in more places, more often, than the unforgettable speeches of our unlamented leaders were ever heard. The naive might well believe that the noble heart of Russia throbs solely to the beat of disco in these transmutative days. Capitalism is a marvelous system, but when it comes to its contemporary artistic fruits I stand fast on the side of the Black Hundred.

"Energetic American music," Sonya said, slapping out primitive rhythms against her knees with her hands, singing along with her favored tribesmen. "*Ahnee naa yah.*" At first I foolishly believed that *nya* was one of the words chanted by the lunatics as they made bestial love to their instruments, but that could not be— Americans never say no, even when that's what they mean.

"Sonya, turn it down, it's like needles in my head. What is it?"

"'Smells Like Teen Spirit,'" she said. She caressed herself between her legs and placed her fingers at my nose, so I might be mollified by her scent. "Smells like me." Taking my right hand off the wheel, she guided it gently into her lap. My nimble digits pushed aside her Italian lingerie and, seafaring, sank into her briny wetness. "Devil."

Yes, that. "Angel," I replied. That, too.

ב

My wife, Tatiana Sergeyevna Boroda, and I live in a magnificent if decaying structure that proudly wears the Russian
Revival swaddling of its centenarian birth. Designed as a residence
for Moscow's most illustrious stratum of citizenry, it served for
many years following the Revolution as a *communalka*, a Glorious Proletarian Stew, a human borscht roiling with unsavory in-
gredients. Our six-room apartment bears traces of hundreds of
former tenants: parquet floors are scarred where flimsy walls lent
scant privacy; sealed pipes in the kitchen once leaked gas into the
vicinity of five stoves; etched into the bathroom tile is the scurrilous directive of a former dweller troubled by fellow residents, who
were evidently not possessed with enough Stakhanovist fervor in
fulfilling their cleaning plan. By the sixties, suitable workers' palaces had been lashed together in the suburbs to host the masses,
and the flat was renovated. We moved here in 1975, after our
wedding trip to Sparrow Hills.

Sometimes at night I awake, thinking I hear our apartment's
onetime tenants shouting at each other to turn out lights or remove muddy boots from the hall, and then believe I hear vicious

curses in response. When the bones of our arthritic home snap in and out of place, my imagination runs mad, and I detect in those creaks and groans the crash of doors underfoot and the howls of past residents dragged away once again to answer for their crimes. I do not think such reveries unusual, for all walls in Moscow scream in the night.

Come morning, I see outstretched hands at our bedroom window. Unlike so many such hands in our city, these belong neither to beggars nor to robbers. On either side of the window are statues of goddesses, although Tanya perceives little of classical heritage in their lissome charms. More cynical than I, she believes the naked women to be the architect's favorite whores. Years ago a government theorist extolled the glories of our Soviet atmosphere, proclaiming its cleanliness to be greater than that of Arctic ice, its essential ethers more healthy for children than the purest oxygen. Our window's sad defenders belie his hyperbole. One has lost a breast to the corrosive air and the other a buttock; their faces and arms are pitted as if by smallpox. Both are black with soot, suggesting that they spend their long nights stuck in chimneys. Yet even in disarray, the goddesses hearten me each morning; like all that is Russian, they retain their beauty, however thick the palimpsest of filth.

It grieves me to tell you that the view past the goddesses is not as seductive. Allow me to describe the vista with which I am confronted each morning. During the thirties, at the command of Stalin, the Transformer of Nature, Tverskaya Street—Gorky, then— was widened to allow the free passage of tanks in the event their presence proved advantageous. In front of our apartment house another building was constructed, one larger, in Stalin Gothic style. (If you knew nothing of Stalin, the architecture could tell you.) Stalin Gothic expropriated the most grandiose features from each architectural school and employed them simultaneously. The resulting designs were made more inspiring by the copious use of party symbols worked into the carved iconography. Our building proffers sylphs to the appreciative gaze of passersby; the other, dead-eyed workers fettered with bonds of wheat.

Separating the structures is a courtyard, in which residents of both buildings walk their dogs, disassemble their cars, and make essential private arrangements. Our bedroom faces a man's bedroom—if he has a wife, we've never seen her, and heaven knows no woman should be so unfortunate. He is fat and in his sixties, I would say. He chooses to drape himself in the manner of the goddesses when he rises, and in that state I see him every morning. Imagine greeting each day seeing Khrushchev naked. To encounter such a hallucination in the *banya*, or bath, where one steams away the woes of the world, is expected if not desirable. But this! He moved in last spring and at once began continually parading in his dawn attire; I cannot imagine him clothed. In deepest winter, frost covers the window with ice ferns, and I am usually spared this brain-fogging sight; but this January's weather had been unnaturally warm, and there was no frost. As he appeared this morning he opened the *fortochka*, the small inset window within a window. Taking his rod in hand, he aimed carefully before firing. His stream arced down to the muddy snow below.

Tanya was in the kitchen preparing breakfast. "He's pissing out the window!" I shouted, unable to believe the scene playing before my eyes.

"*Who?* Khrushchev?"

"Like a horse." I judged him to be a rural lout who'd amassed riches through disreputable agencies and who now aspired to a lush life in deluxe surroundings while remaining willfully ignorant of city ways—but this was too much. Could he not use the *sink* if his toilet was broken? These days the whole of public Moscow is inhabited by the raw and uncultured, but being forced to confront the farm behavior of peasants in my own bedroom was more than I could bear. Opening my own *fortochka*, I berated him. "Hey!" I yelled through the small opening. "You're not in a barn! I'll call the authorities." Khrushchev, startled, peered up as he finished his business. Then, leaning down, he screamed back at me through his urinal, across the courtyard.

"Suck a foreskin!"

The old bastard's cheek was astonishing. It is not pleasant to admit it, but I descended to his level. "You're fucking my brains!" I shouted back. "*Bydlo!* Dolt!"

"I'll go up your ass with soap!" he replied. People below employed their own rich phrases as they contributed to the clamor, demanding that we shut our mouths.

"Stupid bastards!" they shouted up to us. "Communists!"

"Fuck a pig," he said to me, making crude gestures as we continued our stimulating debate. "I need you like a prick needs an alarm clock!"

"Kulak! Fucking peasant! I hope yours freezes off in your hand!"

"*Max!*" Tanya said, appearing as if by magic beside me, closing the *fortochka*. "What is this foolishness? Don't you know everyone in Moscow can hear you?"

"Did you hear what he called me?"

"I heard what you called him," she said, drawing my neck-tie tight with hangman's grace as she knotted it for me. "You're *both* uncultured. Come and eat, unless you're going to stand here all day chatting with your friend."

"That lousy peasant."

"What difference is it to you what he does with his thing?" she said, working my gold cuff links into my sleeves. "He wants to stick it out the window, let him. Hungry crows will peck it off."

"He acts like a dog in the street," I continued, following her into the kitchen.

"Men and dogs always stick their things where they don't belong," she replied, examining me as if I were suitable for vivi-section. Her look subdued my anger enough so that I might feel fear. I carefully studied Tanya's impassive countenance as she ladled eggs and sausage onto our plates, feeling anxious rather than saddened that her emotions were so masked. She was asleep when I came home, the past evening. Often she was awake when I crept home after nights of erotic pleasure, but so far my ever-believable excuses had forestalled discovery, if not suspicion. Still, I often worried that through overuse I had honed too sharp an edge onto my invention and that someday, called upon without warning to employ my swordsmanship, I would swing my weapon too reck-lessly and cut off my own head.

"You came in late last night, didn't you?" she asked, her eyes as opaque as the eggs before me. A favorite song of Sonya's blared over the radio, its tune perfunctory, its message incompre-hensible.

"When I returned to the office countless problems faced me," I told her, deafening myself to the song's incoherent, evoca-tive words, blinding myself to the images of Sonya they conjured.

"Once I start working, it's impossible to stop." She sat sphinxlike. "Your beauty stirs me this morning," I said. "I tremble." Tanya glared at me again, but then accepted my compliments for what they were and smiled. She adjusted with unwrinkled hands a Chanel scarf that encircled her unlined neck. I wore another of my fine suits, and she too was attired in splendid business wear: a deep blue blazer, a gray wool skirt, black leather boots as soft as my car's upholstery. She'd had her hair done at an expensive pavilion the day before, and white no longer threaded her russet tresses. My wife's beauty was a mature woman's beauty, but none the less glorious for that. If it had only been in her nature to more freely express the emotions in her soul, and so respond to me as I could have responded to her, perhaps others of her sex would not have had the luck they so often did, employing their crafty wiles.

"Save your flattery for Khrushchev," she said, spreading jam on a thin slice of bread. "What problems can't your worthless staff handle? Fire them all and get new ones. So many good people need work."

"My workers are irreplaceable specialists," I reminded her. "If they fail me, I apply an iron hand." She laughed. I happily let her delight in taunting me; it distracted her and caused me no harm. "Call me Stalin," I said. Tanya laughed again, although long-ingrained conditioning caused her to at once lift a finger to her lips to shush me.

"Some dictator," she said, retrieving business documents so she could examine them before going to work. Reassured that my crimes had again escaped detection, I opened the *Moscow News* and pored over enthralling accounts of the spectacular accomplishments of the world's most progressive society. The Brain Institute denied that it held Anastasia's. A parliamentarian was gunned down in the Metro by persons unknown, and the city militia assured the public they would track down the assassin as if he were a filthy rat. Ufa's citizens were sickened by mysterious fumes; the populace suspected the Army of burning chemical weapons nearby, though the Army denied responsibility. Throughout the near abroad, in Chechnya, in Tadzhikistan, in Nagorno-Karabakh, parched hates continued to be quenched with new blood. If I wished to have pizzas delivered to my office, Pizza Hut would now charge me only forty hard dollars. There was a photo of Michael Jackson and a suggestion that he is perhaps an alien brought to earth by one of the UFOs that always are seen only in the provinces. I never imagined that one day I should miss finding in the morning journals the masterful oratory of Chernenko, photographs of women holding corn, and long essays celebrating the overfulfillment of steel plans in Magnitogorsk.

Without taking her eyes from her papers, Tanya asked a question. "What do you think about the girl?"

"Girl?" I repeated, as if the word were unfamiliar to me. I lifted my own newspaper higher, cloaking my face. "What girl?"

"Little coma girl," Tanya said. "In Ekaterinburg. Heartbreaking."

I lowered my newspaper. "What happened to her?"

"Her dog ran away and can't be found." I found the article and an accompanying photograph. The little girl posed with her dog, a boxer. The uncredited photographer demonstrated his mastery of light by giving them numinous haloes, as if girl and dog had been beatified, or at least awarded extraordinary prizes by the former Politburo. "She evidently loves her dog very much. Her sadness is so great that she went into a coma."

"How is that possible?"

"Who comprehends mysteries of the mind? I am no psychologist. The dog's been gone for four days, and she's been in her coma three." She turned down the radio until we were no longer at the mercy of its idiot prattlings. "The whole city devotes its attentions to being of service to her family."

"What else have they to do in Ekaterinburg?"

Tanya frowned. "Hunting parties are searching for her pet."

"There can be a lot of meat on a dog," I remarked, certain the beast had already been thrown by rustics into the stewpot.

"It's a tragic situation," Tanya said. "You shouldn't make jokes. Psychics are applying their talents to the search round the clock." I saw that it was nine, and I laid aside my paper, preparing to leave. "There's something I need to ask you."

"It's late. I should be at work."

"Sit here and talk to me," she said, raising her voice. "This is important."

Her harsh look revealed her intent. Too late, I perceived the trap. With cunning worthy of our harsher rulers she'd waited until I'd lulled myself into a fool's notion of security before producing the list of my crimes. How could I imagine I would constantly outfox her? I would never have said so, but Tanya knew me even more intimately than did my mother. Myriad questions set my mind aflame. How had we been discovered? A note, slipped into a pocket and forgotten? An overheard phone call? An informant, perhaps one of my employees? Or possibly something more evanescent? I thoroughly washed my face and hands last night before coming home, as always, so that Tanya would not detect Sonya's personal fragrances. But had she smelled Sonya on me even in her sleep? It no longer mattered. I was captured; there was nothing to do but confess. "I understand," I said, accepting that my skull would shortly receive her bullet.

"There's a problem at my workplace, and I need your advice," she told me. "What is the matter now? You look as if you're about to faint."

"A moment of light-headedness," I muttered, disbelieving my good fortune but readily accepting the whims of fate. "The air. So stuffy inside."

"The window's open," she said. "If you ate breakfast you wouldn't feel bad."

"The tale of the little girl so disturbed me, I was unable to finish," I explained, with my fork shoveling what I hadn't eaten into my mouth. "Her dog. So tragic."

"Don't eat so fast," she said, slapping my arm.

"Of course," I said, slowing my movements, edging more closely to her that I might listen attentively to her words. My reprieve came so unexpectedly that throughout our conversation I had fantasies that I'd entered into a sustaining coma of my own and was only enjoying soothing dreams before rudely reawakening into our gray, muddlesome world. "What is the problem, my small bird?"

"We've contracted with a new group of investors who are driving us mad," she told me. "No matter what we suggest they put their money into, they find fault and refuse. All the same, they make it crystal clear they want to do business. What are we to do?"

Tanya ran a consulting company, which I financed for her. With reliable friends with whom she had worked for years in the Ministry of Foreign Trade, she advised businessmen who wished to invest hard currency in our prospering country. Once her clients selected an investment program, Tanya and her staff facilitated necessary arrangements with essential agencies and departments. Her approach in dealing with institutional fiends was not unlike mine, for she had learned her most subtle and effective techniques from me. "We're running out of ideas," she continued. "We offer imports, exports, steel, agriculture, retail. They turn up their noses and tell us find something else, please."

"Do they continue paying your consultation fees?" She nodded. We smiled.

"It arrives by messenger every Monday," she said. "Only Iosif has met with them directly; he knew someone who knew them."

The name was unfamiliar. "Who is Iosif?"

"A new employee. Very promising, I think."

"Does the political situation disturb them?" I asked. It amazes me that so many investors are struck dumb with fear when offered the chance to put money into our nation. Intelligent financiers from the far abroad whose opinions I respect rarely comprehend that it *does not matter* how our political situation turns out, if it ever does. There is no reason to believe that the solid business practices we have long employed in Russia throughout all regimes would be more than momentarily disrupted. Sometimes we Russians are so straightforward in our actions that outsiders cannot help but misunderstand us, I think—our honesty confounds them.

"Perhaps, but if so they think it impolite to mention," she said.

"Why would they show such courtesy?"

"Do you ever read anything but business chronicles? Science has proven that Asian brains are structured differently from ours. The frontal lobes, of course."

I stood corrected. "What are they, Japanese? Korean?"

"Representatives of the Sultan of Brunei," she said. "All necessary documentation has been provided."

"Brunei?"

"Would you talk to my associates and advise them on how to proceed?"

"Of course." As I shut my eyes a heavenly vision worthy of the mystics came to my mind: a rushing torrent of money, and I leaping salmonlike through it. From my wide reading I understood that the wealth of the Sultan of Brunei is limitless. Patriotic fervor gripped me. I comprehended at once that his representatives should under no circumstances depart from our struggling Motherland without leaving something of themselves behind. "Perhaps I can make safe recommendations for investments."

She arched her eyebrows. "Safe for whom?"

"For everyone," I assured her, kissing her on the cheek. She grabbed my face between her hands as if to tear it off, digging her fingernails into my skin before kissing me, glancingly, on the lips.

"Thank you, Max," she said.

"My dove," I told her. "Anything for you."

Then I left my happy home, breathing cold, refreshing air as I stepped outside, my soul warmed by the love of two women. On such pleasant mornings I walk to work, strolling down Tverskaya before turning east onto what was Marx Prospekt and is now Mokhovaya, although the signs remain unchanged. Khrushchev's apartment block has a grand public archway that gives access to our muddy court. As I transversed the gloomy portal I found the building manager's wife taking a broom to drunken beggars as she defended her rampart of trash containers.

"Idlers!" she shouted, swinging her knout. "Crawl back in your holes!"

Most of the sots were too pickled in alcohol to make a coherent reply. An older one tried, but his tongue lolled too loosely in his toothless maw to allow him to form words. "*Kyuhy–k'hui–kyuhh!*" he mumbled.

"Parasites! Drunks!" She swatted him on the head, a teacher correcting an egregious student, and chastened the others. "I'll call the militia!" But the squalid are as inventive as they are eternal. The one struck dumb by drink tried to scratch insults into the passageway's marble with an empty tin of pork roll. Making my way to the boulevard, I exited this drama as unimpressed as the most demanding critic.

By daylight Tverskaya teemed with a multitude of *sovoks*—human dustpans—as our great helmsmen once, in private, called the proud Soviet people. Throngs of provincial shoppers, and not a few Muscovites, muscled their way along the broad sidewalks. Capitalists—not people who line the street selling treasured heirlooms purchased for resale the week before but machines so named, a tractor whose two crab arms pinch up and carry away snow—were clearing the boulevard to allow motor traffic to pass unhindered. In my golden youth *stilyagi*, or hooligans, rechristened Tverskaya Broadway. (*Stilyagi* wore pegged pants, Elvis hair; their coats were so padded you could shoot them and they'd not know. They listened to rock and roll on the bones, as I did, and were always arrested, as I never was.) Tverskaya, Moscow's central boulevard, is beautiful beyond measure but has nothing of Broadway about it. I have never visited New York but I have seen photographs, and I feel assured in saying nothing in Moscow resembles New York.

One of my banks was parked outside the Central Telegraph Office. There are dozens of new financial institutions in Moscow— DialogBank, Tokobank, Rosselkhozbank, to name but a few competitors (Menatep, of course, is far above us all in terms of power and reach, but considering the background of its operators that should come as no surprise). Many are run solely to satisfy criminal designs, but not the Comrades' Bank, which I own with two colleagues once employed by the competent organs. Our seven mobile facilities make loans, exchange foreign currency, and provide invaluable services for resident and tourist alike. The guards recognized me and didn't aim as I approached. Most of our stalwarts are Afghanistan veterans, battle-hardened and impervious to temptations that enemies of productive people may offer.

My co-investors and I know who to bribe and how often, and thus far we had avoided the random assaults that so often beset even the most corrupt financial institutions. Too, word circulates freely throughout criminal circles regarding prophylactic measures we have taken to safeguard our banks. If mercenary brigands were to attempt to rob one of our facilities, you see, the entire van would blow up the instant the teller pressed his foot against the alarm button in the floor. For reasons of security, of course, we never arm our tellers with a complete understanding of our advanced antitheft technology.

Waiting for me was my day-to-day supervisor Arteim, an Armenian. The main reason Muscovites hold irrational prejudices against those sharp southern entrepreneurs is because there are no better businessmen. Arteim and I met in the late seventies; we had mutual acquaintances involved in what was afterward called the Fishy Business. Ministry of Fisheries bureaucrats had formulated a scheme using fruits of the sea as items of barter and bribery, enabling themselves to fatten for years on the spoils. The cabal dissolved in frenzied finger-pointing and tearful confession after keen-eyed customs officials accidentally discovered thousands of tins of Sevruga labeled for export as low-grade herring, in brine, for cats.

Arteim and I were innocent of provable involvement with the plot and so escaped the accusations of all but the most suspicious. It saddened us to watch our associates be snatched so unexpectedly from public life, but we consoled ourselves afterward with knowledge that could not have been gained except through experience and have since enjoyed fifteen years of profitable friendship.

He stood with an unfamiliar man beneath a framed photograph of Milton Friedman. Our associate Telman (who is also Armenian) insists that the economist's troubled mien be hung in all our facilities to reassure American customers—I suspect most of them think it a photograph of Lenin they haven't seen before. When he greeted me, Arteim showed not as much chrome as he generally reveals when he smiles. The stranger was tall and wide and wore an orange jacket fabricated of leather so laughably false it would not be used for insulating apartment doors. It gleamed as if buttered, and one worn elbow was patched with electrical tape. I observed sizable bulges at his sides and took comfort in the proximity of our guards. "We have a problem, Max," Arteim said.

I introduced myself. "Ivan Ivanovich," the stranger replied, the tone of his voice suggestive of a broken oboe. It was all I could do to contain my hilarity, hearing such a pseudonymous name. He looked as if he came from the Far East, or at least from some distance beyond Irkutsk. We shook hands. Ivan Ivan's paw was damp, as if he kept it beneath rocks when not using it.

"Let us enjoy frank and open debate regarding our concerns," I said, opening a drawer in Arteim's desk, taking out glasses and a bottle of ten-year-old Noyag brandy. "Shall we toast our desire to attain mutual satisfaction?"

"Too early," Ivan Ivan said, his reeds squeaking. I placed the bottle and glasses back on the desk. It was unfortunate that he abstained; drink so often has a soothing effect on uncultured hooligans, so long as their superiors provide limitless amounts of essential nectar. "Celebrate later. Your associate and I disagree. I think you can settle this matter."

"What's the problem?"

"It is complex," Ivan Ivan said, slouching against the wall. I wondered if he would leave a greasy spot on the paneling. His jacket's leatherette was as squeaky as his voice. "Our monthly collections. It is shameful to deal always in cash, don't you think? Such disreputable light is cast upon our great friendship."

"Money doesn't smell," Arteim interjected. I saw that his own sidearm was in handy reach, which troubled me. He carried it always but never used it, and if the spirit of the Wild East suddenly seized him I doubted he could remember which was the right end to hold. "Valera never suffered such humiliation, seeing us. Is that why he no longer comes? Was the shame too great for him to bear?"

"Where is Valera?" I asked. In the prison without walls that Russia has become, it is often difficult to remember with which criminal gang one is dealing unless its members have given you reason to never, ever forget. Valera, and now Ivan Ivan, represented one of the more reasonable mafias. Valera was an affable lout who could not refuse a proffered drink. Thinking of him, I recalled his nose, or should I say the half that hadn't been cut off. "Promoted?"

Ivan Ivan lowered his eyes. "Death arising from a chronic ailment."

"Who shot him?"

Before our visitor could avoid telling me, Arteim interrupted to make a more plaintive inquiry. "Why will you not take our money?"

"It cheapens our friendly relations," Ivan Ivan claimed. "I'm not saying no money ever; that would be foolish. But there is more in life than money."

"A remarkable thesis," I said.

"This is not my belief alone. Our entire group is concerned."

"Are you in a spiritual crisis?" Arteim asked, sneering. "Troubled with the fate of art in a degenerate world?"

I raised my hand; my partner fell silent.

"May I be forthright?" Ivan Ivan asked. "Life is filled with enough humiliations. At present there is something we need more than money. We know you have great access to many things."

"Do you mean strategic resources?" I asked, inferring without exertion that he sought electric samovars or refrigerators or other such consumer opiates. He carefully slid his hand beneath his jacket, moving with caution so as not to alarm our alert guards. Instead of armament, he drew forth a doll.

"You recognize?" he asked, as though without his kind prompting we would be at a loss to identify the small mannequin. When Moscow's numberless prostitutes fail at disguising themselves as Madonna they try to look like Barbie, with as much success. The doll he clasped in his fist was no less scuffed and bedraggled than her impersonators, as though she had been recently taking pleasure with her male doll compatriots or possibly with Ivan Ivan himself. "Some desirable items money cannot buy, as even you prosperous gentlemen know."

"You need Barbies?"

"Do you not believe our dealings would be more soul-rewarding if sometimes we traded for what enriches the drab lives of our families instead of mere common currency?" His eyes grew wet, as if he stood facing the wind. "We do what we can in these hard times. My colleagues are not as wealthy as I may appear."

For the first time I noticed an ugly wen on the side of his head and found it impossible to take my eyes away. "You want dolls for your families?"

"Our little girls," he said. "They cry themselves to sleep."

It disheartens me to tell you that Arteim's expression softened at once. Southerners jerk like puppets when emotional strings are pulled. "I have two little girls," he said.

"I hope yours don't weep their nights away," said Ivan Ivan. Even his wen appeared to be throbbing with pain. This masterstroke eroded our position of strength; upon hearing such a deeply felt sentiment Arteim toppled squarely onto the side of the little girls.

"How could I know your situation?" he asked. "You didn't tell us until now."

"Sadness froze my lips," said Ivan Ivan.

"Probably we can create the right conditions," I interrupted, anxious to assuage this heartbreak. Arteim was so overcome he excused himself, walking away to find a cloth with which to wipe his brimming eyes. "How many do you need?"

"Not many," Ivan Ivan said, recovering with breathtaking speed. "Four–five hundred." He scratched his wen. "Even now I can hear them crying."

"You must fear drowning in a flood of tears," I said. Barbies sell on the street for fifty dollars, in stores for eighty; I could buy them for ten. Thanks to Arteim's soft heart and head, I would soon see five thousand dollars fly through my window en route to this cadre of thugs and their illusory little girls. Possibly the dolls were to be stuffed with heroin and exported, and that irritated me; I had never sought deliberate involvement with would-be pharmacists of the people. "Something can be done, I'm sure. But I am no wonder-worker."

"I know you'll do everything possible." He returned Moscow Barbie to his pocket, pulling open his jacket and allowing me to better glimpse his unimpressive weaponry.

"Without question." For a moment I wished that I could direct my guard to shoot him on the spot—however, a rash businessman is a dead one, soon enough. "For now, why don't we use traditional cash stipends?"

"I think that would be all right."

"Let me leave you with a happy memory," I told him, stepping over to the teller's compartment. Taking two hundred-dollar bills, I held them against the light to make certain they were genuine. Of late, two-thirds of the dollars passing through Moscow are counterfeit. "You're sure you don't find it too demeaning to accept this in lieu of Barbies?" Ivan Ivan shook his head and hastily stuffed the cash into his pants. "Good-bye, then."

Arteim returned as Ivan Ivan, his wen, and his squeaking jacket made their exit. "How could you suck up such idiotic lies?" I asked him, infuriated.

"Why are you berating me, Max? Think of those poor children. Have you no emotions?"

"That lout makes a sucker out of you while I'm standing before you. How could you be such a fool?"

"How can you deny small girls simple joys?"

"Five hundred small girls?" I said. Arteim frowned. "He and his colleagues are evidently national heroes of production."

"The fucking swindler," he said. "Using small children to take advantage."

"How many times have I told you? Keep emotion separate from business. Do you ever listen? My God!" In keeping with my advice, my anger speedily cooled. We have been through so much that on those infrequent occasions when his business sense is not what it should be, I can always find it in my heart to forgive him.

"I'm sorry, Max," Arteim said, plainly abashed. "Should we kill him?"

The emotional strings to which Southerners jump are as often made of razor wire as of silk. "To what end?" I inquired, and of course he did not answer me. Not once had I found it necessary to have anyone murdered; not every Russian businessman can make such a claim. "Possibly we can turn this deal to our benefit. Let us think how to satisfy the lousy peasant without losing our shirts."

"Should I track the Barbie market?" Arteim asked.

"Go ahead," I said. "We'll undoubtedly find the solution to this needless problem." He grimaced, fearing my anger, and I was contented enough by his appropriate reaction to say no more. "Look into something else for me. A crematorium called Glow of Life at Nicholas Archangel, in Reutov. There are troubling things going on there, I think. Find out who the investors are, if you can."

"Is it a market with potential?"

"Limitless."

My office was a short distance away on Nikolskaya Street in Kitai-Gorod. From trustworthy officials I rent the third floor of a six-story building once used to house superfluous files of the Ministry of Agriculture. The structure was put up in 1963 and has aged as well as any constructed during that era of giants. Windows streak with rust, concrete erodes into sand, the roof retains so much water that mushrooms could sprout from its asphalt. There is an ever-widening gap between the outer wall and the floor in my office; I can drop a pencil into the gap, and it will reach the basement in seconds. Last autumn a steel panel fell from the facade, crushing two strollers and decapitating another (partially, vertically). Since then, I waste no time lingering at the doorway of the building. But office space is in short supply, and sometimes you must leave yourself in the hands of merciless fate.

Allow me an advertisement (an infomercial, I believe they are now called in America) for my central operation, founded four years ago. The Universal Manufacturing Company supplies a demanding public with needed documents. My trained specialists are accomplished at preparing notarized reports, business contracts, banking records, panegyrics issued by long-dead worthies, audits of production achievements worthy of material reward—in short, any paper that eases citizen life and warms bureaucratic hearts (excepting those aforementioned funerary officials, who are difficult). We can produce historic Soviet documents drawn to suit the demanding specifications of foreign journalists or officials. Prices are on a sliding scale; we would not charge a poor grandmother the same as the BBC or MTV. For now, the Universal Manufacturing Company deals strictly on a hard-currency basis. We use all modern overnight-express shipping services.

"Good morning, all," I said, walking in. My well-paid staff joyfully responded, raising their heads from their desks, some for the moment pushing aside their lights and tools and engraving equipment. The long row of gentle *babushki* I keep busy preparing the small red folders in which internal passports are housed clucked and fluttered when I walked by them, as if they were hens and I a potent rooster. My senior workers smiled at my approach, and I gave them hearty greetings, stopping sometimes to inquire about a few long-term projects. "How's it going?" I asked Fyodor, who worked on a project that held great interest for British researchers.

"Mr. Philby has outwitted his superiors left and right," Fyodor said, riffling a sheaf of superb-looking documents, "but now he wishes to atone for his errors."

I clapped him heartily on the back. Tomas, an excellent scribe who for many years worked in the competent organs in Nizhni Novgorod, raised his hand as I walked by, calling for my attention.

"Max?" he asked, showing me KGB documents to which he'd devoted unwavering attention for days. "I need only appropriate signatures."

"Pass it to Mischa, he can do them in his sleep," I said, studying the paper; it was perfect. Tomas's assignment necessitated his producing a host of documents suggesting that CIA agents in Minsk foiled KGB attempts to brainwash Lee Harvey Oswald during the noted assassin's stay in our all-welcoming country. These documents were intended to eventually reach a well-known Chicago scholar, or so our middleman informed us. History can be so much more flexible than Lenin ever supposed; last May, Tomas supplied a California researcher with papers proving the precise opposite.

"The stamps are correct?" he asked.

"Reconfirm with Valentina." In our contemporary world, past events are nothing more than zakuski, from which one selects delicious appetizers according to one's particular taste, and it pleases us to cater. The Universal Manufacturing Company can prove John Kennedy shot himself, as long as we are paid in advance.

When I stepped into my office suite my administrative assistant, Ludmilla, was already there. An aggressively responsible woman in her sixties, she believes deeply in her heart—as we all of us do here at Universal Manufacturing—that disturbing facts should never be too long hidden and thus relays unpleasant news every morning before I can even say hello.

"You have visitors and you'll not want to see them," she told me.

"Who are they?"

"Evgeny, for one."

My younger brother. "Why is he here?"

"It would be beneath him to tell me, or so he seems to believe," she said, making a sour face. "Impress upon him that I am no public lackey. He's in your office."

"He won't be for long. Who else?"

"Dmitry Mikhailovich Gubin."

Sonya's husband. "Where is he?"

"He went for a walk when I told him you hadn't yet arrived. Said he'll return at ten. He must talk to you, he insists. I told him he has no appointment and therefore it will depend on your discretion."

"Did he say what he wanted?"

She shook her head. "He appeared nervous."

As any man might appear, coming to shoot his wife's lover. That, of course, was my initial unfounded reaction. For a moment I almost took my bulletproof vest out of the closet, but aging amateurs such as Dmitry rarely aim for the head, at least not on the first shot. I tried to throw off my gnawing fears. He could never have discovered our situation on his own, and Sonya would never confess. But what if he had? What if she did? At once my suspicions returned and began feeding on themselves. No emotion is so gaily self-cannibalistic as paranoia. I glanced behind me, in case he had crept back into the office, intent on revenge.

"Send him in when he returns," I said, and stepped into my office. Evgeny sat in my comfortable chair, resting muddy shoes on my mahogany desk and perusing an issue of *The Economist*. With brusque motions I shoved his feet back to the floor where they belonged.

"Max!" he exclaimed, quickly rising so that I might take the seat he so courteously warmed for me. "A great opportunity presents itself."

"Stop treating Ludmilla as if she were your lickspittle," I said. "We have no serfs here. Do you fancy yourself one of the false Romanovs?"

"She doesn't like me, Max. I have done nothing to her. She stares at me as if I were a spider, as if I'm evil personified."

"Stupidity personified, perhaps. What do you want? It's too early to listen to your mad ideas."

"Investors are interested in my park," he said. "It could mean big money for both of us. Is that too mad for you to hear?"

Evgeny is our family's holy fool. My brother will always be dear to me, but since childhood he has done all he can to test my love. For inexplicable reasons he perceives himself to be a master businessman, a financial whiz, my entrepreneurial equal. Evgeny could funnel money into a penned goose and never see a kopeck of it again. During the Brezhnev years, when even the little coma girl could have made millions of rubles while lying unconscious in her bed of trauma, Evgeny lost money in harebrained schemes. Under perestroika, when the lowest *zug* could get a handout from intelligent Westerners as long as an acceptable hatred of communism was feigned, Evgeny landed himself repeatedly into debt. Yet

I must be fair and admit that he is not so much stupid as merely cursed with a soul innocent of guile. As a child he took too closely to heart our mother's fairy tales, and if today you were to tell him you had a magic hen for sale, he would open my wallet without a second's hesitation. "Who is crazy enough?" I asked.

"Americans," he said, almost hopping up and down with excitement. I must also admit that his most recent idea is not without merit. For two years he had devoted unstinting effort to developing a Western-style theme park to be located outside of Moscow. From a Polish consortium he borrowed money to purchase the land, and I had interest enough in the concept to sink seventy thousand dollars into preliminary construction. As of that morning, of course, only one building had been partially built.

"Were they on a tour bus?" I asked.

"They're from Texas," he said, and then, in English, "Howdy, partners." Before hearing his call to the world of high finance, Evgeny wanted to be a cowboy. So often I wished that our parents had given him the horse he beseeched St. Nicholas and the Snow Queen to bring him. "They want to invest much money."

"How did you meet them? What references do they have?" Proportionately, there are as many criminal Americans in Russia at present as there are criminal Russians, but not even the most respectable are here because of altruistic desires to assist our hard-beset people. Americans are our main competitors, uninterested in Russian prosperity and might unless it serves their purposes; only a fool denies it. Their business acumen is rarely as sharp as they think it to be, but Evgeny is perhaps the only Russian who could be constantly outwitted by Americans.

"Through your friend Gyorgi Ilyich," he said, mentioning the name of a friend in the Ministry of Foreign Trade whose judgment I trusted. He had an unfortunate tendency to pass along information he thought useful to Evgeny without warning me beforehand. Granted, in the hands of anyone other than Evgeny the information could probably prove fruitful. "I haven't met them. We spoke by phone. They stay at the Metropole and are utterly reliable, he says."

"I want to meet them as well. I should assist in your presentation, I suppose?" My beloved brother nodded his head so rapidly I feared it would shake loose of his shoulders. I no longer allowed him to face wolves alone when they came seeking fresh lamb. "When is a meeting scheduled?"

"In a few days."

"You can't tell me?"

"I left my appointment book at my office."

"All right," I said, sighing. Always, I am encircled by fires onto which I must piss unending streams of money. Ludmilla appeared at the door.

"Mr. Gubin has returned," she said.

"Have him come in. Good-bye, Evgeny. Use the side exit."

"Thank you again, Max." As he bolted from the room, Dmitry Gubin entered. At a glance I saw he was unarmed and so at least felt assured of my physical security. To look at Dmitry, you would not have guessed he was incomparably more prosperous than he had been when he worked at the Ministry of Internal Affairs. He was flamboyantly nondescript. His old Hungarian suit was so stiff it might have been lined with cardboard, and his shoes had never come into proximity with leather. Dmitry's hair, what there was of it, was a greenish-gray blond. His hands, speckled with liver spots, showed nails bitten to the quick. It was lucky for him he had as much money as he did, for otherwise Sonya would not have looked twice at him except to laugh the louder.

"Come in, Dmitry Mikhailovich," I said, although he had already sat down. There is no excuse to forget one's manners, however base the behavior of those around you, but most of my countrymen will never learn this. "How can I help?"

I braced myself to suffer, and thereafter deny, a torrent of accusations; but fate continued to be kind, and it soon became apparent to me that he had not come to discuss any unfortunate discoveries he might have made. "I need to retain your specialists for an assignment, if you are willing to take me on as a client," he said. "Is your office secure, Maxim?"

"Absolutely," I said. Every day two of my experts swept the office, protecting against electronic infiltration by malcontents, or spies wishing access to our trade secrets. "Talk freely to me, as if you were in your own apartment."

Judging from his expression, that was perhaps not so assuring a thought as I might have intended. "Three friends and myself are setting up a new operation," he began. "They worked in the old Department for Combating Theft of Socialist Property." I smiled. Dmitry may as well have confessed the crimes they'd not yet committed. The aforementioned department was corrupt even by Soviet standards; volunteers for such combat uniformly left the battlefield burdened by the fruits of victorious pillage while at arms. "We will export souvenirs from Russia to Brighton Beach, New York, in exchange for hard currency."

"Souvenirs?" I repeated. "How many surplus medals and balalaikas does the world need?"

"A host of available markets remain," Dmitry said, his mask as solemn as before. "Our group is funding the operation, with some assistance by silent partners. We intend to work in partnership with another group responsible for oversight."

"One of the more dependable mafias?" I asked, but he made no direct reply.

"Single representatives from our two groups are presently hammering out specifics of our partnership. These negotiations will conclude by the end of February. What I need done needs to be done before then."

"Broader investigations will be undertaken at the conclusion of negotiations?" Such was standard procedure; one can be no less careful in choosing partners for business than for marriage—should be more careful, in most cases.

"Exactly," he said. "The representatives will exchange complete membership information and afterward will make background checks of all participants. Once the reliability of those involved is assured, the contract will be signed, we'll meet for formal celebrations, the program goes forth. Standard procedure."

There was of course a great deal Dmitry was not telling me, but that was as it should be. "I congratulate you on your initiative, but you've not come to boast of your marketing prowess. What do you want us to do?" I paused long enough to give him a most necessary caveat. "Don't relate information which doesn't directly bear upon the proposed assignment."

By making that statement and preserving it on tape, I could later defend myself against charges of conspiracy, if charges were for any reason ever filed—my lawyer assured me that it is a fool-

proof procedure. (I have a new lawyer, now.) Dmitry stared at me
for an interminable time before speaking. Again, I felt a disconcerting chill along my spine; this was prelude, I thought anew, a
distraction before his attack began—but I was wrong. Leaning forward, whispering, he said, "I will have to give you *some* background. You remember the railroad scandal?"

"Of course." The railroad scandal was, I think, the most
breathtaking swindle perpetrated during the Brezhnev regime;
granted, the competition is fierce. A railroad through Georgia was
proposed and designed. The go-ahead was given. Every kopeck
of the millions of rubles allocated for the project was siphoned off
during the four-year period of so-called construction. In most of the
world, secrets known to more than one are no longer secrets; but
in our incomparable land, millions know secrets and they remain
secrets. The multitude eventually involved in the scheme not only
conspired to pretend that the railroad was being built, continuing
after its theoretical completion to claim that the railroad truly existed, but went one step—a staircase!—beyond by providing and
forwarding to the unsuspecting agencies solid proof that the imaginary railroad was one of the most productive in the Soviet Union. I
have read much in western magazines recently concerning the supposed new field of virtual reality; has there ever been any other kind
in Russia? "You were involved?"

"Very much so," he said, his eyes wary as a cornered rabbit's.

"This casts a shadow over present situations?"

"Very much so," he repeated, sighing as if guilt caused him
physical pain. "When deputy ministers are themselves involved,
is it so shocking that those under them would also be? I was no
mastermind, no Napoleon of crime, but if advantage could be
taken, you took it." Unexpectedly his face lost its lines of care, and
I could not imagine what elation seized his heart until I realized
he was under the impression he was confessing to one who in spirit,
if not in act, was but another stalwart in corruption. "You remember those years, Max. The most of the most."

"I am not threatening you with the gulag, Dmitry. What is
your point?"

From his brow he wiped fear's morning dew. "I am telling
you I was but one of many semi-innocents, that is all. Unlike most
of the idiots involved, some of us saved our money so that when

Andropov's dogs came sniffing, we could buy needed influence. But money wasn't enough, sometimes. It's been all I could do to live with my conscience, since."

"Lived well, I'd say."

He ignored my remark. "Pressure was put upon us by the competent organs. We were given an opportunity to redeem ourselves by serving our nation patriotically through the sharing of information. I did what I could, several of us did. We passed along potentially useful facts regarding a key cadre of plotters in Tbilisi, of whose existence the authorities were unaware. Its members were prosecuted and convicted and shipped to Archangel, excepting the one who was executed. My God, Max, you wouldn't expect Georgians to thrive in such cold country." He shuddered as if he too had for too long been flash-frozen.

"They survived and have returned?" I asked.

"Understand that my present associates, who were innocent of involvement in the railroad scandal, were the ones who initiated our current deal. Once it was under way, what could I do?"

"You're telling me the group with whom you'll be in partnership includes the same Georgians you helped send to prison?"

"Some of them."

"Are they aware of your guilt?" I asked. "If not, they'll ascertain your complicity when they look into the records."

"Precisely my point," he said. "They don't know me yet; I would have been nothing to them at the time. It was only a happy accident that I knew of their involvement. Not so happy, now. I was told the reports I made were entered anonymously, but who knows for sure? When the Georgians make their search, they may find suggestive material. It would be only human for them to leap to conclusions."

"Why don't you make new deals, with safer partners?" I asked. "That's my recommendation."

"This deal is unmatchable, Maxim," he said. "An astonishing opportunity."

"To peddle souvenirs like a pensioner in street markets?"

"*Blyad!*" he shouted, and hot words erupted like lava from his mouth. "There's money enough in this deal to enable Sonya and me to leave this insane country!"

"That's your intention?" I asked, knowing I revealed no

disconcertion in my features. Sonya had told me nothing of any plans to emigrate.

"What kind of life are we living here, Max? We are prosperous, sure. We command respect. We enjoy business success, we own fine apartments, we possess priceless treasures. We live like kings, but we live in a pigsty. Here shit, there shit. What kind of life is that for human beings?"

"These are Russia's most difficult hours, Dmitry, but—"

"But what? Wait till the future? How long have we heard such lies about our radiant future? Look out your window, tell me what our future will be."

"What I was going to tell you is we should make what we can of the present," I said. "Let's put the future behind us."

"I am trying to make everything I can of the present," he told me. "You say not to tell you more than is necessary. Very well, it is necessary that I be in on this deal, whatever the dangers. It is necessary that the records are corrected. The world waits for me, and I want to go there." Dmitry halted his tirade and paused, gasping for breath. "Can you do the job?"

"Of course, but it is complex," I said. "Several thousand documents will be involved in such a case as you describe. They must be found, destroyed, replaced. Plus checks in KGB records. Maybe in SVRR, or even the GRU. All this to be done in a month and a half. And I don't have to tell you, the bureaucrats with whom we deal will have to be greased until they're slippery as eels."

"That doesn't fuck me," he said. "No one but you can even grasp the enormity of the problem, much less solve it."

"The problem itself is not my sole concern. Georgians are dangerous. The idea of working with them even at a distance troubles me."

"Certainly I sympathize with your fear," Dmitry said.

"Then you understand why I cannot—"

"One million dollars, American. Three hundred now, the remainder once our deal is concluded. Would this sum bolster your courage?"

Though usually I am as adept as Tanya at cloaking honest emotions beneath a facade of cool impassiveness, I feel sure Dmitry discerned the shock I felt, hearing him name his sum. "Why do you need money to move if you can provide such a fee for our services?"

"For our project my group, not I, have funding sufficient for our needs. What do you say, Max?"

The pashas and beys of the Sultan were yet waiting to be greeted. But who could predict how they might respond to my enticements? One million dollars, and I could hear every bill rustling like leaves in the wind. "Give me until tomorrow to decide."

"He has whispered these dreams in my ears before. Why should I believe him?" Sonya asked me that evening, in the tiny apartment off Arbat Street I rent specifically to assure undisturbed privacy for our evening trysts. "My darling, it's too ridiculous to warrant consideration. He and I are not leaving Russia, don't worry. You and I are capable people, sure, but what would Dmitry do, anywhere else?"

"He has his talents," I noted, but I remained unconvinced that I could enumerate them, if called upon to do so. She stroked my arms with feather's touch and rubbed her legs against mine as if to set them ablaze. There aren't words enough for me to say how dearly I love my wife, for all our trials, but I would be lying if I didn't tell you that when I was with Sonya I wished to be nowhere else. Already once that evening we had made mad love, and now she bided her time while I regained my strength.

"Just to smuggle his priceless treasures out of Russia would cost him the money he is already busy counting," she said. "Dmitry is so smart, he is stupid. And these partners of his are no wiser, I assure you."

"He's told you nothing about this project?" I asked again. "Not even a hint?"

She shook her head. I felt unspeakable delight, marveling at my goddess's gold hair gleaming in the room's winter moonlight. "Why should it matter that you know what they're up to? Isn't it written in your contracts that you should know nothing about nothing?"

"This is different," I said. "Too many uncertainties. There's this involvement with Georgians. His cagey references to silent partners. And so much money. There is something dark under way, I think."

"If Dmitry wants to give you this mountain of money, take it," she said. "I would prefer that you were the one so burdened with wealth."

"If he's involved in malfeasance you're involved as well, my angel." Embracing me, she raked her fingernails along my sides. The stimulating pain she inflicted with her talons made me more aware of my apprehension. "You may be burned if he's juggling fire." It was difficult to speak with an extra tongue in my mouth; I pulled away from her. "This project may keep him in such proximity to me that it may be harder for us to see each other. Have you thought of that?" Striking with astonishing speed, she hit her target with unerring accuracy, once more fastening her lips onto mine. We kissed as if to inhale each other's souls. "Look, if his plan succeeds, and he's serious, he'll leave and take you with him. And I'll have helped him take you from me."

"Why should I leave unless I want to?" she asked, bringing her face so close to mine that I thought I glimpsed ball lightning leaping between our eyes. "I'll go nowhere I don't want to go. He can juggle whatever he wants."

"It could be dangerous."

Sonya stopped my mouth with a nipple, quieting her infant. As she bade me suck she pushed my head and shoulders against our bed's headboard. A small *matryoshka* doll tumbled onto the mattress. "There is danger walking down any street," she said. "Danger here with you too, I think."

As she took my ear in her mouth she carefully replaced her doll on the headboard, which was lined with our room's *poshlaia*, an army of *matryoshkas*. *Matryoshkas* are Russia's own Barbies, small wooden dolls that hold, nestling within them, a series of progressively smaller wooden dolls: open the first and find another, and then another. Traditionally, each doll is a replica of the one that encases it, but in recent years the artists are perhaps reacting as artists often subconsciously do to transformations in their societies, as the peasant smells the storm in the wind. When you open a *matryoshka* of contemporary vintage, there is no foretelling what pleasant or unpleasant discoveries may be found within.

"Mutual danger," I said.

Sonya revealed her teeth and then turned away, crawling serpentlike to the foot of our bed. She curled over the edge, placing her hands on the floor. My eyes were drawn to the end of Sonya that conveys the purest and most essential expression. She wriggled her backside, as if her unseen front half were helplessly caught. My response to that particular action of hers was Pavlovian: my well-worn implement rose up to beg unconditionally for its honeyed treat. "Decadent Western music should accompany our sins, don't you think?" she said, switching on her tape player. I grimaced as she added her own atonal purr to those deafening American yodels. Backing up, lifting her hips, she spread her long legs so I could better focus on the apex of her pyramid.

"Come pin your butterfly."

"*Koshka!*" I exclaimed. Making a great leap forward, I buried my face in her underbeard, and as I lapped up her sweet nectar, tasting of mushrooms and honey, her feral moans counterpointed those of her favored artists. Rolling onto her back, she seized my neck with her hands as if to break it, arched her spine, and clamped her legs around me, pinching my sides in an iron grip. During our maniacal storm of passion she gasped, shrieked, wept, and gnashed her teeth. She flailed her arms so wildly she left bruises where she struck me, but I barely noticed and couldn't have cared less (I would take pains later to be sure Tanya did not see them). It was hot work in the sweatshop. The Bolshevik Alexandra Kollontai (whom romantic if wrong-headed revisionists have recently called Lenin's mistress) is notorious for having said that in our unprecedented revolutionary society sexual intercourse should be no less necessary, or more remarkable, than the act of drinking a glass of water. I could not imagine that Sonya's thirst would ever be slaked.

Afterward we lay on damp sheets, clasped tightly, as if we could burrow beneath each other's skin. Her music, mercifully, came to an end. We listened instead to the argument of the couple who lived next door and to trucks grinding gears as their drivers sped down the lanes of the nearby Garden Ring.

"Tell him you'll do it." Her voice was a moist whisper.

One million dollars. "I don't know."

"Tell him. Believe me, I won't go with him if he emigrates. And if there's danger in what he does, who better to protect me from danger than you?"

Hundreds, perhaps thousands would be better equipped; that is, after all, what security forces are for. "He'll be constantly lurking around. Even the blindest hog finds truffles."

"Dmitry could be in the next room now and never know we were in here together, naked. He is too preoccupied with his grand schemes. With his treasures. Tell me, how could he ever know of our love?"

"If you tell him."

Sonya ran angel's fingers along the length of me. "One raven never pecks out the eyes of another."

"I'll speak to him tomorrow," I said, as she started to lick my neck. Gunshots, outside, sounded as celebratory fireworks. What a joyous city is Moscow.

3

The empty street was gray and rain-slick. Eddies of fog blurred a single streetlamp's cone of light. A black Chaika with tinted windows pulled to a screeching stop at the curb. A uniformed military intelligence officer opened the door, the rock pile of his face thrown into shadow by his cap's shiny brim. His mitts were the size of beer mugs. "Get in," he demanded, in heavily accented English. "We've been looking for you."

Evgeny and I shared warm smiles of profound satisfaction. I had not seen the infomercial before and was at first entirely pleased with what he and my acquaintances at Cinema House had produced.

"Don't argue," the officer said, taking his place in the car, pointing his finger and glaring directly at the lens as if the camera sat fettered in the back seat. "You must go to Sovietland!"

Our three-Texan audience shifted in their chairs, doubtlessly impressed by the actor's apt portrayal of a cruel Communist operative. In quotidian life the actor, a friend of Evgeny's, was employed as a security guard by SVRR, the successor agency to the KGB—a watchman who watches the watchmen, as it were. For his performance he received twelve hard-earned dollars.

"We're going to Sovietland!" the happy family imprisoned in the car replied, cheering. The two small children were ideal, but Evgeny failed to cast the parental roles with actors or actresses blessed with a true American look. The young husband, grinning, showed a jawful of steel, and his wife wore more eye makeup than the most pathetic prostitute. Their matching T-shirts were emblazoned with English words: HAPPY FOOLY HAVE A CASUAL BEAT LIFE. Costume supervisor Evgeny Borodin supplied these fashionable garments from an inexhaustible cornucopia of leisure apparel he'd earlier obtained from a crafty Japanese wholesaler, in exchange for irreplaceable icons our family owned for generations.

"Sovietland is a most dependable part of the recipe for recuperation," the officer intoned. "In Sovietland, we will check the victorious march of capitalism and turn back the wheel of history. Hey, you, have a great time!"

The fifteen-minute film mixed contemporary scenes of the aforementioned players with Soviet documentary footage of May Day celebrations, Young Pioneer parades, economic festivals, and like bacchanalias, as well as artistic sketches and architectural designs illustrating the proposed thirty pavilions and rides of Sovietland. Jubilant music taped off soundtracks of old American industrial films obtained from the Ministry of Foreign Trade film library provided pert accompaniment to the scenic visuals.

"Streets are safe, prices stable, rents low, jobs guaranteed," the officer told the tourists, through the magic of traveling mattes seeming to show them a thousand tractors arrayed in martial formation.

"We must be in heaven," said the tourists.

"Ha-ha-ha-ha," the officer replied. "No, we must be in Sovietland!"

We held the video's premiere in Evgeny's spartan office on Herzen Street, which I rented for him so he would always have a place to eat lunch and bring women. The three Texans devoted unwavering attention to our presentation. My beloved brother, however, apparently believed the audience to be incapable of fully appreciating the more understated aspects of the proposal; repeatedly, and against my better judgment, he added annotative commentary in an English that could by no means be called fluent.

"Only souvenirs for sale will be terrible Soviet Union products," Evgeny noted loudly. "Tourist staff will be surly and unpleasant, great specialists in nonobtrusive service." The Texans shook their heads, hearing his assurances, and I slapped him hard on the back, making pantomimic gestures that he should not utter another word.

"Hello, Miss Soviet Union," the officer said. In amazement I watched him introduce the tourists to Evgeny's girlfriend, Irina, a nineteen-year-old Kiev model and karate teacher bereft, as far as I knew, of thespian talent.

"What is she doing in this?" I angrily whispered to my brother. He ignored me, intent on explicating the scene to our guests.

"Miss Soviet Union personifies beautiful land, untapped ability of younger generation, and bountiful goodness of Russian women," Evgeny proclaimed as Miss Soviet Union struck poses that well displayed bountiful curves. "She or someone like her will be welcoming visitors with hearty hugs." For inexplicable reasons his doxy began executing wild leaps onscreen, flinging herself in all directions. "Her skill in kicking enemy heads with feet serves to emphasize maidenly charms."

One of the Texans held his hand over his mouth, as if to keep from laughing or vomiting. The officer and the tourists, thankfully, took leave of Miss Soviet Union. Drawings of stylish pavilions limned in the Constructivist manner of Chernikhov appeared, anteceded by grainy footage of a Ukrainian feast.

"Staff will be outfitted in favored Soviet garb," Evgeny continued. "A funny feature will be that some double as secret police. If guests are overheard criticizing Communist system they will be taken to realistic prison. Sentences will be only half-hour instead of life, sure," he explained. "Psychological provocation adds pep to plate of plenty."

At last the park model in its entirety appeared on camera, a detailed miniature of which even Hollywood's skilled wonder-workers would be proud. There, built to scale, were the Tatlin Tower, which visitors would ascend to enjoy spectacular panoramas; the Central House of Refreshment for the Benefit of Peoples, which would purvey exquisite delicacies and simple provender in the traditional manner of our quartermasters; the Guest Workers' Hotel, where Sovietland tourists could experience socialist life for as long as they could bear it; and the rest of the rides and exhibits. An architecture student, otherwise underemployed, had prepared the tiny models, which were of a fineness not seen in the buildings constructed in Moscow in the last twenty years.

Yet I felt overwhelming shame and humiliation, for Evgeny had chosen the moment of filming to wander aimlessly across the rear of the set, towering above it as if he were a hideous monster intent on stomping the park flat. "Why weren't you edited out, you idiot?"

"We were running low on film."

The officer, tourists, and Miss Soviet Union reappeared, this time accompanied by cohorts wearing filthy moth-eaten costumes. I couldn't believe my eyes! It was all I could do to keep from heaving my shoes through the TV screen. Although I had repeatedly, and severely, denounced Evgeny's notions of having Western-style park mascots at Sovietland "to gladden children's hearts," as he put it, he nevertheless decided to feature them in the promotional film. Judging from their addled, stumbling waddles across the screen, pitiful hirelings in vodka's charge had essayed the key roles of Mischa the Russian bear, Mister Twister the evil American capitalist, Kolobok the little round breadloaf, and Marlboro the pack of cigarettes.

"The supreme aim of Sovietland is the fullest satisfaction of man's material and cultural needs for tremendous never-ending fun," said the officer, embracing Mischa.

"Come have your way with us," said Miss Soviet Union, fending off Kolobok.

"We see you there," the tourists threatened. The assembly waved at the camera, and the film ended. I switched on the overhead lights, stunned by what I had seen. Cinema House's denizens had known exactly what was needed, a sophisticated pitch designed to attract potential investors, but with Evgeny's incomparable assistance they had produced the sorriest farce. The three Texans sat quietly, staring at the blank TV. It shames me to admit that I grew as angry at them as I was at Evgeny, imagining the compassionless joy they surely took in our incompetence. As I prepared to make profuse excuses for the miserable sights we had forced upon them, the oldest of the three spoke, a distinguished white-haired gentleman named Tyler who bore not the remotest resemblance to a cowboy.

"I think it's a *marvelous* idea," he said. "Like nothing any of us have ever seen before, I can tell you."

"You think?" Evgeny said, his eyes as shiny as a sick dog's. "Wonderful! Wonderful! It will be marvelous place, I promise."

The two younger Texans, full-figured men in tailored suits, took their turns speaking. "I'm impressed. I'm real impressed. We all are," said the pinker one, whose name was Chip. "Real impressed."

Then Walter, the third and by far coldest member of the party, asked a question. He was so grim that initially I thought he was their bodyguard, not their senior accountant. "Who are you targeting?"

"Oh, nobody will be shot for real in Sovietland," Evgeny assured them.

"Foreign visitors will visit," I interjected. "People who never knew what our life was like and are curious. Tourism is booming in Russia, now that borders are free and open, and will continue booming."

"How?" asked Walter. "It took us three months to get visas. Lowlifes shook us down all the way through the airport. When we checked in at the hotel, the manager told us there was no room service unless we wanted prostitutes. The bellboy wouldn't leave our room, when we finally got one, until we gave him a twenty. He wanted a fifty."

"These good folks don't run the hotel, Walter," Tyler said.

"Look, if Russia really wants tourists you ought to look at how China treats people."

"We cannot deny, many are uncomfortable with our new freedom and behave badly as a result toward foreigners," I explained. "Very regrettable. In our country foreigners once were holy cows, but too often now, sitting ducks."

The three of them stared at me as if I had related a charming but incomprehensible folk superstition. "Something that bothered me was your saying the park staff would be surly and unpleasant," Chip said. "Why buy the cow, holy or not, when you get the milk for free?"

"No, you are thinking of agricultural pavilion," I said, correcting him. "We expect strong domestic trade. Many Russians are unwilling to lose contact with forty years of life. Their nostalgia will increase as time passes. Our people do not want to feel like relics of lost era. Our Sovietland park will allow them to once again enjoy what they think they miss."

"Tourists will be very at home in Sovietland," Evgeny added. "Not visible in filmed model are fiery steam baths and zoo of wax animals."

"We can't pretend that presently our countryfolk are not hard beset," I said. "But many leisure-seeking Russians can afford quality merchandise and top entertainment. We intend to fulfill all needs."

"But how long can it last?" Tyler asked. "How can we be sure that once Yeltsin goes, whoever gets in next's not going to make Sovietland seem good by comparison?"

"In that event, we expect attendance would increase," I said—they had no glib retorts.

"This will be no Euro Disney, gentlemen," Evgeny said. "Sovietland will be enormous success. We will drown in money."

"Every cent we'd put in would be taxed away at current rates," Walter said. "Or it'd be stolen. Drowning hardly seems the problem."

"Well," Tyler said, standing, "we'll give it some serious thought."

"Serious thought will be wonderful," Evgeny said, shaking their hands vigorously, as if pumping would bring their money to the surface. "You have my number printed on fine cards I give you." The cards I had had printed to his specifications for him read, in English, EVGENY BORODIN, *General Successful Business.* "Soon as possible, let me know decision. But be hush-hush, gentlemen, walls have hearsay."

"We'll let you know," Tyler said. They donned their coats and new fur hats and stepped out of the office, leaving nothing behind.

"Isn't it marvelous, Max?" Evgeny asked me as he took his videotape out of the machine. "We've done it! They think our idea is mind-boggling."

"You'll never hear from these Texans again, I guarantee you."

"Then why would they have told us how impressed they were?"

"How many times have I told you? Americans are like Japanese, they never say no even when they mean it. They smile when they stab you." My harsh words had the predictable effect, and his balloon deflated at once. It was almost impossible for me to tell Evgeny truths he needed to hear, for when I did his reactions made me instantly aware of how regenerative were the fables in which he chose to believe. "Look, this afternoon I'll be meeting with Tanya's associates. They have clients seeking good investments. I'll make a recommendation."

"Bless you, Max," Evgeny said.

"And listen to what I tell you. Don't ever show that film again to anyone. It makes everything about this project look like the work of halfwits."

"Perhaps there were excesses."

"Perhaps," I repeated, utterly disgusted. "How can the ambience of Sovietland be what you claim with stupid mascots roaming about, harassing helpless people? And what purpose did it serve to have your sweet kitten play a featured role?"

"It pleased her parents."

"But no one else. Keep her away from cameras when I'm paying for film."

He stroked his goatee, which he grew in his teens in honor of Father Lenin and retained to enable the world to be at once cognizant of his intellectual nature. In truth it made him look like the Satan in an amateur puppet show. "That brings to mind unavoidable matters, Max," he said. "The electricians are demanding two thousand dollars to cover costs of outlets, payable today. Work progresses at an astonishing pace on the first building, I want to tell you."

"I'm sure," I said, extracting crisp, verifiable hundreds from my money belt. Anytime I know I will be seeing Evgeny, I come prepared. "Let me see what happens this afternoon. Maybe I can do some fast talking, and we won't need any film."

Faint hope. "I fervently honor my brother's wishes, Max," Evgeny said. Ignoring his fraternal rhetoric, I embraced him and left, wishing I could relieve myself of memories of that morning's grotesque humiliations as easily as I could relieve myself of money. A common tale in our military folklore is the rumor of the soldier stationed in close proximity to large microwave installations, who within minutes finds his vital organs simmering in his abdomen like a pungent stew. Each time I have business dealings with Evgeny I think I suffer internal trauma nearly as great. Although we Russians are a notoriously emotional people, I have long taken pride in the smooth aplomb I can affect when thrown into demanding situations, but allow me to spend a half hour with my brother and I will be practically pounding on the walls screaming. Our father had no belief in either of his sons and called us worthless *stilyagi*; I'd long since proven him wrong. Surely, this is why I continue to devote myself to furthering my brother's success, unlikely though it is that he will ever have any.

"Any calls?" I asked Ludmilla when I reached my office.

"Your friend Lev Anatolevich Toloconnicov, from New York," she said. "He was going out but said he'd gotten your message. Would you like me to try putting a call through so that you may speak to him?"

I shook my head. "No. By the time you reach him I might be in conference with Tanya's associates." They were scheduled to arrive at two, although I suspected they would be late; like so many of our countryfolk, they have no notion of time. "I'll try when I get home."

Lev, a good-natured fellow whose single failing had been unshakable faith in the inerrant truth of Communist dogma, worked with me for many years at the Ministry of Culture. With the onset of perestroika he foresaw the inevitable result and so without warning escaped to New York—when surrounded by tigers, don stripes and growl. I heard from him only twice, since he emigrated. He first wrote that he worked as a cabdriver, visiting romantic cities such as Boston and Newark on his days off and submitting lengthy appreciations of Shostakovich to a Russian newspaper. Six years later he wrote again, sending me his address and phone number (he lived in Brighton Beach) but neglecting to tell me what he was presently doing. I'd left a message on his answering machine the night before, asking if he could enlighten me as to the present demand for Russian souvenirs in America.

"Mr. Borodin?" Masha Datlovskaya said, appearing at the door. "When you are free, I need to show you something in these Gubin documents."

"I am always available to you, my pet." Ludmilla stared at me as if I were a sewer rat, but I ignored her, for Masha and I have never shared intimate communion. She is an intelligent woman, one of my most capable workers, and thus not one I would chance to lose through senseless dalliance. But I won't deny I enjoyed following her as she led me to her desk. Her lovely rump is broad as a mare's, and although I am no farm boy, no molester of beasts of the field, the artful swaying of her flanks evoked memories of my first sensuous stirrings, visions as evocative as any peasant's affectionate recollections of his swaybacked mounts. I remembered trips to the circus: the smell of dung and roasted nuts; the arc lights and the green spots they left in the eyes; my father's rousing laughter at the cavorting clowns and bears; my mother jamming my hat more tightly over my ears; Evgeny's incessant wailings; and, most powerfully, my childish inability to decide whether the horses or their bejeweled equestriennes had the more beautiful buttocks. Masha sat down; my mind turned to thoughts of my absent rider.

"It is complex," she warned me, retrieving a stack of documents from the recesses of her desk. "These were recovered from the Ministry of Internal Affairs. This morning I began examining them, seeking the trail of Mr. Gubin."

"And you're finding a highway instead?"

She nodded. "These are bookkeeping records, apparently genuine accounts rather than whatever was presented to the Ministry of Finance. As you predicted, they give leads to laundering procedures. Funds initially channeled through the Tbilisi office of the Ministry of Railways continued on to a remarkable number of other agencies before—"

"Being converted and diverted into private hands."

"The dispersal method is more sophisticated than anything I have come across before," she said. "I'm really quite impressed."

In its essential framework, the railway scheme worked in the manner of all such schemes of those profligate days. Ministry of Internal Affairs officials—Dmitry and his superiors, in this case— having received permission from above (that is, their bribes were accepted) to go forward with the project, reached an agreement, (necessitating more bribes) with Georgian officials and their henchmen in the Ministry of Railways to oversee the theoretical construction. The locals hired workers who agreed (more bribes here, surely) to oversee preparation of appropriate documents: production charts, accident reports, orders for strategic materials, and other ephemera. Internal Affairs tracked the plan's seeming fulfillment, reporting to those superiors (bribes would possibly be involved) that all progressed on schedule, simultaneously assuring that not a ruble went anywhere save into the pockets of those involved.

"What is so sophisticated about their method?"

"Usually one or two channels only are used through which to funnel money," Masha said. "Here at least seventeen were employed, none on more than one occasion. Had the plotters not been so greedy, there is no question their financial turpitude would have gone undetected. Money was transferred through the Ministries of Agriculture, Foreign Trade, GUM, Ferrous Metals—"

"Half the gross must have gone for bribes," I said. "How much in all?"

"Impossible yet to tell. Hundreds of millions of rubles were in the stream. It would still have been too obvious, you know, if they'd sent diversions through a single agency. Mr. Borodin, did you realize some of the money was transferred through Melodiya?"

I shook my head. "Not at all. You're certain?"

"Absolutely. I haven't come upon references to the Ministry of Culture itself." Meaning, she had not yet come upon references to me. Melodiya, for those of you who are unaware, was the state record company. While in existence it issued hundreds of millions of records. In Moscow they were sold at Russia's largest record store, a mammoth facility on New Arbat where, certainly, records most desired were always out of stock. "I've been tracking the flow of money by cross-checking references to specified individuals, and one of these was a Melodiya worker. Take a look at what I've found."

While working at the Ministry of Culture I dealt constantly with Melodiya and its apparatchiks. At no time did I recall anyone in its administration being arrested, or even interrogated, in regards to the railway scandal. But if they had been, it would not have been something I needed to know.

"Who was the Melodiya contact?"

"Oleg Norinsky. Did you know him?"

"He was the auditor," I said. "Typical bureaucrat. We had limited contact."

Melodiya was not an especially corrupt agency, but I should be forthright and confess that as a benefit of my ministry position I, like many, made a considerable amount of money skimming profits off record sales. I was not a greedy, heartless bastard, and so I rarely took more than I could readily use. Before condemning me for my freely admitted theft, keep in mind that in our perfect Soviet society where everything belonged to everybody, nothing belonged to anybody and was therefore free for the taking. In comparison to most, I exercised superhuman restraint. The chickens I repeatedly chose to pluck were the Happy Guys, a hideous ensemble of insipid hacks. Groups who trimmed their hair and decibel levels and purged their repertoire of offensive songs enjoyed full benefits of state support. The Happy Guys were exemplary of such artistic frauds. They foisted off onto a desperate public saccharine ballads such as "Moscow Suburb Nights" and also songs intended to sound like Beatles songs; so they might have sounded, had the Beatles been as banal. Wherever the Happy Guys are now, I trust they are no longer smiling.

"Here. Melodiya exports to Teheran, 1976 and 1977," Masha said, passing me a sheaf of sales statements. "All agencies involved in these machinations used Iran and India in converting rubles into semi-hard currency, rials and rupees, before reconverting them into dollars and banking them away outside the country. I am guessing these figures are perhaps not greatly realistic."

With knowledgeable eyes I perused the documents, seeing entries for the Moscow Symphony, the Kirov company, solo cellists, flautists, and the like; there were also notations of supposed album sales of Alla Pugacheva, the Forest Brothers, Flamingo, and other purveyors of auditory kitsch. "An informed guess, I think," I told her. The sales totals appeared outlandish, although I cannot speak with unquestioned authority—Alla Pugacheva, for example, sold over 150 million records, not exclusively in the Soviet Union. But never, even under the Shah, would export sales to Iran have been greater than domestic sales, and that is what these statistics suggested. While browsing, I came across a listing that struck me as a maul strikes a steer in the slaughterhouse.

"What is it?" Masha asked.

"The Happy Guys never sold so many records." According to these astounding statements, over eight million of each of their too-numerous albums had been sold in Teheran. Not in a thousand years! I had examined their true sales statistics every month for ten years, yet evidently someone was skimming off layers of nourishing cream before I even saw the bucket.

"You've never seen these?"

"Certainly not." I wasn't astonished that secret transferrals of cash might have been processed through Melodiya; but the scale of this was mind-boggling. Obviously, monies in theory payable to those tone-deaf imbeciles had been instead subsumed into the thieves' outflow. I was enraged; how much money that rightfully should have been available to me had gone elsewhere instead?

"Keep me informed if you find anything else as remarkable."

"Of course," she said, and coyly smiled, fluffing her black, curly hair. "I am pleased to be working on such a fascinating assignment."

"No one else could do it as well. Thank you, Masha Chuchmillevna."

I returned to my office. Hers was an unpleasant finding, but in a sense this was not the greatest surprise to have arisen from Dmitry's assignment. No sooner had my workers started carrying out this undertaking than an unforeseen factor evinced itself. Heretofore, in neither my business nor at the Ministry had it ever disturbed me that we trifled somewhat with *causality*. By this I mean we had always looked upon our revisions of historical truth as discrete events. One week we could prove that the American Rosenbergs were Soviet spies, and prove the opposite one week later, and to whom would it ultimately matter? But the nature of Dmitry's assignment required that in supplanting original documents with our replacements, my workers had also to alter every cross-referential record, for the Georgians would examine all pertinent material. This time we could not simply paint rosebushes over the photographs of those fallen out of favor; we had to create a new, whole, consistent reality that could be thereafter photographed and rephotographed without suspicion by anyone who desired to play cameraman. Still, my workers and I are long steeped in Soviet tradition, cognizant of history's infinite mutability and the versatile use   which its lessons may be put; we would meet the challenge.

But the awareness that these bastards had cheated me out of my just thievings wore at me as water erodes stone. It occurred to me that my former associate Sokolov could perhaps elaborate on what Masha had found beneath the rocks; possibly, too, he knew how to find this conniver Norinsky. Sokolov was for years a director of Soviskusstvo, which was Melodiya's distributor. He had since been swept into the city's maelstrom, and I had no idea onto which shore he ultimately washed, if he hadn't drowned. I resolved to leave the search to Ludmilla, a master investigator if there ever was one.

"Mr. Borodin," she called out. "Gubin on three."

"Dmitry?" I asked, lifting the receiver of phone number three—I had six, which would impress without evincing delusions of grandeur. "What is it? What do you want?"

"Maxim, can you hear me?" he shouted. It sounded as if he were phoning from the floor of a steel mill. I held the receiver farther from my ear and realized that the rhythmic thumping that inflicted so much pain was intended to be music.

"Where are you?" I shouted back.

"Disco Inferno. A delightful new establishment near the Hotel Rossiya. A first-class facility." By that he meant there was a ratio of one stripper for every two patrons. He slurred his words; obviously, he had been drinking.

"What is it, Dmitry?"

"With my partners I am arranging a meeting with one of our investors a week from Monday, at the baths. He wants to meet you."

"Who? What investors?" I screamed, growing hoarse as well as deaf as I attempted to make myself heard.

"Our silent partner," he shouted back. "Not as silent as we like, sometimes."

"Why should I meet him?"

"He may have his own projects for you one day," Dmitry said. "I gave you highest recommendations. Will you join us when we meet?"

At any other moment I should have said no, never. Such commingling of public and private sectors may be a sensible option for some entrepreneurs, but not for those of us in the field monopolized by Universal Manufacturing. It is safest for us to live by the tenet that too much insight into the reasoning behind a customer's need for specific documents will prove disturbing, if not dangerous. "What kind of projects?"

"Ultimately rewarding projects," he said. "We'll steam our cares away, if nothing else. What could possibly happen?"

"All right," I said, realizing that it had been months since I'd been to the baths; what could it hurt, after all?

"I'll set it up, then. Is work on the documents progressing smoothly?"

"I told you so yesterday. Why do you drive me mad with your constant interrogations? You think we're not capable?"

"It is easier for you than pissing on two fingers, I'm sure," he said, laughing loudly and drunkenly. "We should broaden our business relationship, I think. Let us have dinner together this evening, you and your wife, Sonya and me. Meet us in our lobby at seven. There is a fine Armenian restaurant near our building."

"I have no idea what Tanya's schedule is," I lied. "She may be busy. I don't know if I can reach her."

"The music is so loud here, I can hardly hear a thing," he shouted back. "We will see you tonight."

Without warning, Sonya appeared in my office doorway. Ludmilla was telling her not to disturb me, but of course my koshka paid no heed. Lifting her arms as if she were a diva acknowledging the wild applause of adulators, Sonya slipped off her mink coat. She is wholly conscious of the effect her beauty has upon me and invariably wears ensembles to enhance what is already breathtaking. That afternoon she wore a remarkable outfit, a red leather jumpsuit that fit her so tightly she appeared to have grown a crimson skin. Upon each breast was a yellow hammer and sickle. Black calfskin boots rose over her knees; an ammunition belt with golden bullets encircled her waist. She appeared to be personifying the Communist super sex goddess Oktobriana, whose frenzied adventures, in samizdat comics in the sixties, aroused a million onanistic fantasies among the golden youth, myself included. "Dmitry, I must go," I said. "Work awaits me."

"I'll not keep you," he said, and brayed once again; his wife took the tip of my nose gently between her teeth, as if to nip it off. "Meet us at seven, in the lobby."

I dropped the receiver into its cradle as if it were burning hot. "Don't you know I was talking to your husband?" I asked her. "My God, what is this? What are you wearing?"

"Don't you like it?" she asked, slinking alongside me; her leather made not a squeak as she moved. "Why were you screaming? What does Dmitry want now?" Ludmilla slowly pulled my door shut and locked it. She did not approve of my behavior, but she has a commendable sense of responsibility to her employer.

"He wants us to have dinner together tonight. Tanya too. What a horrible idea."

"I think that would be a delightful evening," she said, sitting astride me, wriggling into my lap as if to screw herself onto my pole. "Will you be uncomfortable, having us both in the same room with you? Can't you handle two women at one time?" She brought her face close to mine. Her hair tumbled down in a storm of gold, blinding me.

"Where did you get this sausage skin you're wearing?"

"It's a present."

"From?"

"You," she said, laughing, and I realized she had once again craftily employed my American Express number for her own purposes. Sometimes, seeing my bill, I would rage that two or perhaps three mafia bands had somehow broken into my account, only to discover afterward that Sonya had gone on an impromptu shopping spree and, afterward, neglected to tell me. "It's Moschino. A uniform for shock workers who slave in gold mines."

There was nothing proletarian about her movements at that moment. "Change clothes tonight before we get there," I told her. "Tanya will call you a hoyden, a cheap prostitute, if she sees you dressed like this."

"Why? Because she barters for daywear and not nightwear? *Nichevo*."

"What a wicked thing to say." She brushed her lips against my eyelashes, making me blink all the faster. "What did Dmitry think?"

"He was *very* pleased. When he asked where I got it I told

him he bought it for me." My hands had somehow found their way to her suit's zipper, but she eased them away. "Forgive me, my darling, but we can't. As I was starting to put it on this morning I saw that Auntie came to pay her visit. But I wanted to wear it to see what you think." Lifting herself off my lap, she knelt beside my chair. "Madam Palm and her five daughters should perhaps comfort you in the meantime."

Before I could stop her—were I fool enough to try!—Sonya unfastened my trousers and ran her fingers along my virile member as if playing sprightly airs on a flute. Only then did she apply her prodigal embouchure.

"Devil."

It may seem to you that I spent most days at play with Sonya, but this was not the case. Man does not live by wife alone, true, but I swear to my less worldly readers that having a mistress is unquestionably more difficult than having a wife. Carrying on the most desultory tryst requires an enormous investment of time, greater even than the amounts of money and emotion that must also be spent. In the past, whenever my former mistresses became too demanding of my free hours, I would break off the relationship, unwilling to be at anyone's mercy; but I could not imagine a day spent without Sonya. For her, I structured my schedule so as to always allow time enough to enjoy passionate encounters. But my attentions spoiled my clever vixen, who reveled in the power she had over me. Often she broke off engagements at the last minute, pretending to be unavoidably detained, then appear at the most inopportune moments, aware that however much I huffed and puffed she would still escape punishment for her childish behavior. What could I do? I seized opportunities for earthly bliss as they arose, as evanescent as the perfume left in the air of a room through which a beautiful woman has walked.

"Mr. Borodin," Ludmilla unexpectedly called through the door, rapping loudly as she unlocked it, rousing us from our lascivious pleasures. Sonya pulled herself upright before Ludmilla could throw open my office portals, and I as quickly closed my pants, catching tender skin in the zipper. "Representatives from your wife's company are here."

"Marvelous," I said through clenched teeth, painfully freeing my vital part with the hand she couldn't see. "Is Tanya with them, by chance?"

"Unfortunately, no," she said. In her voice I detected more than a hint of sarcasm. "Do you care to see them?"

"I've been anxiously awaiting their arrival," I proclaimed, making sure they could hear me, gesturing meanwhile to Sonya that she should take her coat and slip unseen out the side door. She chose not to grant my wish, but instead took her mirrored compact from her purse and began reapplying lipstick, red as our country's old flag. Ludmilla shook her head, turned, and left the room.

"Are you ashamed of me?" Sonya asked, retrieving her coat from where she had dropped it onto the floor. "Why should I scurry off like a rat?"

"You heard who they are," I was saying as Tanya's associates entered. There were three men and one woman, Alla Yurasova, a longtime friend of Tanya's and mine. She was not a person in whom I wished to raise warranted suspicions. When Alla saw Sonya, she gave her a look that could have cut her in two, but my koshka acted as if she didn't care. One of the three men was years younger than the others; I recognized Anatoly and Roman, but this youth's was an unfamiliar face. All three of them wore fine suits (mine, Zegna, better); the stripling wore gray kidskin gloves which he chose not to remove. He and Roman stared at Sonya as if they saw God, and Anatoly grinned and giggled nervously.

"Sonya Maslovska Gubina, this is Alla Melnikovna Yurasova, Tanya's co-worker," I said, introducing the women. The men introduced themselves, stammering out their names; the youngster's was Iosif Fedotoskich Kostikov. His face was as barren of sentiment as any criminal's. Something about his gloves bothered me. "Sonya was just leaving."

"I was dropping off papers for my husband," she explained. "It's very good to meet you, but I must be moving along."

"A pity," I said. "Tanya and I look forward to seeing you and Dmitry tonight. For dinner."

"The four of us," she said, flashing her teeth.

"That's right," I said. "The four of us."

In a whirl of fur she took her leave. I told my visitors to be seated. "I hope we're not interrupting anything, Max," Alla said. Her stare troubled me.

"No, no, certainly not," I assured her. "Now then, let's get to it. From what Tanya says I understand these Bruneian representatives are willing to invest but have thus far declined the options you've presented. Do you know why?"

"It's been like reading the minds of statues," said Alla. She was Tanya's second-in-command and usually dealt with representatives of European nations. She was Tanya's age and dressed in the same cultivated Western style. We always got along well—too well, sometimes—which was good, although the way she usually looked at me made me imagine she always (with reason, granted) suspected me of crimes she'd not yet been able to prove. "You're the one who meets with them, Iosif. Tell Max how they behave."

If weasels had a voice, the voice would be Iosif's. "I make proposals; they smile and shake their heads," he said. "They are very particular, but I think they are not impossible to please."

"They are scared, I think, but don't want to say. A question of face, perhaps," said Anatoly, a dark Adonis who personified all that was most masculine, even though Tanya told me that outside the office he lived an enthusiastic, if secretive, homosexual life. His healthy aura (money's cologne) attracted the most conservative financiers like flies. "I think they want to invest in something that can't be expropriated if our leaders decide they've had enough experiments in democracy."

"If." Alla laughed. "When."

"Some experimenters," said Roman, the firm's bookkeeper, whose face possessed the affable gloom of a bloodhound's.

"So you're telling me they need an investment guaranteed to remain uncompromised, whatever our political and social conditions," I said. "Something with great common appeal, unaffected by revolutionary upheavals."

"We suggested television," Alla said.

"They smiled," said Anatoly. Iosif said nothing; his gloves annoyed me all the more, the longer I looked at them.

"Let me tell you an idea that occurs to me," I said. "What about a theme park, loaded with thrilling pleasures and amusements?"

"Like Gorky Park?" Alla asked.

"No, not at all. What's there? Nineteenth-century amusements, every one, save for a few tawdry new exhibits."

"Like Mount Rushmore?" Roman asked, meaning the park's one-sixth scale replica of America's Mount Rushmore, in plastic, which had been recently completed; no one could say why such a thing had been built, save to provide an attractive backdrop for our politicians to stand before during the coming election campaign and proclaim their steadfast belief in the ideals of democracy.

"No, I mean a contemporary theme park. Everyone loves theme parks. Siberians would stand in line until their eyes froze if one was on the Arctic Circle. Africans would risk catching horrible plagues to have fun. I've seen pictures of Arab World in Kuwait City, built since the war. Mines everywhere, and still a smash success. Look at the continents of entertainment provided to the masses in America and Japan. Look at Euro Disney."

"The Russia of theme parks," said Anatoly, whose voice was deep and raspy. He must have begun smoking and drinking while still a swaddled baby to have so admirably cured his throat. "Billions lost and nothing to show but monuments."

"Mindless propaganda disseminated by second-rate French competitors. Typical lies of wreckers. What do we have comparable in Moscow for our citizens and foreign tourists? Gorky Park? What else do we have? The Theater of History, with those idiotic wax exhibits?"

(Exhibits showing our national figures in the unlikeliest groupings: Ivan the Awe-Inspiring cradling Pushkin in his arms while Stalin looks on, smiling; Vysotsky serenading Brezhnev; Beria and Skuratov playing chess while Czar Nicholas stands nearby, his head half shot off.)

"How else will children learn of their noble heritage?" Alla asked.

"Are you saying we should suggest a Moscow Disney to our investors?" Iosif asked, tapping his knees with gloved fingers. Why did I so instinctively dislike him?

"Not as such," I told them, and then told them more.

As is often the case, the sole person not left speechless in awe by my brillance was my own beloved wife. "How could you have the nerve to make such an idiotic proposal?" Tanya asked me that evening, as we drove to Dmitry and Sonya's apartment. Though I was in no rush to get there, I could not bear her harsh accusations and so proceeded at top speed. "How could you get my firm involved with any project of Evgeny's?"

"My devoted wren, you asked for my help," I said, ever alert for militia in hiding. A sizable percentage of Moscow's constabulary spend their shifts pulling over helpless travelers, accusing them of nonexistent traffic violations, and threatening to perform on-the-spot alcohol blood tests with filthy rusted needles unless the drivers fork over baskets of money. I've never been snared in such a trap but have seen it happen to others—Arteim, in particular, is plucked constantly by our motorway gestapo. "Your partners outvoted you, true? Evidently they favored my idea. You tell me your investors were also captivated by the notion, yes? Is my imagination overworked?"

"No," she admitted. The Bruneian representatives were ready to invest; the theme park concept was one to which they had wholeheartedly responded.

"So why complain so bitterly?"

"They'll realize their error in the morning and fly home on the first plane," she said. "Wait and see."

"You should enjoy your success, my dear."

"They can pour all the money in Brunei into this park and still never ride the first ride. I know I'm right, and so do you. I was so furious with Alla."

"My pigeon," I said, patting her knee; she jerked it free of my gentle touch. "At least admit I solved your problem."

"And caused a multitude more, I'm sure."

"Deal with those when they occur, *if* they occur," I told her. "Evgeny is an idiot savant, perhaps, not an idiot. This idea of his is not a bad one, or else I wouldn't have thought it worthy of your partners' attention. Do you suspect me of suggesting it only to palm Evgeny off on someone besides myself?"

"Why should I suspect, when you give me so much proof?" Her anger didn't trouble me; her bile would be soothed once the first payments arrived from the Bruneian representatives. "We're in Sovietland now, we'll be there fifty years from now. Why pay? It's crazy."

I parked the car beneath a working streetlamp. After removing the accoutrements and locking them in the trunk, we strolled across Patriarch's Ponds, a small, lovely park in the western part of the central city which readers of *The Master and Margarita* will readily recall. Few parks are nowadays safe to walk through after dark, but for years this neighborhood has been one where party bigwigs and mafia chieftains live, and the measliest hooligan knows not to show his ugly face here. Dmitry and Sonya lived in a posh salon in one of the orange-brick Stalin Gothic apartment blocks overlooking the park. They moved in after they were married, taking a flat once owned by the Second Deputy Minister of the Interior. I imagined Dmitry pulled an orchestra's worth of strings with his old superiors to obtain housing in one of those ugly buildings.

"It is a beautiful night," Tanya said, her voice no longer acidic with life-shortening vituperation. I accepted her sudden calmness with peace and equanimity. Peering up through dead trees into heaven, we saw the stars shining so brightly that not even our city's mephitic air could obscure the light they'd emitted, eons past. "Perhaps you are not too wrong, Max."

"At least everything is under control. What more can we ask?" I took her arm in mine as we walked; this time, she did not pull away. "Do you remember years ago, when we used to come here?"

"What grand days," she said. Both of us stopped walking at precisely the same time; we stood alone, but together, in the center of the park. I—we—recalled our first kiss, thirty years earlier, one August evening in Patriarch's Ponds. We reenacted that happy event; my mind erupted a cascade of images. On summer Sundays we would ride downtown from the university, watch fireworks on the river, enjoy treats of pear soda and ice cream, in night's dark arms sample such intimate pleasures as she would allow, and always we were grateful to live in the most forward-seeing and scientifically advanced society on earth. How often she gazed into her mirror shards of memory to assuage the succession of gray days since, I can't say; I glance at mine only in passing. It is a blessing that memories are buried with the brains that hold them; no film, no photo, no written account can retain the sharp edges memories possess when they rattle around loose in the head, repeatedly cutting into the mind. How many times can you be wounded by a single experience? But no analgesic is as effective as nostalgia.

When we reached their apartment I pressed the buzzer to let them know we'd arrived. From the park's vantage point, the encompassing buildings appeared as impregnable and finely maintained as they ever had, but up close, it was easy to see that not even this hermetic neighborhood had existed entirely unchanged in the midst of the vaster transformation. Graffiti scrawled across the entranceway read HOLY RUS PRESERVE THE ORTHODOX FAITH. When the door unlocked we stepped into the twilight illumination of a single low-watt bulb. Drips echoed through the lobby's cavern, and everything smelled overpoweringly of mold. I expected a guard to be stationed within, but in fact there were three armed soldiers in uniform seated at the *druzhina's* old desk. They raised their automatic weapons as we approached; our innocent appearance meant nothing. After examining our identification, they grinned broadly but neglected to lower their weapons.

"Why did Dmitry want us to meet them downstairs?" Tanya asked as we stood in stygian gloom. "Aren't we good enough to be allowed into their home?"

"He owns numerous valuable art items, I've heard," I said. Sonya told me that for the past six months he had spent each night in his treasure room, as if his sleeping presence assured that his bounty would remain secure. "I think he's excessively fearful of their being seen."

"Why would you have such possessions if you wanted no one to see them?"

"What if by mistake he showed them to some scoundrel who later returned to steal them? There's nothing of snobbishness in his secretive actions. Certainly he has nothing to be snobbish about."

"What prizes does this connoisseur collect?"

"Icons and jewelry, I suppose. Statuary, maybe. Precious metals. Even at the Ministry, he was collecting. Probably that's how he obtained his finest prizes."

"How so?"

"Many of his treasures are expropriations, I'm sure," I said. Ninety percent, Sonya claimed, although as far as I was aware she had no way of documenting this. "Items improperly acquired by their former owners, evidence recovered from criminals, and the like. He's still actively amassing collectibles, from what I hear. Everything is turning up on the market in these troubled times."

"Greetings, good friends!" Dmitry cried, appearing from behind a shattered wall that separated the lobby from the elevators. Sonya followed several paces behind, again bundled in mink but now wearing a stunning black outfit. I am no fashion arbiter, but even I can recognize Chanel. She'd pulled back her hair in a tight bun (a styling I do not like, as to my eye it makes her head resemble a shiny gold onion). The boots she now wore were low-heeled and rose no higher than her calves. Rarely did she dress so conservatively; had I not known her, but only saw her walking down the street, I would have looked more than once but felt no cavemanlike urge to take her.

"It's good to see you both," she said, embracing us gently, as if we were covered with sores, and offering light pecks on our cheeks. "How long it's been."

We walked to the restaurant, a short distance away. Many expensive black cars—Mercedes-Benzes, Volvos, Jaguars, and even a few old Zils, the Soviet Cadillac—were parked along the curb, some guarded by drivers, some left unprotected; all would be safe as long as they remained in the neighborhood. Our conversation was purely social, and we spoke of nothing important. I kept close to Tanya's side, far from Sonya; both women were so quiet, and Dmitry unreeled such a never-ending line of pointless chatter, that I almost forgot they were there.

"The food these Armenians prepare is a gourmand's dream," Dmitry said, professing great familiarity with the restaurant. "Each time we come here, it is even more superb than the time before. Just like the old days. You know how impossible it has become to find a good restaurant in Moscow."

"When was it easy?" Tanya asked.

"Oh, there used to be such places in the old days. We had connections in the Ministry." Did he think no one in any other ministry had been capable of even finding bread? "How we lived. Always, the most of the most. Ah, here we are."

No signs noted a restaurant's presence; not a light shone in the building. We crept down a slippery flight of iron stairs waxed with ice. With gloved hands Dmitry pried open a handleless steel door. Inside was a glowering old bastard, wearing a stained overcoat, parked in front of the enclosed entryway. Bristling brown mustaches grew out of his nose. He and Dmitry exchanged familiarities.

"*Nichevo*. No tables."

"Yes, tables. We have reservations. Let us in."

"Who are you? Foreigners? Jews?"

"Don't make me whack down pears with my prick. We have tables."

"Go back to your shithole and see who's waiting for you."

"Keep talking, you'll lose your voice as you've lost your mind."

"It won't fuck me."

Several minutes of this entertainment passed before the gatekeeper suddenly surrendered, stepping aside. Dmitry effusively greeted the proprietor of the establishment, a supposed Armenian who, judging from his swarthiness, spent his childhood under a much brighter sun than had either Arteim or Telman. He pointed sullenly at one of many empty tables. "Very much like the old days, Dmitry," I admitted. The only other customers were three Japanese businessmen draining bottles of cognac—five fallen soldiers lay at rest in their table's debris—and, sitting in the center of the room, a paunchy man of indistinguishable age (between thirty and seventy) and a plump girl with dyed-blond tresses who was perhaps a full decade younger than Sonya. His baggy suit made him look all the fatter, and her tight zebra-striped skirt provided slight protection against harsh weather. She repeatedly crossed and uncrossed her legs, allowing us all to be aware of her lack of underpants.

"These harlots think they own Moscow," Tanya whispered to Sonya as we sat at a table situated beneath the room's only window, which offered no view; it had been painted over and was encircled by blinking colored lights.

"Disgusting," Sonya said with palpable distaste. Dmitry and I could only nod our heads in agreement.

"The food is delicious here," he said, making gestures above the zakuski provided us as if to bless the pickles, peppers, and radishes, dark bread, minced fish and onions, lumps of sheep's cheese, and strips of dried meat. Bottles of fruit soda and mineral water awaited pouring. Clean dishware and cutlery were provided; the table's salt and pepper shakers, we saw, were miniature busts of Brezhnev, decrepit old Uncle Lyonya, the Great Hero of Malaya Zemlya—manufactured in Finland, according to the mark on their undersides. "Order whatever you like, I have already taken care of the bill."

"Marvelous," I said. He made his first perfunctory attempt at gaining the confidence of a waiter. To my utter shock, a young server totally unskilled in nonobtrusive service sped fleet-footed to our table.

"We'll start with shashlik—impaled delicacies called shish kebabs in the West, I understand," Dmitry told him. "Beef or lamb, which do you have?"

"We have coypu," the waiter said.

"Excuse me?" Tanya asked. My sly koshka slid a pickle suggestively into her mouth, calling to mind distracting images, as she undoubtedly intended.

"Coypu in filets, breast of coypu, haunches. A most attractive meat."

"What is coypu?" asked Dmitry.

"Mouth-watering and tender. The healthiest of animals."

"What does it taste like?" Sonya asked.

The young fellow was initially baffled by her question but readily recovered and replied. "Like coypu."

"Coypu shashlik, then," said Dmitry. "Potato salad. Butter?" The waiter shook his head. "Caviar?" Again, the negative. "Three bottles of vodka."

"*Three?*" Tanya asked.

"What is an evening without vodka?" Dmitry said. "It clears bad blood. I forget, Max, how women prefer sipping tea or Pepsi-Cola."

"Do you believe everyone wants to drink as much as you do?" Sonya asked her husband as the waiter quickly returned with chilled water of life.

"Why not?" Dmitry asked, pouring each of us a glass. He had not seemed drunk until that moment; then I remembered he had been drinking when he called from the club earlier. Once that awareness was clear in my mind, it was hard to look at him without seeing him barely able to keep himself from weaving from side to side in his chair. "To our great business success," he said, raising his glass. We joined him. "*Na zdroyve!*"

A party of six men entered the restaurant, five giants accompanying a lone midget (in truth a small gentleman of normal height, if of slight build). His companions were as broad as they were tall and wore black leather coats that brushed the tops of their black boots. The giants had the bearing of Cossacks and the dark hair and parchment-pale skin that so often distinguishes Georgians.

"To our beloved wives," Dmitry said, refilling our glasses. "May they love us dearly, whatever our faults."

Again, we drank. The new party took seats at a table not three meters from us and shouted for service. Two older waiters and the proprietor himself ran pellmell to grant their desires. The small ringleader's minions removed his astrakhan-collared coat for him, revealing natty attire and a breastplate of medals pinned to his jacket. He wore as many decorations as old Uncle Lyonya himself had worn; it was said our late leader had medals tattooed on his chest to match the ones on his suits, so even when naked he could not forget how important he was. Of all our past masters, I think I remember Brezhnev most fondly—admiration must be paid to one who not only invented the wartime exploits for which he received his king's ransom of decorations but in some cases the wars themselves.

"Look at the old goat," Tanya whispered to Sonya, and for a confusing moment I thought she was speaking of me. "If she doesn't rob him, she'll kill him. That will teach him a needed lesson."

My wife was referring to the all-too-likely couple, who prepared to leave. The girl struck a haughty pose while allowing the fat old man to pull her coat around her. They ignored the laughter of the Georgians, who gaped at the girl's legs and uttered rude remarks. In the face of such commentary (bestial, nonessential, traditional), her manservant intelligently chose to play the role of mute eunuch rather than avenging warrior. The men laughed all the louder as the couple walked out. Then, hideous racket blared over unseen loudspeakers; what some call music had evidently been requested, and the proprietor obliged.

"Fucking Georgians," Dmitry said, filling our glasses. The noise was so great that I knew none of the men had heard him— that pleased me.

"We are fortunate women to have such husbands," Sonya told Tanya, her eyes twinkling. "Distinguished older men are the acme of masculinity."

"Paragons, considering," said Tanya, "but still all the same. The young ones want money, the old ones want sex."

Sonya looked at me, and I looked at Dmitry. "How do these people rate such service?" he was saying, apparently to himself.

"You are so young," Tanya told Sonya. "Will you be having children?"

"I am not possessed of a maternal temperament," she said. "I don't think it would be wise, and Dmitry agrees."

His face flushed with humor, anger, and drink. "My first wife and I thought we were fortunate to have children, until they grew older. Then we realized the horrible mistake we made. To maturity," Dmitry said, laughing and lifting his glass. "Everyone. You must!" Already I felt as if I had drunk more than was desirable; true, for a Russian I am not much of a drinker, but this is an advantage in business. Tanya and Sonya reluctantly took up their glasses as well; it would have been rude, had we not joined in. "Everyone loves children until they have them."

"You should not say such things," Tanya told him.

"Oh, Russian women," he said, vodka opening his throat wide. "If you cared for Russian men as you do Russian children, we would not have half the troubles we do."

"Russian men *are* Russian children," said Tanya, and she and Sonya laughed. Some in the party of Georgians stood up and began dancing with one another to the big-beat Armenian disco sound, shouting and stomping their boots. I felt as if I were locked up in a zoo.

"Max seems full grown to me," Dmitry went on. "If you had ever had children, you would know."

"We had a son," Tanya said sharply. "He is no longer with us."

Dmitry's face sagged as if it were wax and he had too closely neared fire. "Forgive me," he said. "I hadn't realized."

"It isn't something we talk about," I said, staring blindly at him in order to avoid Sonya's stare, for I'd never told her either.

"How old was he?" she asked my wife.

"Eleven," Tanya said. "A strapping young boy."

"I had no idea," Dmitry said, continuing to stare over at the Georgians.

"What happened to him, Max?" Sonya asked. The cheers and the shouts of the Georgians grew almost so loud as to drown out these undesired questions.

"He's alive, in the past," I said, perhaps with too much vehemence. "Better he should stay there."

The young waiter interrupted, arriving with potato salad and more bread. "Coypu is sizzling," he told us. "Five minutes more."

Meaning, forty. The Georgians sang along with the hideous music, clapping their hands. In Sonya's face I saw a look directed toward me that I had never seen before; there is no single word in any language, as far as I know, for such a mixture of pity, anger, and undesired mistrust. She would want to know more about my son the next time we met, I knew, and I did not want to tell her.

For what seemed hours none of us said a word, hushed more by the uninvited appearance of ghosts than by the ever-increasing gaiety of the Georgians. Tanya sneered as she passed the potato salad. She never favored Caucasians, not even pale light-eyed Georgians indistinguishable from the sons and daughters of Russia; she refused for years to let me bring Arteim or Telman to our apartment, at last relenting enough to allow them entry into our kitchen but no farther.

"Look at them," Dmitry said, so loudly that even the kitchen staff could have heard him. "Riding into paradise on someone else's ass."

"Take care what you say, Dmitry," I said, leaning across the table so that he could hear me without my having to shout.

"God, Max, what's happened to us?" he moaned.

"We have drunk too much, that is what has happened."

"Our country I'm talking about!" His wavering mood unnerved me, but I refused to let my fear show. There is no period of drunkenness more dangerous than that hour when you are no longer able to readily distinguish the emotions you remain able to feel, and animal rage seems as appropriate as joy or sorrow.

"Perhaps we should concentrate on eating and in that simple way satisfy the purity of our souls," I said, and tasted the potato salad. The potatoes had been left in the ground, I think, for several unhappy years. "Indescribable."

Waiters appeared, lugging broad salvers laden with shashlik swords speared with chunks of tempting meat, delivering them to the now-exhausted men rather than to our famished group. "What is this?" Dmitry yelled; luckily, he could barely be heard over the mind-destroying sonic blasts. "We were here hours before they were. Where is our food?" No waiter paid him the slightest attention.

"Would you shut up?" Sonya said to him, in a sterner voice than I had ever heard her use. Tanya laid down her fork; she looked at me, and I could tell she wanted to leave as much as I did.

"We are Muscovites," Dmitry announced, bombinating as if addressing a Party congress. "Not Asian trash."

Perhaps none of the men had heard? Casually glancing their way, I saw that at least two had; they were patting their companions' shoulders and pointing at our table. "I am telling you to say no more, Dmitry."

"It burns the hell out of me," he said. "Three hundred thousand rubles I pay them, and who gets served first?" He stared directly at the men. "*Chuchmeki!*"

All the Georgians were listening now but made no threatening moves; I gave thanks to whatever powers that be that they had spent their energies in dance, minutes earlier. The so-called music stopped playing; the small man, their ringleader, called over to Dmitry. "You should be careful what you say when drinking, friend."

"Friend?" Dmitry repeated, and before I could stop him he added unnecessary commentary. It is rude enough to tell strangers that they should mind their business if they have shown no true interest in your own, but it is even more unwise to employ earthy idioms when so doing. "You're not being fucked, so don't wiggle your ass!"

Although not all Caucasians are adept at Russian, it was at once clear that these were fluent. The fiercest-looking giant rose from his seat wielding a shashlik spear, seeming ready to put our meat on his spit. Dmitry made no further remarks.

"May I have a word with your leader?" I asked, lifting my arms, holding my hands palms outward so they could see I intended no sudden gestures. The giant paused where he stood. The smaller man got up, dabbing at the corners of his mustache with a napkin as we walked toward each other.

"I must offer sincere apologies for my drunken and ill-mannered business associate," I told the man, standing passively before him, as if I were the smaller wolf exposing my throat to the larger. "He is a boor. An outcast. There is no excuse for what he said. Please, if you accept my deep and lasting regret for this unfortunate occurrence, we will leave and no longer disturb your happy group."

He regarded me silently for a moment. "Drink can get the best of even the most reserved," he said, extracting from his pocket a fine silk handkerchief. "Russia is a country with room enough for everyone, don't you agree?" I nodded vigorously. "It saddens us that so many of your fellow citizens disagree." With artistic movements worthy of a pantomime artist he carefully opened the corners of the silk. Within the soft bed nestled an assortment of human teeth—molars, incisors, bicuspids—some filled, some perfect, two capped with golden crowns. He shook the teeth in his hand as if preparing to roll them for luck. "Your friend has an endearing smile. He can keep it."

"Thank you for your understanding nature." The man smiled, nodded, and returned to sit with his companions. For an instant I thought I would pass out but managed to keep my head. When I looked at Dmitry he must have known that had he said another word, I myself would have run him through with a shashlik sword. Although our dishes had at last been brought to us, I said we should go and no one argued. As I put on my coat, temptation got the better of me (as it sometimes does) and I tried a bit of coypu. Since that evening I have ascertained that a coypu is a small fleshy rodent; from personal experience, I can tell you it is possibly more savory than earthworm or mole—possibly.

4

Experiences such as we enjoyed at the Armenian restaurant remind me that, even when young, I realized Russia will never hold the position it deserves to hold among the majestic empires of history as long as Russians drink. Our masters, be they Tatar, Czar, or Soviet, have forever proclaimed that one day our multitude would rule the civilized world and all the spinning planets, but as long as half the country is unable to stand erect without physical assistance from the other half, what is the use of such lunatic delusions? Three small glasses of vodka kept me shaking through the next afternoon; and though I am no drinker by my countrymen's standards, it is not as if I am allergic to Satan's gift. How will Russians attend to even perfunctory errands when so many see an untapped bottle as nothing more than refreshing mouthwash? I fear the necessary transitional stage between communism and capitalism remains that of alcoholism.

I was not looking forward to my appointment with Dmitry and his associates, though at the time I thought the threat of more drink was the worst facing me. In the meantime, I intended to distract myself with more pressing matters: contacting Lev in New York, finding Sokolov and wresting the truth of Melodiya's shady dealings from him, keeping Arteim hot on the trail of the crematorium's tyrants. (If they were supplying their clients with cigar ash, yet burning the bodies as they obviously were, what were they doing with the *genuine* ash and bone? The more I pondered the matter, the more it troubled me.) As always, seeing my koshka was my most essential need. But the morning after the debacle, snow began to fall.

Westerners who dismiss Marx, yet pay homage to Freud's nonsensical scribblings, call Russians masochists for feeling stimulative excitement at the sadistic grip winter fastens upon our throats, but only the perverse take pleasure in strangulation. Even as we were escaping uninjured from the restaurant, our secrets unexposed, a vast amoeba of cold was sloughing south from the pole; it absorbed the city within its mass for three days and nights. Moscow had not known such a blizzard in years. Women armed with flexible iron spears pried ice from the tramlines, capitalists worked double-time carving tunnels down the boulevards, but it was to no avail. Roofs fell beneath the weight of angel feathers, gray stone and red brick grew white as snow accumulated vertically on walls, snapped power lines hissed and sparked atop the drifts, and unwary travelers screamed piteously for help as they were swallowed up in quaking bogs of snow.

Then the temperature dropped until there was no temperature. Siberians, in winter, are used to their breath shattering in the air as it issues from their mouths, falling as chiming glass to the ground; so too did Muscovites hear such tintinnabulation through each endless night. The papers repeated as fact tales of children innocently opening *fortochkas* and dying on the spot as they inhaled lung-freezing air; stories of factory workers uncorking their bottles and taking hearty swigs only to collapse, throats iced shut by vodka; rumors of wolves seen in the suburbs, padding silently between tower blocks in search of night ramblers. In the media appeared reports such as could only appear in our matchless country:

> We regret we are unable to give you weather. We rely
> on weather reports from the airports, which are closed
> because of weather. Whether we are able to give you
> weather tomorrow depends on weather.

Yet, as criminals returned to prison slip at once into familiar routines, so within hours Moscow's populace remembered the love they felt for their wintry gulag and how keenly they feel its absence. When they passed foreigners in the snow-smothered streets, blue and snuffling and cursing that no coat they owned was warm enough, good Muscovites frowned as if in empathic sorrow; but the moment the immigrants slogged off through the drifts, my brothers and sisters beamed with knowing smiles. The xenophobic among them (a majority, I fear) undoubtedly hoped our harsh winter would again repel the invaders, leaving us once more alone unto ourselves, for no one is as deserving of Russia as Russians. As Russians think of Moscow, so the world thinks of Russia—the cynosure of evil, a fount of spirit-maiming regulations, the devil's winter hideaway—but like so many of my countrymen who know these stereotypes possess some validity, I could not live anywhere but here. Why this is so cannot be scientifically measured; perhaps it can only be ascribed to inexplicable chemical reactions, such as those which occur when I give thought to my wicked angel.

For this reason, I did not wholeheartedly relish that week's frost fair—the first day was the worst. There have been innumerable times when I have gone thirty-six hours without seeing my sweet koshka, but not for years had I spent each of their minutes penned inside my apartment in the company of my beloved wife, who even in close quarters remained as fearfully unheated as our building's lobby. When, beset by afterimages of Sonya lingering sharp-edged from the night before, I placed willing hands on Tanya's still-firm body in faint hopes that I could rouse her to fulfill her wifely duties, she frowned as if I were a shivering tourist passed in the street—then smiled slightly and walked away.

Our phone lines, blessedly, continued to work; I distracted myself from the long legs wrapping tightly around my mind by trying repeatedly, and without luck, to reach Lev. At nine I received the call I had awaited all evening. Tanya remained in the room throughout our conversation, but that was as well; by then, had I as freely expressed my lust to Sonya as she expressed hers to me, we would have burned the ice off the lines.

"What a terrible storm," I said, speaking as if to a business associate. "How is it over your way?"

"Our apartment is so overheated I have taken off all my clothes," she slyly told me. "Can you believe it, Dmitry has gone out? Maybe he will freeze to death."

"He ingests enough antifreeze to prevent it, I think," I said, attempting unsuccessfully to deflect the maddening images she catapulted over my walls. "Where did he go and why?"

"To meet with his partners. One of them called; the next thing I knew he was putting on his coat, rushing from our flat as if it were on fire."

"Don't talk so long on the telephone," Tanya said. "You think you're still at your job? Act like this is your home."

"I am on fire," Sonya said. "Thinking of you makes me burn."

"We're good and warm here, too. Very cozy."

"My fireman's hose would cool my flames."

"Hurry up," Tanya said. After a few more minutes I did, replacing the receiver in the cradle with a hand as heavy as my heart.

When I returned to my office on Wednesday I found my workers, save for Ludmilla, spiritedly applying themselves to assigned tasks. (My irreplaceable assistant was suffering from influenza caught the day before, during her trek to or from the office—she alone had come in on Monday, performing her duties with commendable fervor.) I treat all my workers well, and they respond in kind; some stayed at their desks for as many as seven hours each day, fulfilling the requirements of Dmitry's contract. By Western standards, true, this is not a pressing schedule, but I should note that in my firm as in all Russian firms even the hardest-working of my employees rarely works a full American day—otherwise, when would they find time to stand in line to buy essentials? True, shortages are not as extreme as they were during Soviet days, and if I want to buy a new CD player or fine Brioni suit I have only to walk the short distance to GUM and there hand over my money; but if I need bread or gasoline you'll find me on the line with everyone else. For the foreseeable future, this continues to be an unavoidable aspect of our quotidian life. The work still gets done.

It saddened me that morning not to see Ludmilla. Had she been there she would have made an attempt, however unsuccessful, to prevent my brother from entering my quarters and seating himself in my chair. Evgeny even had the cheek to put his snowy boots, no, not on top of my expensive desk but on the arm of a brocaded antique settee I reserve for the hindquarters of valued clients, and not for his imbecilic majesty's ass. I moved so quickly to shove his feet away that the rest of him followed, landing hard on the floor.

"Every morning growing up I saw you, first thing!" I shouted. "Will it continue this way until I am dead and in the ground? What is the problem now?"

Evgeny arose from the floor as from a luxurious divan, fumbling as if for grapes. "The Bruneians have never seen snow."

"And?"

"It concerns them," Evgeny said. "They won't leave the Metropole."

"Are they worried about losing their healthy suntans?" Taking my place in my chair, I picked up the telephone used exclusively for long-distance calls to America, intending again to try calling Lev. "Did they think dusky maidens would serve them coconuts and fresh fruit the whole time they were in Russia?"

"Of course not," Evgeny said. "They're worried that work on the project may be further delayed. Would you meet with them and assuage their fears?"

"I haven't time," I said. Thus far I'd not met the Bruneians face-to-face, but I was in no frenzied rush. At Tanya's direction Iosif (whom I continued to find inexplicably dislikable) made the formal presentation with Evgeny, taking care that the Bruneians should neither see my brother's masterful propaganda film nor be subjected to his enlightening lectures. "Have Anatoly take care of it. He can talk the tail off a horse."

"He did, but I perceive lingering suspicions. Max, how often do even we Russians see so much snow?"

"They'd better get used to delays, whatever the weather," I said, hearing the expected busy signal at the other end of the line. This didn't mean that Lev was there. It will not surprise you that even now there are no more than one hundred overseas telephone lines available to the tens of millions of Russians wishing to speak to someone—anyone—somewhere else. Interminable periods of time are wasted staring into a receiver's mouthpiece, earpiece fastened against the head as if with glue, before contact with the alternate world can be made. At least my office phones are of Western make, which enabled me to press an automatic redial button and switch on the speaker to hear Lev if, against all odds, the call finally got through. "I suppose work is presently at a standstill?"

"Work progresses even as we speak," Evgeny said.

"How can anyone do outside work in this weather?"

"Our workers are capable and handle unforeseen problems well."

"Keep in mind you're not speaking to a Bruneian. Look, show them the ongoing work when the weather clears. Make them dizzy with success."

Evgeny holds in readiness, for times of trouble, an expression of melancholy suited to bring hot tears to the eyes of those who know no better; this was the expression now confronting me. "That will be difficult for at least a month, perhaps longer."

"Why?"

"The roof was finished on the first building a week ago. Interior work was under way. When it was all completed I planned to bring everyone out so that together we could fling our caps high."

"What happened?"

"It collapsed," he said, adding, "the roof, not the building."

"Under the weight of snow?"

"No, you will laugh when I tell you it collapsed several days before the storm, in bright sunshine." He awaited my laugh for some time before proceeding. "The construction supervisor informs me he cannot rely on the foreign materials used. Undependable quality."

"He has a special source for obtaining reliable Russian materials, I'm sure." My brother nodded. "A token of our esteem is required?"

"It would honor them."

"I'll be honored when these Bruneians begin taking full responsibility for financial matters," I said, opening my wallet. "Have you seen this building, with or without roof?"

"Of course," he said. "Interior repairs are nearly done."

With banker's alacrity he counted the bills I gave him. "Two thousand more would speed completion, I believe." My harsh stare convinced him to content himself with a less hurried timetable.

"Did they rebuild the roof before starting anew on the interior?" I asked, curious. My brother's eyes flickered quickly from side to side, as if he were watching a top-seeded tennis match.

"That would seem a sensible way to do it," he said, answering my question. In Russian architecture as in Russian life, to first build the house and then the foundation appeals to the masses as a reasonable approach.

"Good-bye, Evgeny. I have work to do."

"Do you think you could perhaps speak to the Bruneians?"

"I can't be of service at present. What do you think, I sit here in my office all day waiting for the phone to ring so I can enjoy pleasant conversations?"

An unexpected click echoed over the phone line; then I heard a faint, distant voice. "Hello?"

"Lev!" I shouted into the speaker, quickly picking up the receiver. "Can you hear me?"

"Maxim?" he said. "Max, is that you?"

I hastily waved Evgeny away and he left, my money heating his pockets. "Yes," I said. "Yes, it is. Can you hear me?"

"Well enough," he said. When a friend in a foreign land places a call to Moscow (or vice versa), the friend may as well be on Mars, or on the far side of the grave, so bad is the connection. To speak over our vital ether requires constant repetitive intonation of each statement and patient understanding that twenty seconds will pass before anything either of you have said will be heard by the other. "How are you?"

"Splendid," I shouted. "Business is booming over here, don't listen to propaganda. You?"

"Boundless success," he shouted back at me. "People pound at my door day and night, seeking help."

"What are you doing?"

"Consulting," he said. "Consulting and law, the most popular jobs in America. My clients pay me one hundred dollars an hour. Many clients. Always they pay in check form, and I always pay my taxes, always."

"What do I care?"

"It's good for people to know," he said. "You understand. *People*."

"Oh, of course," I replied, remembering that in America all phones are regularly tapped by agents of the state. "It's good you always pay your taxes. Tanya is also a consultant. What is your field of expertise?" An especially prolonged pause followed, and I gathered that Lev did not care to tell me over the telephone. "I'm sure no one can match you in thoroughness of knowledge."

"What do you need, Max? What was this question about souvenirs?"

"How is the market for them there?"

"Russian souvenirs? Badges, posters, *poshlaia*?"

"Exactly."

"Does the ocean need water?"

"A client of mine will be shortly engaged in exporting souvenirs to New York, or so he tells me. What do you think of this?"

"I think he should use his money to buy a hat and keep his head out of the sun. Every Russian in New York has a trunkload of this kitsch. There is no great demand, no one cares about poor Russians anymore. Too much bad press."

"Chechnya?"

"You got it," Lev said, shouting over the thunder crackling through the line. "That; Yeltsin drunk all the time; the usual. Russia is passé, people move fast here. There are more popular countries. Is your client working independently?"

"He seems to be involved with Georgians," I said, disconcerted but not surprised by what he told me.

"They're not exporting souvenirs, then. Which Georgians?"

"Criminals."

"Doesn't help. Find out their names if you can, I will tell you which branch of mafia he is dealing with. Keep your own nose clean."

"Don't worry."

"How is Tanya? Who else are you fucking?"

His candor troubled me, and I chose not to make a direct reply. "I am quite content. How about you?"

"Not so good, Maxim. Women here take insufficient interest in the masculine world. Very sad. And Russian women turn into Americans the second they get off the plane. You can suffer grave humiliation, acting rashly. Even with prostitutes," he said. "I must go to work now. I ask to be considered a capitalist."

"What would Lenin do?"

We both laughed. "Call me when you know more," he said.

"Oleg is a wastrel, a malcontent, a reprehensible layabout," Sokolov told me when we met to have lunch in his office, the following Monday. "But useful. He has his failings, but I live with them." He smiled and lit a black Sobranie. I admired his double-faced gold cuff links as he buttoned his jacket's sleeves. "Remarkable, the way he makes numbers dance to his will. Very useful." It turned out that Sokolov was enjoying astonishing success. His company, All-Russia Informative Partners, provided statistical information of reliable flexibility for both government agencies and the private sector—*You Want What We Have* was its motto. Oleg Norinsky was one of his many employees. "If there were misrepresentations of the sort you describe going on at Melodiya, he would know," Sokolov continued. "It comes as a shocking surprise to me."

"Of course."

For thousands of years there have existed in Russia viruses that inflict chronic mental laryngitis when they infiltrate the brain; afterward, memory no longer speaks. All citizens have suffered this affliction; those who pretend to be vaccinated against its effects are often the most notorious carriers of infection. Other countries have known related plagues, but our specific national strain, mutating in accordance to the tenets of Lysenkoism, adapts as easily as it thrives.

"Why is he not here working?" I asked as Sokolov rose to get his coat.

"In Oleg's world, Monday is the day you spend drinking in order to recover from the weekend," he said. "Usually he recovers at work, but not always. I know where he'll be. We'll go there, but I should tell you I have reservations."

"What is the problem?"

He retrieved his copy of *Izvestia* from his desk and handed it to me. "Page six, the horoscope column. I'm Gemini."

Reader, understand that even the most enlightened Russians direct their lives by the forecastings of astrology, geomancy, divination, and similar hermetic arts, arts not constantly favored with unlimited respect in the so-called modern world. Remember, there was no Renaissance here in Russia; neither was there Reformation, nor Enlightenment, and even the great Victorian materialist age mostly passed us by. Many times, only cosmic explanations, bereft of Western rationale, enable my countrymen to understand why things happen in our country as they do.

Under Gemini, I read:

> Don't expect anything good today. Unpleasant people
> will set the tone at receptions. A bad home life will
> worsen.

"You understand my foreboding."

"Ridiculous," I said. As you undoubtedly guessed, I entrust no faith in medieval explanations of worldly woes. Tanya constantly tells me that I will one day comprehend the perils of my skepticism, but she may as well predict that before the End Times we shall all grow curly tails and root through muck for our dinners.

"What does yours say?"

Under Capricorn, I read:

> This is a largely dangerous day. You may have trouble
> with your kidneys. No one will pay attention to you.
> Tighten security on your delivery trucks.

"I have no delivery trucks, and my kidneys are fine."

"So far," he said, and walked to the door. "Let's go."

Although the building that housed his company was of recent construction, admirably situated on the gardenless Garden Ring, the adjacent neighborhood was not so well maintained. Had our leaders boasted so unceasingly of our flaws as they had of our glories, they could in honesty have proclaimed Moscow's slums to be the least progressive in the world. In furthering an awareness of the gruesome conditions in which capitalist societies allow their people to live, as students we were shown photographs and given detailed accounts of New York's Bronx, Rio's hillside shantytowns, Calcutta's teeming alleys, and the rats' tunnels in Hong

Kong's infamous Kowloon Walled City, metropolitan stews worthy
of the pen of a Gorki or a Hugo. The hives of Moscow are airier,
with splendid views, and in them almost the entire populace lives.
But nestled near the commonplace ten-story sinks of iniquity,
sprinkled among five-story *khrushchobas* (Khrushchev's concep-
tion of workers' housing, providing to our citizen nobles four walls,
a floor, occasionally a ceiling), you sometimes find single-story
wooden structures, untouched since the Czar's day. In a maze of
streets we came to one that housed a beer hall, and therein Sokolov
sought his wandering boy.

Snow blackened with soot was piled high on either side of
the entrance to a depth of three meters. We stamped the slush from
our boots and went inside, shoving open the heavy metal door,
descending two wooden steps to a wet, creaking floor. The finer
the establishment in Moscow, the less penetrating will be the scent
of urine perfuming the foyer. Entering a beer hall always makes
you think you've thrust your head into an airport toilet.

"He's here?" I asked.

"I'll find out."

The room was packed sardine-tight. No one paid attention
to us, our fine clothes notwithstanding; in daytime, even in
Moscow's contemporary ruins, these kinds of people are too intent upon drinking themselves blind to spend much time plotting
criminal stratagems. Behind the bar the innkeepers, short of
glasses, filled empty milk cartons brought in by the clientele. Many
drinkers poured vodka or vials of Red Moscow perfume into their
beer, fruitlessly attempting to improve the taste. On a table near
the bar was an array of appetite-whetting food, free for the taking—week-old chunks of bread, dessicated fish strips, sausage bad
enough to drive the cats away. A ceramic stove unevenly heated
the room; those nearest could have enjoyed a refreshing sauna,
had they brought rocks and buckets of water; denizens farthest
from the warmth lay on the floor, resembling mammoths in perma-
frost. There was, at least, no disco.

"Have you seen Oleg?" Sokolov asked a barman who was
engaged in filling empty vodka bottles with beer from a hose.
Tattooed tears issued from his cold marbles. Behind him, affixed
to the wall, was a sign scrawled in ink, saying:

TODAY'S EXCHANGE RATE $1 = 1 KILO OF RUBLES
ETERNAL GLORY BE TO THE VICTOR PEOPLE!

"Over there," the barman said, sweeping up change from the countertop with a knobby fist. We looked. Oleg Norinsky appeared to be sixty, although he was perhaps only in his forties—he was by no means a man of mature years when he worked at Melodiya. He sat at the end of a long wooden table, staring into the abyss that lay past his carton of beer. Thinning the brew with vodka, he raised it to his lips with shaking hands. His hair was matted; his suit grimy with mud; sores on his cheeks freely bled.

"My master of statistics," said Sokolov.

"He must be breathtakingly competent, on the job."

"Today obviously isn't one of his better days. I don't know his sign or I would check *his* horoscope and ascertain *his* troubles."

We took seats on either side of him.

"You've been keeping us waiting for you, Oleg," Sokolov said. Norinsky drank his nauseating potion, seeming to neither hear nor see us. "You're not devoting your attention to business problems, are you?"

"I am thinking about life," Norinsky said, enunciating his words with the too-careful precision of the constantly drunk. "Why are you bothering me? Who is this, a representative of the competent organs? He looks familiar."

"This is an associate of mine, Maxim Alexeich Borodin. When he was with the Ministry of Culture he worked closely with many of your Melodiya associates. He hopes you can provide him with information."

"They always want information," Norinsky said, turning toward me. His breath would have killed a goat. "You are a representative of the competent organs, to be sure."

I ignored his drunken taunts, wishing to keep our conversation brief. "When you worked there as an auditor," I said, "you oversaw financial records involving sales, I understand. I should say apparent sales, perhaps."

"It's a blur to me," Oleg said, wiping his mouth with his frayed sleeve. "Everything these past few years has been a blur. My father had an eye disease, what is the name? Glaucoma. Vision closes in like an enemy. Perhaps I am suffering from *glasnostma*,

yes? What a life, what a life. Our world has shrunk to the dimen-
sions of an observation slit."

"Aren't you ashamed of yourself, pickling your brain in
alcohol?" Sokolov asked, leaning over on his left. Oleg shook his
head.

"Monies were evidently distributed to Melodiya by way of
the Ministry of Internal Affairs," I said, "and marked to be circu-
lated through a number of accounts, including those of the Happy
Guys."

Oleg grimaced, as if he were about to be sick. "My God.
May they never be heard by anyone again."

"Do you remember if a specific person in or out of Melodiya
was directing this money laundering?"

"You confuse me," he said. "What are you asking?"

"Did you ever hear of an Internal Affairs apparatchik
named Dmitry Gubin?"

"You *are* with the organs. Stop faking, you faker."

"Treat my associate with respect, you drunken bastard,"
Sokolov said.

"This name Guber means nothing to me. Look, what I did
meant nothing to me even when I was doing it. Why should I care
now? What fascinates you about this ancient history? Are you
writing your memoirs for a Western publisher?" Norinsky laughed,
spraying me with his spittle.

"How much money went through the Ministry of Culture
itself?" I asked.

"Do you miss your tribute?" Norinsky asked. "With dolts
like you in charge, no wonder the country fell to pieces."

"Shut your pig-ignorant mouth," Sokolov said, making a
motion with his fist as if preparing to cuff his employee. "We are
not as low as your companions, I don't think."

"Almost."

"These transferrals through the Ministry of Culture were
done without my knowledge," I continued. "Do you remember
anything improper?"

He laughed and sipped his beer. "Ask me if I remember
anything proper," he said. "I remember how you were screwing
the Happy Guys. Everyone except the Happy Guys knew, poor

fools. They didn't deserve fine dinners, trips abroad, exotic drugs, whores with hot buttocks, did they? No, save such earthly delights for ministers and their ass lickers."

"The Happy Guys took their share, believe me," I told him, attempting to keep my temper in check.

"But they weren't alone," he said. "Listen to me, none of this fell into my sphere of personal concern. You could have stolen each other blind, for all I cared. I was but a cog."

"My sources have documentation that claims over two hundred million of the Happy Guys' records were sold to Iran. Obviously, there were no such sales."

"Who can guess at the secret pleasures of the ayatollahs?" Norinsky asked, weaving in his seat.

"Were more than two sets of financial books being kept?"

His eyes widened, as if he spotted elephants behind my shoulders or even felt the coils of the snake as it gripped ever more tightly. "*Two* sets? An encyclopedia. Everyone needed useful figures to boost their accomplishments or conceal malfeasance. How do you think I became such an expert?"

"But who was ultimately responsible?" I asked, raising my voice.

"In the Soviet Union? Benevolent employer, let me praise you for bringing this hilarious comedian here to entertain me."

Seizing him by the necktie, Sokolov extracted him from his chair's embrace as if lifting an oyster from its shell. "No one is laughing." After being dropped back into place, Norinsky brushed his stained lapels and adjusted his collar with dirty fingers, barely deigning to glance at us as he neatened his tramp's attire.

"No," he mumbled. "No one in Russia will laugh again until we cleanse the evil around us." Rising so quickly from his chair that he almost pitched forward onto his face, he threw out his arms and called upon his sullen compatriots to pay heed to his words. "No one. Am I not right?"

Those who were able hoisted their drinks high. Sokolov and I looked on with increasing amazement as Norinsky drew himself erect and enjoined the crowd to pay heed to his ever-more-energetic oration.

"Hear me, friends, our country is a criminal paradise. But these *businessmen* are the biggest criminals of all."

"You said it," coherent members of the rabble responded. "Hear, hear."

"He is a very good worker," Sokolov said to me.

"Brothers!" Norinsky's fellows listened closely now; even the mammoths stirred to life. The barmen fumbled for their knouts and truncheons, in the event passions grew too heated. "The time of these bastards is coming to an end! Our Army will save us! Our people will rise up! Join me, brothers! Sing our anthem!"

All the louts began muttering the lyrics of a song that one presently hears only at gatherings of fossil Bolsheviks in Red Square or at the old Lenin Museum. As a child, I'd never learned the words of the Soviet National Anthem; by the time I entered school, they'd been outlawed.

> *Be true to the people; thus Stalin has reared us,*
> *Inspired us to labor and valorous deed!*

"A good time to leave," Sokolov said, standing up.

> *Our army grew up in the heat of grim battle,*
> *Barbarian invaders we'll swiftly strike down. . . .*

We eased cautiously through the crowd, taking care not to step on stray feet. Twice we were confronted by beery hooligans who tried to block our way, making what they imagined to be threats. Finally we reached the door and emerged into invigorating cold. Ignoring the catcalls behind us, we hurriedly walked through afternoon's long shadows until we reached the Garden Ring. An unending stream of trucks raced along the ring, cargoes hidden beneath green tarpaulins.

"How can you retain such a time bomb?" I asked.

"Don't take him too seriously," Sokolov said. "Ultimately he threatens nothing but his liver. As long as he does his work when he's in my office, he can do what he likes once he's out." He lit a black cigarette, shot smoke through his nostrils, and smiled. "Listen, I've been thinking about what you've told me. Don't you imagine Esenin was the conspirators' man in the Ministry itself?"

A thin contrail of fine gray ash streaming from the back of

a passing truck was ground beneath the wheels of successive trucks into the icy pavement. "You're probably right."

"Who knows who might have been involved at Melodiya," he said. "Everyone there probably took a cut, one way or the other."

Esenin had been my superior at the Ministry of Culture during the years I worked there. "If he wasn't dead I'd ask him."

"He'd have never told you."

"His eyes would tell."

Let me digress and offer you an illuminating story about Esenin, who—I trust—presently gives suck at Satan's bosom. Although he did not nest in the highest branches of bureaucratic trees, he had access; he was a close friend of Brezhnev's wicked daughter, Galina (how close, one never asked). For his own daughter's wedding reception, Esenin asked to borrow Catherine the Great's china tea service, so his guests would be impressed by his good taste and his power. His request was granted. Several hundred bottles into the festivities, a celebrant dropped an eggshell-thin cup. Hearing the sound of shattering crockery, imagining that the good-luck toast to the newlyweds was at last being given, the other guests at once hurled every irreplaceable piece into the fireplace. Huzzah! At Galina's command, Uncle Lyonya's underlings directed the Hermitage curators to swallow their loss and be happy. Typical; but Esenin had the gall to file a property damage claim, payable to the Ministry of Culture, and he received reimbursement! The voucher was conveniently made out in his name, to facilitate the process.

"Don't judge Oleg harshly," Sokolov said, preparing to take his leave. "I've seen him worse."

"I'd never stand for it from one of my employees. Beat your own, scare the stranger."

"There's no need for me to exact punishment. Oleg's curse is that he never blacks out from drinking." He dropped his cigarette into the nearest drift. "Shame keeps him healthy. He'll be in tomorrow, first thing, and never say a word the rest of the week. A model worker."

"Why are you not at your business?" Tanya asked me when I called her, later that afternoon. "What are you doing? You're not drinking, are you?"

"Certainly not," I said. All I had to do was walk past an empty glass, and afterward my thoughtful wife would spend part of each day for a month berating me with concern. I rolled onto my back; a golden sun peeped beyond my raised legs as if from behind clouds. "As I told you, I'm en route to the baths, to meet Gubin and his associates. At present I'm here at the Ministry of Culture, checking on the reliability of our sources."

"Are you the only one there? Why is it so quiet?"

"It's nearly six; they've all gone home." Sonya thrust her head between my legs and opened her mouth, but I foresaw no upcoming pleasure—the contrary!—for I could tell she was about to make some mischievous, easily overheard remark. "I'll try to be in by nine."

"Come in whenever you like, as you always do," Tanya said; as I couldn't see her, I had no way of knowing the spirit in which she offered her remark. Her voice held even less emotion than her features ever did. "I must work late tonight also."

"Be careful, my pigeon," I said, pushing Sonya's face against my lower region; save for piping squeaks, I succeeded in muffling anything else she might have unwisely had to say.

"Use your time wisely," Tanya said. "Remember what I tell you."

"As always."

The moment my wife hung up I lifted my hand from Sonya's head. She drew away from me violently and rose from our bed, perceptibly angered. For an instant I thought she would hit me; she didn't, and almost as quickly lay back down.

"Angel, she might have heard you if you'd spoken."

"I had nothing to say," she said. "Am I a doll you throw around at will? Have you no respect for me?"

"I have the most wholehearted love and respect for you, koshka," I said, trusting that my sincerity would be evident. "Believe me, I didn't mean to behave in such a common manner."

"Are even the best of you peasants at heart?"

I guessed that she meant Russian men in general but thought it wise not to ask—she might think I didn't know. "I'll never again be so uncultured. Do you forgive me?"

"No." Then she changed the subject of our conversation to an entirely different, more undesirable matter. "Why did you never tell me about your son?"

"It was years ago, and a tragedy. It has no bearing on our lives."

"What other secrets do you never tell me?"

"My sweetness, please, I don't want to talk about it."

"When we were first together you always told me how much you enjoyed being with me, because we could talk so freely. Do you remember?"

"That's still true," I said. "Without question."

"How often do we talk now?" She allowed her voice to slip into its highest register. "Hello, Max, how are you?" Then, she lowered it into the deepest level she could manage: "'Koshka, koshka,' boom boom boom. Any more, when you want to talk, you must talk to Tanya. You want to fuck, you fuck Sonya."

"That's not so," I said, pulling her closer, brushing my fingers along her tender skin. "I've been so busy lately. So many problems. And your husband—"

"He has nothing to do with this. Max, how can we be as close as I've thought we've been with you keeping secrets from me?"

"That's the only thing I've never told you, I swear. It was a disheartening situation, my sweet kitten. Even Tanya and I never talk about him. It serves no purpose. Do you understand?"

She shook her head. "But no other secrets?" I shook my head. She rested her head against my chest, tugging at its hairs with her fingers, closing her eyes as if to dream. "Will you tell me, one day?"

Never, ever. "I'll try."

Sandunovsky's Steam Baths, an extravagantly decayed establishment on Neglinnaya Lane, in Moscow's center, was built almost a century ago. Chekhov rented a room there, undoubtedly devoting hours spent within to tinkering with the watchlike mechanisms of his classic dramas; afterward, lingering in the hot room, trying to clear his lungs of their poison. Plaster flaked from the building's grandiose facade, exposing gray brick beneath as a lovely woman's skin shows pale and mottled through the runs in her hose. From the chimneys wafted coigns of steam, clouds of more benign nature than, say, a crematorium's billowing smoke.

"Our partner is running late," Dmitry informed me as we checked our outer wraps with the *banya's* ill-tempered old grannies. He and his associates—Tibor, Mikhail, and Vlad—had been drinking, although in comparison to Norinsky they could have passed as teetotalers. His compatriots had worked together in the Department for Combating Theft of Socialist Property for so long that you might at first glance have supposed them to be triplets. A closer look showed them to be nothing more than the interchangeable gears of office machinery they had, through time and proximity, become. "Let's go in. He'll meet us inside."

From a pensioner we purchased entry tickets and, from another ancient biddy, bundles of birch twigs. Although we had visited these baths many times, we gaped as always at the lobby's mindlessly ornate Russian Rococo decor. Dust that blackened the gilt of the uppermost entablatures and moldings might have been tracked in by Chekhov himself, wafting over time from floor to ceiling. Tumorous bags of soiled laundry sandbagged cracked, yellowed columns; a hallway floored with red and green tiles led to a broad marble staircase beyond. We climbed the stairs to reach the men's section, watching women make their way to their own quarters. I will not deny that I uninhibitedly admired their beauty, but in a more gracious and subtle way than did Dmitry's companions, who nudged one another, winking and leering bug-eyed, making low remarks such as those whose contact with women is limited (or nonexistent) inevitably make. One young woman, a stunning brunette who was almost as attractive as my koshka, especially attracted their attention.

"Look at the ass on her," Tibor said. "I bet she fucks like a crab."

"I could club her blind with my prick," said Vlad.

Mikhail smiled and prodded me in the side. "Don't you wish we could push her under a streetcar?"

Men speak openly of their darkest urges in private, to be certain, but that did not excuse his remark, which was of the foulest sort, used exclusively by the most uncultured. Pushing a woman under a streetcar means to gang-rape her until she dies. When they all began snickering like schoolboys I felt driven to let loose my fury. "Have you daughters or wives?" I asked them; they nodded, appearing confused by my question, or perhaps by my ice-cold voice. "Would you like it if I was to see your most beloved on the street and turn to you and say, I'd like to fuck her ass so hard she could tongue my cock clean as it came out her mouth?"

Had I said *mothers*, rather than the aforementioned relatives, they would have killed me on the spot. My understated phrasing had the desired effect—they were silenced and glared at me as if I were a hog among sparrows.

"Max, Max," Dmitry said, clapping his hand on my shoulder. "Please excuse my beloved associate. He is overly prudish, regarding matters of the flesh." They laughed. I joined heartily in their good cheer, warmly slapping Dmitry across the back, trying not to think about the disagreement I'd had with his wife and the troubling conversation afterward that so sapped our animal passions. "Come, let's go. The bath awaits."

After entering the vast changing room, we took off our clothes. Broad wooden beams befitting a manorial hall braced the ceiling; the assuring glow of streetlights shone through the stained glass windows. I noticed that Tibor wore circular bandages on his arms and back, which in homeopathic theory guarantees vibrant health. I would as soon put my trust in leeches. Sitting down on high-backed wooden benches, we swaddled ourselves in sheets kept hanging on convenient hooks. Candlelabra attached to the ends of the benches cast buttery light; I believe they were intended to heighten the attractiveness of the bathers, but the effort failed. Whenever I am at the baths I always feel surrounded by a regiment of naked Khrushchevs, Romans bereft of empire.

We bought snacks of dried salt fish and stepped into the bath itself. Hundreds of men paraded through the primeval mists, gently scrubbing themselves, swatting their backs with twigs as if to brush away flies. Men lying on their stomachs allowed masseurs to work abrasive coffee grounds into the interstices of their muscles, emptying pores of accumulated filth. Filling yellow plastic bowls with hot water from taps on the wall, we scrubbed and rinsed ourselves. "Tell me about this silent partner of yours," I said.

"Haven't you told him, Dmitry?" Tibor asked.

"It hasn't been necessary for you to know his precise background until now," Dmitry said. "You might have formed unwarranted prejudices in advance of—"

"Who is it?"

"Pavel Petrenko," he said. "His party provides us with a supplemental source of regular income. In return, we intend to help fund their party with a percentage of profits from our sales."

"Petrenko? You mean the People's Party of Hammer and Steel?"

"Is that its name?" he asked his associates. The four of them suddenly seemed almost deliriously nervous. "Probably so. Excessive melodrama. Come, let us move into the hot room."

Entering the sauna, we danced across the scorching floor, trying not to burn our feet. In the center of the room was a staired wooden platform rising toward the ceiling. Our party lingered below, listening to the snaky hiss the stoves emitted when watered. The higher you climbed on the platform, the higher the temperature rose; at the top, plum-faced masochists ecstatically flagellated themselves with twigs.

"Petrenko and his party are fascists," I said. "They're Nazis."

"More to the point, they're lunatics," Vlad said. "You'll see."

"He makes Zhirinovsky look like Gorbachev. In the name of heaven, how did you get mixed up with them?"

"We needed additional backing; they needed a long-term source of income," Dmitry said. "Therefore we satisfy our mutual needs. Synergy, I think it's called. It isn't as if we're supporting them on our backs."

"You just told me they'll be sharing your profits."

"If there is income," Dmitry said, blinking his eyes against the heat. "They understand the risks."

"What do you mean, *if* there is income?" I asked, growing hotter than the stoves. Dmitry pulled his sheet more closely around him. "You don't expect profits?"

"Of course, but their expectations may be less realistic than ours."

"Does Petrenko know that for all intents and purposes he'll be working in league with Georgians?"

Dmitry shook his head. "Don't tell him."

Let me explain that of the dozens of political parties presently in existence in our land, the People's Party of Hammer and Steel is the most notorious. If its candidates—Petrenko is the only

one, I think—won Russia's highest offices in the upcoming election (the one that is always going to be held next year), it intended
to waste no time writing its party platform into law. Included in
the platform were such surprising proposals as issuing every Russian family a weekly case of vodka; building stainless steel walls
around the entire country and a clear plastic dome above it, thus
securing our nation against Western sneak attacks; recapturing for
Russia places we have never possessed—Norway, Tibet, Arizona—
and supplying secret technology for the "psionic x-ray bomb" to
the Bosnian Serbs. The PPH & S also proposed to expand offensive weapons production, break existing treaties, imprison foreigners, and ethnically cleanse our traditionally problematic minorities,
but so did the majority of parties.

"I'm guessing the Georgians are equally in the dark about
Petrenko and his minions?"

"You understand why we hesitate to tell them."

"Do you have the brains of an ox?" I said, aghast by what
I was hearing.

"We needed cash transfusions; what could we do?" Dmitry
asked. "I assure you, the antagonistic groups will never interact."

"Why does Petrenko want to meet me? Obviously, you've
not told him the truth about what my company is doing for you."

"We've left it unstated. Basically, he wanted to meet you
to be sure you were a good Russian."

"Not Jewish," Tibor added.

"Believe me, Max, there's no need to worry."

A bass voice boomed out of the opaque steam. "Worry
about what?" The speaker appeared, naked save for a sweat-
darkened fedora, his arms clasped across his chest. Years ago, when
I was in the Army, I was stationed as an interpreter in what is now
Kirghizstan, near the Chinese border. Many times we heard native
tales of the primitive man-ape which supposedly yet lives in the
unexplored mountains nearby, a possible survival from the Nean-
derthal Age known as the *almas*. Looking upon the lantern jaw
and heavily furred body of Petrenko, I perceived that the enigmatic *almas* had evidently been captured.

"Good to see you, Pavel," Dmitry said, and they embraced.
"This is our printing facilitator, Maxim Alexeich Borodin."
Petrenko seized my hand in his, squeezing hard as if to break
bones; I was familiar with this obnoxious trick and quickly returned

the favor. Satisfied by my reaction, he engulfed me in a greater grip, pressing his thick, damp torso against me for some moments longer than I thought necessary.

"This is my aide-de-camp, Gyorgy Debalov," Petrenko said, putting his heavy arm around the shoulders of a younger man who came out of the fog to appear at his side. "The leader of my private guard, the Hawks." Debalov was a hooligan with short blond hair, swimmer's musculature, and the air of one who spends dull moments etching his initials into strangers' arms with a razor. Gauze was wrapped around his manly root. "Pardon this horse's foreskin, he's had it bad with a Parisian head cold. Stuck his prick in a bad cunt." Petrenko laughed, climbed up, and squatted on a wooden ledge at the apex of the platform; Debalov pitched a bucket over the stove, splashing us with scalding drops of water. "What of it, Gubin? What's taking so fucking long, getting these shipments under way?"

"Keep in mind the well-known inefficiency of capitalism, Pavel," Dmitry said, assuming the submissive attitude that came so naturally in the presence of those from whom he needed something. "Everything will move by March first."

"What's the delay?" Petrenko asked. Debalov climbed up and took a seat beside his superior.

"The mafia, for one thing," Dmitry said. "The usual payoffs."

"Pay them off in what we're exporting," Petrenko said, breathing deep of the rising steam. What did this mean? I wondered, but said nothing. Dmitry glanced at me as if to judge my reaction. Seeing that I had none lessened his palpable fear.

"Nothing's printed yet," he replied. "Nothing will be until the last minute. In the meantime, we must deal with them. All have access to authority."

"And we don't?" Petrenko asked. "My God, Yeltsin can't handle these lice he's bred. What a sorry situation. Once we are in control, we will crush these gangsters like bedbugs. Nothing will be left of them but spots of blood."

Dmitry nodded cheerfully, in unison with his associates. "The glacierlike slowness of bureaucrats presents problems as well," he continued. "Max is dealing firmly with them, however. He's doing a job worthy of highest admiration."

"Everything must proceed faster, all the same. Asses don't

move till you kick them." Petrenko stared down at me from his aerie, his face a looming purple balloon. "You, Borovik. Why can't you push these papers through more quickly?"

"Borodin," I said, correcting him. My head was swimming in the room's unbearably hot air. "My company is proceeding in accordance with the timetable Dmitry provided."

Petrenko retrieved a bottle of vodka from the folds of the sheet Debalov carried and, opening it, took a long swig. "Listen to me, did you just pop out of a cunt? Do what I tell you and get this job done."

What job could he possibly mean? What had Dmitry told him? "I do what I'm asked to do."

"Like a trained dog," he said. "Where are your brains, in your ass or your head?"

Sick of his tedious barnyard talk, dizzy with heat, and infuriated by his despicable insults, I responded at once, without hesitation (or, to be honest, thought). "Watch your fucking mouth, you walrus prick," I told him, staring up at him through the fog. "When it's done, it's done. Fuck off until then."

Had Koba himself, the Greatest Genius of All Times and Peoples, suddenly appeared in a sulfurous cloud at that moment to drag us all down below with him, Dmitry and his associates could not have looked more horrified. Debalov stood up, preparing to descend. Petrenko stared at me, his face as empty of intelligent expression as a stuffed animal's; then, shoving his hat farther back on his head, he began to laugh. "Excellent," he said. "Excellent. I appreciate your candor and admire a man who gives as good as he takes." He rose, stepped down the platform, seized me by the arm, and yanked me up to his level. "You must sit with me and drink. I insist."

Thrusting his bottle into my hands, he made it clear that he would not be pleased unless I took a deep draft. Here at the apex of the platform, I felt as if I were sitting on top of the sun. The bottle burned my hands when I touched it, and the vodka was almost boiling. When I drank, I seared my throat with fire. For an instant I thought my body would reject Petrenko's gift, but before this could occur I luckily recovered my composure. Flinging an arm around me as if I were his dearest companion, Petrenko guzzled down the rest of the bottle's contents.

"I can tell you are a man who can take punishment," he said. "Most people are spoiled, afraid of punishment and ridicule. How can you know joy if you don't know pain? One of our key goals is to return the gift of pain to our people."

"What idiocy," I said. Alcohol affects me all the more powerfully when I am being simultaneously parboiled, and I was somewhat more forthright than ordinarily I would have thought wise. "Simply to get bread they stand in line for hours in the cold. Isn't that enough pain?"

"That's not pain, that's life," he said. "True pain makes for strength, and it is clear our people are no longer strong. They've been ruined by Western degeneracy. Our people need the sort of pain they experienced in the Great War. Noble pain, where the sting can be relieved only by steadfast devotion and excessive zeal. They'll shape up in no time, believe me."

"You think we should have a new war?" Debalov handed him a fresh bottle. I glimpsed Dmitry and the others at the bottom of the platform, looking as horrified as before; their forms shimmered miragelike in the excessive heat. Debalov's expression did not change either; he continued lusting after me with homicidal desire. I tried to avoid catching his eye.

"There are simpler ways of accomplishing our goals," Petrenko said, passing me the bottle after taking another long drink. "When we take control, we will have a new tourist slogan ready for the world. *Don't come to Russia, let Russia come to you.* What do you think? I tell you, we will soak our feet in every ocean. Look here, tell me something,"

"What?" I asked, taking another drink, hoping to replenish vital fluids. Some moments earlier I had stopped sweating, a dangerous sign. Favoring me with another dewy hug, Petrenko placed his lips close to my ear.

"Gubin," he whispered. "Is he a yid?"

"Not to my knowledge."

"Are you certain? He has the conniving personality. Respectable intelligence, of a sly sort. A connoisseur of art. You've noticed his nose, of course." I shook my head. "The pores," he said, tapping his own sizable proboscis. "Very large. Often a telling indicator." Once again, my ear almost disappeared within his mouth as he closed in. "Is he circumcised? Then we'd know for sure."

"I've never looked." Petrenko slapped my shoulder so roughly I almost fell off the platform.

"Liar. You can't fool me, every man takes a sensible interest in such matters," he said. Taking his own prick in one hand while seizing mine in his other, he squeezed it not quite as hard as he had squeezed my hand. "We are *very* Russian, anyone can tell."

He released me, possibly reconsidering his unexpected action, and I started edging away from him until I realized I was only sliding closer to Debalov. Taking more of a sensible interest than is usual for me, I saw plainly that Petrenko was a graduate of one of our fine security establishments, for the shaft of his generative organ was spotted with black lumps—when not breaking rocks, prisoners often while away their days inserting lead shot beneath the skin of the male root in order to give their lovers extra pleasure.

"Look, why else does he hide himself beneath that sheet? You know why?" I shook my head. "If he didn't, everyone would see for sure that he's a yid."

"Unless he's Muslim," I noted. It was clear from Petrenko's bemused expression that this notion had not occurred to him. Thinking as quickly as I could, I came up with what I believed might be a way to get us out of the hot room without exposing myself as one who lacked masculine toughness. "The steam is too thick in here to see clearly. Maybe we can get him into the pool."

When he smiled he revealed better teeth than I would have expected. One of his front incisors was gold; there was an indistinct design cut into its surface. "I like a cunning thinker. Men!" he shouted. "To the pool. Let us be like leaping salmon!"

We staggered out. I gasped, grateful beyond words to be able to breathe again, and trailed the group, barely capable of walking, hoping that after I joined them in a cooling dip I could excuse myself and go home. "There will be no lonely women in our Russia," I heard Petrenko saying. He grasped Debalov's neck, pinching it soundly as if to make him yelp. "This cuntsufferer won't know what to do with his prick till it heals," he said, and Debalov giggled like a schoolgirl. "Watch him, or he'll sneak over to the women's section." I suspected that the women faced little danger if he did.

All except Dmitry plunged into the pool when we reached it. To Petrenko's clear dismay he remained seated on the side, tightly wrapped in his sheet. "Gubin," Petrenko shouted, breaking the surface of the water. He was not wholly uncultured; he'd removed his hat. "You don't swim?"

"Not well."

"Get in!"

"Gladly," Dmitry said, flinging himself into the pool, screaming in agony as he sank. When in time he bobbed to the surface, his lips were blue as a bruise and he shivered like a whipped pup. Petrenko circled shark-like around him, periodically descending beneath the waves, but, judging from his sorely disappointed expression, he was having no success in ascertaining Dmitry's anatomical state. Deciding I'd enjoyed these capers long enough, I hauled myself from the pool, gathered my wrap around me, and walked to the crowded changing room. The cooling waters had not effected a full recovery from my time spent in the hellish sauna, and so, sitting down, I closed my eyes and sought solace in blessed quiet, disturbed only by the room's all-pervasive conversational undercurrents.

Before I could get up and retrieve my clothes, unfortunately, my evening's companions spilled into the changing room, new bottles of vodka at hand. Petrenko, his hat replaced on his head, sat down with Debalov on the bench across from me; Dmitry and his associates took their place on my side. "We will by century's end develop a modified lord-peasant social structure, I think," he said to Petrenko. "This is inevitably a spontaneous result of capitalism; look at America. There, people ascend to their natural levels as cream in milk."

"Or shit in water," Petrenko said, downing more vodka. "Capitalist parasites and nation-fuckers are always able to buy themselves the best seats, just like under communism. Capitalism and communism reduce all human endeavor to economics; neither are suited for Russia." He grabbed my knee and tapped it with his fingers as if to see if I were ripe. "Look at the results. Look what we have now. The worst of both worlds. Something new is needed."

"Petrenkoism," I offered, and, sadly, he adored me all the more.

"No, no, I am no egomaniac, no self-aggrandizer," he said, smiling. "Do I look like a Communist, Max?" We laughed; I could visualize the titanic statues he would surely raise in honor of himself. We rubbed soothing powder, kept handy in open buckets for the use of customers, into our shoulders and chests. The powder was gritty, which did not seem right, but perhaps the baths had been denied access to its usual suppliers. "With the help you and Gubin have offered us, we will shortly have matters set aright. Our people debase themselves, amassing Western currency. Once the currency is as debased, they'll understand the error of their ways."

A theorem came to mind; all it needed was proof. "It will take vast numbers of fake dollars to affect the American economy to the desired degree, of course," I noted.

"Keep your printing presses rolling twenty-four hours a day if need be," said Petrenko.

I looked at Dmitry. "Rest assured, I'll do what must be done." He avoided my gelid stare. So, this would-be future Czar obviously believed that the documentation I was facilitating was counterfeit American money. How could Dmitry be such a fool as to have given this impression? What were his intentions? Without my consent, he was readying my own grave while he simultaneously dug his. The nerve he had, to expect me to willingly participate in his mendacity when I knew nothing about it.

"Excellent. I expect efforts worthy of Stakhanovites from everyone who works for our party," Petrenko said. "It won't be easy, my friends. There is no sea without water, no war without blood."

He was as drunk as Yeltsin now, as were Dmitry and his partners. Debalov, on the other hand, had touched not a drop all evening. He sat quietly alongside his master, Behemoth hard by Woland, watching us as an anaconda watches a pig, foreseeing a delicious dinner. "We'll crush our enemies, the enemies of Russia," Petrenko continued, his voice rising. "We'll suffer no lily-livers; we'll hang men by the balls and women by the cunts until they beg for mercy. We'll dance on their bodies to the music of bones cracking underfoot. All *zhopniks* and yids, soulless Americans, screeching women and sexual perverts, black bastards from the South—"

He trembled but was not cold. I have never seen a man look happier. "Armenians?" I asked. "Chechens? Azeris?"

"Fucking Georgians!" he screamed. "*Chuchmeki!* We'll stack them up like lumber."

Undoubtedly he could have spewed his wrath for hours, and would have, if he'd had the chance. But at that instant, guns began to fire on the far side of the room as, I supposed, several different gangs decided to make more exclusive one anothers' membership lists. "God help us!" Dmitry screamed, and ducked. Even as we threw ourselves to the floor, dozens of sheeted men were hurtling through the steamy air with unsuspected grace, appearing in the magic of the moment to be filmed in slow motion; I thought of a pod of mighty whales, enthralled by and rejoicing in their limitless power as they broke the surface of the misty waves. All around us we heard a sound resembling that of a battery of peas being spat against plastic sheeting. Splinters of wood spiraled up, shot off the benches where we'd been sitting, seconds earlier; windows shattered as if in a cyclonic windstorm. Throughout the duration I constantly patted myself, searching for wounds, fearing each imagined twinge to be the grace note of a fatal chord.

As suddenly as it began, the firefight ended. The room took on the silence of a country church. Dmitry's face was as pale as a corpse's; when he opened his eyes, he found himself staring into mine. He, and many others, had shat themselves, and that odor mixed with others more noxious permeating the air. "Don't lie to your fucking investors about me hereafter," I told him, shocked by how my voice, a well-modulated baritone (or so I have been reliably told), presently sounded to my ringing ears as a wobbly, breathless tenor. "I'll turn you over before you can blink."

He started to cry. "My God, I'm wet. I'm shot, I'm shot."

Seeing no bloody stain, I felt his pillow-soft stomach through his sheet and then examined my hand. "Vodka," I said.

"What's all this fucking and dancing going on in here?" someone shouted, and then we heard other authoritative voices. "Militia! Nobody move!"

Everyone who could, of course, stood up at once. At first it was difficult to perceive the scale of the aftermath. Frigid air pouring through shattered windows thickened the room's steam;

heads swirled through the mist like specks of pepper in soup. Militiamen rushing into the baths hoisted their rifles and aimed to fire upon surviving miscreants. "Everyone is forbidden to leave!" their commanders bellowed through their bullhorns. "Investigations are proceeding!"

The state's defenders kept us from the immediate field of battle, but when the steam cleared I glimpsed perhaps a dozen sprawled bodies, blossoms of red garlanded round their winding sheets. Their twisted arms and legs resembled a child's carelessly knotted shoelaces. Medics hurried past, carrying a man on a stretcher. His intestines, blown free of his body by automatic fire, had been piled atop his chest so they would not be misplaced. "Max," Dmitry said as he allowed me to help him stand up, "I think you made a favorable impression."

Petrenko's hat was askew on his head until Debalov adjusted it for him. He waved an unbroken bottle of vodka, demanding that I take it from his hands. "To a fucking memorable evening," my new friend muttered, collapsing heavily against me. He vomited. I drank.

5

"Why would we want Romania? Nobody lives there but Italian gypsies and vampires. Such unnecessary countries have nothing to fear from the People's Party of Hammer and Steel."

Petrenko was on live television the next morning at ten, appearing on a magazine show on Channel 2times2. Our escapades of the evening before notwithstanding, he looked as if he had enjoyed twelve or fourteen hours of refreshing sleep, and not once did the interviewer trick him into saying anything he didn't intend to say.

"What about Finland?"

"The Finns shiver like feeble women when they hear the name Petrenko. We spit in their eyes. Let them go on drinking and sharing intimate moments with their reindeer. What do we care?"

At first I believed that either Petrenko had superhuman powers of recovery, or else the show's makeup staff had been trained by the preservation specialists who tend to the Livid Lenin (Mr. Waxy, as our late leader is known to the disrespectful), for he looked so healthy he might have been dead. Watching him more closely, I realized that the reason Petrenko could so impressively and expansively expound upon his theories was that he was still drunk.

As he continued to rage, I held my phone receiver close to my ear, listening with intense concentration to Dmitry explaining the process by which I became an accomplished counterfeiter. "Maxim, you concern yourself too much with these details. Why should it matter to you?"

"You don't see why it would bother me that he believes I'm committing a capital crime?" I asked, trying not to shout, not trying very hard.

"Don't you understand? He will not put all criminals to death, only those who haven't been of assistance to him." Dmitry slurred his words, and I imagined he too had not yet sobered up— or else he'd already started on his morning rations.

"Are you calling me a criminal?" I felt no compulsion to understate my worries.

"Of course not, Maxim, don't scream—"

"Why did you even tell him about me?"

"A slip of the tongue."

"You mean you were drunk."

"Alcohol had nothing to do with it," he claimed. "Although I cannot deny that Petrenko's presence inspires me to drink more than I should. Surely you can sympathize."

"Go on with your fables."

"He was pressing me unmercifully, wanting to know who was producing the counterfeit currency, so-called. Considering your business, your name naturally came to mind. The moment I mentioned it, I realized the mistake I'd made. At once he insisted upon meeting you."

"You assure me none of your people are involved in actual counterfeiting?"

"Certainly not. Petrenko had to be fed soothing fantasies in order to get him to go along with our plan."

"You don't see a danger in that?"

"Maxim, you told me you don't want to know more about our business than you have to know, yes? So look, do your job and let us concern ourselves with such matters. You won't have to involve yourself with Petrenko again, unless of course you wish to set up separate business arrangements with him."

"Why should I want to do such a thing? Especially if he expects me to be supplying him with nonexistent counterfeit money? You don't think he'll be disappointed and seek me out once your lie is revealed?"

"It won't be revealed," Dmitry insisted. "Look, he never needs to actually see the currency, only the profits due him. As long as he has real money in hand, why should he be unhappy?"

"Only last night you told me he may not be so lucky," I reminded him. "That you weren't sure that he would receive any profits."

"Maxim, I thought smart businessmen were always looking for new markets," he said, ignoring the unwelcome intrusion of fact. "He's happy; let's keep him that way. You know, for your personal benefit I elaborated upon the full array of services your company offers. The possibilities fascinate him."

"Thank you so much for sending me such clients," I said. "There's something else here I don't understand. You told me you would be transferring souvenirs, true? But listen, I have it on good authority that the market for Russian souvenirs in America is sated."

Dmitry hesitated, as I expected, before responding. "Not entirely."

"This assignment of yours grows less attractive the longer we work on it."

"Then think of your fee and nothing else. Doesn't that seem the most sensible approach?"

"Hereafter don't involve me so directly in these schemes of yours," I said. "Be mindful, I could consider it a contract violation."

"It was an accident, Maxim, it won't happen again. Remember, I had only the best intentions."

"Hell is paved with good intentions."

After we hung up I returned my full attention to Petrenko, who was crowing like a rooster. Until I listened for a minute or two I couldn't comprehend what subject presently so excited his emotions; he kept repeating "Big! Big! Big!"

"The cost of such a dome is estimated to be, perhaps, five

hundred trillion rubles," the interviewer noted, interrupting him. "Considering the present financial situation of our nation, do you not think that this could be problematic?"

"Some of your listeners may prefer to believe I am speaking of a metaphysical dome," Petrenko replied. "So be it. There is ultimately no reason that it be constructed of such primitive materials as steel or plastic. My advisers assure me that advances in science will soon allow us to install an antimatter barrier that will fully encompass our borders, once we decide what our borders will be. Intruders will be reduced to women's face powder."

"Would you tell us more about this so-called antimatter barrier? This concept sounds somewhat magical."

Petrenko waved away the question. "The technology is too complicated to be readily understood," he said. "But do not worry, protective barriers of some sort will be built once we take power. Such barriers are necessary to insulate us against outside infection, as the Berlin Wall once kept West Berliners from sneaking across to enjoy the fruits of socialism."

"West Berliners could come and go at will into East Berlin," the interviewer pointed out; Petrenko rolled his eyes, as if he had been told the sun was hot. Ludmilla knocked at the door and stepped into my office.

"Mr. Bazhenkov is here to see you."

My client entered, and we shook hands. Bazhenkov had been recommended by a mutual friend. His needs were simple—a few documents pertaining to late-seventies decrees of the bastard Suslov—and he did not mind waiting until my people finished working on Dmitry's project before we attended to his. He might have been formed out of dough: walk any street in Moscow; see a thousand who look exactly like him. His suit, however, was like no others I have seen. It was double-breasted, expertly tailored, made of the finest woolen cloth—and was the color of an old carrot, pulled fresh from the soil. Without doubt he selected his muddy-orange suit believing it would inspire respect, yet the whole time Bazhenkov was in my office I could not help but wonder why he wasn't also wearing a false red nose and wig. It amazes me, what my countrymen choose to spend their money on, once they have money.

"Gennadi Nikolaiech, I hope all is well with you," I said, gesturing that he should take a seat.

"Not at all," he said, in such lugubrious tones that at once I feared he had suffered business reverses and kept his appointment only to tell me that he would not be able to retain my firm any longer. "So tragic. You heard, of course."

His expression led me to believe that all the Bazhenkovs save himself had been brutally murdered in their beds. "What is it? What happened?"

"The little coma girl," he said, tears wetting his eyes. "In Ekaterinburg. Dead."

She'd been in her unproductive state for so long I hadn't remembered she was still alive. As I sympathized with Bazhenkov I strove to affect a suitably mournful expression. "Heartbreaking."

"Never awoke, died yesterday. So sad. And then two hours after she was admitted into heaven, her dog was found. He returned to her building on his own."

"Heaven gives, heaven takes," I said, and pointed again to the seat I offered him. "Perhaps we should turn our attention to matters of this world."

"Look," Bazhenkov said, sitting down, glancing at the television screen, gesticulating when he saw Petrenko. "There's the man for Russia." His sorrow was at once vanquished. With my easily distracted client I watched his shining knight.

"Simple arithmetic," Petrenko was telling the interviewer. "If we kill ten million people, the remaining two hundred and ninety million will be much happier because we did."

Bazhenkov grinned and clapped his hands together, as if applauding a seal for having caught a fish. "Which people?" the interviewer asked.

Petrenko shrugged. "The guilty know themselves, when they look in the mirror."

After attending to the day's business I let myself freely anticipate the tableaux of passion in which I would soon be striking poses. As I sat at my desk, gorging my mind on reveries of Sonya, I stared through the window at the world beyond. Above the roofs of nearby buildings was a cloudless sky, clear as blue ice; the temperature had risen enough above freezing that the black hillocks bulwarking every curb had finally begun to thaw. The dripping limbs of the courtyard's birch tree scratched at heaven; carrion crows, ruffling their feathers against the wind, leapt along the branches, nipping at unseen buds. This was my favorite time of the year, when Spring stirs into half-consciousness, thinking it too dark and cold yet to awake, yet knowing it must. Of course, the joys of the season would be most manifest once Dmitry's assignment was finished and he paid the remainder of his million-dollar bill.

Sonya came to the office at four, which allowed us three hours to share in exuberant frolic. The weather was so pleasant, however, that we decided to stroll the short distance from my building to our nest of love. As we reached the street she took my arm in hers and pressed herself close against me. For a fleeting moment I foresaw only pleasantries ahead; then she spoke. "Let us be like the Peripatetics and talk as we walk," she said.

"Talk about what?"

"Your son."

A brisk gust of wind nearly lifted the hat from my head as we turned the corner; I felt as if icicles slid unseen down my back. "I've told you before, Sonya, I have nothing to say. Why do you continue to bring up this subject?"

"I'd think a man could talk for days about his only child. If you don't want to tell me what happened to him, then tell me what he was like."

We entered Lubyanka Square; both of us reflexively looked toward the building. In the minds of Muscovites there is no blacker pit than this small office structure. Its dungeons have been empty for years, but if buildings absorb the evil that occurs within them as tissue blots ink (and remembering the night sounds in my flat, I think they do), there could be few places on earth more redolent of the lower depths. In Lubyanka, citizens were shot for failing to inform on their families, for being a party member "by accident," for collecting foreign stamps, for using nonexplosive arsenic to blow up nonexistent bridges, for plotting to stir volcanoes into activity throughout the Soviet Union, timing them to blow up simultaneously, destroying the nation—were shot for being alive.

"There's not much to tell. He was like any young boy, boisterous and proud."

"Was he like you?"

"How can I tell you what kind of an adult he would have been? I am no soothsayer, no astrologer."

"You're not on trial, Max," she said. "What I am asking you is was he like you when you were his age?"

"Perhaps. I don't remember what I was like."

Her elbow shot into my ribs as if it were a mallet; young women are often so much stronger than they look. "Were you as evasive then as you are now?"

"Not as much," I said. "My father would have told you I was a worthless hooligan." Beat your own and scare the stranger, my father would have said. "He was no soothsayer either. So how can I say what my son was like? I would undoubtedly be as much in error."

In Lubyanka Square is an empty, graffiti-covered pedestal upon which once stood Dzerzhinsky, the founder of the Cheka, Lenin's secret police. The statue, a bronze representation which looked like pig iron (had it been gold, it would still have looked like pig iron), was sculpted in the Mister Big Pants style of all Soviet monumental figures—by that I mean the idealized monster is seen to be evidently wearing the outgrown clothing of an older, larger brother. The night the putsch failed, three years ago, his statue was the first to come down. I recalled with satisfaction the sight of the crane hauling up Iron-Hard Felix by his neck, letting him hang as his victims might have hung, had they not instead been shot.

"Tell me, why are figures in Socialist Realist art always looking over their shoulders?" she asked. I felt relieved that she had decided to move on to a different subject, although it puzzled me why she would ask a question to which I should have thought anyone in Russia would instinctively know the answer.

"Paranoia. Somebody is always coming up behind them."

She nodded and smiled. Her feigned guilelessness had fooled me once again. "Then they could all be statues of you."

"What is that supposed to mean?"

"You don't trust anyone. Not even me. I hate you for that, sometimes." We headed south, making our way through the crowds on Mokhovaya. On our left were shop windows. Displayed for sale in one were Parisian ensembles, fitted perfectly onto headless mannequins, and a selection of Chanel purses and bags; in the next, tin whistles and three dusty six-liter jugs of vinegar. "What kind of future do we have, Max?" She sighed and started to pull away from me, but I held her arm tightly, and after a moment she relaxed and we remained locked together. "You don't trust me enough to tell me of the joys and sorrows of your most personal moments. How can I believe you love me as much as you say you do?"

On our right, across the broad avenue, was the TSUM department store and the store once known as Children's World. The souk that has sprung up on the surrounding sidewalks appeared larger each time I passed. Naturally there were numerous kiosks, but there were many more individual traders, thousands perhaps, offering goods of every description: large-scale retailers with racks of clothing, appliances, and kitchenware; provincial farmers selling fresh chicken and winter vegetables for outlandish prices; Southerners, Northerners, Siberians, and Far Easterners, each offering the specific goods of their region; students selling off family memorabilia, middle-aged couples disposing of household necessities no longer thought essential, sad-eyed elders offering for trade or purchase a bottle of Polish shampoo, a medal once proudly worn on May Day, or a puppy.

"Sometimes I shouldn't even trust myself, koshka," I told her. She rested her head against my shoulder as we walked. Old biddies glared at us, struck mute with envy of our youth. "I trust you more than I trust anyone else."

"Even your wife?"

"In some ways," I said, speaking truthfully; she appeared to believe me. "Koshka, if I don't choose to tell you about my son, it has nothing to do with whether I trust you or not. I can't explain it to you more clearly than that." Whether or not she believed me, I couldn't say, but it was a statement she seemed to accept. "One thing I can tell you, I was a good father to him."

"Did I say you weren't?"

"No, of course not. But I was a good father, no question." She gave me a most quizzical look. "Not the best."

"But not the worst."

Could I honestly say that? I didn't know. I should never have taken him to the West. "Let's talk of other matters. Please, my angel. Please."

From the calm expression on her face I could see she would take me off the spit for a while; I'd been cooked enough to suit her taste. "All right," she said, stopping before an entrepreneur's small table. "Buy me something."

"Anything you wish." I had no difficulty understanding or fulfilling this particular desire of hers. The dealer watched us closely as she examined the merchandise he displayed, keeping a hand tucked beneath his filthy coat. At last Sonya selected an especially grotesque object, a small porcelain hippopotamus painted white, with gold tusks, eyelashes, and toenails; it was evidently a smoker's accessory, for in its back was a cavity ready-made to hold the contents of a pack, and in its mouth another hole, which would allow the ceramic creature to share a fragrant *papirosi* with its owner.

"How much?" I asked the dealer. He grinned, showing a dismaying lack of teeth in his upper jaw.

"Three thousand rubles or two dollars."

"Fifteen hundred rubles or one dollar," I offered.

"Two thousand rubles," he replied.

"Eighteen hundred." We agreed, and I handed over a stack of candy wrappers. Sonya held the hippopotamus up to her face as if she planned to kiss it, but she recovered her senses in time and returned her new item of *poshlaia* to the dealer. He placed it within a tissue-filled box. She kissed me, and then took a compact from her purse, to check her lipstick in its mirror.

"We should get to our flat, I think," my koshka whispered. "If we see cosmetics for sale, I need a new compact. The powder I have is too gritty, almost like toothpaste."

I should here try to explain for my Western readers what, exactly, *poshlaia* is—those who have not grown up with its taste, bitter on the tongue, find it hard to know its savor. *Poshlost'*, in itself, suggests the trivial, the vulgar, the noncultured; it infers a banality obscene yet dull, evil yet mundane, yet a banality that comes so naturally and is as necessary to the Russian soul as love or hate. A set of *matryoshka* dolls on a parlor mantelpiece is *poshlyi*; so too a woman who weeps at the sight of cheap postcards illustrating cats entangled in yarn. But I am not strictly speaking of kitsch, or even lovers of kitsch as you may think, for that too severely circumscribes the concept, which applies as much to our lives as to our arts. That which is *poshlyi* makes life bearable without making it worth the trouble of being alive; *poshlaia* turns life into a habit. The most specific and typical example of *poshlyi* behavior I can think would be that of a married couple who continue to make love long after their desire for one another has faded away. After the Revolution, our farseeing leaders fervently attempted to rid the country of all that was *poshlyi*; in so doing, however, they only ensured that all that was Russian would forever after be *poshlaia*.

Sonya and I passed the Museum of History and the Lenin Museum—both presently closed for repairs (of the kind not easily accomplished with hammer and nails)—and, as we did, looked between them into Red Square toward St. Basil's nonet of domes and spires, a quarter kilometer distant from where we were walking. Directly ahead of us on the left were Kremlin walls, the color of dried blood. A crocodile of people queued to await entry into Lenin's mausoleum. Evgeny asked me, not long ago, if I thought I could strike a deal with the government to have Lenin relocated to Sovietland, but I refused to admit I'd even heard his ridiculous question. Better they should leave the Leader of Free Peoples where he is and, if upkeep proves too dear, install a roulette wheel in his chest and turn the mausoleum into yet another casino.

The scene here in the hub of the wheel looked at first glance as it always had, but recent changes were evident if you cared to see them. Everywhere I looked, I saw Westerners, notably Americans, flatfootedly stumbling along, studying the marvels of our alternate world, imagining they understood a tenth of what they saw, unaware of how, to criminal eyes, they willingly stood as exposed as chickens ready for the pot. Yet I couldn't help but suspect that these new tourists possessed a more sophisticated mindset than American guests of past years (miserable delegations from socialist organizations, trade union tour groups, flotillas of university students), all of whom happily allowed themselves to be dragged by the nose by Intourist girls, snapping up lies they were thrown as if they were bones.

The least of threats to tourists were two small boys lurking nearby, waiting to pounce upon likely victims. "Señorita," one cried out to Sonya, in the inexplicable belief that she was Cuban. She clutched her purse, but neither runty brigand moved to snatch it. "Money for rubles?"

"Beat it, you hoodlums," I said, shaking my fist. "*Fortochniks*. Begone!"

The most recent generation evinces no pretense of love for its elders. "Stick your head up your ass!" the older of the two brats shouted. "Prickface!" screamed his companion. I shoved my hand into my coat's inner pocket as if reaching for a gun. Without a second's hesitation the boys turned and vanished into the crowd.

(A *fortochnik*, you should know, is a small boy employed by a gang. The older gangsters shove the boy through unlocked *fortochkas* of ground-floor apartments. Once in, he unlocks the door and allows his companions to enter. *Fortochniks* carry icepicks and, if they find anyone at home, kill them by stabbing them in the temple.)

"You looked like an old granny," Sonya said, laughing and stabbing the air with her own fists. "You're as red in the face as a radish. Ignore the hooligans."

My anger faded at once. "I'm not that old."

"Not at all," she said, and we walked on. "Moscow isn't like it used to be. So much is shabbiness and ruin, and no one cares."

"You sound like an old granny yourself," I said. "Eventually there'll be no better place in the world."

"You believe that?"

"It won't happen overnight."

My koshka grinned without smiling. "But in the future, no doubt."

"Sooner." Without a doubt, my optimistic nature led me to hold such a cheering belief. You can't *always* expect the worst, I thought at the time; but what I didn't yet understand was that I should have.

That night Tanya and I lay in our bed in a semblance of peace. I am not ashamed to tell you that I always slept naked, as prolonged pressure of night clothes during sleep inevitably causes premature withering of the male organs. Tanya, on the other hand, was swaddled tightly within her flannel floor-length gown, resembling a gigantic baby. If at any moment her body bumped against mine, she drew away at once, as from poison ivy. As I lay there, staring at the ceiling, my thoughts—without conscious effort or intention—turned from tender moments shared with Sonya to the conversation I had had with her, then to memories of my son, and then to my father. I remembered his torrent of complaints directed toward me throughout my youth. There was no question that Evgeny was his mother's son, they were so alike in personality as to be twins; but as for me, it was clear to him that plainly some hereditary alteration (induced from without, in accordance with Lysenko's theories) ensued between sire and foal—that somehow he produced a wastrel, a wrecker, an insatiable fly forever rubbing his legs in piles of Western shit. He would work himself into such despair over God's cruel joke against him that he could recover a sense that the world was not utterly absurd only by lashing me into unconsciousness with his belt, at least until I attained a size greater than his own. I don't have to tell you, it did no good; I went about my business as before, secured good positions at university and in the Ministry after leaving college, and, against his expectations and my desires, became to some degree like him as I aged. But never once did I lay a belt, a foot, or even a hand on my own son. Possibly I should have.

"You heard about the dog." My wife was not asleep, after all. She said this with no forewarning, startling me so that I nearly leapt from our bed.

"Dog?"

"The little girl's dog, in Ekaterinburg. Do you ever pay attention to events you don't profit from?"

"I heard she died, but I'm too old to cry," I said. "What about the dog?"

"He came back to the little girl's building at the instant she died."

Already, in its retelling, history was undergoing its necessary revisions. "I heard something of the sort, but I know nothing else."

"Her mother believed the dog's return was a sign," she continued. "Her father did not and cursed the dog for coming back.

When he saw his mistress lying on her deathbed, he was so stricken with grief that he ran to the apartment balcony and leapt off."

"The father or the dog?"

"The dog, of course. Aren't you listening to me?"

"With rapt attention, my small wren. He was killed?"

In the dark, I discerned her head nodding affirmatively. "Ten floors, what do you think?"

"Will they be buried together?"

"That isn't the point," she said. "There were new developments today. The little girl's mother filed a criminal complaint this morning against her husband, the father, for murder."

"Murder?" I repeated. "He killed the girl?"

"Not the girl, the dog. The dog didn't commit suicide in its grief. The father was so infuriated he picked up the dog and threw it off the balcony."

The more she told me, the more I found myself overcome by the need for nature's nightly restorative. "The authorities agreed to charge him with murder?"

"Evidently the mother's uncle is Ekaterinburg's chief of police. It will be interesting to see what happens." Her story was finished, I supposed, and I closed my eyes, feeling as if I might be instantaneously asleep; but her next statement, unrelated to what we had been discussing, guaranteed that I would spend a wakeful night. "Alla said Dmitry's wife, Sonya, was in your office the day you met with them about the Bruneians," she told me. "What was she doing there?"

God help my pathetic soul, but she'd at last entrapped me. *What had I told Alla?* I couldn't remember; too much time had passed. There could be no escape, not now. At once I understood that my wife's suspicions had been assured. I stammered out a reply, unable to judge for myself how feebleminded it might have sounded. "She was dropping off documents belonging to Dmitry that we needed."

"I see," she said.

"Is there anything so strange in that?"

"Not at all."

I held my breath, hoping I would be able to defend myself once she made her next remark, a sly inference, a direct accusation. She said nothing else; was she so sure of my guilt, and of what she supposed would be my reaction to her interrogation, that she was merely awaiting my full confession? After five or ten minutes passed I edged closer to her and listened carefully to the monotonous sound of her gentle exhalations. Asleep? Out like a snuffed candle.

My workers finished Dmitry's project three weeks later; he called to tell me that the Georgians were happy. He suggested we get together soon and have a celebratory drink, or two, or ten. I agreed, thinking I could at last have a chance to pin him down about his involvement, if any, in the money laundering at Melodiya—neither my capable workers nor my adept investigative team had had any success in digging up enlightening information.

At seven that Sunday evening I went to the Metropole on Theater Square near the Bolshoi, doubtless the finest hotel in Moscow and, I have heard it said, the most beautiful in Europe. Erected at the turn of the century, the Metropole appears to be a splendid palace of nobility, built in Russian Art Nouveau style. The hotel is large, but superb proportions allow you to imagine that it was designed on an intimate scale. A terra-cotta stringcourse of sculpted figures runs along the south and west facades, beneath the top floor and cornice; mosaics in majolica tiles enliven the uppermost stone gables. Rows of chimneys lend the roof a medieval silhouette, and curlicued wrought-iron balconies enhance the building's glory as expensive jewelry enhances a woman's.

In Soviet days, only the most favored guests could stay at the Metropole. After the Revolution, Central Executive Committee meetings took place in the spectacular dining room, and ovations rising to thunderous applause echoed off the ceiling's painted glass canopy, that astonishing translucent tent, each time Lenin or Trotsky spoke. Bukharin and Sverdlov kept rooms in the hotel so they would have a luxurious abode in which to rest between necessary engagements. The famous Irish writer Shaw stayed there in the early thirties, and there Stalin came to see him, discussing at length over six-course meals of fresh vegetables the incomparable perfection of Soviet life. Shaw is of course also recognized as a master satirist, but in no way could this have been considered a meeting of equals. No sooner did he conclude his enlightening visit, stomach full and spirits lifted, than kulaks in Ukraine began to eat their small sons and daughters in order to survive the famine the Father of the Peoples benevolently bestowed upon them.

The Metropole was restored by Finns in the late eighties, thereafter becoming the first Moscow hotel whose prices matched those of Tokyo rather than Bucharest. Rooms presently go for five hundred dollars a night, and the guest list remains exclusive. Anyone, however, can skulk within if they have enough of what I believe is called *attitude* in America: that is to say, a certain bearing arising from greater self-assuredness than most of my country-folk possess. But along with American entrepreneurs with mouths full of promises, European representatives of nonexistent firms, and Asian criminals busy setting up intracontinental trading arrangements, domestic examples of capitalism's more shameful manifestations are also to be found constantly parading through the Metropole's classical lobby, ascending marble staircases, or sitting languidly in finely detailed public rooms.

Most dress expensively, if without taste: mid-level mafia, who are never told they will not be served unless they wear a tie; gamblers en route to casinos, pockets fat with unburned money; would-be peddlers of art, drugs, weapons, and nuclear material, all certified as to authenticity; and, circling vulturelike around them all, prostitutes of the highest level, predominantly brunette save for the few genuine blondes, every one wearing clothing that uncovers them so effectively that they might as well be naked. But in the Metropole, all who are allowed to enter may—for as long as their wallets stand it—pose as affiliates of the golden class.

Dmitry and I sat in the bar at a table with a bottle of vodka, far from the distracting crowd. We shared two toasts; after those, I sipped when he swallowed or abstained from rounds entirely, not caring if he thought me rude. "You must join us at the feast tomorrow," he said. "I told our hosts you will be there."

"Why did you do that? I have no desire to meet these Georgians. Petrenko was bad enough."

"Oh, Pasha." He waved a hand as if brushing away an annoying insect. It surprised me to hear Dmitry use the familiar form of his name; they'd apparently grown close. "You know, to get him off my back I had to tell him a week ago that the shipments were already going out."

"When are they going out?"

"By the end of this week, without question," he said. "You probably want to know when you'll receive the remainder of your fee."

"I expected that we would touch upon the subject."

"Wednesday. I promise you on my mother's grave."

"No later," I told him. "A bank transfer?"

"Certainly not," he said. "You'll be paid in cash."

"You've that much at hand?" He nodded. "What about the Georgians? Or Petrenko? Don't they expect to receive their cuts at once?"

"Everyone will enjoy similar satisfaction, let me put it that way." Picking up the bottle, he refilled his glass and tried to refill mine. "So Sonya and I will see you at the celebration?"

"If possible, I'll stop by."

"They're expecting you, Max."

"Why?" I asked. "What have you told them about me? How thickly are you spreading lies?"

"I've told them you're my personal friend and long-time business associate," he said. "A staunch supporter of Russo-Georgian friendship. Good business possibilities for you, Max, I assure you. The party starts at noon and runs at least a day and a night, you know what Caucasians are like." He downed another glass and as quickly poured himself a fresh serving. What was in him that he tried so hard to drown? "I have to tell you I'm glad this is nearly over. The tension has been unbearable. Constantly fearing something would go wrong."

"That they'd find out who you were, you mean," I said, and he couldn't deny it. "Tell me, Dmitry, who is receiving these souvenirs for you in New York?"

"American associates," he said. "Mostly poor immigrants. We should help our brothers there whenever we can. The place is no utopia, after all."

"Everywhere there are problems," I said. "How do these poor immigrants get the money to purchase souvenirs at wholesale?"

"Their invention is admirable," Dmitry said, avoiding my stare. "As I understood it, Max, the less you knew about our operation the happier you were."

"Our business is concluded, and my curiosity is aroused."

He didn't smile, but neither did he avoid my question. "The receivers will of course be assisted by countrymen more experienced in American ways."

"Mafia?" I asked, not that it was necessary to understand, only confirm. "This is something else you've neglected to tell Petrenko, I bet. My God, Dmitry—"

"It would be ideal to work with angels, sure, but how is that possible? America is a criminal nation; everyone there is a born gangster. It's historical tradition, their spiritual heritage."

"Which is what Russians and Americans have most in common, yes?" We laughed. "Dmitry, there's something specific I need to ask you about. While working on your assignment, a troubling aspect of the past came to my attention. I'd like to know what you knew about it."

"If I remember, I'll tell you."

Habit caused me to speak in near whispers, not that any spy could have heard me over the disco blaring through the bar. "When railroad money was laundered at Melodiya," I said, "it looks as if most went through the Happy Guys' accounts. Was money duly owed them embezzled during the course of those transactions?"

"That would have been possible, but I'd have no way of knowing," Dmitry said. "As I understood the arrangements, it was essential that whoever enabled transfers to proceed in any of the departments or ministries we used took their expected cut. How else could it have been done?"

"Was Esenin receiving a cut?"

"You don't know?" Dmitry asked, pausing a moment, as if taken entirely by surprise by my questions. "Since I didn't know you at the time, I had no way of knowing the degree of your participation when I first came to you with this assignment. I imagined you'd either tell me if you had been involved or not; it didn't ultimately matter."

"I wasn't."

"And you're so much the poorer for it, then," he said, and smiled. "Esenin would have overseen dispersal of the percentages at Melodiya, in any event. He probably wished to preserve your innocence."

For once he had been so straightforward that, alarmingly, I suspected him of telling the truth. In any event, he appeared to know no more than I did, and so I said nothing else. Dmitry stared into his vodka as if within its crystal he could divine his future; when he lifted his head he turned a sadder face toward me, as if he'd not much liked what he foresaw. "Life is more interesting than it used to be, Max, but there's much I miss about the old days. You know the way it was. The most of the most."

"The most of the most for the least," I said. "You're living like white people now, why should you complain?"

His eyes misted as he wallowed in nostalgia. "These youngsters, these foreigners will never know. How could you tell of the marvels of our lives?"

Anyone would find it marvelous, beyond comprehension, a veritable fairy tale—where should I start? By explaining that Russia has so few computers even today because for years cybernetics was deemed a reactionary pseudoscience? That food in state restaurants was so bad because by deliberately making it inedible there would be more left afterward to use in overfulfilling the State Waste Food Plan? What could I tell you regarding the private railroad car used by the Politburo gerontocracy to transport their personal cows and milkmaids when they traveled? How if the old bastards went fishing, scuba divers would lurk beneath the surface of the deep, attaching fat salmon to their hooks? What about Ministry of Science attempts to bring the dead back to life in the belief they would be better workers, once risen from the grave? What about Khrushchev, assured in his Lysenkoistic beliefs that corn could sprout from sand, as pears might grow on mice? Or Uncle Lyonya, presenting a platinum bust of himself, to himself, for supreme sacrifices in improving the lives of the people? Or Chernenko, the esteemed living corpse, always needing prompting to remember the name of the country he led? Or the Greatest Genius of All Times and Peoples, line-editing hack novelists in order to clarify their plots? No, I think the marvels of our Soviet society were too multiform, too rarefied for any to comprehend, even after a lifetime of study or experience. "What days they were," he murmured, nose-deep in shit, convinced it was honey.

"Dmitry, what is really being shipped to the New York mafia?"

"Brighton Beach mafia," he said, correcting me. "Max, this is not a productive line of conversation."

"Is it counterfeit currency?"

"Didn't I tell you it wasn't?" he said, sneering. "Petrenko and his louts think they'll make dollars worthless as rubles by flooding America with counterfeits. Don't they understand the Americans would just print even more money and thus make the bad worthless? Petrenko is no Milton Friedman."

"Then what?" I asked again, hoping he was drunk enough to say, but he wasn't.

"Please don't ask these questions, Max," he said. "There is something I need to talk to you about. I suffer a crisis of the soul. I think Sonya is having a love affair."

Thank heaven my reaction time was slowed by drink! This was possibly the last statement I expected to hear from him, although looking back from my present vantage point I'm astonished that I convinced myself that this should forever be the case. But my luck held, and I was rescued once more; those quadrants of my brain capable only of animal response took over as he intoned his words, and my face signaled no surrender. "Do you know with whom?" I asked.

"No, it's nothing but suspicion, but solid suspicion."

"Why do you think she's having an affair?"

"Scientific reasoning," he said. "The look that appears on her face sometimes, when her thoughts seem to turn to one she misses. During the day she disappears, and I have no idea where she goes. She says shopping, but she spends her entire life shopping, so who can tell? I think she has been dressing for someone other than me, choosing outfits which shamelessly exaggerate her physical features."

Memories of those ensembles reappeared as tantalizing ghosts in my mind. The room suddenly felt hotter, but I wasn't perspiring. Were his suspicions more informed than he let on? Was he testing me to see if I would break down with guilt? How long could he go on; how long could I keep from cracking? During the purges, those accused who refused to confess would be sometimes placed alone in a soundproof room; then, after a time, they would barely hear over hidden loudspeakers a two-sentence conversation—*His mouth is filling with saliva; yes, you can see it form at the corners of his mouth*—over and over again, never louder, for minutes, hours, an entire day. It always worked.

"You've been working too hard, I think," I told him. "Nerves or your stomach produce these feelings. Something physical is taking its toll."

"It's more than that," he told me, his facial muscles going slack.

"Why do you think so?"

"The situation is plain, Max, any fool can see," he said. "I'm much older than Sonya, and she has the beauty of a goddess. Even with my money, it's a miracle she ever went for me. Now I'm afraid it's ending between us. I've always been aware of this possibility, but I never thought it would happen."

"Have you confronted her with your suspicions?"

"No. As I say, I have no undeniable proof. The last thing I want to do is make myself a laughingstock in front of her." He swept his limp green-gray hair from the sides of his head; when he brought his hands away I was amazed to see pale locks still clinging to them. If Dmitry noticed anything unusual in this, he didn't let on. Bits of hair wafted like dandelion fluff to the floor as he shook his fists. "But the possibility makes me crazy with anger. If she's having an affair, I swear to you I'll catch her. And if I find her in the sexual act with her lover, I'll hack him to pieces. With my gun I'll blow off the top of his head as if it were a hat. I'll bash in his brains with an ax. I'll stomp his face into jelly with my boots. And Sonya will watch every minute, I'll make sure of it."

"These are possibly unhealthy fantasies, Dmitry."

"Afterward I'll say to her, Come home and let's have dinner."

"Her response would be instantaneous," I assured him.

"My passionate love for her allows these thoughts to torture my soul. If she is having an affair, and I'm sure she is, I can only hope she'll see the error of her ways before it's too late."

"Bear in mind, Dmitry, if you were to come upon Sonya and this so-called lover and react as you have told me, punishment afterward would be swift and harsh. This isn't France, you know."

"I know." He sighed. "Realistically, I'd have to kill them both, then myself."

"Who does it benefit, saving a dead face?" I asked, hoping I could perhaps pound sense into his thick head. "Be sensible. If you discover hard proof your wife is involved in illicit behavior, confront the parties involved in the most emotionless manner. In that way, secure your position. What if this theoretical lover is younger than you, larger, or crueler? Then who'll wind up jelly?"

"I know you're right, Max, but it's difficult." He poured another drink. Undoubtedly he would not express such Tatar desires when sober; vodka is always bloodier than blood.

"Tell her how much you care about her," I said. "That heartens women."

"She must swear eternal fidelity to me alone."

"I'm sure she'll react as she thinks proper. It's getting late, Dmitry—"

"When I wake up and see her in the morning," he told me, "her eyes, her hair, her ethereal form, I think to myself, How lucky can a man be? But now I can't get these suspicions out of my mind. I see her, and then at once I visualize her mouth encircling some fucker's prick. I have to practically bite my fist to keep from smashing it into her face."

His wry badinage began to pall. Had I not have needed to explain myself too fully afterward, I should have liked to do nothing more at that moment than smash my own unbitten fist into his tired, lying old face. "If she were guilty of nothing, what purpose would that serve?" I asked.

He poured another drink. It is hard to be identifiable as an alcoholic in Russia, but Dmitry exerted superhuman effort to be so recognized. "She'd understand why she should behave," he said.

"Vodka is doing its talking for you. Deal with her lover, if she has a lover," I told him. "The rest takes care of itself." My assuring words evidently had the calming effect I intended them to have. Perverse as it may sound to you, I had no difficulty saying them; in our country we have had long experience employing words whose meaning is subordinate to their value—sometimes we believed there could be no other kind. "I think you should call it an evening, Dmitry."

"I'll be fine"—swilling his drink, splashing some on his cheap suit.

"Very well," I said, not adding that I hoped he would be fine only until he paid me the money he owed me; otherwise I didn't care what happened to the bastard, not after the way he talked about his wife, my koshka. After leaving the bar I stopped long enough in the lobby to call Sonya, on my own phone.

"He's drunk and talking violently," I told her, after informing her of his suspicions. Dear girl, she was blithely unconcerned by my warning and was truly astonished (and pleased, no doubt) that I took his threats so seriously.

"Every time he gets drunk he starts talking that way, you've seen him in action," she said, laughing. "For years he's suspected me of everything, even when I've been completely innocent." It was hard to imagine her in such a state, but I tried. "I'm supposed to be scared? Don't worry, my strong man, he merely blows wind from north instead of south. Pay him no mind."

"You should be careful, just in case."

"I'm bigger than he is, remember," she said. "He hits me, I hit him back harder. He hits me again, I kill him. Then he'll learn his own lesson."

I allowed her to convince me; then we exchanged heated farewells. It was after eleven, and I phoned my evening driver to pick me up, for though the Metropole is not a twenty-minute walk from my apartment, Moscow's streets are not without hazard at night. Glancing into the bar once more before leaving, I was surprised to see Dmitry, not only still there but still conscious. I left him alone, hoping that eventually that night he would crawl all the way into the bottle and not go home.

Stepping into the crisp air to await my driver, I waited near the entranceway for safety's sake. The slovenly night doormen were engaged in striking deals with a cabdriver; a gang of four Azeris, or so they appeared in the dark, lurked menacingly at the curb beyond a streetlight, awaiting opportunities. A flock of young prostitutes of the sort once called currency whores (a thin dollar was thick enough to pry apart their legs), having been denied entry into the Metropole, swooped down upon a pair of men—Bruneians?—leaving the hotel, cawing loudly and pecking the arms of the unwary travelers. All the girls bore the faint resemblance to Barbie to which I've alluded; one, especially *au courant*, had shaved her natural eyebrows and drawn in their place thin arcs, seemingly with iodine. The men, wisely, held aroused passions in check and attempted to break away from the harpies before their clothes were torn from them; sadly, they raced directly into the welcoming arms of the southern cadre. No sooner did the thugs fall upon the pair than the girls launched their own assault. With the doormen and cabdriver I watched, entranced, as a fight broke out between hooligans and whores over who had priority. In the midst of the contretemps, militiamen drove up in a holding vehicle to rescue the hapless foreigners, tires squealing to a halt. The officials heaved the tourists into the armored back of their black crow and sped away. Sometime before dawn the men would be released, probably somewhere in the distant suburbs, their wallets lighter for having paid off the officials with sizable bribes to avoid being arrested for creating a public disturbance. If they were lucky, they wouldn't have been raped. Oh! our incomparable Russian life, in this new epoch of human progress.

It did not please me to see that Tanya was awake when I got home. As I drew near, to press my lips against her hair as she turned away from me, she stepped back. "Is there something wrong, my pigeon?" I asked. "You're up so late."

"There is something we need to talk about."

"A business problem?"

She shook her head. For a fortnight, she had been moodier than usual. Her emotional state shifted repeatedly, from seeming catatonia so profound she appeared incapable of thought, to a state of contained rage so intense, yet so wordless, that I worried she would have a stroke. As she would never tell me what troubled her, I could only imagine she was undergoing physical transformations women her age suffer. Lifting her hand, she bade me to follow her into the living room, which I did. She closed and locked the French doors behind us, drawing the lace curtains over the glass panes. I cannot tell you why my suspicions weren't aroused except that perhaps, after numberless rehearsals, when my time came to take the stage I froze. Possibly that corner of my soul most needing confession and repentance seized control of my brain, causing me to ignore natural suspicions. Maybe my allotted time simply ran out.

There were sheets and a pillow on the sofa. This troubled me. "Is someone staying over tonight, my sweet one?"

"I have something I think you'll want to hear," Tanya said, and directed me to sit down on the sofa. She took her Walkman off a nearby table and placed it in my hands. "You'll be as fascinated as I was, I'm sure."

"What is it?" I asked, fitting the headphones over my ears.

"Listen and then tell me."

When I switched on the machine I initially discerned rustling sounds, as of a ream of paper being thumbed, then heard the squeaking of chairs above the recorder's gentle hiss. Then a conversation started coming over the wires, passing through the tiny speakers directly into my head.

Koshka, I was saying, my voice wavering in pitch, *I want you. I'm exploding inside.*

Darling, explode, Sonya said, her voice muffled, as if she were speaking from beneath blankets or through pants. Succeeding moments were wordless although interpretable. My wife stood tapping her foot against the floor. The nihilist in my soul commanded me to rush from the room as quickly as possible, breaking down the doors in my haste, but realistically I knew I could never commit such a cowardly act. After a few more seconds I took off the headphones and placed them, and the recorder, on the table before me. This was the moment I'd long dreaded; there was only one thing I could do.

"Has someone convinced you that this is my voice on the tape?"

She responded to my question in a way I would never have predicted. With speed few boxers could match, she slapped my face so soundly that I almost fell off the sofa. "*Explode!*" she shouted. "Go on, then! Two can explode!"

"How did you obtain this so-called conversation?" I asked, rubbing my hand against my cheek, thankful she hadn't broken the skin with her rings.

"My associate Iosif," she said, staring at me; I would rather have confronted the eyes of any murderer. "Pay the people who sweep your office better, Max, if you expect to enjoy a secretive life."

"That little bastard bugged my *office?*" I asked, infuriated, but a second slap curbed my appetite for debate.

"I know you've had affairs before with cheap whores, don't deny it," she shouted. "But this! Meeting her in your office! Obviously your entire staff assists you in lying to me. My God, Max! You made me have dinner with her!"

"That wasn't my idea," I said. "Why are you making these rash accusations? Look, it isn't difficult, manufacturing conversations." It didn't seem likely that I could make a believable case, but I tried. "Who is this Iosif? For all you know he was put up to this by business enemies of mine."

"Iosif is dependable, Max, that's why I had him install the bug," she said. "This is a record from life, no question. Why do you deny it?"

"Have you had the tape subjected to scientific tests?"

"Loyal as a tomcat, timid as a hare!" she shouted. "Can't you admit your actions? I listened to the entire conversation, such as it is. Any fool can tell nothing has been edited. You think me *less* than a fool? It broke my heart to hear that tape, you monster. How long have you been with her? How long, Max?"

That was it; there was nothing I could do but surrender. "April."

"Almost a year. Time for a new one, don't you think?" she asked. "How can you do this? Treating me so shamelessly? All these years, and who knows how many women?"

"And with whom do I remain?"

"You bastard! You don't respect me!"

There is no greater or more painful accusation that one spouse can hurl at the other in our country. "Don't say such a thing. I have the highest respect for you."

"Then why do you follow these bitches like a dog? One woman isn't enough for you, no, you need a harem. You think I never realized? I didn't *care?*" She balled her fists as if preparing to strike me again. "Why do you think I insisted upon going into business for myself, rather than depend on your largess? I didn't want to be left to starve like a pensioner when you left me for some young whore."

"Sonya is no whore."

"Have you ever had her over here?" she asked. "Has she been in our bed?"

"Never." I spoke unfiltered truth. "There's much I'm guilty of, but that would be sheerest disrespect to you. Something I'd never do."

"Shut up!" she screamed. "She means more to you than the rest, I can tell; don't tell me she doesn't. Are you planning to leave me for her?"

"I've never wanted to leave you, my angel, I swear to you. Believe me when I say I'd never abandon you."

"How can I believe anything you tell me?" she asked, picking up the recorder and throwing it at the wall, shattering the housing and breaking a hole in the plaster. "Even when I present you with undeniable truth you try to lie your way out of it. Do you even know what truth is?" Tanya wasn't crying, which troubled me; nothing in her face implied that she felt anything but the most undiluted rage at that moment, and I could think of no way to calm her. "Did you have to bring your mistress to your office? Do your workers see you betray me every day? Do you fuck her on your desk?"

"Not every day." She tried to slap me again, but this time I caught her wrist. I held her tightly until she calmed down enough to scream before letting go.

"If I told you to stop seeing her you wouldn't, would you?"

"Tanya, please."

"Would you?"

"I want you both," I answered, in absolute honesty.

"You can't have us both!" she shouted. "You must decide." For an instant I thought she would cry, but she was too accomplished in controlling unseemly emotion; the shades fell over her eyes, and by will she allowed her features to take on the warmth of marble. "Whatever you decide, I will remain your business associate. It's up to you as to whether you want me as your wife."

"You're giving me an ultimatum?"

"Exactly," she said.

"You don't want me to move out?"

I wouldn't have called the expression on her face a smile, but it came close. "No, Max, you stay here and decide." My cheek felt remarkably sore when I touched it. "Don't worry, you're not bleeding." With that she turned and walked out of the room, shutting—and locking—the doors behind her.

I am no *starets*, no holy man, no doomsaying Cassandra; apocalyptic visions do not bombard my waking life, and premonitions of coming days never force me into making millenarian prophecies for which I can be held accountable. But later that night, when at last I fell asleep, leaving my troubles behind in the sunlit world, I dreamed. In my dream I possessed the power of ubiquity. I dreamed of Moscow and the radiant future it had been denied in waking life, and this is what I saw.

Many-storied buildings rose throughout the city, their designs a thousand years ahead of our time: oval towers bridged by skywalks, glass pyramids glowing like braziers, bundles of steel tubes held aright by guy wires, gold-domed cylinders of granite and green tile. Through the black iron latticework of the Tatlin Tower ascended a cyclopean glass ball into which was etched a map of the world, each country made of sparkling red rubies. Rising above all was the Palace of Soviets, three hundred stories in the style of the tower of Babel; at its apex was an aluminum statue of Lenin, one hundred meters high. Two red searchlights beamed constantly from his eyes, directing all into the path of his mesmeric stare. Squadrons of ten-engined airplanes with half-kilometer wingspans soared in formation through the night sky, their fuselages emblazoned with Socialist Realist figures illuminated by tail-mounted searchlights, their loudspeakers endlessly blaring agitprop into the atmosphere. Autogiros buzzed like bees over the city; carmine zeppelins cruised in elegant progression high above black clouds curling up from ten thousand smokestacks. Boulevards twenty lanes wide ran from the Kremlin in every direction. The river, enlarged by voluntary prison labor into a deep ocean harbor, provided Moscow with a seacoast almost Bohemian in its grandeur. Ships docked to load up our national products, goods transported from Stalingrad, Stalinsk, Stalino, Stalinbad, Stalinir, Stalinkan, and Stalinovo, goods to be sent forth to a waiting world: caviar and sables, vodka and *papirosi*, heroin and hashish, plutonium and red mercury, balalaikas, *matryoshkas*, lapel pins, rayon banners, platinum busts of our leaders, and coypu. Posters of milkmaids, gymnasts, weight lifters, folk dancers, tractor drivers, miners, soldiers, and all for whom labor is a matter of honor papered every building's facade. Red neon signs mounted to the Kremlin walls proclaimed:

CANNIBALIZATION IS FORBIDDEN
LET'S CATCH UP WITH AND SURPASS AFRICA
WE'LL OPEN A WOMEN'S SHOP
THROUGH WHIPPING TO SOCIALISM
WHO IS KILLING WHOM?

As I watched, Moscow's surviving citizens emerged from their buildings. In silent procession they marched into Red Square. From every streetlight hung friends of relatives of enemies of the people. Trams ran on bone lines. In bookstores, works sold were bound in the skin of the authors. Skulls sprouted from the earth like mushrooms in the city's great parks. Impaled upon the spires of Stalin's seven skyscrapers were the swollen heads of old Bolsheviks: Trotsky, Zinoviev, Kamenev, Radek, Bukharin, Rykov, and Krupskaya.

The assembled populace applauded wildly as they watched the moon, gleaming like chains, white as a silver fist, rise high over Sovietland. No one in the crowd wanted to be the first to stop clapping. The ever-intensifying ovation continued; palms stung, fingers swelled, blisters burst. People clapped the skin from their flesh. Tendon sprang loose of muscle, muscle slipped from bone, and still the applause grew louder. Bloody spray resettled as opaque fog, enshrouding the crowd. As the people vanished within the red cloud, they continued to cheer the moon for having delivered the darkness they craved. In the moon's face was the silent, mustachioed face of the Father of Night: the man after our own hearts, the man who missed nothing, the man who forever found you out, the man who knew you better than you would ever know yourself.

Why did no one realize that if we built hell on earth there would be nothing to look forward to?

6

"Will we stay long, Mr. Borodin?" Ludmilla asked as we walked to the celebration the following afternoon. As Sonya would be attending with her husband, and Tanya (I was sure) wished not to be seen with me at present, I asked my loyal assistant if she would accompany me. With perceptible reluctance, she agreed. "There is much work to do at the office."

"We are not presently in the office," I reminded her, holding her arm so that she would not slip and fall on ash-covered ice. "Call me Max, please."

"Impossible," she said. "Our professional relationship would be damaged. But let me say to you, in my opinion, you should not be attending this party. It doesn't matter who they are, Georgians are dangerous."

"You don't even think they're human."

She nodded. "Show me reliable evidence that would convince me. And I don't have to tell you, I don't think much of Mr. Gubin."

"Certainly you think less of his wife," I said, and she nodded again. "We'll eat a little, have a drink, then leave."

"Georgian spices set me afire inside. I'll take a glass of wine to help thin winter blood." She fell silent, and I hoped she'd run out of advice—no such luck. "I don't see why you should further involve yourself in his nefarious schemes."

"I'm not involving myself. Dmitry has placed himself in the midst of delirious complexities. I'm curious—"

"Curiosity kills."

We walked on. Dmitry's Georgians lived in one of the few neighborhoods of Moscow that the most snobbish European (even a Belgian) would without hesitation call attractive, an area of twisting streets absent of socialist spoor lined with ochre houses near the western Boulevard, below Tverskaya, above Herzen. Our boots slid beneath us as we trudged past eighteenth-century villas, nineteenth-century mansions, and churches three hundred years old. After the Revolution, Communists expropriated the magnificent homes in this neighborhood for their personal use, and while some continued to live in the residences their grandfathers had stolen, many of these splendid old structures had been recently sold (at heart-stopping prices), to other countries to serve as consulates or to the flashiest representatives of the new *nomenklatura*: stock traders, Menatep executives, security specialists and, certainly, mafia bigwigs. Foreign workers—foreign, because working—scurried across the roofs of nearby castles like squirrels, installing slate shingles and repairing glazed-tile chimneys.

"What are we coming to?" my assistant asked. "Georgians living in such exclusive surroundings. My God."

"If they have the money to live here, why shouldn't they?"

She struck me in the chest with her white-gloved hand. "They should be hung from streetlamps."

I wondered how much I should tell Ludmilla about the problems Tanya and I were having; my assistant was blessed with perception so acute as to be supernatural, and it was impossible to forever hide the situation from her. When I struggled into the office that morning (feeling as if my back had been broken during the night; our sofa did not substitute for a billowy feather mattress), Ludmilla at once inquired if my wife and I were having difficulties. "Aren't we all?" was my reply, but that didn't satisfy her; I knew she would bring up the subject again, intent on driving me to admit my crimes.

Before leaving that morning, I had asked Tanya if she was feeling more affectionate, but her only response was to glare unforgivingly at me until I turned my face to my cereal. I weighed the impossible choice before me. Could I abandon my wife? Of course not. It may seem fantastic to you, but hear me, my love for Tanya was too strong; something that always comforted us was the certainty that we would be there for each other when death came tapping at our door. But it was unthinkable to me that I could live without my koshka. I felt as if I'd been told to decide which leg I wanted to keep.

"I should be truthful," I told Ludmilla as we entered a narrow lane lined with skeletal trees. "Tanya and I are having marital troubles."

"It doesn't surprise me," she muttered. "Mrs. Gubina is the cause, I am guessing?"

"To a moderate degree."

"Not that you want to hear my advice, but I tell you to leave her alone and enjoy the life you have. With absolute respect: to my mind, the more years a man accumulates the more stupid he becomes. We women become smarter; you can no longer fool us. We take our revenge wiser if not happier."

"Thank you for your respectful advice."

"Follow it!" She gestured with such exuberance as she spoke that I had to grip her arm all the more firmly, to prevent her from pulling us both to the ground. "Every old man turns into a Myshkin, abandoning the world to abase himself before God. And what is the God of most? Foolish young girls. These men have—what do you call it?—Oedipus complexes. Don't deny it. Idiots, every one of you. Believing you'll absorb precious life energies through proximity. The only thing being absorbed is your money."

I should tell you, I preferred Ludmilla's enchanting interpretation of Freud to her sage wisdom regarding the foibles of elderly men. Thankfully, we had reached our destination. "These matters can wait for later discussion. We're here."

She suddenly realized where we were. "My God! These beasts have taken over Petrovsky's house?"

"Evidently. Look, let me do the talking while we're here. Our hosts may not take your observations in the spirit in which you offer them."

My reliable assistant gave no indication that she heard anything I said. On our right, a high wall ran the length of the block, its flaking plaster painted in a palimpsest of anti-Asian obscenities. Giant bedsprings of razor wire topped the uppermost heights of the wall, securing the grounds from assault. Two guards clad in leather black as their hair stood by the gateway, drawing on cigarettes as they watched us approach. The smaller of the two positioned his meter-wide body in front of us as we came up, drawing his pistol from its holster.

"Who asks you here?" he snarled, in a Kazakh accent. I hastily presented the engraved invitation that was delivered to me that morning, pulling it from my coat pocket with broad gestures, so he would not fear I reached for a weapon. He studied the words as if surprised to see that communication by writing was possible. An unpleasant scar, reddened by cold, ran between his eyes. Thick mustaches protected his lips from severe climate. Half of his left ear had been lopped away by someone wishing a souvenir by which to remember him, and his knuckles had been fractured and re-knitted so often that the backs of his hands were nothing less than slabs of bone. "Pardon formalities," he said, stepping aside. "Welcome to you." His equally fearsome partner unlocked the steel gates and pointed toward the house, a short distance along a muddy driveway.

"How do you know we'll be safe?" Ludmilla asked.

"Don't worry." Parked along the drive were some thirty American motorcycles, the vehicles themselves barely visible beneath decorative overlays: shiny tin badges, party insignia retrieved from trash heaps, filthy stuffed animals, Goodwill Games banners, enamel buttons, gilded casts of women's breasts, animal horns, icons of contemporary vintage, and framed portraits of rock stars. A platoon of Kazakhs, the cyclists themselves, never took their eyes off us as we walked past. Most had Kalashnikovs slung across their broad chests; some carried swords in scabbards tied to their belts. Each Kazakh guard wore with his black leather outerwear a white shirt and black leather necktie.

"Look at the brutes," Ludmilla said. "Thirsty for blood."

"Don't annoy them."

"It disgusts me to think that this trash lives in the Petrovsky house."

"Have you ever been inside?" She shook her head. "Neither have I. Let us feel lucky to be allowed entry to such a historic structure."

The house was built in 1895 for the famed tradesman Petrovsky, a leading exporter who sold fine Russian furs to buyers in America, Britain, and France. Architects of the period vied to outdo one another, building structures ever more dreamlike or, in the case of Petrovsky's house, hallucinatory. A three-story yellow box was barely distinguishable beneath ornamentation of mad extravagance—I deliberately choose that adjective; the detailing was of a complexity seen most often in the artwork of the insane. The crenellate cornice appeared to be melting; columns supporting a central stepped pyramid (topped with a copper globe) were wasp-waisted, with multiple waists; small knobs of rock spotted the marble facade as if the edifice suffered from stonepox. No two gold-framed windows were the same size or shape. Petrovsky's house was overlaid with terra-cotta friezes, stucco entablatures, ceramic mosaics; brass gratings, stone terraces, stained glass; turrets and steeples, porches and balconies, ogees, oculi, and oriels. There was no other house like it in Moscow and, as far as I knew, in the world.

"You know the story of Petrovsky and his mistress," Ludmilla said. "A telling lesson."

"One I don't need to hear." In 1905, as Petrovsky prepared to enter as a member of the new Duma, his mistress murdered him. Here I would have to agree with Ludmilla and tell you he deserved it, for he committed a gratuitously stupid act: seducing her young daughter, evidently for no other reason than because she was at hand. When his mistress discovered what he had done, she lost her reason. With a woodman's ax, she chopped him into bloody meat; then, having avenged her daughter, she poisoned herself with arsenic.

"Old men, young girls," she said. "Always the same situation."

"I am not yet a Big Mac."

She gave me a piteous stare and shook her head as if to marvel that one she so admired could be so ignorant. "Not yet."

We ascended slick granite steps; the oaken front doors swung open. "Hello, guests," said the Georgians' greeter, another

Kazakh, one who at first sight looked twice the size of the gatekeeper. A more lingering examination revealed that a substantial percentage of his mass resulted from his wearing a black leather jacket beneath a knee-length black leather trench coat. The Kazakh was placid as a cow; when he smiled, he revealed ivories powerful enough to rend the limbs from living animals. "My name is Mels."

"Mels?"

"My father's name, which he bequeathed to me. Stands for Marx-Engels-Lenin-Stalin: Mels. I think he believed it would do me good to have such a name." He laughed loudly as he bowed; his rifle swung out from beneath his coats in a vaguely obscene manner. "In the name of our hosts, I would like to welcome you to our happy home. Please, allow this lady to take your wraps."

A beautiful young Georgian woman, whose high, firm breasts broke every gravitational law, came forward to retrieve our outerwear. She said nothing, but I would not call hers nonobtrusive service. Ludmilla was far less impressed by her performance, I think. "Are you in charge of these guards?" I asked.

"They obey our great leader, as do I, but I oversee them," Mels said, slapping himself on the chest as if it, and not his leather clothing, was bulletproof. "We are a band of lighthearted brothers. We stay safe together in this dangerous city, afloat in hot blood."

Did he mean the brothers or the city floated so uncomfortably? I decided I shouldn't care. "What did you and your friends used to do?"

"We were state-supported wrestlers on the Alma-Ata team. Now no support, no state, no wrestlers. No Alma-Ata! So we became experienced security consultants. If you would, please now accompany me to the feast."

Leaving the foyer we entered a grander room floored in green marble. The smooth white plaster of three walls rose upward to form a vaulted ceiling, unbroken save for a single row of stained-glass lunettes. High above our heads bas-relief snails, butterflies, and birds crept and fluttered across the snowy arches, in seeming accordance with obscure zoological symbology. In the fourth wall, farthest from us, was a jasper fireplace large enough to broil a wisent. The gilded pier mirror above the mantel was burnished by years of wood smoke; leering jade trolls served as the mantelpiece's caryatids. To the right of the hearth was a cascading staircase, a sea wave stone-frozen. Its every structural element—newel post, winders, balustrade—had been sculpted from a single block of pink marble. Lamps rose at spaced intervals from the curved railing, their bronze stems exploding into glass blossoms of yellow and mauve.

But the room's fountain was what held our attention in a death grip. "You like?" Mels asked us, extending a leathery arm. "Our great leader's prize, made especially for him."

The fountain—solid gold, or at least gold-plated—was three meters tall but retained a certain delicacy in the context of its surroundings. In the center of the floor stood a pedestal thick as an oak, braided in the style of a peasant woman's tresses. Balanced atop the pedestal was a gilt cockleshell a meter and a half across, filled to its scalloped brim with bubbling water dyed a deep blue. From the midst of the roiling waves lifted a pyramid of unlikely beasts and legendary figures, all tangled together. Crabs gamboled with satyrs, storks pecked vermin from the flanks of centaurs, apes stood astride manticores, grimacing Neptunes armed with tridents speared giraffes, and laughing naiads spread their legs to welcome the finny lusts of dolphins. Standing atop the grotesque heap was a naked woman, sparkling gold, wearing an antlered helmet and lofting an assegai. Her body's features were as detailed as a medical illustration. Kneeling at her feet were winged elves of indeterminate sex, burying their faces in her groin and buttocks, hungrily paying homage with estimable fervor. From the warrior woman's nipples two threads of blue water arced into the pool below.

"My God," Ludmilla exclaimed, staring in horror at this unique manifestation of nouveau riche taste. "I have never seen anything so unsavory."

From unseen speakers housed in the base of the braid issued a thumping beat whose perpetrators would have gone unknown had Mels not named names. "Techno," he said, tapping the heel of his heavy boot against the floor in time with the pounding. "Come now, you must be announced. May I have your full names, please?"

We told him, and he led us toward mahogany double doors to the right of the staircase. Sliding open the doors, he stepped inside. "Maxim Alexeich Borodin and Ludmilla Matrosovna Savicheva!" he proclaimed, in a stentorian voice. The dining hall was, like the antechamber, two stories high and of equally lavish decor. The fireplace was malachite, its hearth blue Delft tile. Crystal chandeliers, glittering glass whisks of light, hung from the beamed ceiling. Heavy brown draperies hid those within from the world without. The walls were upholstered in red leather, which contrasted agreeably with the black leather of the Kazakh guards standing at attention around the room. At a banquet table covered with platters, salvers, and tureens sat some thirty people, not all of whom were Georgian. A few I recognized as high government officials; also in attendance were five army officers in full dress uniform, their medals shielded by crisp linen napkins, and one Orthodox prelate. At the head of the table sat a young man so pig-plump he looked ready to burst, not only out of his expensive suit but also his skin—our host, I guessed. Near him were Dmitry, his three partners, several empty seats, and Sonya. Hanging on the wall nearest our host, behind his head, was a life-sized oil portrait of the most notorious Georgian, the Leading Light of Communism.

The plump man rose to greet us. "Allow me to welcome you to our home," he said, clasping my hands in his. I can no longer estimate the age of the young at a glance, but I should not have imagined him to be older than thirty. "I am Lavrenty Zhordanich Mzhavanadze. Dima speaks well of you." It surprised me that the man employed the diminutive of Dmitry's name. Mzhavanadze turned to Ludmilla, took her hand, and kissed it. She was not flattered by his attentions. "These seats are reserved for you."

We sat directly across from those we knew, Ludmilla standing erect as a Czarina until our host drew out her chair. Dmitry's three worthless partners grinned as if they were already drunk, greeting me so effusively they must have thought I liked them. I looked across the table at Sonya; my koshka, of necessity, vanished behind a wifely mask. She smiled at me with no wilder passion than she might feel pinching a loaf of bread to make sure it was fresh. Her gray dress fit so closely as to suggest she had cashmere skin; I would have willingly blinded myself, staring into her sunburst of hair. As I gazed upon my sweet one, I knew again that I would not live without her. I cursed the fact that while we were in the presence of Ludmilla and, especially, Dmitry, I could not tell her of Tanya's directive.

"Where's your wife, Maxim?" he asked.

"Her own business needs constant attention. If these matters concerned her, she'd be here, believe me."

He gave me an oddly disconcerting smile and lifted forkfuls of lamb from a pot of delectable stew. "I'm glad you were able to join us. How are you, madam?" he asked Ludmilla; she snorted, sounding like a pony left out in cold weather.

"Good to see you, Max," Sonya said, biting off a hot pepper short of its stem; seeing her allowed me the greatest happiness I'd had that day. Strangers sitting to our right passed platters of food. A Kazakh inadvertently soaked the tip of his necktie in my glass of champagne, as he leaned over the table to supply Dmitry with a refill, but offered no apology. "As always."

Our fat host hoisted his glass. "A toast!" he shouted. The crowd hushed and swiveled as one to face him, as if they were steered by a single lever. "To lasting Russo-Georgian partnerships."

"*Na zdroyve!*" everyone said, tossing back their drinks. Kazakhs hastily replenished the empty vessels. "Filipp Ilyich Spirkin, of Kiev!" Mels announced. Mzhavanadze excused himself from our conversation, rushed over, and threw his arms around his newest guest. (I realize that most of my Western readers will never be able to sound out Mzhavanadze, however long they try; even we Russians have difficulty with Georgian names. So I refer to him, hereafter, as Nadze.)

"I hate Georgian champagne," Sonya said; but my angel would drink Dom Pérignon like water, given the opportunity.

"Try the grape vodka, a special treat of their country," Dmitry said. "Much better. Very dry."

"And strong as the kick of a horse," Ludmilla said. "Have a taste, perhaps, but no more unless you want to be like these drunken men. The wine is quite good."

Sonya looked at me and smiled; I bit my tongue and turned away. Nadze continued to stand with Mels at the entrance of the room, greeting other new arrivals, not all of whom lingered to enjoy fabled southern hospitality. Several overlords of Moscow's militia stopped by long enough to give Nadze small gift-wrapped envelopes; following a series of warm embraces, as if between brothers, they slipped away. Moments later, one of Yeltsin's most trusted advisers appeared, presented our host with a sealed billet-doux, and vanished. He was followed by an executive in the Moscow branch of British Petroleum whom I had met several times at social functions. He saw me, I saw him; neither of us acknowledged the presence of the other. In every case, with every visitor, there was first a presentation to his Georgian highness and thereafter a show of supplication that stopped short of kissing either Nadze's diamond ring or his ass.

"Georgians are famed for their hospitality," Dmitry said, easing spice-rubbed cubes of shashlik from a sword. "Treat them right, they treat you right."

"Always?" Ludmilla asked, staring at the portrait of Stalin.

"Well, often."

"Eat something, Ludmilla," said Sonya, spooning up black caviar and pickled mushrooms. "Everything is wonderful."

"These acorns in syrup will be enough for me," Ludmilla said, spearing one on her fork and placing it in her mouth. "Piquant." Having made her pronouncement, she laid down her utensil and sipped her wine, having received the refill for which she'd signaled. Most of the guests seemed to be much more famished than my assistant; some of them behaved as if they had not had a meal since childhood. I watched, fascinated, as one peasant ate an entire hen, cracking open each bone so as not to lose a gram of marrow. Seeing Dmitry conferring in whispers with his three partners, I leaned across the table to chat politely with Sonya.

"Tanya told me last night of an interesting discovery she made."

She understood. "Interesting but unpleasant?"

I nodded, watching Dmitry from the corner of my eye. "She's offered me an impossible choice."

"One you'll have no trouble making, I'm sure." She inserted another pepper slowly into her mouth. The pony sitting next to me gave another, louder snort.

I felt a tap on my shoulder, as if from a militiaman. "Maxim Alexeich," Nadze said as he returned to the table. "Move closer to me. I've looked forward to meeting you. Sit here; let us discuss business propositions."

Ludmilla shook her head as I shifted to a seat next to our host. Dmitry watched me; whatever his truest emotions were, he kept them so bottled he gave no more indication of possessing a soul than would a store mannequin. His partner Vlad stood up and spoke to one of the Kazakhs.

"Bathroom?" he asked, and followed the guard out of the room.

"Lavrenty Zhordanich, I am more honored than I can say to be in your splendid presence," I swore, speaking in the most formal manner. Nothing pleases gangsters such as Nadze more than shameless toadying, and so I abased myself to a degree he would find acceptable. This is not an easy thing, reader; to believably offer such unfelt fealty takes years of practice. Early in our marriage, after we attended an event at the Palace of Congresses, Tanya told me that if she knew me only from having watched me that evening, she would have thought I'd been taught in childhood that there was no better place for my head than beneath a superior's foot (and, yes, my father tried to beat such lessons into me). "But this does not seem the time and place for a common entrepreneur such as myself to discuss trifling business matters with so important and powerful a figure."

"Maxim Alexeich, few common entrepreneurs own seven banks. Get off your knees. Let us speak looking in each other's eyes."

"One bank with seven branches," I said, correcting him. "I still wish to affirm that it graces me to be with one who commands such evident respect."

"Would that one among us be capable of commanding the respect he commanded," Nadze said, gazing with unaffected emotion at the portrait. "A toast!" he cried out, and again we heeded his words. "All Georgians and friends of Georgians, forever feel in your hearts the living presence of our greatest leader. To Iosif Dzhugashvili, to Koba, to Stalin!"

To the exterminator! We all raised our glasses and drank to the memory of he who erased sixty million. I should like to believe that the act of stating the words *To Stalin* was what caused my tongue and throat to start burning; but I must be honest and admit to you it was nothing more than raw grape vodka that cauterized my esophagus.

"Surely you aren't Communists?" Ludmilla asked Nadze. I tried to shush her before she said anything more offensive, but a different voice served to distract our host.

"Fuck, no!" shouted a younger Georgian, seated farther down the table. From his expression, I knew he realized his error even as he made it. Nadze glared at the man as if he cursed the

day of his birth but appeared otherwise unperturbed; then he lifted
his hand, placing a fingertip to his lips.

"Language," he said, in a near whisper. Two Kazakhs
seized the man's arms, drew him from his chair, and bore him out
of the room. After the door swung shut behind them, Nadze turned
toward Ludmilla, lowering his head as if in obeisance. "Madam,
may I ask your forgiveness for the uncultured behavior you have
witnessed today?"

"Slum language in the public sphere no longer shocks me,"
she said, holding up her glass of wine for another refill, her fourth;
a Kazakh gladly obliged. "You didn't answer my question."

Nadze smiled and cocked his head to the right, as if his
neck were sore. "We gave you such an impression? That we were
Communists?"

"Wasn't Stalin?"

I found it unbelievable that she was bringing up such a
delicate subject at a table of (undoubtedly armed) Georgians.
Sonya, too, looked to be no less shocked, but her husband and
his partners retained stony faces, gazing on steadily as if watching
the ballet.

"Happenstance," Nadze said. "We salute him as a great
Georgian, a great leader, as one who left us with a mighty heri-
tage. The common people loved no one more. Look anywhere in
Russia today: what you still see, what you'll always see, is Stalin.
The beautiful buildings, the Metro, the nation's industries."

"All ruins."

Nadze shrugged. "Can a dead man do more than inspire?
But if Stalin were here today, mind you, Russia would again be
the strongest country on earth."

"Why wouldn't he want Georgia to be the strongest country on earth?" she asked.

"Tigers don't live on mice."

I was distracted by an overheard fragment of conversation.
An army officer walking behind me was speaking to one of the
Georgians: "—claiming they'll ship five hundred into New York by
way of Hamburg." My suspicions rose, but I heard no more, for
then Ludmilla asked an unbelievable question.

"You don't believe that if he were our leader today, all of
you would not be in prison?"

At that, even Dmitry and his partners took horrified notice. I am not a man of violence, but I considered stomping sharply on her foot, in hopes that pain would silence her. But Nadze took what she asked him very well; knowing Georgians, I'm sure the fact that it was merely a woman who had made such a provocative remark enabled him to slough off excess anger.

"*Nichevo*," he said, after a moment. "Nearly everyone in our country has been in prison at one time or another."

"Some think he would be doing a smart thing, putting us in prison," a Georgian said. Everyone at the table laughed uproariously.

"Or stupid thing," said Nadze, who—although he continued to laugh—thought it wise to introduce a fresh subject of conversation. "Bring out our women and children," he proclaimed. "It is time for them to join us."

Mels disappeared through the doors that led into the antechamber; then, moments later, in a torrent of screams and laughter twenty-odd Georgian children flooded through the room, their weary mothers adrift in their wake. The fathers greeted the little ones with passionate embraces, leaving their mates to take seats at a separate table thoughtfully provided for the families. Nadze's two dark-haired boys, no older than six, ran across the room and leapt shouting into his lap. He locked an arm around each of their necks as if to lovingly choke them into unconsciousness.

"Where has Vlad gone?" Dmitry leaned over to ask Tibor. "What is taking him so long?"

"I'll see," his partner said, standing and speaking to one of the Kazakhs; then they too left the room.

"Maxim Alexeich," Nadze said, affectionately patting the heads of his baby birds as they chirped madly, begging for attention, "my sources inform me that you enjoy much business success."

"Small-scale success, to be entirely truthful." When gangsters sidle over to you, making idle conversation regarding your personal finances, it is a safe bet they are not asking in order to compare your standard of living with theirs. I would have been surprised had he not inquired of my situation at some point during my visit—to that degree, gangsters are not so different from businessmen such as myself when it comes to seeking out new

investment opportunities. Still, I didn't plan on telling Nadze anything beyond what he could discover on his own. Instead, I thought
it wise to emphasize how continually I skirted the rim of bank-
ruptcy's abyss (in fact, this had not yet happened, but we all know
how happily truth exists, relieved of the burden of supporting fact).
"We've not experienced serious trouble so far."

"With whose outfit have you contracted for your essential
protection?" he asked, ruffling the hair of his boys with stubby
hands.

"Papadin's," I told him, and he frowned. Aram Papadin
headed the Russo-Armenian mafia with whom many businesses,
including mine, throughout the Kitai-Gorod neighborhood dealt.
Arteim and Telman had known him for years, enabling us to strike
a particularly favorable deal when we chartered the Comrades'
Bank. I got on fine with Papadin; I never saw him. Ivan Ivan (who
you recall was so fond of Barbies) was the representative of
Papadin's assigned to us, and since our initial meeting he'd given
us no trouble. Papadin's was not a gang with whom Nadze's minions would willingly tangle—Nadze knew that, and so did I.

"You've agreed to a fair rate of payment?"

"As good as one could desire."

Holding his hands perpendicular to his face he formed a
steeple with his fingers and peeped down at his boys through the
belfry. "How is the market for documents?"

By imagining that I possessed a countenance of rock, I
managed to hide the degree to which this question disturbed me.
If Nadze was familiar with the Universal Manufacturing Company,
could he not be equally cognizant of the work we had done for
Dmitry? For a moment I considered pretending that I took his
question as a general observation, rather than a specific inquiry,
but I had an intuition that such an approach would only confirm
suspicions already held.

"The international market is doing well. But here in
Moscow—" I shrugged, hoping to imply that the need for documents in the domestic market was not as robust as the need, say,
for droshkies (that is, horse-drawn sleighs). "Even if demand
increased, there is only so much material that can be readily
accessed."

"Unless supply is adjusted to meet demand." Nadze lowered his children to the floor. They dashed to their mother, a frail

Georgian woman who picked them up. She must have been younger than her husband, but already her chin sagged into her neck, which sagged into her breasts, which sagged against her stomach. She looked as if she were melting from the ears down.

"Easier said than done," I noted.

"Excuse me one moment," he said, standing. I hadn't heard Mels announce the newest arrival; Nadze evidently recognized him before he could enter. When I looked across the room, I was not greatly shocked to see the little dentophilist whom Dmitry had insulted in the Armenian restaurant. He and Nadze embraced and spoke briefly—I gathered he was not staying.

Ludmilla called for a refill. Sonya stared straight ahead with dead eyes, as if her soul absented itself while her body remained where it had been directed to sit. Dmitry leaned over Tibor's empty chair to speak to me. "You and Lavrenty appear to be getting along well," he said.

"Did you realize he is apparently aware of what the Universal Manufacturing Company does?" I asked, not loudly. From the dazzling play of emotions on his stricken face, I gathered he didn't. "No?"

"What did he ask you?"

"Nothing specific. He's been distracted. I'm not bringing the subject up again, believe me."

Dmitry picked at the food on his plate with a fork. Nadze took leave of the diminutive gangster and started back to his seat, but before he got very far a Georgian associate stopped him. They conferred for a few moments; he handed Nadze an envelope as he left, one not wrapped in shiny paper. Nadze read the missive within, slid it into his jacket, and returned to the table. "Maxim Alexeich, perhaps you could tell me something about your wife's business."

"Her consulting firm?"

He shook his head. "Consultants are common as thieves these days. No, I refer to an investment her firm has recently made."

Was he speaking of Sovietland? That project was under no one's protection, not yet. Naturally, the contractors Evgeny hired had their own connections, but no one had attempted to move in on either us or the Bruneians. I think most mafias erroneously believed our theme park to be such an inconceivable concept as to not be worthy of their attention (which, considering known mafia investments in action films, Vietnamese brothels, dog breeding stables, and psychokinesis research facilities, should give you an idea of how ludicrous they thought our project to be). The thought that Nadze might have questions regarding the business or holdings of my blood relations had not occurred to me. How could I have been so stupid and ill-prepared as to not be ready for this inquiry? Obviously, troubling events of the night before had left me too addled to foresee the likelihood.

"My wife and I keep many aspects of our lives separate," I said, circumventing truth when possible and speaking with as much aplomb as I could muster; surely I would manage to keep enigmatic anything I happened to know. "We find this a sensible arrangement in most circumstances, and particularly when matters of money are involved."

"Maxim Alexeich, husbands and wives should be of one flesh, not live in tense coexistence," Nadze said, expressing almost maternal concern.

"Call it détente," I said. "I'm afraid I can tell you nothing about her investments. She and her partners use their profits as they deem appropriate."

"In all honesty, I have the knowledge I need regarding the details of their investment," he said. "But I would like to discuss with them their long-term plans for the columbarium."

For the first time in many years I could not judge how well I hid my reaction. "Which columbarium?" I asked, perhaps too carelessly.

"The Glow of Life, in Reutov," he said, and laughed; in our country there are many cheerful young men, and Nadze seemed to be the happiest of them all. "Please excuse me, but this is an embarrassing position for me. I hadn't expected to be giving *you* information pertaining to your wife's financial holdings."

"I'm equally surprised."

"Her firm is the largest single shareholder in the columbarium, with a forty-nine percent interest. They made the purchase last month. The employees own the majority of shares, and their cooperative administers the operation." He leaned forward, gripping my arm as if he were an old and trusted friend come to arrest me. "Not well, I should add. The cooperative is experiencing certain difficulties. Some of their decisions were not thought out very well, and they—" Halfway through his sentence, he decided to avoid relating superfluous details. "Now I don't have to tell you, this is a growth industry. In the right hands, an investment in the business could make a tenfold profit, maybe more."

"What do you intend to do?" I asked, knowing his plan, whatever it was, had been already set into motion. Just then there was nothing I could say; I was too dumbfounded by the information he threw so casually into my face. For weeks, Arteim had tried to excavate the names of the monsters who owned the crematorium—and who should turn out to be one of them but my wife? She'd learned too well the business rules I'd taught her: the need for secrecy, the courage to put money into unlikely fields, the technique of creating necessary demilitarized zones between possession and owner. But now something else bothered me more; it spoke too clearly of the capabilities of Nadze and his men that they'd found her out.

"I would like to meet with her and discuss the possibility of working with her firm."

"In what way?" I asked. "Even if the purchase has gone through as recently as you say, they've undoubtedly hired protection in the meantime."

"You misunderstand me. Certainly we should not think of expropriating her firm's holdings without her consent," Nadze said. "Ideally, we would purchase the workers' interest. They'll be agreeable; I am not worried about that. What do they know of running such an operation? Many of the employees have very specialized abilities, and—let me speak candidly—their skills are only going to waste. Doubtless, they could be more fruitfully used in other areas of our organization."

"Doubtless," I replied, thinking of the tattooed beasts, imagining their wealth of talents. Did Tanya have any idea of what she'd gotten herself and her firm into? I had to talk to her, the sooner the better—but considering our contretemps of the past evening, would *she* talk to *me*? "By any chance, have you spoken to her yet about your ideas?"

"I wanted to meet you first," he said, shaking his head, clasping my shoulder with his paw. "We can work out a beneficial arrangement, I think, one that will please us all. Later, we'll discuss this matter at length. At the moment, however, please excuse me while I fulfill my responsibilities as host." Nadze stood and shouted across the room to his favored Kazakh.

"Mels! Enough of zakuski. Bring forth the entrée."

Four of the biggest guards strode with Mels across the room, toward the kitchen. In their absence the guests spoke only of the imagined splendor of the entrée, guessing—betting, too—how memorable it might prove to be. Even Ludmilla put down her glass of wine (one glass, eight refills) to await the presentation. Light again shone in my koshka's eyes. I regretted having told her of Tanya's demand in such a cryptic, perfunctory way; surely, dismaying scenarios of what might be occurring were burning in her mind while she pondered the ramifications of my warning. Her husband, I noticed, was plainly disinterested in Nadze's presenta- tion; he and Mikhail stared at the empty chairs of their partners, whispering to each other, looking not nearly as assured as they had when I arrived.

"My friends," Nadze cried out as the kitchen's double doors flew open, "let me welcome you properly!"

Mels reemerged, carrying a broadax almost three meters long, resting the oaken haft against his shoulder as if it were a rifle. His right hand wrapped comfortably around its wood; the room's chandelier lights glinted off the mirrored surface of the silver blade, high above his head. Heretofore I'd seen such a weapon only in the Kremlin Armory or in Eisenstein's *Alexander Nevsky*. Were they intending to reenact the death of Petrovsky? Then the four other Kazakhs came out of the kitchen, wheeling a steel cart the size of a Zhiguli's chassis. Upon the cart, encircled by crisp-skinned suckling pigs, lay the roasted carcass of a steer: a veritable aurochs, cooked to perfection, black-brown, glistening, steeped in fragrant, bubbling sauce. The Kazakhs rolled the cart into position along- side the table, and the guests sitting nearest turned fully around, so as not to miss an instant of this bizarre medieval spectacle. Heat rising from the beef fogged Ludmilla's glasses. Nadze pointed a finger at the leader of his Praetorians, and Mels raised his ax with both hands, lifting it high over his head. For a disconcertingly long time he held the weapon aloft, absolutely vertical; then, as if he were a Tatar warrior sounding a charge to his brigands across the windswept steppes of Rus, he emitted a bloodcurdling shout and with all his strength brought down the blade.

"*Hyaaaggh!*"

Sizzling juices, hell-hot, spattered the faces of the closest guests, who screamed like lovers enjoying sexual congress. The children cried, two Georgian wives fainted. As the steer was cleaved in twain, vents of steam shot geyserlike out of the crevasse, searing the prelate and two military officials. Four roasted sheep prepared in the eastern manner (with head) continued to simmer within the beef; the sudden change in air temperature, and the force of Mels's ax plunging through into the surface of the cart itself, caused the sheep to burst open as well, exposing roasted chickens stuffed into each one. The suffocating aroma of delicious Georgian spices nearly cloaked the sharp odor of some of the guests. For an instant no one seemed to know what to do—even Nadze appeared to be lost—so without a moment's hesitation I rose to my feet, lifting my glass as if it were an ax.

"*Bravissima!*" I shouted, and the crowd (save for unconscious women, bawling children, the prelate and two generals rubbing lumps of butter over their deep-fried arms, and a Georgian who'd thrust his face into a tub of potato salad, hoping to cool his burns) applauded so wildly at this unforgettable evocation of old Georgia that they could have put any Party Congress to shame. Nadze patted me on the back and returned to the table, acknowledging the plaudits offered.

"I should like to see a kitchen that can prepare whole oxen," Ludmilla told Nadze, who didn't sit down. Never before had I heard her slur her words when speaking, but never had I seen her so drunk. "May I ask to be given a tour?"

"My dear, I must say no. Only men are allowed entry."

With tremendous effort, Mels pulled his ax free of cart and carcass, bracing himself by pressing his boot against choice shoulder cuts. "Men!" my faithful assistant said to our host. "Imagine, men running around loose in a kitchen. It must be a regular hog lot in there."

"I tell you what," Nadze replied. "I need to speak to your employer alone. The kitchen would be an excellent place for us to hold our conversation, I think. When he returns, he can tell you all about our facilities. How does that sound?" His suggestion did not appeal to me in the slightest, but it looked as if my opinion would not be a decisive factor. Ludmilla gave another snort and held out her glass. Mels poured; he stood directly behind me, bottle in one hand, ax in the other. "Come, Maxim Alexeich, this won't take long. You too, Dima."

At least I was not the only one unpleasantly surprised.

Dmitry's eyes opened so wide I saw the entirety of his black irises, afloat in reddish-white pools. He stammered, as if his tongue had somehow caught on his teeth, but finally spat out a few words, demonstrating the quickness of thought I found it ever more difficult to admire. "I'm sure the kitchen is a miracle of technology," he said, "but subtleties in the culinary arts are lost on me, I'm afraid."

"We also need to talk, Dima," Nadze said, sounding not as affable as he had, moments before. "Come along."

Dmitry found himself practically lifted to his feet by the Kazakhs to his left and right. I nodded to Mels, letting him know I needed no like assistance. He walked with me as I followed Nadze and Dmitry toward the kitchen. Most guests did not note of our departure, being too busy devoting close attention to the joints of meat deposited on their plates. I glanced across at Sonya, who looked quite disturbed by our being called away. I smiled and strove to feign a mood of blithe unconcern. Ludmilla was busy wresting a bottle of grape vodka from one of the servers. Neither Vlad nor Tibor had returned to the table; Dmitry's remaining partner, Mikhail, sat alone. He was shaking, as if he were cold.

"What a splendid house, Lavrenty," Dmitry said to Nadze as we left the dining hall. "Does it satisfy your needs?"

"The walls are very thick."

Either the kitchen was a recent addition or else several older, smaller rooms had been combined into one and remodeled by stylish Italian designers. Never in Moscow had I seen such a cooking hall. Walls, ceiling, and floor were whiter than fresh-fallen snow; there were five refrigerators, three ovens, three dishwashers, each encased in matte-finish aluminum, and enough sinks to supply a hospital morgue. Built into one side of the room was a fireplace that could have held three steers of the size served to the guests; the spit within continued to glow red. Hanging from the ceiling or affixed to the walls were copper molds, brushes, knives, ladles—every imaginable cuisinary tool. Nothing in the room appeared to have come from east of the Danube. Twelve kitchen workers assembled as Nadze entered, doffing their toques, lining up for inspection in order of seeming importance, from the head chef (an older man with spade-shaped beard, even fatter than his employer) to the cooks' apprentice (a sapling-thin boy, twelve or thirteen, with bandaged fingers and a face powdered in flour). Mels shut the doors behind us as we entered the kitchen, locking them tight.

"Gentlemen, you've outdone yourselves," Nadze said. "An astonishing presentation. My highest congratulations to you. Tell me, who is the pastry chef?"

"I am, master," said a butter-greasy man in the center of the line.

"The desserts are chilled?"

"At the precise temperature."

"Excellent," Nadze told him, tying on an apron. "In a kitchen, who knows what might spill?" he explained. On the front of the apron was a silk-screened tiger. "Mels! Unlock the vodka."

The kitchen kings trailed ratlike behind Mels as he led them to the far side of the room. The moment he threw open the pantry (a room half the size of my flat, it looked) they rushed forward as if to board the sole lifeboat on a sinking ship. Once they were inside, embracing their bottles, Mels closed and locked that door as well.

"Even now, I like to come in and fix dinner myself for my men," Nadze said, grinning as if he were deliriously happy. "I was a cook in the Army, but that is not the place for gourmandizing, as I don't have to tell you." He strutted through the kitchen with the air of an admiral visiting a new-christened battle cruiser. I couldn't help but imagine how displeased Ludmilla would be when told of the spotlessness of the facilities. "Maxim Alexeich, I would like to get your opinion."

"Concerning?"

"Do you believe that if two parties enter into a formal arrangement, both parties should thereafter aspire at all times to fulfill the requirements of that agreement? Does this not seem to you inarguably sensible?"

"Without question," I said. "The smallest child would understand."

"But if one party fails to live up to his responsibilities, this could be problematic, yes?"

"It stands to follow."

Mels stared into the glass window of an oven door, seeming to think it a television. Nadze picked up a butcher's knife and a sharpening stone and began to whet the utensil as he continued to speak. "Now, Dima. If one party not only fails to live up to the requirements of the agreement but actively works to the detriment of the same as well, very big problems must arise, don't you think?"

The walls and doors of the room must have been extremely thick; although the dining hall was not ten meters from where we were, the only audible sound I noted in the interval between question and answer was the hum of the fluorescent lights overhead. "I'm not sure I understand, Lavrenty," Dmitry said. "What is your point?"

"Dima, do you have a low opinion of the intelligence of those with whom you work?"

"Why ask such a question?"

Nadze laid down the knife and stone. "What happens to the mouse who thinks he outwits the cat?"

"Lavrenty, I'm afraid you've lost me."

"No, no," Nadze said, "we found you. We know who you are, Dima, and what you've done. We're quite aware of unfortunate actions you've committed in the past. We've been quite aware for some time."

Dmitry did well, keeping his face free of emotion, but I foresaw that he would not be able to do so indefinitely. "What actions?"

"You remember Konstantin Iremashvili? Arrested in the railroad scandal? Executed as an example to the people for theft of socialist property? No? Your partners must remember him, Dima. They facilitated the warrants against him."

"Who was Iremashvili?" he asked. "The name is unfamiliar—"

"My cousin," Nadze said, sitting down next to a meter-wide cutting board. "Maxim Alexeich, allow me to compliment you and your firm. You performed a superlative job for Dima. If we hadn't known who he was before we entered into this arrangement, we might never have found out afterward, thanks to your excellent work. A shame it went for naught."

Dmitry had no immediate response—I don't know that I would have, either, had I been in his situation. Of course, at that point I had no idea yet how dire my own situation might be. "Why did you proceed with the agreement if you knew what he'd done?" I asked.

"Maxim Alexeich, wouldn't you?" Nadze asked. "Business is business, and not without risks. I hoped that, as a matter of honor, Dima would admit to past crimes. If he didn't, we were willing to overlook it. We cannot always expect to shake clean hands. But what you've tried to do, Dima, is astonishing. People call us cynical, but compared to you we are innocent lambs."

"I wish I had a better understanding of your accusations."

"Did you think we would be fools enough to allow your subcontractors to ship containers to New York without first making sure of the contents?"

"What are you saying?" Dmitry asked. "You mean to say you've already checked them? The containers were only ready this morning."

"I heard of them this afternoon. What do you think my men found in the containers?" Dmitry shook his head. "Ballast. Quite worthless ballast, at that. Seventy-five thousand copies of Brezhnev's war memoirs, fresh from the printer's warehouse, untouched for twenty years."

"Those worthless pigs!" Dmitry exclaimed. "Thank God you caught them."

Nadze looked at Mels, and they laughed so loudly that they could barely catch their breath. "My God, Dima, what are you telling me?"

"These shippers, they've stolen the material they were supposed to ship," Dmitry said. "It's obvious."

"Is it?"

"I swear to you on the souls of my parents. They've pulled a fast one on us, the crooks. Look, we should go feed them their pricks."

Nadze leaned over and rummaged through a drawer; in a moment he found a pair of steel scissors that ended not in sharp points but blunt-edged clamps. The tool was used perhaps to remove potatoes or onions, one at a time, from boiling water—I am not an expert in food preparation. "But who was the one who subcontracted the services of these so-called criminals?"

"I accept full responsibility for hiring them, Lavrenty Zhordanich. Don't you see? They must have made an arrangment with one of the other mafias. They stole the valuable material and left worthless ballast in its place. We should beat the truth out of them, if need be."

"We did," Nadze said, standing up and walking toward Dmitry, clicking the prongs of his tool together as if playing Cuban castanets.

"And what did they say? Who did they tell you provided the ballast instead of the material?" Dmitry asked. Nadze pointed at him. "Then they've lied to you. They have. You believe them and not me?"

"Your subcontractors tell us they loaded the goods they were told they'd receive." Mels ambled over to where Dmitry and I stood. It heartened me, somewhat, to see that he'd set aside his ax; all he now carried was what appeared to be a thin taper made of stainless steel. "Told by you."

"You're saying you find their word unassailable?"

Nadze waved a paper in Dmitry's face. "Dima, you're only sinking deeper into your own revisionist quagmire. This was delivered to me not twenty minutes ago."

"What is it?"

"One invoice for seventy-five thousand copies of Brezhnev ballast, at two rubles per volume. Do you recognize your signature when you see it? Here, look. At the bottom."

Dmitry examined the document closely, as if it were a complex legal contract, written in a language with which he had scant familiarity. "Forgers are everywhere in Moscow these days," he finally muttered. "Max can affirm that; he has considerable experience along this line."

"Maxim Alexeich, does this look like Dima's signature?" Nadze asked, showing me the paper. The scrawl was plainly his.

"It appears to be a signature resembling ones I've seen," I said. "It would only be fair, however, to reconfirm my—"

"A forgery," Dmitry repeated. Nadze sighed.

"You claim this is not your writing?"

"A ridiculous fraud. Look, I'll tell you what you want to do—"

I heard a hissing sound, as if a gas burner had been switched on. From the tip of the steel taper Mels held shot a steady blue flame. "Dima, I *know* what I want to do," Nadze said. "Please excuse us, Maxim Alexeich."

Moving quickly, as if he were on a privatized assembly line, Mels pushed Dmitry to the floor, pinning his hands flat, holding him down. Nadze seized his nimbus of hair in one hand and jerked back his head. Mels reached down and squeezed Dmitry's jaws open, and then he and Nadze exchanged tools. Mels thrust the potato plucker into Dmitry's gaping maw, clamping his tongue between the two ends of the instrument and locking them in place. Then Mels pulled with such force that I thought he intended to tear the tongue from Dmitry's mouth; instead, Nadze adjusted the taper's flame and directed the fire at its glistening red surface. In a very short time I began to smell my client cooking (an aroma not as enticing as the steer's, I must tell you). Dmitry's eyes nearly popped from their sockets; in agony, he made irreproducible noises that I knew were human only because with my own eyes I saw who was making them. Nadze pressed a button at the base of the taper, cutting off the flame; Mels released his grip on his implement. I watched in horror as Dmitry rolled back and forth, thrashing his legs, howling like a dog and pressing his tongue against the cool floor, trying to relieve his pain.

"Nothing as hot as a mouthful of lies," Nadze said, placing the taper on top of the nearest oven. Mels whistled a merry tune and spun his tool around his thumb as if it were a pinwheel. "Maxim Alexeich—"

"Call me Max," I said. "Please."

"Max, I'm sorry you have to be an observer of these proceedings. You can see I'm a reasonable man, but look what we're up against. He owes you money as well, doesn't he?"

"He does," I told Nadze, not for an instant allowing myself to reveal the slightest hint of fear.

"You possess finer sensibilities than Dima, I believe. I will like working with you. Tell me something. What did he say we would be shipping to New York?"

"Souvenirs."

He smiled. "What do you think we plan to send?"

"It's none of my business."

"Under the circumstances, it is and it isn't," said Nadze. "Dima? Feeling better?"

It startled me to hear Dmitry choke out any kind of sound; I should have thought he'd be unable to speak for weeks. "Bastard."

"Amateurs, amateurs. How do you Russians expect to run a country when you don't even understand basic rules of the marketplace?"

"Why treat me this way?" His enunciation wasn't perfect, but Dmitry could make himself heard, if you wanted to hear. "These foul accusations."

Nadze shook his head in disbelief. "What do you think, Max? Does Dima have an aversion to truth, or does truth have an aversion to him?"

"Listen," I said, hoping against reason that there could be a fast escape out of this. I cursed Dmitry for having gotten me into the situation in the first place, cursed myself for so willingly going along. "Dmitry and his partners are plainly over their heads here. Why don't you settle your differences, whatever they may be, call off the agreement, and afterward go on your separate ways as before?"

"An excellent idea, Max."

"We fulfill contract," Dmitry said, as well as he was able— we ignored him.

"In truth, it's the course I'd decided we'd take." Nadze took my hand in his, clasping it tightly. "Thank you for offering to serve as an objective party in this difficult matter."

"No, I didn't mean—"

"Keep sharp eyes on him," said Nadze. "Make sure he does what we tell him to do. Make sure what he tells us is true. I know I can count on you."

My God, but this was an assignment I had no desire to take on. "Why would you choose me to oversee his atonement?"

"Let me tell you again, Max," he said. "I know we can count on you."

He didn't explain why he knew, and I wasn't thinking clearly enough to wonder why—certainly, I should have.

Dmitry lay face down, panting and moaning. "Dima," Nadze shouted to him, "you're so bad at fooling others, why are you so good at fooling yourself?" Dmitry shook his head, pressing his tongue repeatedly against the floor. "Listen to me, Dima, our agreement is off as of this moment. We shall make other arrangements to ship the material in question. Our plans must move forward unhindered, we are on a *schedule*. Understand?" Dmitry nodded, keeping his tongue on the floor. "Your oafish conniving has caused us unacceptable delays. You've let us down quite badly, Dima. At the very least I must insist upon reimbursement."

"What?" he asked, lifting his head, croaking like a frog.

"You must return not only the money but also the material we advanced to you on loan. Regard yourself lucky that this is all we demand. Your associates have assured us you know where the money is, where the material is, that you alone oversaw its safeguarding."

"When? When'd they tell you?"

"Thirty minutes ago," Nadze said. "Aliev and Medunov"—Vlad and Tibor—"are in general agreement concerning this matter. I do not know yet what your third associate has had to say; he was removed from the dining hall after we left. I would be surprised if he told us a different tale."

"What've you done to them?" Dmitry asked, trying to drag himself to a sitting position. Neither Nadze nor Mels (nor I, to be candid) helped.

"We'll be holding them here until you bring us what is ours," Nadze said. "Collateral. You're familiar with the principle, I'm sure. They'll be safe, Dima, don't worry. Look, if they were Georgians and in the hands of the militia, they'd already be dead. You have no reason to think we will treat them so maliciously. Why would we do that? There is probably much they can tell us which will be of interest."

Dmitry closed his eyes. "When'll you let them go?"

"It's three o'clock," Nadze said, checking his watch: a Rolex, as I don't have to tell you. "We expect to see you and Max here tomorrow afternoon, at three, with our money and material. Your fellow conspirators will be released at that time."

Again Dmitry tried to stand and at last succeeded. "If I am going to watch him for you, I need to know what material you are talking about," I said to Nadze. "What was advanced to him besides money?" He had no ready answer. "By any chance, will the material returned to you be added to what is being sent to America?"

Nadze glanced away, looking toward the pantry, while he spoke to me. "A high probability, yes."

"What is it?" I asked; then, remembering the army officer's remark I'd overheard, offered the answer I suspected. "White gold?" During the Khrushchev era, when doomed attempts were first made to implement Ukrainian-style agricultural techniques in the Central Asian socialist states (despoiling those once-rich lands, turning the Aral Sea into a lifeless desert strewn with abandoned ships), white gold was the official term for the Uzbekh cotton crop. In recent years, however, the phrase is applied almost exclusively to the region's superlative heroin.

He returned my stare and gave me a broad smile. "Seventy kilos of finest purity. I knew you'd be a hard one to fool, Max." Dmitry's tongue hung from his mouth, revealing a blackened circle in its center. "Let us return to the celebration. People will wonder what has happened to us. Mels, unlock the doors."

His assistant released the kitchen staff before allowing us to leave; they stumbled out of the pantry, tripping over one another as they listlessly returned to their workplace. "Tell me something," I asked. "In which room did Petrovsky's mistress murder him?"

"You know the story!" Nadze said, expressing the thoughtful host's appreciation of the interests of his guests. "The dining hall, of course. The poor man. Doesn't it seem to you that the presence of ghosts heightens the atmosphere?" .

Sonya's face brightened, the moment she saw us return. Ludmilla swayed in her seat, as if struggling against a strong wind. Possibly she'd had additional glasses of delicious grape vodka in our absence. Dmitry gave no indication that he had suffered any experience more painful than having seen the hearth on which the steer (now no more than a pile of gnawed bones) was roasted. His third partner, Mikhail, was not in his seat, having of course been lured away in our absence. Nadze gave the women warm smiles as he strolled by.

"Probably we should be heading on," I told Ludmilla, placing a hand on her shoulder.

"Yes, yes. Back to work," she said. With no small effort I pulled her from the chair, encircling her waist with my arm so she would not fall down.

"Have a pleasant afternoon, friends," our host said. "Mels, see our guests out."

"Max," I heard Dmitry calling out behind us, slurring his words to nearly the same degree as did Ludmilla. "We're leaving, too."

"We look forward to seeing you again," Nadze told him.

As we went into the entrance hall we saw the young woman

standing there with our coats—undoubtedly Nadze had suspected we would not wish to tarry much longer at the party. Mels bowed as we left, his gun again swinging out from beneath his coats. Once outside, at the foot of the stairs, I took Dmitry by the arm and gently pushed Ludmilla into Sonya's embrace. "Excuse us." By her expression I knew she could tell something terrifically unpleasant had ensued, out of her sight. "Your husband and I must confer for a moment before we leave."

I steered him a short distance along the driveway, far enough away that we could not be overheard. The Kazakhs on duty watched us closely but soon perceived our harmless intentions. "Max," Dmitry said, holding his mouth open as if the rush of air against his tongue might lessen his pain, "I'm sorry."

"Fuck yourself," I told him. "Look what you've gotten me into, trying to swindle these crooks. They were never fooled for an instant."

"I can't believe those bastards," he said, and for a short foolish moment I thought he was wisely agreeing with me. "Stealing material right off the dock."

"Enough of your lies," I said, astonished by his incomparable mythopoeic abilities. "Understood?"

"Max, why would I lie?" With a certain sorrow that I was not better able to contain my emotions, I seized Dmitry by the lapels, almost lifting his feet off the gravel. Sonya gasped; the Kazakhs roused themselves and paid close attention to us. As I answered him, I spoke as softly as I could.

"I'll be at your apartment in the morning by ten. I'll send over some of my guards to keep watch. They'll make sure you don't leave. Are you going to do what they want you to do? What *I* want you to do?"

"Of course I will, Max. I have to get my associates out of their clutches." He sighed, as if unable to comprehend why I treated him so badly. "You're giving me less credit than I deserve."

"That isn't possible."

After seeing that Ludmilla got home safely if unconsciously (her husband appeared less shocked by her condition than I would have guessed), I phoned Arteim, telling him to send guards to Dmitry's apartment; if my client were to try sneaking away, they should shoot him in the hand or foot—I wanted to keep him alive, at least until we paid our second—and, I hoped, final—visit to these Georgians.

The afternoon was cold; the sky, the color of an old sheet. I left the old neighborhood and its empty streets, lined with silent well-guarded houses, and strolled the river-wide length of New Arbat, down sidewalks twenty meters across, past the world's largest cinema, largest bookstore, largest restaurant; past fountains that could have held whales and past acromegalic buildings so out-sized the apparatchiks they housed could have entered as children and left as old men without transversing the same hallways twice. A demonstration was ongoing at the White House. Diehard Communists—slobbering pensioners, malcontent skinheads, and representatives of the armed forces—gathered to await the television cameras: screaming denunciations, waving signs bearing scrawled anathemas, holding tattered posters of Lenin and airbrushed icons of the onetime Supreme Standard-Bearer of the Proletariat. Pathetic fools, I thought, and walked on, my anger evergrowing.

My anger did not spring solely from Dmitry's nefarious, imbecilic actions, although the thought of being forced to serve, however briefly, these drug-smuggling mobsters made me despise the day I agreed to take on his assignment, in return for money I would now never see. The longer I thought upon the decision of my wife and her associates to invest in such an establishment as that crematorium, supplying its monsters with unneeded money while opening themselves up to the predatory desires of the likes of Nadze, the angrier still I became. When the sun sank, I finally walked back to Tverskaya, saw her car in the garage, and rode the elevator upstairs. Entering our flat, I saw Tanya sitting at the kitchen table, enjoying a hot bowl of kvass soup.

"We have to talk."

"I called your office," she said, keeping her eyes lowered. "I was told you and Ludmilla had gone out for the afternoon. Was that the best you could do?"

"What are you talking about?"

"It's obvious where you've been. Did you make your decision?"

"I haven't been with Sonya," I said, infuriated by her groundless suspicions, however understandable they might have been. "I mean she was there, but—"

"Liar. So we have nothing to talk about," Tanya said, rising and going over to the sink to wash her bowl and spoon.

"Call Ludmilla and ask her where I was." No sooner did I complete my sentence than I realized that my loyal assistant was presently incapable of speech. "Call her tomorrow; she drank too much this afternoon."

"Have you lost your talents for lying? Ludmilla doesn't drink, you know that. How stupid do you think I am?"

"Would you please listen to me?" I shouted.

"Why should I, if these are the tales you're telling? And lower your voice, can you? Do you want the neighbors to hear our quarrels?"

"Who'll hear, Khrushchev? Look, we went to the feast these Georgians held to celebrate their agreement with Dmitry. Sonya was there with *him*, not me. We barely spoke. The problem is, the Georgians found out who Dmitry was and—"

Without warning, she slammed the bowl into the sink so hard that both shattered. "Stop it. I've had enough of these fables."

"It's truth!"

"Does her husband know about you?"

"No, I don't think so. Tanya, listen." She started to walk out of the room; I caught her, seizing her arm more roughly than I ever had before—do not misunderstand me; I had no desire to physically hurt her. "You must listen to what I have to tell you. It's important."

"Let go!" she screamed, jerking away. "Adulterer! Beast! I'll never let you touch me again."

"When have you let me?" I shouted, pressing my face against hers. "Those Georgian devils are after this crematorium of yours!"

Did she hear me? At first I couldn't tell, for while I tried to keep my grip on her left arm, with her right she picked up a stove pot and slammed it against my head. I wasn't hurt (due to a fortuitous combination of hard skull and Soviet metal), although I was stunned. She ran down to our bedroom, shutting the door and locking it from the inside before I could recover. There wasn't a chance I'd be able to break it down, and unlike many of my countrymen I am not good at picking locks. I pounded on the wood with my fists, shouting through the door.

"Tanya! Come out of there! Please!"

"Leave me alone!" she screamed. "I told you to make your decision. I guess you made it. Bastard!" It was difficult to listen to her concluding remark; never had I heard my wife use such language before. "*Pig fucker!*"

"These Georgians are on to Dmitry. I think he's in great danger. Their leader wants your crematorium. These people are dangerous, they're criminals."

"What right do you have to be asking questions about my firm's investments? You don't own them; you can't take them from me. They're mine."

"I don't want it, the Georgian does. He told me about the crematorium; he already knows. Don't you understand the danger you're in? *We're* in?"

"Our firm has protection. Leave me alone, Max, just go away. You can't imagine how much you've hurt me."

"These Georgians will hurt you worse," I said. "Who arranged such protection? Who?"

"I'll ask you again, Have you made your decision?"

"Can't you be quiet and listen to me? You don't understand—"

"I understand our situation is the same. Until you come to your senses, I have nothing to say and I don't intend to listen. The parlor is prepared for you."

"My God, Tanya, don't do this."

"Sleep well."

My temper almost slipped loose of its ties. "I wish—" Wish you were dead, I almost told her, but I caught myself and said nothing of the sort. Years ago I'd sworn I would never say anything like that, ever again, and I never break a promise to myself. My energy left me, as if sapped from without; for the moment, I could only accept the situation as it was and hope she'd listen to me the next morning, before it was too late. "My small bird," I said, "I wish you'd forgive me." She didn't; our bedroom door stayed locked, and I saw her no more after that.

7

I awoke in agony the next morning, unable to move; with prolonged effort I managed to shift enough to relieve pressure
on my compressed spine. The pain was so great that I almost called
out to Tanya, so she could assist me in rising; then I realized she
would undoubtedly be in no mood to help. By hooking my foot
beneath a table I was able to slowly lever myself aright. When
sensation returned to my limbs, I felt as if they were being rubbed
down with hedgehogs. I sat on the edge of the sofa, listening to
my vertebrae click into place as I craned my neck. The sun was
up; bars of light and shadow thrown by the half-shut window blinds
painted me in prisoner's stripes.

When I returned from the water closet I raised the blinds
and, peering out the window, was blessed with a morning vision
such as I had never seen before. In Khrushchev's building, in an
apartment on the floor directly across the courtyard from ours, I
saw a naked young woman. Probably she had just awoken and was
unaware of anything save her immediate surroundings. She stood
half turned toward the window in her room, combing her black
waist-length hair. I fixed the girl in my sights for as long as she
was visible; after a minute or two (I still recall each second) she

laid down her comb and walked into another room where, sadly, I could see her no longer. Hers was a ice skater's figure, with powerful thighs and calves, and you could have balanced a cup on her buttocks.

The instant she disappeared, I noticed the degree to which the sight of her aroused me—but then I felt a cool draft on the back of my neck, and my interest lessened. Turning, almost falling over an ottoman, I found that our apartment door was not only unlocked (I'd locked it myself before turning in) but ajar.

"Tanya?" I shouted down the hall and ran to the bedroom. That door was also open, and so I was not as shocked as you might imagine when I discovered she was gone. From the disarray of the bedsheets and duvet I gathered she'd slept there, most of the night. It troubled me that I'd not heard her leave, although such was my mental state that I couldn't yet imagine I wouldn't see her again. An unpleasant realization soon intruded itself into my mind. Searching our closet and our dresser drawers, I ascertained that her clothes had not been removed; the dust on our suitcases remained undisturbed. Then I saw a note on the nightstand. Her handwriting, no question.

> *M,*
> *Do whatever they want. I will be all right they say but*
> *I don't believe them. Why didn't you warn me?*
> *If I didn't love you I would have you killed for this.*
> *T.*

Her words—no question about that, either. No one could ape the mind of my wife or feign her adeptness at commingling affection with threat. *If I didn't love you I would have you killed for this:* our marriage, in a phrase. Beneath her note, there was another one, unsigned, bearing a single sentence scrawled in an unrecognizable hand:

> *We look forward to seeing you.*

I wished now I had taken an ax to our bedroom door the night before to better impress upon my wife my warning. As I stood in the room where we had slept away so many otherwise profitable hours, holding the notes in my hand, I felt a sudden tightness in my chest; until it passed I feared I was having a coronary seizure, but evidently it was nothing more than heartburn. How many times during their years together do married couples fall in and out of love? I couldn't count the number of dead moments Tanya and I had shared, yet however often I was lured into exuberant flings with other women more sparkling with life, once their glamour faded I invariably returned to the arms of my wife. There is no scientific rationale to explain this, any more than there is to explain why a horse always races back into its burning barn, but both are facts. Tanya knew when she made her demand that I couldn't or wouldn't leave her. Divorce is like murder, harder to commit than to consider; and I think the aftermath of the former hurts twice over, for its protagonists are also the survivors. We both knew she would be the one with whom I remained, my overpowering love for my koshka notwithstanding.

(So I convinced myself by the end of that morning, although I would not be human if I did not admit to since having had second thoughts.)

Before making necessary phone calls I took out the reader I keep in my desk at home, a basic model that speedily reveals evidence of bug infestation. In ten minutes I'd checked everything in the apartment; I was sure I'd discover at least one of the phones to be tapped, but I didn't; in some ways that was more disturbing than my wife's disappearance. If nothing else, were they not interested in my reaction?

I called Sonya. When she answered the phone I knew she was safe, and we exchanged heartfelt emotions. "Is he there?" I asked.

"Still asleep."

"That prick on wheels can *sleep* under these circumstances?"

"What did they do to him?"

"What did he tell you?"

"Nothing," she said. "Next to nothing. What happened to his tongue?"

"Cat got it."

"Max!"

"I'm sorry, but I'm not going to say he didn't deserve what was done to him. What specifically did he tell you, my angel?"

"He said there was a misunderstanding. A theft perpetrated

by his associates that somehow ruined his big deal. He accepted full blame and now he tells me he has to go back and clear up the problem this afternoon."

"He thought he could swindle them and got caught at it," I said. "That's what happened. He stole their money, God knows what else. They're holding his associates prisoner, probably whipping them into butter. Nadze told me to come back with him and make sure he does what he's supposed to do."

"You? Why?"

"At the time I didn't know," I said. "Now I suspect because it's tied in with something else. I think they've kidnapped Tanya."

"Kidnapped? What do you mean, you think? Don't you know?"

"She's gone, there are notes left, and one is definitely not in her handwriting; her clothes are here," I said. "When I came home yesterday I tried to tell her what had happened but she wouldn't listen to me; she only wanted to know if I'd made my decision."

"About me?"

"That's right. What puzzles me is that if she was kidnapped, whoever did it left no transmittal devices behind. That makes no sense unless something scared them and they had no time."

"*Did* you make your decision?"

Were they both going to start hounding me? "Sonya, it's impossible to even think about such matters at present. Don't worry, my angel, I'll never leave you."

"But why would you want her?" That was not the first time she asked me that question; I wondered why she asked it now. "*They* want her, I mean. Why would they want to kidnap her?"

"Remember the crematorium in Reutov? When you came to surprise me."

"Of course. That terrible place with the tattooed men."

"Tanya's firm owns a sizable part of it. The Georgian told me this yesterday when he had me sit next to him. He—"

"I heard. I was listening," my ever-surprising koshka informed me.

"Obviously this is their way of moving in on her, and on me as well."

"So you're going over there today too?"

"I have to," I told her. "It was incredibly stupid for Dmitry to get involved with these Georgians, but now he's not the only one. Look, I'll be over at your apartment by ten. If he acts as if he's going anywhere, stop him. Are my guards there?"

"Everywhere," she said. "I thought those apes were here to kill us until Dmitry told me they were yours. God, Max, I miss you." Her voice was full of tears as she spoke. I closed my eyes, to think of her; but the instant I did, that scampering nymph from across the courtyard hopped lightfooted through my mind. "I'm scared. I love you so passionately."

"Everything will work out," I told her, mentally routing the intruder in my head, foolishly hoping such a cliché of fantasy would calm my koshka's fears. "Look for me at ten." We hung up. Even in the midst of this distressing situation, hearing Sonya's voice nearly drove away thoughts of Tanya. But for the moment, that could not be: whatever our personal difficulties, my wife and I had important business arrangements that could not be as easily disrupted. For as long as she was in danger, my wife needed me most. We would settle our personal problems afterward, perhaps not to her liking, perhaps not to mine, perhaps to no one's, but they would be settled.

As I dialed Evgeny's number, I glanced out the window to the building beyond and of course saw no one save Khrushchev, stumbling through his flat in his traditional wardrobe, his hairy gut seeming to wobble by itself when he walked as if it were an independent host trying to break free of its parasite. The phone rang a dozen times before my brother's small pear, Irina the movie star, answered.

"Who rings so early?" she murmured, yawning deeply. "Can't you tell time?"

"This is Evgeny's brother, Max," I stated, using the commanding tone of voice I employ with the most recalcitrant bureaucrats. "It is gravely important I speak to him."

"Is your house on fire? Call back, we're barely awake."

"Did you hear me? Put him on at once."

"Be quiet, I'm not deaf." The receiver fell with a *plumpf* onto something soft—Evgeny's head, perhaps. Then I detected the rustling of damp sheets and muted giggles, followed by the sound of human engines revving before they shift into higher gear. Apparently my brother had no desire to waste valuable time conversing with me when he could instead be indulging in ignoble frolic.

"Get her breasts out of your mouth and pick up the phone, you feebleminded bastard," I stated loudly into the receiver, intending that he should better perceive my mood.

"Sorry, Max, I was sleeping like a rock," he insisted as he picked up the phone, begging for mercy before I'd even thought of applicable punishment. "What's the matter? Is something wrong?"

"Why else would I call?" I asked, expressing myself at top volume. "Tanya's been kidnapped."

"Are you serious? How? Who's responsible?"

Before I could tell him I looked out the window once more and saw the young woman again, naked as before, standing in Khrushchev's apartment. She was cupping her breasts in her hands as if to show off her nipples. Show them off to whom? Why was she there? She couldn't be his wife. His *daughter*?

"Max?"

"Gangsters are responsible," I told him, unable to shut my eyes to this vision. "The Georgian mafia."

"What? Max, what are you saying? How did you get involved with them?"

"I didn't originally. One of my clients did." It would do me no good to tell my brother too much about the situation; his poor brain could have never stood the stress. "Then it got more complicated, and now we're boiling in the same soup."

"Have you contacted the authorities?"

While I sat there, holding the phone and staring out the window, desire once more tried to throttle reason and throw it to the ground. I am no *skoptsy*, someone who physically mutilates himself in order to restrain natural if unbidden urges; still, I cannot deny the mixture of shame and embarrassment I felt, drinking in her form, assaulting her with my eyes. It is especially hard to admit that I was being overwhelmed by lustful notions for an innocent stranger while my wife was held against her will by vicious criminals—but there is no reason I should presently lie to you.

"Max?" I heard my brother shouting. "Where are you? Max! Have you notified the authorities?"

"These crooks *are* the authorities," I told him. "Listen to me. Until I've resolved this, don't leave your apartment. Possibly the Georgians will try to kidnap you as well."

"Me? What have I done?"

"Nothing, but neither did Tanya. I'll make sure you have

protection, but stay where you are. These Georgians are capable of anything. You'd better keep your pigeon there with you."

My directive pleased him to an inordinate degree. "Is that an order, Max?"

"Treat what I tell you with utmost seriousness. I'll call and keep you informed as need be. But for now go nowhere, do nothing."

"Whatever you say."

Even as I lowered the receiver I heard their lubricious giggles starting anew. Before making my next call, to Arteim, I looked out the window again—and yes, what should I see but the young woman warmly embracing Khrushchev. God help her, they were both naked. How? *Why?* He extended a spindly leg, and she straddled it as if it were a horse, moving back and forth in such a way as to make her masturbatory intentions clear. Khrushchev grinned; he looked like a hippopotamus, waiting to be tossed a cabbage. The horror was too great, and I rushed forward to pull shut the blinds. Before calling Arteim I tried for several minutes to excise all carnal thoughts from my mind.

"They know about Universal, they know about the banks," I told him, once I explained the situation. "Execute plan C." This meant he would arrange to have our banks' capital holdings electronically tranferred for the duration to our Liechtenstein account, keeping only enough hard money on hand to satisfy the demands of our depositors and customers. "Sweep for bugs. Go to Universal and have them close the office. Everyone should take a short vacation until this is settled. Ludmilla probably won't be there today, she wasn't feeling well yesterday." Probably she wouldn't wake up until this afternoon, and I couldn't begin to imagine what her hangover would be like. "Make certain all major records are encrypted as they should be. I don't want them to have access to our client list."

"What about your wife's firm?"

"Do nothing," I said. "They're on their own."

"Should I ask Papadin for assistance?"

"No. Give him some idea as to what's going on. Keep it general. We may need him, but being in his debt in such a matter wouldn't be that much different from being tied up with these Georgians." Arteim, Telman, and I rarely employed the services of our protector's specialists, or of their more murderous countrymen, although under the circumstances I knew every option should be readily available for us to employ. But if you're not a puppet, what need have you for strings?

"Done, Max," Arteim said. "You know you can count on me."

"I appreciate it more than I can say," I told him. "Start checking around with those who deal with these Georgians. Conceivably you might be able to ascertain where she's being held. It's not likely, but try."

"I'll have Telman work on it."

"Don't use cellular phones unless you can't help it," I said. "Send guards over to my apartment. I want no visitors in my absence."

"You'll want accompaniment when you go to see these Georgians, of course," he said.

"No," I said. "They have a battalion of Kazakhs guarding their house. They could hold off an army assault for a week. We'll have to trust in fate."

"As you say. When the transfers are made, you want me to call you?"

"I won't be around a phone I can trust once I leave here. You know I trust you, that's good enough. I'm leaving momentarily. Get those guards over here."

"Rely on me, Max."

Curiosity overcame me; before getting dressed, I pulled aside the blinds and looked once more across the courtyard, but I saw neither Khrushchev nor the young woman. There was only one inference I could make; the thought of such a beauty willingly submitting to the desires of such a peasant, such an *ugly* peasant, saddened me. What could I do? I had trouble enough controlling my own life.

I didn't think it wise to be seen walking freely through the streets, so I rode to Dmitry's in my Mercedes, leaving at half past nine. There were no parking places on the street, so I pulled through his building's arched driveway into the trash-strewn swamp in the rear that served as parking lot—its mud, thankfully, was still mostly frozen. I saw one of my brawny stalwarts standing watch at what, in our country, is called the black entrance: that is to say, the rear door people actually use to get in and out of their building. All seemed calm enough, but no sooner did I secure the car than I heard a too-familiar voice.

"Max!"

Turning, I was appalled to see a face I'd hoped never to see in the flesh again. Petrenko waved cheerfully as he slogged across the parking lot, his hulking catamite in tow. For outerwear, he wore a calf-length army coat and, rather than a sweaty fedora, a fur hat which gave the impression that a marten was sleeping atop his head. The earflaps bounced up and out in time with his plodding steps, as if the creature, dreaming, was thrashing its legs, chasing imaginary prey.

"Max!" he said again, nearly cracking my ribs as he embraced me. "What an unexpected pleasure to see you! Have you also come to grind this weasel's prick beneath your thumb?"

"Dmitry?"

Petrenko nodded and spat on the ground. "He is filthy mud between my toes," he said, kicking away one of the beer bottles lying at our feet. Looking at Dmitry's building, he pointed at my guard. "Maybe he is more sensible than I think; he must expect visitors. Who does he think he is? Some mafia bigwig, with thugs to protect his lying ass from the hand of justice? Gyorgy will break their heads like eggs."

His companion wouldn't last a minute against the smallest of my men without having his own head removed and handed back to him, but I saw no need to note this explicitly. "That's one of my guards, Pavel," I said. "I stationed several here to make sure Dmitry didn't get away."

Petrenko's eyes widened in amazement; tiny blood vessels crackled the glaze of his whites. "Brilliant, Max. I stand in awe of your brain."

"I am guessing you haven't received any money from him?"

"Precisely," he said. "Let's go upstairs and kick his ass from hell to breakfast."

The presence of these lunatics complicated matters beyond reason but, try as I might, I couldn't think of an easy way to lose them. Petrenko so freely employed melodramatic words and gestures (the favored crime of Russians) that it was impossible to guess whether he planned to berate, beat, or kill Dmitry. As with the Georgians, this situation demanded reaction rather than action—certainly I would do what I could to talk him out of choosing the last of those three aforementioned options. "Rough treatment won't get us far, Pavel. We should use our wits."

"He'll fold like paper at the sight of me. Everyone knows Petrenko is Russian power personified." Shaking a fist at the sky, he struck one of the most commonly seen Socialist Realist poses—struck it well; I suspected he practiced often in front of mirrors. "Petrenko makes world shit in pants."

"Let's go upstairs," I said, never knowing what to say to someone who speaks of himself in the third person.

"Very well, Max. It's good to see your blood is hot as mine. Listen, when we get upstairs, we should shut away his wife in a quiet room. She doesn't need to see what we must do. Decisive, emotionless action sickens the stomachs of women. But as soon as we have him to ourselves—" He slammed his fist into Debalov's open palm. "He'll crack like a hymen."

"I think he'll see reason more easily today, Pavel," I said as we walked by my guard; I nodded to him as we passed, but he did not loosen his grip on his Kalashnikov. "To be truthful, I avoid violence if at all possible."

"Max, no. It's healthy as breathing." The lobby's tomblike dankness was especially unpleasant so early in the morning. On my previous visit I imagined patterns barely discernible on the wall to be floral stencils or designs of a decorative nature; in daylight, such as it was, I saw they were nothing but blotches of mildew. No member of the building's security force made his presence known, and I wondered if, the night before, they had unwisely gotten into a heated argument with my own guards. "How much does he owe you?" Petrenko asked as we climbed the crumbling stairs that led to the elevator.

"Too much," I said. A car's doors yawned open, and we crammed ourselves in. Petrenko pressed down the floor button until it clicked, locking into place. "What excuse has he given you for not turning over any profits?"

"He hasn't." The car vibrated like a tuning fork as it rose. "He told me the shipments started last week; that means I should have received our first payment yesterday. Did I? No, certainly not. Can his kind ever tell the truth?"

"Pavel, I believe he's had problems that were beyond his control," I said. "Not that I'm making excuses, but that's why I've gone easy on him so far."

"If he doesn't have something for me this morning he'll have some fucking problem, let me tell you. He is a walking moral vacuum." I tried to picture such a beast; the sole image that came to mind, however, was that of the olive-skinned young woman I'd seen from my window—I hastily shooed her away. "He never even showed me examples of the material so I could judge its quality. Have you any with you?"

"Any what?" I asked; then recalled that in Dmitry's imagination I produced counterfeit dollars to serve Petrenko's schemes. "Oh, yes. Of course." Reaching into my wallet, I removed a genuine twenty-dollar bill. "He hadn't shown you? I'm not surprised." Snatching the money from my hand, he carefully examined it. "What do you think?"

Without warning, he planted wet lips on my cheek. For an instant I feared that while they had me trapped between them in that coffinlike elevator, my new bosom friend would become even more recklessly demonstrative in his affections. "Max, if I didn't know better, I'd swear this was real," he said, pressing his fat against me. "What a fucking master you are."

"You'll find none better."

With a shuddering lurch the car braked to a stop. When the door slid open we saw two-thirds of a meter of greasy shaft showing between the floors of the hallway and of the car. "More typical quality workmanship," Petrenko said in disgust. With considerable exertion we managed to hurriedly extricate ourselves—too often in such a situation, the contraption will suddenly return to life, crushing would-be escapees or worse (only a month ago, a man was helping his aged mother out of an elevator when the door closed shut on his neck and descended; his head fell into her carrier bag, and weeks passed before she recovered the power of speech). No sooner were we out than the elevator shot upward at high speed, its door remaining open. "There will be none of these tubular guillotines in our Russia," noted Petrenko. When the two guards on that floor recognized me, they relaxed and stood at ease, lowering their eyes as we walked by them.

Sonya opened the door when I rang the bell, and we entered. She was more than a little startled to see my traveling companions, who exuded the faint aura of having come to murder everyone in the household. "Where is he?" I asked her.

"Down the hall," she said. "In his office." His treasure room, she meant. In their living room I saw expensive furniture: a sofa, three chairs, tables, and lamps; a glass-doored wall unit; a Japanese television (domestic models, such as those of Raduga, are notorious for exploding spontaneously); and two unwatered rubber plants, their leaves weighed down by dust. Had it not been for the books and *poshlaia* loaded into the wall unit, it might have been a hotel suite, and not a five- or even four-star suite at that. I had never been in their apartment before and didn't regret it; I felt as if I were crawling into bed with them both, the moment I walked in the door.

"Have you met these friends of your husband?" I asked as we took off our shoes. She shook her head; I had no doubt she recognized Petrenko. "Dmitry!" I called out loudly, so he would hear. "Someone besides me is here to see you."

"I'm going to the kitchen," Sonya said. "You men don't want me around while you play your little games."

"Get out here, Gubin!" Petrenko screamed, tossing his coat to Debalov. "There's no escaping responsibility. Where is my first payment?"

Dmitry didn't answer, and I began to worry that he would try to escape through a window—I had no doubt he could, if necessary, convince himself that he could survive a nine-story drop. "Pasha, I didn't expect you," we finally heard him call back. "Give me a minute."

"I'll give you my fucking boot in your fucking head if you don't come out now," Petrenko said, stepping forward.

"Here, I'll handle this," I whispered to him. "Dmitry," I shouted. "Pavel is due his profits on the shipments that are going out. Surely you must have forgotten. Let's clear this up, why not?"

"Here I come." Two doors left open in the hallway blocked any view we might have had of his treasure room. I heard huffing and then a mysterious creak as he closed his secret repository.

"Hurry," I said. As Dmitry came down the hall he started to cough. He held a small wooden box; his hands were whitened, as if he'd been kneading dough. He coughed so violently that a button of phlegm shone at the corner of his mouth.

"Gubin, stop fouling the air with your filthy germs," Petrenko said. Evidently, he had decided not to express his anger in a subtle or even indirect manner. "Where is my payment?"

"Pasha, I've experienced some unfortunate delays. You will have to take my word on it, I'm short of hard currency today."

"You're telling me you don't have my money?"

"Not immediately at hand, no."

"Bastard! *Private property owner!*"

"But I have something else for you in the meantime, until the money does come through," Dmitry said. "Please, Pasha, let me explain."

"Explain what?" Petrenko asked, his face beet purple. "Explain you screwed me? Go swing an elephant's balls." Throwing his hat to the floor, stomping his sock-clad feet, he gave himself wholly over to frenzy, as if in his anger he forgot where he was and imagined himself preparing to address an adoring crowd. "What is this? You think I'm a Westerner, some capitalist prick bought off with lies and honey? Have you no respect for me? Does anyone in this country stand by his principles?"

As hypnotizing as was Petrenko's performance, Debalov proceeded to distract and confound the three of us by voicing a stunningly unexpected opinion. "Pavlik Morozov," he said. "We need more like him."

"What? What are you saying?" Petrenko asked, turning to shout at his robust assistant. "Morozov was a shithead Communist bastard ass kisser."

"He stood by his principles."

(Morozov was the fourteen-year-old boy who, during the early thirties' dekulakization, turned his father in to the authorities for hoarding grain. He was rewarded by those in the small village in which he lived by being gloriously beaten to death— so the story went. Current opinion holds that Morozov's mother talked him into betraying his father and that Stalin, afterward, directed enemies of the people to kill him, so he could better serve the state as a useful martyr. Many grotesque statues of him, since removed, were erected across the Soviet Union to his inspiring memory.)

"He was a snake, like this one before us," Petrenko said. "Learn your history."

"What is it today?" Debalov retorted.

"That is nothing that concerns us here. Once more, Gubin, do you or do you not have profits to hand over?"

"No, but I have something else."

Petrenko almost visibly swelled with air, as when a toad bloats, seducing other toads. "Here. Let me remove my pants," he said, unbuckling his heavy leather belt. We stared on, baffled by his actions.

"Why?" Dmitry asked.

"So you can fuck my ass a second time," he said, yanking his belt free of his trousers. Grasping the ends in one hand, he whipped the perceived malefactor across the face with his home-made knout. "Make it hurt. Like this!" Dmitry clasped the box he carried securely against his chest as he fell into a chair, helpless beneath Petrenko's lashing blows. "Deceiver! Relish your punishment! Enjoy! Enjoy!"

Debalov laughed like a hyena, enthralled by the scene. Petrenko's eyes rolled back in his head, as if in the joy of the moment he experienced religious ecstasy.

"Max, do something!" Sonya shouted, rushing into the room, stopping short when she saw her husband being pounded fork-tender. No matter how deserved I considered this punishment to be, I could not bear to stand idly by while Petrenko proceeded to waste our valuable time. Without hesitation, I grabbed the belt from his hands with quickness a purse snatcher might envy.

"Pavel, stop!" I shouted. He circled to confront me, his eyes aflame with passion. Debalov thrust his hand into his leather jacket, seeming to fumble for a weapon he'd neglected to bring. I stared at them both, daring them to attack and prepared to cry out for my guards to enter and join the fray. Petrenko regained control of his emotions and signaled his companion to be still. That pleased me; after the fact, I realized that had my men received my go-ahead, they would surely have burst in and mowed down everyone in the room. Ten businessmen I have known were shot, and five killed, when their bodyguards allowed their fingers to race too unhesitatingly (and more than once, I think, deliberately) to their triggers. "See what he has to offer, at least."

Petrenko nodded, wiping a shaky hand across his sweating face; he blushed when he realized his pants had dropped to his knees. Dmitry never loosened his grip on the box he held.

Debalov presented me with a grimace so threatening that I nearly laughed in his face. Sonya stared at all of us, saying nothing; I wasn't sure which horrified her more, the brutal violence she'd witnessed or the never-to-be-forgotten view of Petrenko's furry legs and haunches. When I judged he'd calmed down, I returned his belt to him. "I am a man of strong emotions, Max," he said, pulling up his pants.

"Controlled emotions are strongest," I said, and then turned to the other miscreant, speaking calmly yet firmly, as if to a child. "Dmitry, why don't you explain to Pavel why you don't have his money?"

"Of course." I expected he would weave a marvelous tale, and I was as anxious as Petrenko to hear what it might be. Dmitry shifted in the chair he had been beaten into until he found the position that hurt the least. Sonya came over to give succor; it pained me to see her express such concern, but it was, if nothing else, a polite gesture. "The mafias have come down hard on me this week," he said. "They demanded bigger payoffs than I expected. They badly threw me off my schedule."

"So? Who doesn't have to deal with criminals these days?" Petrenko asked. "Once we're in control, there'll be no more interference from them. Give us our money and you give us strength. Keep our money, you weaken us. Very simple."

"How will you get the payments you deserve if they kill me before I can get them to you? Look, these crooks have nearly finished with me. I swear to you on my parents, I'll have liquid funds by the end of this week. Meanwhile, let me give you something from my personal collection to guarantee your loan. When I have your money for you, give it back. If something happens to me, keep it."

"Collection of what?" Petrenko asked, looking around the room; plainly, he didn't know of Dmitry's treasures. "Dolls? China or silverware? What have you got that I'd want?"

Dmitry unfolded white tissue paper within the box he held. "An egg."

"What? Am I a chicken?" Petrenko yelled. I think he was more than ready to employ his belt in an active manner again, but then he comprehended what Dmitry was saying. "A Fabergé egg?"

"What other kind are there?" Dmitry lifted away layers of cotton batting before removing the egg from its protective box. "But

even among Fabergé eggs, there are none like this." He cradled
the prize in his hands.

Unlike most of the eggs I've seen, such as those priceless
examples of the jeweler's art displayed in the Armory (along with
battle-axes suitable to be wielded by Mels, Peter the Great's boots,
and the stuffed moth-eaten horses of the Czars), this one, not much
larger than my hand, was of a memorable simplicity: it did not rest
in a filigreed cradle of gold or a nest woven of silver twigs, or stand
atop a finely detailed pedestal of precious stone, but was complete
in itself. The egg was of white opal, which fired magnificently in
the room's soft light, glinting pink and blue and orange. Six narrow bands of black lacquer encircled the egg at its widest circum-
ference, each band studded with roses made of topaz petals and
emerald leaves. The egg's smaller end was capped with a crown of
chased gold. The larger end contained an oculus, inset in a field
of platinum, bordered by a double row of blue diamonds.

"Is it real?" Sonya asked, but none of us were able to answer or even talk. She was so enraptured by her husband's objet
d'art that she appeared to be on the verge of tears. Petrenko no
longer seemed to be breathing. Even Debalov leaned over his
superior's shoulder, to see what fascinated the rest of us.

"Shiny," he said, as might a rat or crow, were it capable of
speech.

"Pasha, Max," Dmitry said, raising the egg, his hands miraculously steady as he held it before our eyes, "you two first. Here,
look through the opening at this end. Go on."

I could not believe what I saw when I stared through the
oculus. The lower half of the egg's interior was carpeted in gleaming mother-of-pearl; the upper half was lined with sapphire, inset
with nearly a hundred diamond chips, appearing as a cloudless
night sky. In the heart of the egg was a single ruby cut into the
shape of a round red-sheeted bed. Tousled blankets of salmon-
colored coral dripped from its edges onto the nacre below. Two
ivory figures lay on the bed, a man and a woman, both naked. They
were frozen in the act of performing mutual oral pleasure upon
each other, the woman above, the man below. Never before or since
have I seen visual art which so perfectly meshed contrary aspects
of the human spirit—the sublime and the ridiculous—into a single
expression which combined, as effortlessly, highest art and lowest kitsch.

"With a magnifying glass," Dmitry said, "you can see that the detailing of the ivory lovers is worthy of Chinese masters."

"Where in God's name did you find such a thing?" I asked. Petrenko was left wordless, a pleasant state in which to have him.

"I can't be too forthright as regards its recent history," Dmitry said, allowing Sonya to peer through the opening. She gasped, seeing the tableau within. "Everything is for sale in Russia. I was in the right place, at the right time, when the offer was made to me."

"I am no expert, but I see no mark," Petrenko said, finally speaking. "How can you be sure this pornography is by Fabergé and not a contemporary artist?"

"No one alive is capable of such craftsmanship," Dmitry said. "Believe me, it's genuine."

"What can you tell us about its provenance?" I asked.

"High officials of Czar Nicholas's court intended it to be a present for the Czar's beloved uncle, Edward the Seventh of Great Britain, for his sixty-ninth birthday," Dmitry said. "A worldly man, and a notorious appreciator of womanly charms. Being a man of religion, the Czar obviously never approved the design himself."

"We should all walk as closely with God as he did," Petrenko said. The two of them lifted their eyes toward the ceiling, ignoring the fact that it had not done Czar Nicholas much good to be so accompanied. Still, their piety was admirable.

"Edward died before it could be presented to him," Dmitry said, replacing the egg in its box, rewrapping the protective layers. "Afterward, apparently, it was thought best to hide it from the Czar. Yusupov, Rasputin's assassin, seems to have had possession of the egg for a time, before the Revolution. Afterward, who can say?" He shrugged. "One million dollars, I paid. A bargain."

"No wonder you don't have my money," Petrenko said, but Dmitry's next statement kept him from saying anything else.

"In the West it could bring—what? Five, ten, twenty times that," he said. "Hold on to it until I can give you your money, later this week. I promise you."

Dmitry placed the box in Petrenko's hands. The idea that this gorgeous, ridiculous egg would be even temporarily in the possession of such a fool broke my heart. I feared I would never see it again; and hereafter, there could be no object in this world I'd want as badly.

"It's immoral and unwholesome," Petrenko said, once more gazing through the oculus, "but desirable. Very well, Gubin, I'll hold on to it. We both know this treasure wouldn't be easy to sell, I think, or else you wouldn't hand it over so cheerfully. You'd better have hard money for me by the end of the week."

"You'll have it," said Dmitry. "I swear."

Petrenko and Debalov left not long after, their anger mollified. When Dmitry recovered, he went without speaking to his treasure room. In his absence I sat next to Sonya on the sofa, close enough that we could speak in confidence, far enough apart to allow us a moment to reconsider before giving in too heedlessly to temptation. "You told him about Tanya?"

"This morning, when he woke up," she said. "He didn't seem surprised."

"No?" Already I had begun to think it likely that Dmitry was responsible for calling Nadze's attention to my wife and her firm, prior to the feast; had he also known of their investment in the crematorium? Certainly I had no reason to believe he knew in advance she would be kidnapped (should I say, had no proof), but that was a possibility as well. If I came upon evidence that he was directly involved in her kidnapping, he would regret it, if only for a short time. "What did he do when you got home?"

"He lay down for a while after medicating his tongue. That's a horrible burn, Max. What did they do to him? He wouldn't tell me."

"It's not pleasant to recount," I said. "Maybe later. What else?"

She didn't appreciate my thoughtfulness but didn't press me. "After an hour or so he got up and went to his treasure room. Around nine the phone rang; he got it. I don't know who called. Then he returned to his room and stayed there until midnight. Then he came out and went to bed."

"That was all?"

She nodded. "What's going to happen, Max?"

"With luck we'll go over, Dmitry will make amends, I'll tell Tanya to hand over title to that crematorium and she'll be released, his partners will be released—"

"His partners?"

"He didn't tell you that either? The Georgians kidnapped them as well, holding them to give him an extra reason to do as they tell him."

"My God," she said. "What if you don't have luck?"

"I have to believe we will. They're dangerous criminals, not inhuman monsters. Nadze seems to like me enough to listen to what I have to say, as long as I tell him the truth. That was your husband's problem; telling the truth is an act contrary to his nature."

We heard Dmitry coughing; instantly, I stood and walked to the far side of the room. He emerged from the hallway carrying a brushed-chrome briefcase and pushing a medium-sized metal trunk along the floor with his foot. "You'll want to check these, I suppose," he said to me.

"That's what I've been told to do." Opening the briefcase, I discovered that it was packed tight with crisp hundred-dollar bills. I quickly flipped through a selection of wrapped stacks to be sure he'd not interspersed genuine notes with sheets of blank paper. Then I pointed to the trunk. "White gold?"

"Look for yourself if you don't trust me."

I decided that comment warranted no response. Taking my handkerchief from my jacket pocket I wrapped it around my hand, opened the lid, and saw dozens of glassine bags sealed tight, stuffed plump as goslings with gray-white powder. I didn't check the purity of the powder; I had no desire to put my fingerprints on those bags. Closing the lid, going to the door, I called in one of my guards and directed him to carry the trunk down for us when we departed.

"Don't leave the apartment for any reason," I told Sonya. "My guards will remain on duty."

"I'll be back," Dmitry said, and we left. I gave my guards directions to shoot on sight anyone whom they perceived to be posing a threat. This was not a time to be overly generous in giving strangers the benefit of the doubt. After putting the cases in my car I took the wheel; we drove the short distance to the Georgians' house.

"I had better leave their place with my wife." He made no response. "They kidnapped her, you know," I reminded him.

"You seem suitably concerned," he said, and before I could ask why he made such an insulting remark, he pointed to his mouth. "Can't talk. Tongue hurts."

"The pain must come and go."

He chose not to risk further unnecessary injury and said no more, even as the guards admitted us through the gates of the Georgian stronghold. We parked and got out; Dmitry carried the briefcase and I half-dragged, half-carried the trunk as we walked to the house. Mels greeted us no less cheerfully than he had done the day before.

"Welcome, friends. Please, allow us to relieve you of your burden." Two of his stockier Kazakhs took the cases from us, lugging them out of the entrance foyer.

"Hello, Dima, Max. May I offer you a drink?" Nadze asked, walking in from the antechamber. The woman with weightless breasts again took our outerwear. Our host wore a navy blue suit as well cut as the one he'd worn the day before; I noticed that not all the buttons on his jacket sleeves were buttoned, evidence of the very finest tailoring. He shook our hands as if we were old friends.

"Vodka," Dmitry told him. "A large glass."

"You can have a flagon, if you'd like." I declined his offer, seeing no reason to celebrate until this deed was done and my wife was safe again in our apartment. Nadze signaled Mels, who dashed off and almost immediately returned with a half-filled tumbler. "Right on time. That pleases me. Dima, you'll be happy to know we've already hired new parties who will satisfy our shipping needs."

"My subcontractors were responsible for thwarting our mutual goals, as you know," Dmitry said. "So be it." Had he already been drinking that morning? His mood was most unpleasant, and—I perceived—not solely because of the pain in his tongue. Nadze gave him a look the charitable might have called a smile. "We've brought you the money and the material that you were kind enough to advance. Allow me to prove I'm a man of my word."

"Remarkable theorems need remarkable proof," Nadze said. "Follow me."

We walked with him through a door that led off the entrance foyer, the same exit the Kazakhs used when they carried off the cases. Mels trailed us, offering no overt threat. Nadze guided us down a seemingly endless hallway whose walls were paneled from ceiling to floor in carved, burnished teak. At the end of the passage was an unmarked door, which Mels unlocked. "After you," he said. As we crossed the room's threshold I saw at once that its walls were shrouded with black canvas. The floor was pinkish marble. Unlike the public rooms, this chamber had no exquisite moldings, no ornate plaster decorations; there was nothing in the room save for the briefcase, the trunk, and three wooden chairs. Mikhail, Tibor, and Vlad sat in the chairs, but they could not rise to greet us; they were bound, gagged, and lashed to their seats with ropes. Seeing us, they looked as children might look, glimpsing their New Year's tree yet still fearful that the presents beneath the glittering boughs held naught but stones. They struggled to no avail. Their faces were bruised and lacerated. Mikhail's cheekbones appeared to have been crushed; Tibor's right eye was swollen shut; Vlad's nostrils bled freely—I am no forensic specialist, so it was impossible to guess how recently they had been slit.

"What is this, Lavrenty?" Dmitry asked. "You swore you wouldn't hurt them."

"Wouldn't kill them," Nadze replied. "So how about it, Max? Has Dima behaved himself?"

"I think he has," I said, deeply unnerved by the condition of Dmitry's partners. "Where is my wife? You haven't treated her like this, have you?"

"Why should we, Max? We know what she has to offer us." He squatted, opened the briefcase, and fanned the bills with nimble banker's fingers. "The count appears to be right. Very, very good."

There was a knock at the door. Mels opened it, looking out to see who was there before turning back to Nadze. "Your visitor has arrived."

"Marvelous!" he said, arising with shocking ease, considering his weight. "Dima, here is someone who has been especially looking forward to meeting you."

The man who entered was as tall as Mels but carried only half as much weight. His walk was a fluid shuffle, the gait of an animated scarecrow. He wore a trench coat over a gray single-breasted suit cut in the soft-shouldered American style, glasses with small round tortoiseshell frames, and wing-tipped shoes so buffed that they appeared to be made of brown glass. His black hair stood straight up on his head, as if he lived in a state of perpetual fear. Judging from his skin's pasty whiteness, he had no blood.

"Valentin Samoilovich Bok, of New York City, formerly of Tiflis," Mels announced before leaving the room.

Nadze warmly embraced the new arrival. Dmitry's brow was wet, and his own color was not as ruddy as it had been, minutes before. "Valentin, this gentleman is Maxim Alexeich Borodin, and this is Dmitry Mikhailovich Gubin. Max, Dima, when I called Valentin to tell him what had happened, he decided to come to Moscow and be assured that our problems worked out to everyone's satisfaction. How was your trip, my old friend?"

Bok ran a long-fingered hand through his brushy pompadour. "Fucking miserable," he said. "To get out undetected I first had to go to Toronto. Then to Helsinki, then here. Fucking airplanes! Poison air, that stewardess gestapo, mind-destroying videos. You know what they gave us to eat? You know?" Nadze shook his head. "Quiche *soup*. Was supposed to be quiche, but it didn't set. I almost threw it in the girl's face when she served me. Seventeen fucking hours trapped in that hellbound cartridge of death."

"You traveled under your name?"

"Certainly not," Bok said. "Yours."

"Excellent, excellent," Nadze said, lowering his head as if anticipating—hoping—it would be struck. "How is Brighton Beach?"

"Better than two years ago, certainly. Republican administrations favor the small businessman." He looked us over as if measuring us for our coffins. Bok's eyes were porcine, mud-brown, as bereft of soul as an animal's. "I am very badly affected by jet lag, so let us settle these matters as quickly as we can. Where is the material? Is everything as it should be?"

"Let's take a look." Nadze threw open the lid of the trunk. "At a glance, this appears to be what we hoped to find."

"So it seems." Bok took from his pocket a switchblade knife and flicked it open. Nadze extracted a bag from the middle of the trunk, several rows below the top layer. He handed the bag to Bok, who sliced it open with his knife. Sticking his forefinger into the gritty gray-whiteness, he drew it out and touched the tip to his tongue, closing his eyes as might a wine connoisseur, testing an untried vintage. "That's it," he said. "Try another." Nadze prepared to take another bag from the heart of the trunk when his associate suggested otherwise. "From the top, this time."

"You think so?" Nadze asked; Bok nodded. Dmitry polished off his vodka in one gulp, a choking draft that seemed not to trouble him. His eyes grew lusterless; they were no longer bright enough to even be glass.

"I'm so surprised to see you here," he said to the Georgian. "I didn't expect to be meeting you in this way."

"Nor did I," said Bok, touching his finger to his tongue, checking the second bag and frowning. "Much of importance depends upon this." He handed the bag over to his subordinate, who also took a taste and similarly frowned.

"Oh, Dima," Nadze said, shaking his head. "The workings of your mind are beyond me."

"My friends, what are you saying?" Dmitry asked.

"This is fine quality," Bok said, holding up the first bag he'd opened; then he pointed to the second bag. "That is talcum powder."

"With quinine, possibly, or other extraneous additive," Nadze said. "Very gritty. Almost dusty. Nonetheless, I must tell you I am very impressed, Dima. Most people would have placed the genuine material in the top layer and hidden the fraudulent underneath. Very cunning."

"What are you saying?" Dmitry asked. I found it hard but not impossible to believe he'd tried to swindle them again so soon.

"You must not have sold it; we'd have heard of such a sizable amount coming onto the market," Nadze said. Bok continued to check the bags, his frown deepening into a look of purest disgust. "Obviously, you've decided to hold on to our material a little longer. Did you believe we wouldn't find you out?"

"Are you telling me that some of this isn't genuine?" Dmitry asked, his expression as guileless as before. "I don't understand. Everything is exactly as it was when I took possession. Do you think there was possibly a substitution beforehand?"

"Not a chance," Bok said, dropping the twelfth packet he'd gutted back into the trunk. "Every bag you were given was one hundred percent pure."

"Ninety," Nadze said, gently correcting his superior. "What are you telling us? Are you claiming someone stole our genuine material while it was in your possession and replaced it with whatever this is—baby laxative, milk sugar, whatever—right under your very nose?"

"That must be what happened," Dmitry said, gripping his glass so tightly that I thought it might shatter in his hand.

"It didn't," Bok said. "Try again."

"Perhaps they know," Dmitry said, looking at his associates, who struggled mightily to shake their heads; they knew what he was next preparing to claim. "Untie them. Let's discuss this like gentlemen, and not movie gangsters."

For some time I'd detected an unusual sound, that of pebbles rattling in a can; I ascertained the source. Dmitry's associates trembled so vigorously, with such constancy, that their chairs' metal-tipped legs were beating a rhythm of fear against the marble floor.

"Gentlemen?" Bok repeated. "Are you insane?"

"They might have told you anything," Dmitry continued, pointing at his battered partners. "I'll be frank. This distrust of my word sickens me."

"Dima, your friends here have told us repeatedly that you were in sole possession of the material from the time it left our hands," said Nadze. "We know they're telling the truth. What are you telling us?"

Dmitry shook like a cornered dog before he finally found the will within himself to recover. He continued holding the glass tightly in front of him, as if certain it would prove to be a useful weapon. "Max, you prepared it for me," he said. "Were you aware of any problems you didn't tell me about?"

For an instant I couldn't believe what I was hearing. This was too unbelievable—and I don't have to remind you that I do not live my life always with unwavering faith in the benevolence of my fellowman. There was no one, evidently, he would fail to indict in attempting to distance himself from his own unforgivable crimes. "What are you claiming, you lying bastard?"

Nadze, I hoped, knew better than to believe Dmitry; the expression on Bok's face as he looked me over, however, was not at all comforting. "I warned you, Valentin," Nadze said. "Dima, are there abler fabulists than you anywhere in Russia? In the world? You're saying you didn't prepare the material for us?"

"I don't understand, Max," Dmitry said. "Do you have amnesia? You and Sonya packed the trunk for me last night, while I recovered from my injury."

"Last night?" I repeated; never before had I actually witnessed anyone attempting to rewrite history while it occurred. "*Sonya?*"

"My wife," he said. "You know her well, Max. You know her much better than I would have ever imagined."

At once it was clear to me who had called him, the night before, and what she told him. Dmitry bore a maddeningly un-emotional look on his face as he made his softly voiced accusations. The conversation we'd had at the Metropole returned to me; I supposed he'd taken my advice and decided not to let his passions get away with him when at last he discovered and confronted his wife's lover. "I don't know what she told you, but you know I was not over there last night," I said to him. "Stop trying to save your worthless skin."

Bok's irritation plainly grew in an almost geometric progression as he watched our exchange. With great dismay, I noticed that he wore something beneath his trench coat which, judging from its shape, was highly suggestive of powerful weaponry. I wondered how badly jet lag affected him.

"*Please!*" Nadze shouted, but then spoke as calmly and pleasantly as before, asking another question. "Dima, are you saying Max replaced our genuine material with this substitute last night without your knowledge?"

"Obviously, this is what happened," he said, feeling more assured. "He and my wife often make personal arrangements that don't involve me."

Nadze shook his head sadly, slowly, then grinned so broadly I could count his gold molars. "Dima, it may bother you, but it doesn't bother me if Max is fucking your wife. *I* would like to fuck your wife. Valentin, if you were to see her, you would want to fuck her too, I promise you." I couldn't decide which one of us Nadze most wanted to disturb by so freely relating his desires. "Let me be truthful, Dima. If I were your wife, and given the choice between you and Max, it wouldn't be you," he continued. "Yesterday afternoon after leaving our celebration, Max drove his charming office assistant directly to her apartment. Then he drove to his own apartment, where he stayed until he left this morning at nine-thirty. Our people watched his building closely and continually, taking care not to be seen by his people. Max went nowhere else last night, certainly not to your apartment." Nadze walked over to Dmitry and placed a hand on his shoulder. "One more try? How about it?"

For what seemed an eternity—half a minute, I suspect—

Dmitry tried to produce the words his lips formed, but made not even a mouse's squeak. He rubbed the tumbler he held as if its feel soothed him in his time of need. "Then he must have done it when he came over this morning," he said, holding truth at arm's length until the last. "The criminal stands before you, can't you see that?"

"Yes," said Bok, bringing out from beneath his coat a sawed-off pump-action shotgun.

"Valentin, don't—"

Shoving it beneath Dmitry's nose, Bok fired both barrels into his face. The result was not unlike what happens when children pop a water-filled balloon—would it had been water that splattered the room. Bok's shiny shoes must have had slippery soles; the recoil sent him tumbling backward, and he almost fell. I hit the floor hard, the instant I saw Bok's weapon appear; Nadze leapt away, again demonstrating that nimbleness so often possessed by stout men. At first I feared the blast's concussion had punctured my eardrums, but by the time I stood up my hearing had already returned to me. Dmitry's body lay face upward—no longer much of a face, or even a head, for that matter—a full meter from where he had been standing. Behind him, the black canvas looked as if vandals splashed the contents of a paint can against it. Dmitry still clutched his glass, although it was now no more than a handful of bloody shards. I felt a pat on my shoulder and turned to see our host behind me, once more on his feet.

"He didn't suffer," Nadze opined. Bok took two new shells from his pocket and reloaded his shotgun before turning to confront Dmitry's three associates. "Valentin, I think maybe you should have a calming drink before—"

"You know where our material is?" Bok screamed, not bothering to remove the gag that blocked Mikhail's mouth before aiming the gun at his nose.

"Don't, Valentin," Nadze said, sticking his fingers in his ears. "The noise."

A moot point: in an instant, Mikhail and Tibor found themselves in a state resembling Dmitry's; I need not trouble you further with specific details. After reloading once more, Bok was courteous enough to allow Vlad to join his associates, so that the quartet could remain in partnership even in the afterlife. Then he circled around and jammed his gun's barrels against my own brow.

The metal was so hot it seared my skin, but I didn't move a centimeter. "Speak," he said. I shut my eyes, certain I had no more than another second of life to relish.

"Valentin, no!" Nadze shouted. "Not him. How will he help us if he's dead?" Bok didn't take the gun from my forehead, but neither did he fire. His glasses had fogged over with tension and rage. "Put down the gun and allow me to handle this. Put it down, Valentin. Put it down."

Bok removed his thumb from the triggers and lowered the gun until it pointed toward the floor. "Yes, it would be stupid to kill you."

"I agree." My voice sounded unnaturally high-pitched as it eked free of my throat.

"Max and I will have a frank discussion of the problem," Nadze said, placing a hand lightly on his associate's shoulder, steering him away from me, taking his gun. "Everything will be taken care of. My God, Valentin, look at you. Look at your clothes." Bok stared down and studied the front of his jacket, his pants, and his coat, all of which were soaked through and dripping red. "I hope that wasn't an expensive suit."

Bok took off his glasses and rubbed off their fog on an unstained portion of shirtsleeve. "I get them wholesale."

"Probably you should go clean up," Nadze suggested. "Long day." He then turned his gaze to the field of battle around him. "If you would, Valentin, send in Mels and some of his men to take care of this."

"I'll do that," Bok said, turning on his heel so briskly he almost slipped in the blood.

The suddenly pervasive smell hit us both at the same time; I thought I was going to vomit, and Nadze's face took on the pallor of a dead fish. "We should continue our discussion in more pleasant surroundings," he said. Arm in arm, we left the room, passing Mels and several mop-and-bucket men, and walked down the hall. My forehead stung painfully, and I wanted to get to a mirror and see how badly I'd been burned; even so, I was glad to still have a forehead. "Valentin is an emotional man, Max. He has been under much stress lately, and I have heard that living in New York only exacerbates a bad temper. Please excuse his outburst. It was quite unpleasant, however necessary it might have been."

"Is he always like this?"

Nadze shrugged. "He hates to fly."

"What have you done with my wife?"

"Max, I want to be wholeheartedly honest. I think you have a reasonable sense of the world as it is. You have no false delusions of either grandeur or innocence, unlike Dima. I enjoy working with capable businessmen such as yourself; you understand the opportunities life can offer. We can work together."

"I try to be realistic," I said; no matter how much I focused my attention on what he was saying, I couldn't keep my arms from shaking, and my nausea had not yet left me. "Look, I would like to leave here today with my wife. Leave safely. What is the problem? What do you want from us?"

"We need to discuss this situation Dima left us with," Nadze said. "First things first. It's a shame that reliable men invariably have to clean up the mess the incompetent leave behind."

"You expect me to resolve Dmitry's affairs?"

"Who else do I have left to turn to? No matter what he claimed, I believe you when you say you were not involved in his final scheme. If it was a matter concerning us alone, this unfortunate situation would not be as problematic, but what can you do? You can't change history."

The route we took this time led us into the dining hall, which appeared much larger when we were the only ones present. The leather-covered walls kept our voices from echoing through the emptiness, as we took seats (neither of us suddenly able to walk any farther—a delayed physiological reaction, I'm sure) at the now-cleared table and continued our conversation. "I can't speak for Valentin, but I fear he may have found Dima's accusation more believable than I do. He's not had direct experience with our late schemer until this afternoon. You understand what this means, of course. By helping me, you will be helping yourself. Valentin will have no need to concern himself with you, once all is as it should be again."

"And how am I to arrange that?" I asked. "Do I have to remind you that, from my point of view, my wife needs the most help at present?"

"Of course. All I am asking is that you bring us the material Dima chose not to deliver. Bring it here tomorrow, at this same time."

"I have no more idea than you do as to where it might be."

"Sure, you know that; I know that. Valentin doesn't know that. In any case, you're in a better position to find out more quickly than we are. I have complete faith in your resourcefulness, Max."

"I'll do my best to find it."

"Your all, Max," he said, for the first time looking at me as he had looked at Dmitry. "Do your all."

"May we please discuss my wife's situation?" I asked. "Why was it necessary to kidnap her?"

"We were informed she might not be willing to listen to us with an open mind." Informed by whom? Dmitry, no doubt. "Also, considering the task we assigned you yesterday, it occurred to me that it would not be a bad idea to make sure she was at hand, in the event anything went wrong. Collateral, you know. As it turns out, that was a good idea, though certainly not through failure on your part."

"Why can you and I not discuss this and work out an agreement now?" I asked. "Obviously, I'm standing before you with my pants down. Tell me what it is you want; let me arrange the details. There is no need to keep my wife prisoner. She has done nothing to hurt you or your business."

"Maybe, maybe not." Nadze extended his hands in a gesture of helplessness. "But first things first. I'm afraid she'll have to stay where she is for now, for our peace of mind. We'll solve Dima's problems; then we'll solve her problems."

"Solving my problems in both cases," I noted.

"You could look at it that way."

"It's hard for me not to think of Dmitry's associates." Even as I referred to them, the memory of the horrific aftermath returned to me with such force that I felt my stomach convulse and barely controlled a fresh onslaught of nausea. "You understand how concerned I am about her safety."

"Don't worry, Max, you have my assurance she won't be harmed. As long as you carry out the assignment with which we've entrusted you, she'll be fine."

"Why should I believe what you tell me?"

"For the same reason we trust you enough to let you leave," Nadze said. "*Nichevo.* I think we understand our mutual concerns. Would it make you feel better to speak to her? She could tell you herself how she is being treated."

"Why can't I see her?"

"It would seem an act of kindness to let you do that, but in truth we've found that in these cases visual contact tends to have the opposite effect. Very disruptive to the smooth process for which we strive. Follow me, let us go to the front foyer. We'll call her from there."

We left the dining hall, passing through the antechamber and past that grotesque fountain. Its recorded music, thankfully, was not blaring that afternoon. "Max, did you realize that, had we not caught him, Dima intended to leave the country last night?"

"Seriously?" Nadze nodded. "Where was he going?"

"His pilot was unwilling to tell us. After several of Mels's men spent some time with him, I'm afraid he was no longer able to tell us." He shook his head. "I'm sure you've confronted the problem of overzealous staff many times in your own business. But without question, Dima planned to make a getaway, weighed down with stolen loot."

"With or without his wife?"

Nadze looked at me and smiled. "She didn't tell you?"

"Of course not," I said, at once grasping the inference he could have made. "Why should—"

"A ribald joke," he said. "Forgive me, Max. I have no idea if she was to go with him or not. Perhaps you should ask her, if you're curious."

As we stepped into the entrance foyer I saw the young woman who oversaw winter wraps; standing nearby, holding the coat she'd already given him, flirting with her as if he had all the time in the world to waste, was the last person I expected to see. Nevertheless, I must have succeeded in hiding my astonished reaction.

"What now?" Nadze asked him; the sharp tone of his voice made me think that he, too, did not plan upon finding Tanya's employee Iosif lurking on the premises, at least where he could be seen.

"I was getting my coat," he said, his eyes flitting back and forth as he tried to avoid my cold glare. For once he wasn't wearing his gloves, and I saw the gallery of tattoos on his hands. "That's all."

What was this so-called colleague of my wife, this marriage despoiler, this amoral betrayer doing here with these Georgians? Clearly, Dmitry was not Nadze's informant; this sneaking cat's-paw was the one who exposed my wife's secrets to the mob. One way or the other I would discover what his game was. Neither Iosif nor I admitted to recognizing the other, and Nadze did not see the need to introduce us—I suspect he realized we might have already met.

"Just a moment, I'll have her on the line for you." He lifted the receiver from a phone on the wall and spoke into it without dialing a number; I gathered that Tanya was being held somewhere in the house. "Put her on," he told whoever answered, and then handed it over to me. "There you are, Max."

"Tanya?" I asked. Nadze was courteous enough to step with Mels to the far side of the entrance foyer; the young woman stayed close by, but it was plain to see her attention was elsewhere. "Tanya, my precious. It's me, my small bird, it's Max. Are you all right? What have they done to you?"

"What have you gotten me into?" she asked in reply, shouting at me with such vehemence as to start anew the ringing in my ears. "Why has this happened? What have you done?"

"Have they hurt you?"

"I wasn't physically molested by the brutes, not that you'd have noticed. You are such an idiot, I think you'd sleep through the end of the world. When they came for me I shouted, I kicked; did you hear a thing? Of course not."

"My pigeon—"

"What are you doing to get me out of here?"

"Everything I can." Our conversation proved difficult, as I suspected it would, but for reasons entirely other than those I'd guessed. There was much I wanted to ask that I couldn't bring up here, where I could be so easily overheard—notably, whether or not, the night before, she had called Dmitry and told him who Sonya's lover was. "So far they won't discuss specifics, and now I have to solve a problem Dmitry caused by his mindless actions."

"My God, let him deal with his own problems. Just get me out of here."

"I would, but he's dead."

"Is that your problem?"

"Tanya, please," I said, angered that she would so berate me while I was trying to assure her safety and secure her release. "It is now. But it'll be settled by tomorrow, and then I can get you out. Then we'll be together again, my love."

"That depends," she said. "What have you decided?"

"Decided?" It was distressingly clear that even in the midst of her grueling experience, our domestic problems were uppermost in her mind. Perhaps they were not treating her so badly, after all. "When have I had time to think about it?"

"Find time or you'll be sorry," she said. Delightful, marvelous; I was being pressured by the kidnappers and threatened by the captive.

"Listen, I'm going to tell Alla what has happened. I may need her help."

"Why bring her into this?"

"It's why you were kidnapped," I said, nearly shouting. "That's what I was trying to tell you last night, and you wouldn't listen to me. These Georgians want to take over your interest in the crematorium, and I intend to tell them they can have it."

"That's not a holding of yours," she said. "Why do they want it?"

"A new source of income. Same reason as you, maybe; why did you want it? You should never have gotten involved in such an enterprise as that place. I've been there; it's a criminal business, no question."

"Don't blame me for that," she said. "Iosif recommended that we make the investment."

Another piece of the puzzle thrown into my lap; this news did not surprise me, as it might have minutes earlier. This would be something else I should be sure to discuss with Alla. "My angel, I'll have you out of there by tomorrow night."

"All right, Max. Do what you can as quick as you can. And make up your mind."

"I will, my small dove. I love you."

My wife made no response, but as I have told you she has never easily expressed any emotion save anger. She hung up, or someone hung up for her, and I handed the phone back to Nadze.

"You see, Max?" he said. "As I told you, she is perfectly fine. As long as this problem is taken care of to our satisfaction, she'll stay that way. What do you think? We are neither ogres nor mindless brutes," he said, slapping me on the back and motioning to the young woman to give me my coat. "Go. Do your duty. We'll see you tomorrow."

8

Sonya took the news of her husband's death with greater equanimity than I might have predicted, but at heart she was a woman who had no difficulty accepting the whims of fate. In the early evening we sat in her kitchen, discussing what had happened that day over glasses of garlic vodka. "Dmitry must have left here this morning thinking it a workable plan," I said. "He could exact revenge against me for having an affair with you, feign innocence of what had been done, and then be given the opportunity again to either bring them the drugs or try and make his escape."

"You think it could have worked?"

I shook my head. "How could anyone ever believe Dmitry to be innocent of anything?" We spoke freely; I'd stopped long enough at my apartment on the way here to make sure that all was still secure and retrieve my sweeper; a hasty check showed their apartment wasn't bugged either. "He did manage to convince this Bok of my involvement, I'm certain. That may prove to be a problem, I don't know. Evidently their men stopped following me, once I came here this morning. Thank God they didn't see me with Petrenko."

Once more I saw that dead-eyed look on Sonya's face. I took her hand in mine, and she encircled me with her arms. As we embraced she gripped me as if she were drowning and wished to drag me down with her into the depths. I should be honest with you and admit that at that moment, feeling my koshka's breasts pressing warm against me, the clasp of her arms round my neck, I knew the decision Tanya expected me to make, even as our lives were at the mercy of these Georgian murderers, might possibly not be the one she expected or wanted. It is true I wanted my dear wife to be freed, but I should note that there are two words for truth in Russian—*pravda* and *istina*—depending on the kind of truth meant; the former implies justice, while the latter bespeaks a faithfulness to being. My newly accepted truth, that I could no longer say I wanted to stay with my wife, was *istina*, truth that could be neither transformed nor denied; justice had nothing to do with it. The problem was, I needed to stay with her. That was *istina*, too.

"If Dmitry had pulled this swindle off, what do you think he'd have done with me?" she asked. "Considering that he found out about us?"

"Had he pulled it off on Monday, nothing." But after today, had he made his escape and left me at the mercy of the Georgians, would he have had her killed? For certainly he would not have murdered her himself. It didn't matter how much he'd blustered about liquidating Sonya and her lover that evening at the Metropole. (Had he been testing me? Had he already guessed, and Tanya did nothing more than confirm?) Ultimately, he was too adept at subjugating emotion for his personal betterment to allow himself to commit such an act. But were someone else to pull the trigger or wield the knife or lower the fist, I don't think, afterward, he would have had difficulties enjoying a night's refreshing sleep. "Otherwise, I don't know. Probably he'd have gone ahead and left you behind, as planned. Then he'd go and live off the fruits of his thievery."

"Did he beg for mercy?"

"If he'd had the opportunity, I'm sure he would have," I said. "It happened too fast. I thought I was done for myself. Bok had his gun right against my skull."

That was perhaps the sixth time I'd reminded her of my painful, disfiguring wound; I appreciated the comfort she gave me. "Does it still hurt?" she asked, carefully touching the burn on my forehead, a reddish-brown brand shaped like a number eight knocked on its side, the symbol of infinity.

"Somewhat, but that's not important. I have to find out where he's hidden these drugs."

"There could only be one place, don't you think?" She stared through the kitchen door into the hall, toward his treasure room.

"If they're not there, I'm good as dead. Can you get it open?"

She rolled her eyes, as if hearing a fretful child's plea for treats. "Certainly he never trusted me enough to give me a key."

"Let's have a look." We got up and walked down the hall. At first glance it appeared that we would easily gain entry. His secret room was secured by a wooden door, and although it was locked I foresaw no difficulties in forcing it open. "Bring me a knife, a thick one, not too long," I told Sonya; she returned to the kitchen, coming back shortly with a medium-sized weapon.

"It works for bread," she told me. I examined the blade and handle.

"This should be simple, if luck is with us," I said, sliding the knife point first between the door and its surrounding frame, a few centimeters above the lock. It went in without much difficulty. Jiggling it downward, I eased it through until enough of the metal was inserted to allow me to pry the knife backward without snapping off the blade. With surprisingly slight effort, I popped the lock. The door swung open, revealing a massive steel barrier set into reinforced inner walls. The three combination locks I saw assured me that if I was to gain entry I would require the service of professionals.

"My God," she said. I tried the handle, in case he'd left it open that morning—he hadn't. "He must have had this thing installed when we renovated the apartment, before we were married. I had no idea this was here, Max. I've only seen the outer door."

"I'll call Arteim," I said. "He knows many capable people."

"Max, meet Suleiman," Arteim said, introducing me to our safecracker. No more than an hour had passed since I told him what we needed, and as ever he acted with alacrity. "The master of masters."

Suleiman slipped off his padded mittens, and I offered my hand in a spirit of good fellowship. He drew back, as if from a flame.

"Please, pardon my rudeness," he said, speaking in a barely audible monotone. "The skin. Professional sensitivity must at all costs be preserved."

Arteim handed me Suleiman's business card; it stated that he was employed as a consultant for the St. Petersburg–based firm of Complex Symbiotic Partners. As to what either he or his firm actually did, I can only theorize that their partnerships were impressively complex and usefully symbiotic. From a distance he judged to be acceptable I examined his master's instruments, which were soft and pink as a baby's ass. His hands were his sole memorable aspect—the rest of him may as well have been momentarily solidified vapor; he was, in fact, so nondescript in both dress and physicality that he faded into nothingness in the mind even as you looked at him. Considering his profession, I imagined this to be an asset.

"Suleiman can read *Pravda* blindfolded," Arteim told us.

"Who can't?"

"No, I mean by placing his fingers on the paper, he can tell you what the words say, literally, without looking."

"Ink is palpable, against the surface," Suleiman explained. "The fingers are never fooled." Sonya smiled, hearing this, but I tried not to reveal my disbelief. The only people supposedly endowed with such powers of whom I had heretofore been aware were of the same ilk as the voyants and shamen, faith healers, spoon benders, and coin levitators who, before new laws were enacted, appeared so regularly on television, pleading for donations. I remember seeing on *Vremya* an old peasant woman wearing a bag over her head, demonstrating her ability to feel through the soles of her feet the colors of the rug upon which she stood. Such so-called miracles of the spirit world leave in awe our country's citizens, whose noble leaders have never been able to tell right from wrong, even with eyes wide open. But as long as Suleiman could do the job, I did not care how he perused his daily journals.

"The room is this way," I said, leading them through the hall to the hidden chamber. "This first door, no problem," I told him, drawing it open to expose the steel vault beyond. "The second, a problem. Can you break in?"

"If God is with us," he said, kneeling, examining the three combination locks. "You've tried the handle?"

"How stupid do you think we are?"

"When I first professionally employed my abilities, you'd be surprised how often I found myself struggling to open unlocked doors," he said, taking hold of the handle himself to judge its immobility. "I learned to inquire beforehand." Having chastised me, Suleiman pressed his ear flat against the metal and carefully twirled each dial several notches in turn, first left, then right. "Five minutes."

"That's all?"

He nodded. I noticed that when he wasn't using his hands he held them away from his sides so that, in the interim, they touched nothing. "Silence will be helpful," he said, and then waited, watching, until we returned to the living room before re-applying his fingers to the dials. Sonya sat on the sofa, Arteim and I in chairs. My seat, I realized, was the one in which Dmitry had been beaten into that morning, before he presented Petrenko with the egg. I repositioned the chair so I could keep an eye on Suleiman's maneuvers. Crouching before the door, he gently caressed its locks with his hands as if they were the most tender parts of a woman.

"What's he doing?" Sonya asked me, whispering so softly I could tell what she said only by reading her lips.

"Silence, *please!*" Suleiman called out. We obeyed his command and so stared at one another as if we were strangers, introduced at a party but forbidden to speak. For a while I watched him work but finally grew bored. I shifted in my seat to better view the collection of household treasures in the glass-fronted wall unit. There were two traditional *matryoshkas* of simple design, fading postcards of gymnasts from the 1980 Olympics, a small framed portrait of Gogol, a ceramic cup with the cartoon character Garfield découpaged on the side, a white faience mermaid with pink-tipped breasts, a gaily stenciled tin wind-up bird, a tiny stuffed dog, red nylon banners from Moscow University machine-embroidered in gold thread, an empty bottle of Chanel perfume (number 19), a pale-yellow bottle of Advocaat, a painted wooden spoon, and a glass paperweight in the shape of St. Basil's Cathedral. All Russians, no matter their social strata, keep prized bric-a-brac on display; the emotion stirred when one gazes upon such objects is *poshlost'*– and this I have already explained to you.

Ten minutes passed; I peered down the hall. Suleiman appeared to be focusing his attentions on only one of the dials, as near as I could tell, and I guessed he had ascertained the combinations of the other two. In her boredom Sonya began idly tapping her knee with her fingers. I gestured wildly that she should stop, supposing that Suleiman would hear the slight sounds as cannonades.

"Gentlemen," he called out, "a moment, please!"

He continued to sit facing the door as we approached him. "What's the matter?" Arteim asked.

"One minute, please. I am calculating likelihoods." Shutting his eyes, he began to rock back and forth, stretching out his arms, humming as if he were a kitchen appliance. He appeared to be processing long series of numbers in his head. It surprised me that such a master as Suleiman would not employ a calculator, but evidently he was a man of tradition. He stopped after a few minutes, sighed, and stared at the door. "It's the relocking device," he said, as much to himself as to us. "It's different from the other two, though I don't know why it should be."

"What are you talking about?"

"Vaults such as this are always constructed to be both fireproof and burglar-proof. Burglar-proofing means relocking devices are installed within the doors, so that if the main locks are forced open, the backup locks slide into place."

"You didn't realize that?" I asked.

"Tell me how I could explain it to you if I didn't understand the principle." I had nothing to say in reply. "Two locks opened easily, but this one isn't responding to my techniques. He must have obtained it from the competent organs. You don't find such mechanisms in public use."

"Then it's hopeless?"

"Of course not. Arteim, please, hand me my bag." My associate passed him a small black nylon carrier imprinted with the word NIKE on the side. "Open the bag, find the power drill and the box of bits. Take the longest bit, and install it if you would." He stared into the bag for some time. "Mr. Borodin, please," he said. "A toothpick."

"Sonya, do you have a toothpick?"

"We have a WaterPik."

Suleiman shook his head. "No, a real one," I said. "Nothing electric."

"Does it have to be wood?"

Again, a headshake. "No." She walked into a room off the hall, shortly returning with a silver box no bigger than a cigarette case. The hammer and sickle, surrounded by sheaves of wheat, were engraved on the lid. "What is this?" I asked, undoing the clasp (it came off in my hands, falling apart in use in the manner of all fine Soviet products). Looking within, I saw a mouse's gold javelin lying upon a white velveteen bed.

"Toothpick," said Sonya.

"Where on earth did you get such a thing?"

"It was awarded to Dmitry for fifteen years of unstinting devotion to the Ministry of the Interior."

"Very thoughtful," Suleiman said. He spoke so softly, it was difficult to hear what he was saying. "Friend Borodin, please, ready my stethoscope and hand me a piece of chalk."

I entwined the doctor's tool around his neck and guided its earpieces into place. He held the chalk in his right hand, while with his left he applied the sounding plate of the stethoscope against the door. "Nobody breathe," he told us. We froze in place, hoping he could do whatever was necessary before we began gasping for air. In less than half a minute he located what he sought, marking an X on the metal with the chalk. "Drill there." Arteim lifted the tool, holding it as if it were a gun, and prepared to bore a hole at the specified site. "Do you know, is there a gas trap installed?"

"What the hell are you talking about?" asked Arteim.

"Sometimes these vaults are designed so that if forcible means are employed to gain entry, poisonous gas escapes and asphyxiates the craftsman," he informed us. "If no one knows, please proceed. There's no other way to find out."

Arteim seemed hesitant. "What if—"

"Keep holding your breath," I said, willing to take the chance. He shrugged and started drilling. In less than two minutes, drill rampant in hand, he drove the bit through into the hollow core beneath the steel plating.

"Stop!" Suleiman directed. "Fine. Now, widen it a little. We can stop worrying about being gassed, I think. All right, stop."

Again, he applied the stethoscope to the steel. "If time-set explosive devices have been activated I'll be able to hear them now." He smiled. "We're safe. Arteim, take the flashlight from my bag. Stand on my right, direct the beam into the hole. Please."

His hands again came into play. Picking up the gold toothpick, he clamped one end between forefinger and thumb, guiding the free end through the small hole that Arteim illuminated. I have no idea what Suleiman did, but whatever it was, he made the act of opening the vault look so easy you could believe any child might have accomplished the task. After a minute he pulled out the toothpick and subtly dropped it in his shirt pocket. "Open sesame."

The handle now moved freely in my hands when I seized it. With greater ease than I expected, I drew open the steel door. Dmitry had hinted at the scope of his collection, but I never imagined he possessed the haul we saw before us. We gasped in disbelief, and even Suleiman, who was probably more used to such sights, looked impressed. Hidden in Dmitry's treasure room were objects I'd heretofore seen only in the Hermitage, or the Pushkin Museum, or in certain of the Kremlin's buildings, such as the Palace of Facets. The vault held no more floor space than nine square meters, and the ceiling was only half a meter higher than my head (I am no giant, believe me), but crammed within was the kitsch of Croesus. There were dozens of magnificent old icons, boxes of nacre and amber, malachite pedestals, cynocephalic figurines from ancient Egypt, examples of the finest Dagestan silver, Art Nouveau crystal vases, exquisitely carved Chinese ivories, Fabergé baubles and bibelots, stacks of gold coins, porcelain vases, exquisite ceramic ware, and miniature marble sculptures. Uzbekh and Turkmen carpets stood on their ends, rolled tight and propped up in the corners of the room. Perched atop a jade pedestal was a one-third life size bust of Stalin, in what seemed at first to be silver but was, I saw in astonishment and dismay, platinum. The effect of seeing so many treasures jammed into one tiny room was not, surprisingly, a sublime aesthetic experience; rather, I felt uncomfortably sated, as if I had eaten at one sitting two or perhaps three entire cream cakes. Dmitry's collection was ultimately *poshlaia*, in its most supreme manifestation.

"My God," Arteim said. "Max, look at this!"

"Something, isn't it?" I asked, crossing the threshold to stand inside the room. The others followed, crowding the vault unbearably; after a few moments of torture, Sonya edged back into the hall. "Koshka, did you have any idea?"

"He never showed me any of this," Sonya said. "Sometimes he took out a single piece and let me look at something he obtained, as with that egg."

"Where did he get it all?"Arteim asked. "How?"

"He must have bought *some* of the pieces," Suleiman said. "It would be terrifically hard to steal so much."

Some of Dmitry's personal possessions, seemingly of less value, were piled on the floor beneath a seventeenth-century rosewood and teak table. He'd left behind a thin Japanese bedroll, an old Tokarev pistol, a glass half full of water (or vodka), and a crumb-strewn plate. A crumpled cloth bag, empty and gray with dust, lay tossed to one side. In the center of the floor were seven small black gun-metal boxes.

"I think I see the greatest treasure of all," I told Sonya, kneeling in front of the boxes. None were locked. Opening the top container, I found it filled with small plastic bags packed tight with snow-white powder.

"Arteim, tell me if this is genuine."

"What is it?" he asked, kneeling down and slitting a hole in a bag with his knife, leaving imprints of his fingers in the powder as he prodded its surface. "Heroin or cocaine?"

"It's supposed to be heroin, I believe," I said. "White gold, from Uzbekistan." He lifted his hand and touched it to his tongue.

"What a bizarre device," Suleiman said, pointing at a combination dial set into the door's interior surface. "Disabled now, I'm afraid. This explains the difficulty I had. Why did he want a lock on the inside?"

"He often slept in here," Sonya explained. Staring up at the ceiling, I saw several vents from which a steady stream of air issued. "He liked to stay close to what he loved most." She smiled. "Maybe he was afraid I'd lock him in."

"My God, Max," Arteim said, licking his finger until it shone in the light. "Fuck my sister! Do you know what this is?"

"What?"

"*Fred.* It's pure fred."

Sonya and Suleiman must have appeared as aghast as I did, hearing Arteim's pronouncement. "Are you absolutely sure?"

"You can't mistake fred," he said. "You didn't expect this?"

"Not at all. Help me carry the boxes out into the hall."

"Should I try the rest?" he asked. "To be certain?"

"No!" I said, loudly enough to make him reconsider before even thinking of sneaking another taste. "If that's what it is, it's far too dangerous."

It is not easy to say what fred is, because no one who knows will tell you. No one will ever read about fred in histories or sociological studies of the Soviet Union, but believe me when I tell you what I know. Fred is not the scientific name of the drug (how it obtained the name of an American man, I can't begin to understand), and unlike most pharmaceutical agents used illegally for diversion by our young people, fred's essential chemical structure remains a state secret buried so deep that I don't believe it has ever come to light. Fred was created by our wise Soviet experts as an agent to be used exclusively in psychiatric hospitals, only on political prisoners. I have heard that the effects of fred are multiform; they depend on the genetic structure, or emotional makeup, or psychological state of the user—maybe all three. You may take fred and find it as soothing as a pipeful of hashish, or you may take an identical amount and never again function as a human being—if you live. Evidently, whatever you are, fred makes you more so, except when it doesn't. How you take it is something else again. I have heard it can be smoked, injected, swallowed, or inhaled; strips of tape may be soaked in a solution of fred, open cuts are made in the shaven scalp and the tape is applied directly onto the skull, serving as a drug-soaked bandage. In the seventies, fred was most often used in apartments known to the cognoscenti as fred houses. The young people said that there were always (as they put it) bad vibes in the walls of a fred house.

And, plainly, fred was what the Georgians intended to export to America. From what I know of Americans, I suspected it would prove popular.

"A remarkable collection," Suleiman said, eyeing the drug-stuffed packets with disdain. "I am pleased to have been of service to you. As regards my fee—"

"I left it open for discussion, Max," Arteim admitted.

"There's a unique instrument in your pocket," I reminded our expert. With a smile he drew forth Dmitry's gold toothpick. "You're welcome to keep it, I'm sure."

"Lovely, but of limited use, I'm afraid."

"I understand," I said, taking it from him and putting it in my own pocket. "What would you like?" I picked up one of the incomparable icons, a glorious image of one of the saints that to my layman's eye appeared to be of medieval vintage. "How about one of these?" But even as I held it in my hands I realized the thoughtless error I was committing, and I was grateful Suleiman seemed not to be the sort who would take my offering as a personal insult.

"Thank you kindly, but I must decline graven images of infidels," he said, and pointed to a gold flask studded with semi-precious stones sitting atop the antique table. "That, however, pleases my eye."

That the flask was worth possibly ten or even twenty times as much as the icon didn't concern me; I hadn't spent my money to buy it. Dmitry's death, in fact, allowed me a chance to recover the six hundred thousand-odd dollars he had owed me—Sonya would not object, I was sure, were I to claim a certain proportion of these riches. But until my future was secured and Tanya released, I could devote little attention to the disposal of the items. Staring at the wealth surrounding me, I knew how imperative it was that the Georgians did not learn of this room's existence. Watching Suleiman examine the flask, still not deigning to touch it, I made another troubling realization. I gestured to Arteim, who'd finished moving the boxes into the hall.

"How can we be sure he won't talk about what he's seen?" I asked. Arteim had obviously not considered this problem before—to be fair, neither had I; how could we have imagined the amount of wealth we would find in the vault? My partner looked at our safecracker as if he were starving and Suleiman a suckling pig.

"You want me to handle it?"

"Do as you see fit."

"As you wish, Max."

We winked at one another. Suleiman held out his bag to Arteim, clutching it between his wrists, and nodded toward a small gray streamlined machine within. "Please. Remove it for me, if you would."

"What is it?" Arteim asked, taking it out.

"Dosimeter," he said, flipping a switch on the side.

"Is this some kind of joke?"

"It's surprisingly useful. Arteim, stand here, please. Hold

it in front of you." My partner lifted the machine until it was in proximity to the jeweled flask, holding it there for half a minute. Suleiman grimaced as he studied the dials. "This is exactly what I was worried about. Very bad."

"What's the matter?"

"We're getting a reading of twenty milliroentgens per hour present in the air," he said, pointing at the dials.

"Radiation?"

"How bad?"

"Twenty times higher than recommended exposure," he said. "It's not good. Arteim, walk over there. Let me get a reading in that area." My partner stepped across and raised the dosimeter above a stack of icons. When Suleiman studied the dials this time, he did not look at all pleased. "Mother of God," he said, his tone as soft and even as before. "We must get out of here immediately."

"What is it? What's it saying?" Arteim asked as we hurried into the hall and pushed the steel door shut behind us.

"Eight roentgens per hour," Suleiman said, glancing over the dials again once we were out; this time, what he saw did not disturb him. "Out here, ten milliroentgens per hour. Not nearly as bad, by comparison."

"Something in there is radioactive?"

"Your so-called treasures," he said. "Happens all the time, of late. In the event buildings or towns need to be abandoned, someone is always happy to return to pick up what was left behind. Collectors are offered astonishing bargains and can't resist, even if they pay a higher price later on. I am guessing some of these items must be from the Chernobyl area."

"The levels are *that* high?" Another memory of Dmitry at the Metropole returned to me; his bringing his hand to his head and coming away with bits of hair. I wondered how many hours, asleep and awake, he'd spent in his tomb.

"High enough to kill, certainly," he said. "Not overnight."

"What about these?" I asked, pointing at the seven boxes. Arteim held the dosimeter above them while Suleiman read the dials.

"You won't be keeping them indefinitely?" he asked, and I shook my head. "Don't sleep on top of them. Otherwise, you should be all right. Arteim, let's check the rest of the apartment for these good people." They walked the length of the hall, testing each room in turn before making a report. "The danger is entirely in the vault," Suleiman said. "Out here is okay, but I would recommend moving."

"Then all of his treasures are—"

"Non-negotiable," Suleiman said. Arteim replaced the dosimeter in his bag. "We should perhaps work out a different arrangement, as regards my fee."

"Naturally," I said, reaching into my pocket, reluctantly taking from my wallet a thousand dollars in hundreds. "Arteim can provide you with more if you need it. That's all I have with me at the moment."

"This is sufficient," Suleiman said. "What an evening, yes? Probably I should be going now. Thank you very much, please, for your courtesies."

We went to the living room. Suleiman drew on his mittens before putting on his coat, and while Sonya assisted him, I led Arteim into the kitchen, whispering so that we could not be heard.

"I don't know how long I'll be gone tomorrow afternoon," I told him. "Come by here at twelve with two guards and pick up Sonya. Keep her with you at all times while I'm over there."

"You're staying here tonight?"

"I'm keeping those boxes in my sight, believe me," I said. "My God, what a day it's been."

"And Suleiman?"

"Let him go home," I said. "He's been very helpful."

It didn't take me as long to reach Lev as I was afraid it would; no more than an hour and a half passed before my call went through. While I waited, holding the receiver, listening to the ether pulse and crackle as signals passed from space into my ear, Sonya continued drinking, pouring herself glass after glass of garlic vodka; I'd never seen her drink as much as she did that night—still, what better way to commemorate her husband? I couldn't help but believe she was more upset by his death than she pretended to be; had I been her, I suppose the loss may even have affected me. In my own way, I was suffering—none of my normal physiological reactions were working as they should have worked. For over an hour after Arteim and Suleiman left I had sat there with my koshka in the heart of every Russian household, drinking and not getting drunk; and now, though it was past midnight, I felt no need for sleep.

"Max, what is it?" Lev asked, when he answered, after I told him it was me. "Nothing about souvenirs, I hope."

"I need information on a Georgian who lives in New York, if you can give me any. He would appear to be a Brighton Beach mobster, and I want to know how much influence he has, there and here."

"Is the line clear?"

Meaning, was anyone else listening. "Yes, as far as I can tell."

"All right. What's his name?"

"Valentin Bok."

"Valentin Samoilovich Bok?"

"That's him."

"My God, Max, he's the head of the Georgian mafia. Surely you haven't gotten involved with him?"

"I have," I said. "He seems very dangerous, and very crazy."

"No, no. He is the light of humanity," Lev said. At first I thought he had become as crazy; then I remembered the inferences he'd made regarding the tapping of phones in America. Doubtless, as was the case here, the government were not the only ones who relied on such tactics to keep watch over their subjects. "I can't begin to describe the kind of luck you must be having if you're involved with Bok."

"I suppose I can't describe it either," I said, following his lead.

"That wouldn't be a good idea," he said. "You're not dealing with the Ministry of the Interior, Max."

"I'd guessed that," I said, my suspicions of Bok's power and clout confirmed, much to my regret. "Let me ask a different question. Do they have fred in America? Do you know?"

"I have never heard of this drug before," he said; certainly he had, since I hadn't made specific the nature of fred, but apparently he thought this answer to be sensible. "Max, probably we should talk another time, if we can."

"Yes. Yes, I understand. Thank you, Lev."

"It's been good to know you, Max."

After he hung up I sat there a moment, thinking of what he hadn't said. "You've finished your calls?" Sonya asked, emptying her glass.

"One more."

She stood up, leaning past me to retrieve an unopened bottle of vodka while I phoned Tanya's associate Alla. My koshka wore fawn-colored cashmere pants, soft and close-fitting, and as she bent over she rubbed her hindquarters against me, her intentions plain. For the moment I had to ignore her, however difficult it might be.

"Hello?" I heard Alla say; I'd woken her, but she knew I wouldn't have called her at home unless it was a matter of the greatest urgency. She was as dismayed as I'd expected when I explained what had happened, and it took me several minutes to calm her down to the point where she could listen to me, but she was the only one of Tanya's associates I could have told. While I believed Anatoly and Roman to be as dependable as any Russian employee, there was no way I had of knowing how well they got along with Iosif and how closely they might have been working with him. But I knew Alla would never again betray Tanya; she always regretted the one time she had. I should make a confession: there was a reason I'd been especially nervous when she and Tanya's other associates encountered Sonya in my office. Alla was very familiar with my behavior when I was in the midst of an affair—ours had taken place ten years earlier.

"I knew Iosif was up to no good," Alla told me. "He has the look of evil. Tanya kept insisting he was all right. She said she'd known his uncle, back at the Ministry, theirs was a good family. You see how much *that* matters! She wouldn't listen to me when I asked her to reconsider."

"His hands are heavily tattooed," I said. "He must have been in prison or has at least long been a partner to gangsters."

"He never takes those gloves off when he's at work. I had Roman follow him into the bathroom one time to see if he took them off even then, and he didn't."

"Did he tell you when he thought he might recover from his illness?"

"No," she said. "When he phoned this morning, he said he'd be in once he felt better. Do you think he'll be back?"

"Don't know. More than likely not. I suspect he's served his purpose. There's something else that's worrying me. Wasn't he your pipeline to the Bruneians?"

"That's right," she said. "Surely you don't think they could be involved?"

"Who knows? Friends of enemies are no less dangerous. Look, if he comes back, act as if nothing unusual is going on. Are you sure Roman and Anatoly can be trusted?"

"They hate him as much as I do," she said.

"Then tell them what has happened but avoid details as much as possible. If Iosif comes in, tell him I phoned to tell you that Tanya is also sick at home. Then watch him, see what he does. He's the kind who falls easily into his own traps."

"What will you do when he does?"

"Collect a trophy," I said. "Keep me informed. We'll get out of this with our skin if we have any luck at all. We have to win her release by whatever means. I can't bear the thought of her being imprisoned by those animals; I can't imagine what they might be doing to her. Whatever happens, Iosif is going to pay for what he's done. I'll leave word with my associates to deal with him if anything happens to me."

"Be careful, Max," she said.

"There should be guards outside your building even as we speak; earlier this evening I told Arteim to get them over there. You be careful, too. This will be over, soon enough."

No sooner had I hung up than Sonya moved closer to me, pressing her mouth against mine. I drew away.

"What's the matter with you?"

"Koshka, no, don't. I have too much on my mind."

She took my chin between her perfect teeth and nipped me. "There's nothing more you can do for her tonight, Max," she said, picking up and placing my hands on her breasts. I felt her nipples swelling beneath my palms. "Make love to me." Closing her eyes, she slipped her fingers between the buttons of my shirt. "I want you. Don't you want me?"

"Koshka, I don't know what they might be doing to Tanya, I–"

"Fuck Tanya," she said. "Fuck me."

"You haven't been a widow half a day yet."

"What a bastard he was, Max. My God, I'm glad he's dead." She pressed her face against my neck so as to better apply her scent. "He never trusted me with his secrets. All the nights he slept with his stupid treasures. If he'd slept with me he'd still be full of life."

"It would have made no difference to Bok," I reminded her, pushing her back, feeling as if I were enmeshed in the tentacles of an amiable octopus. "Dmitry'd still be dead." My instinctual soul desired my koshka badly, while my intellect battled to convince me that this was neither the time nor place for lovemaking.

"I'd have kept him too busy to get in trouble." Why was she telling me such a thing? "Max, fuck me. I'm burning."

"I don't want to hear about how you could have saved your husband. Didn't you just hate him, a minute ago?"

"You think I want to hear how badly you want your wife back?" she shouted, unexpectedly and roughly thrusting her hand down the front of my pants. I tried to break free, but when I tried to pry away Sonya's fingers she gripped my organs tightly, as if preparing to tear them off. "You never tell me your secrets either," she said. "Just like him. Why don't you trust me?"

"Koshka, that hurts," I told her, speaking through clenched teeth. "I do trust you, but there's so much going through my head." I'd never imagined how much strength was in her fingers. The pain was so intense, I was afraid I'd pass out.

"Is there room for me in your head?" she asked, increasing the pressure, her crooked smile as fixed as a doll's.

"Sonya, stop!" I said, seizing the back of her neck and squeezing as hard as I could. "Let go of me, let go!"

"What, you're going to hit me?" she asked, her grip as unyielding as before.

"Let go or I will."

"Do and you'll be an old man with a little boy's voice," she said. "Look, we both let go. All right?"

I nodded. I released her neck, she withdrew her hand from my pants. Leaning forward, I pressed my legs together, hoping I could somehow drive away the dizzying pain. Sonya stood up, rubbing her neck with her hands; then she staggered to the sink, colliding with a kitchen chair en route. With melodramatic gestures worthy of a silent-film actress she turned on the faucets and started washing her hands. She was crying. The pain I felt did not decrease enough that I could walk over to her, but at least I was capable of speech.

"Koshka, forgive me."

"Go fuck your mother," she said, her shaking hands gloved

in foamy suds. She'd never said anything so brutal to me before; I better understood how terribly upset she was.

"It's been a horrible day, my angel. I'm not acting like myself. I never meant to hurt you, believe me. Never."

She said nothing for a minute or two but, instead, carefully dried her hands, devoting prolonged attention to each finger in turn. Tossing aside her towel, she wandered back to the table, half sitting, half falling into her chair. "God, Max, you hurt me."

"You hurt *me*," I said, astonished that I hadn't started vomiting, either from pain or alcohol.

"All this time you tell me how much you want me and not your wife. Then something happens to her, and she's all you can think about."

"Koshka—"

"I understand you're upset, Max, but it hurts me to hear you say these things. I don't want to just be your sex toy, your kitten. That's how you've been acting all day, like you can set me aside whenever you want to. That's how Dmitry always treated me. I hated him for it."

"Why did you stay with him, then?"

"His money," she said. Her eyes may have shimmered with alcohol's glaze, but she spoke with disarming clarity. I have always admired my koshka's realistic view of the world. "Why else?"

We embraced warmly, and almost at once our differences were settled, at least for the moment. This time, I kissed her; she responded without hesitation. "Forgive me?" I asked.

"I shouldn't," she said, but then nodded. "Yes."

"We should go to bed, my precious. We've drunk too much, I think. I know I have."

Her cheeks flushed. She reached for the bottle, intending to pour herself another glass; I pushed it away from her. For an instant she looked as if her temper would flare once more; then she laughed and leaned back in her chair. The skin around her eyes was puffy and red from tears and alcohol; her makeup was smudged, her hair hung over her face. At that moment she looked ten years older than she truly was; I can't tell you how beautiful she still was. I could imagine that I must have appeared to have aged twenty years myself, that day.

"I can't believe he'd have abandoned me like that."

"He'd have pitched you away like an empty bottle," I said. "Who knows why, for certain? Punishing you for having an affair, perhaps."

"If you ever left Russia, you'd take me with you, wouldn't you?"

"Why would I ever leave?" She took my earlobe in her mouth and bit down hard enough to make me jump.

"Good," she said. "I'd like to be with someone who appreciated me."

We hauled ourselves up from our chairs. Perhaps, somehow, I wasn't drunk at all: my head wasn't spinning, and I didn't feel the lightness in my midsection that warned me I would despise the morning, when it came. When we went into the bedroom, I took off my clothes and lay down and shut my eyes, waiting to see if I would pass out. I didn't, and so felt assured that alcohol had not worked its black magic on me that evening.

Sonya had stepped into the water closet, and a few minutes later she came out, leaving her clothes behind. She lay down on the bed alongside me. "Move over," she said, slipping her tongue into my mouth. You know me better now, so I will be more forthright and honest in describing our actions. As I lowered myself atop my koshka and felt her grip me between her strong legs, I detected an unfortunate numbness; if I were to satisfy us both, I would need her help. Memories of our past comminglings didn't help; nor did thoughts of Tanya, nor even of the young woman in Khrushchev's apartment.

"What's the matter, my strong man?"

"I told you there was much on my mind," I said.

This problem did not often occur, but we had through experience discovered an appropriate remedy when it did. "You want me to tell you a story?"

"Yes."

"What story do you want to hear?" she asked. "The Cossacks? The mud?"

"The log."

She rolled her eyes but smiled. I raised myself up on my elbows so she could roll over onto her stomach. Some among you may find humorous aspects to what I shall shortly relate, but it will not surprise me. Years ago I once obtained limited access to

the Lenin Library's collection of Western treatises on sexual response and read what I could on the subject of fetishes. Most case
histories, I thought, might have been jokes without punch lines,
so ludicrous were the situations and narratives, but of course I
believe that those involved may not have seen those aspects as
clearly as a more objective reader. Certainly the investigative doctors had no sense of the human comedy they unfolded before the
world. All that I learned from those so-called masters of the psyche
was that they had no greater understanding of which mental levers
set into motion the mechanisms of erotic fantasy than I did—so I
ceased to be concerned about the particular notions that crept
sometimes willingly, sometimes unwillingly, into my head.

"Now listen carefully because I'm only telling you once,"
she said. "One sunny afternoon in my last year of university, instead of going to classes, I went for a walk through the Sparrow
Hills. I went to a secret lake where I could swim nude and no one
would see me."

"What happened?"

"I come out of the water," she whispered, wriggling beneath
me. "I am very wet and very naked. When I look for my clothes
I'm shocked to see they're gone. What will I do? I wonder. Then I
see a hollow log, and I think maybe my clothes are inside. Maybe
they were carried off by marmots."

She started to giggle. "Too much detail," I said. "What do
you do?"

"I get on all fours to peek in the log," she said. "It's—"

"More detail."

She pressed herself into my groin. "When I get on all fours
to peek in the log my naked bottom is sticking up in the air like a
juicy pear for anyone passing by to see. When I look in the log I
can tell it's sanded and well-polished inside—"

"What?"

"I'm not sticking myself into an old, filthy, dirty log without my clothes on," she said, sounding vaguely—attractively—irritated. "It must have been specially prepared and placed there by
someone, but I don't think about that. I crawl in head first to see
if my clothes are in there. It's dark and round and smooth inside."
I encircled her shoulders in an unbreakable grip; she writhed and
twisted like a snake. "I push myself in as far as my waist but that's
as far as I can get in."

"Why?"

"Because my behind—" I squeezed her, and she elaborated. "My succulent pearlike behind is too plump. When I don't see my clothes I try backing up."

"What happens?" She flicked her tongue along my arms, and spread her legs far apart. I shifted my own body until it was at the right angle—then, success!—she constricted her most pleasurable muscles.

"I stand up and look elsewhere for my clothes—"

"No!"

She grunted, seeming even more greatly annoyed, but she continued. "I try backing up, but I can't. No matter how much I wriggle, I can't get out of the log. I'm stuck. I kick my feet but it's no use. I scream for help. Then I hear heavy footsteps behind me."

"More."

"It's you," she said. "You see I'm completely helpless. You should be a gentleman and rescue me, but you're a brute."

"More."

"A brutish brute. You throb with cruel manhood. You're overcome with hot passion when you see my—"

My seed released itself; I made utterances that were too incoherent to bear repeating. She turned over and covered my face in kisses as I gasped for breath.

"Very satisfying." She sighed. I'd been separated from Sonya in the physical sense for too many days, but that didn't explain the intensity of feeling I had for her in that instant, an intensity which redoubled my awareness that I could not live without her any more than I could live without Tanya, regardless of my wife's ultimatum. With Tanya, I knew *byt*; with Sonya, *bytie*. Again, these terms cannot be exactly expressed in any language other than Russian. (Probably the feelings I had for my wife are equally untranslatable—all I can say, after all, is that I needed the moral authority she exerted over me, even when I didn't want it; not many people actively want their parents, but who would be here without them?) To a degree *byt* refers to our ever-reliable stagnation, the soul-comforting grinding down of our lives, day in, day out, between the wheels of mundane event; while something *bytie* possesses the essence of spiritual being, provides a never-ending epiphany, assures the state of eternal grace. There is earth, and there is heaven, and you want to live in both places at once—

but as Mayakovsky said in his famous suicide note, the love boat crashes against *byt*. However many times it crashes, it will continue to crash, but you keep getting into the boat. Still, I think *bytie* inevitably becomes *byt*, even in heaven. Perhaps I am cynical, but unlike most of my countrymen I have never been mindlessly enticed by prospects of utopia.

Once Tanya was released, I supposed, I would tell her I should see Sonya no longer, but then simply go on as before—until I was caught again, or until my wife tired of me and took the decision out of my hands. Overt, bald-faced lying does not come as naturally to me as it did to Dmitry, but in this difficult world one must be adaptable.

"It's your turn to tell me a story," my dear one said, turning onto her side and stroking my face. "Don't be as imaginative as you ask me to be."

I knew too well what she wanted to hear. "Sonya—"

"Prove that you trust me as I trust you."

"Trust has nothing to do with it."

"Then I'll keep asking until you tell me."

She spoke so forthrightly that I knew she would, and so, in this as in most situations, I went ahead and did as she asked. "What do you want to know?"

"Three questions," she said, "what was your son's name?"

"Alexei Maximovich." I must be honest, however, and admit to you that once I began to talk about my son, I had surprisingly little trouble—possibly the alcohol was at last beginning to fog my poor brain.

"What was he like?"

"He was a strong, healthy boy. Energetic and bursting with life. Completely normal."

Then the third and most difficult question. "What happened to him?"

"It's complex," I said. "I will have to give you some background. Ten years ago I had to go to East Germany, to clear up problems caused by Dean Reed."

Reed (I shall have to tell you, because if you knew, you've since forgotten) was the American singer who, finding no success in his own country, came to the Soviet Union and became, for a time, tremendously popular throughout the Eastern bloc. He died in 1986, supposedly a suicide, but I will always have my doubts. It is as well that he has since been erased from collective memory, for as a performer, I must tell you, he was even worse than the Happy Guys.

"I was told I would need to stay there for three weeks, and that I could bring my family if I wanted," I continued. "I'd been very good, you see, and they wished to reward me. Tanya was working for the Ministry of Foreign Affairs, at that point, and wanted to go but could not get away. It was summer; school was out of session. My son had never traveled outside the Soviet Union, not even to Hungary or Poland. I can't tell you how excited he was when I told him he could go with me. He counted down the days until we left as if awaiting his birthday.

"We flew to Berlin in July. It was very hot. The first two weeks we were there we spent at Reed's country house, what he called his ranch, the poor fool. In the evenings we had to sit and listen to him singing cowboy songs or, even worse, his own imbecile tunes. Hooray for Brezhnev, hooray for Honecker. Incredible, offensive nonsense. My son thought Reed was pleasant but didn't know where to stop. Finally our time there ended, and with relief we came into the city. I had to meet with various people in the bureaus. I was provided with a governess to watch Alexei while I met with some of the most appalling people I have ever had to deal with. If you think Russian Communists were bad I don't have to tell you how much worse German Communists were. When I—"

"You're getting off the subject, Max," she said. "What happened to him?"

"I told you I needed to give you some background," I said, but I could tell she was having nothing to do with my explanation. "Very well. I finished up my business a day early, to everyone's satisfaction. I wanted to do something special with my son, but what was there to do in East Berlin that we couldn't do in Moscow? Just over the wall, however, I knew there were sights he would never forget. I spoke to my hosts and asked if it would be possible to be given permission to go over. I made the appropriate bribes, and we worked out an arrangement. Our hosts knew they could trust us to return, after all. They sent a guard along with us, and we crossed over and spent an afternoon wandering through the streets, going to shops, looking at the people."

"Did he enjoy it?"

"I thought so," I said. "But I'd forgotten what the shock was like. You know what I mean."

"I've never been."

"Not even Finland?"

She shook her head. "I'd love to go west, someday."

That astonished me; her family was not without influence, and I should have thought they would have obtained permission at some point to visit Scandinavia, if nowhere else. "It wouldn't be as disturbing an experience for you, now, as it once would have been."

"What do you mean?"

"But maybe it would," I said, reconsidering. "I don't know. If you haven't been, I don't know if you will understand what I mean. No matter how familiar you think you are with it, it's not the same, seeing that world in context."

After I first left the Soviet Union, traveling to Sweden with my father on a trip similar in purpose to the one on which I took my son (although I was eighteen, and no longer a child), I experienced the dissonant emotions a *sovok* invariably felt upon seeing the West as it actually was, discovering that the parallel world of evil capitalists was in truth a scarcely imaginable utopia in comparison to the bleak society in which he lived. I knew, too, the black melancholy that came over those who, having gone west, returned to the Greatest Society of All Times and Peoples, unable ever again to see it as anything but the greatest lie of all. Eventually I recovered, and it was not easy. So hard, in fact, that I blacked out my memories of those emotions as if with alcohol. By the time I went west with my son, I no longer remembered what it was like, to be confronted with realities that could disturb the mind of even the most hardened adult.

"Tell me, surely you've known people who went west, in the old days," I said. She nodded her head. "What happened to them, after they came back?"

My koshka lay there, staring up at the ceiling. "Sometimes they killed themselves."

"Of course," I said.

"Is that what happened—?"

"No," I said. "But plainly he was disturbed by what he had seen. When we returned to Moscow, he was no longer himself. He stayed inside all the time, lying on his bed. Saying little. Looking at the food we served him as if it weren't fit for hogs. Only later, when it was too late, did I comprehend what had troubled him so. At the time, we didn't know. Finally I thought we should have a doctor look at him. The doctor could find nothing wrong with him, so I pulled some strings and it was arranged that he should go into the hospital for further tests. Tanya didn't want him to go; she was terrified he would never come out. Her family had had bad experiences in hospitals."

(In 1938, at the directive of the Distinguished Academician of Soviet Science and Medicine—that is to say, the Great Leader—her mother's father had been forced to undergo surgery he didn't need and from which he failed to recover; twenty years later a beloved aunt was killed, along with two doctors and a nurse, when her oxygen tent exploded into flames—one of the doctors was so drunk he forgot he was smoking, and the others didn't notice.)

"Eventually I made her see she was wrong," I said. "That was my mistake, but for all I knew the health of our son was at stake. We had no access to the Kremlin hospital, of course, so we sent him to First City."

"What happened?"

For a minute or so I considered whether or not I should tell her; if I couldn't believe it, how could she? "They lost him."

"What are you saying?"

"He disappeared. They said they looked all over for him, but he was gone."

"People weren't disappearing, ten years ago," she said. "Were they?"

"Usually not, but he did."

"What happened to him?"

"We never found out."

"Never?"

"After a year of searching, we finally gave up and accepted the fact that he was gone. This is why Tanya and I never spoke of him, if we could help it. She didn't think I should have sent him to the hospital, needless to say, but what should I have done?"

"Max, it doesn't make sense," she said. "How could your son just vanish?"

There were three possibilities. To those possessed of unyielding rationality, it would seem plain that the hospital had somehow accidentally killed him while he was in its care, and its representatives, for whatever reason, chose not to tell us why or how. And true, at first hearing this seems possible—except that in recent years I had all of First City's private records surreptitiously examined by my undercover experts, and there was nothing in the files they hadn't already told me, long ago. If someone was keeping secrets, it wasn't First City.

Which leads me to the second possibility: Had one or more of my superiors—Esenin, perhaps?—been so disturbed by my impromptu trip to West Berlin that they had made their displeasure known, and executed an appropriate punishment, by stealing my son? But he disappeared in 1985, not 1935; there was no reason for anyone to have done such an outrageous thing—certainly, had they wanted to punish me, they could have done so in much simpler ways. Again, my experts had come across nothing to suggest that any such orders were ever issued.

And that left only the possibility that he left the hospital himself and then, one way or the other, went west. This was without doubt the least likely of the three possibilities, and that is why it was the one I believe most likely to be true. Incomprehensible, unlikely, impossible: yes, it was all these things; but any Russian can tell you that, repeatedly, events have occurred in our country which we cannot believe, much less understand. So that is why I wonder where he wanders today.

"I don't know, but vanish he did," I told her. "So we went on from there."

My koshka stared at me, utterly baffled by what I had told her; while initially she may have felt I was making up my story as I went along, she quickly realized that I was telling her the truth as I believed it to be. "Don't you think you'll ever see him again?"

"Not any more."

"But Max—"

"I've told you all I can tell you," I said. "What else can I say?"

There was nothing else to say, or I would have said it; she seemed at last to accept what I had told her and asked me no more questions. My eyelids grew heavy; but as I began to enter the nightly kingdom, I heard my koshka speak. "I'm coming with you tomorrow."

"If you do, you may wind up joining me in my grave."

"They're not going to kill either of us tomorrow," she said, lifting her arm and pointing toward the hall and her late husband's secret room. "We have too much to offer them."

"Sonya—"

"I don't want you to disappear like that too," she said. "I'll go with you, and if I disappear with you, so be it."

Mels ushered us into Nadze's private office when we arrived, the next afternoon—it told of his character at a glance. His desk, bigger than any minister's, was built of polished mahogany. He had but one telephone, a German model with a dozen lines and fax capability. Hanging on the wall behind the desk was an oil portrait of himself, posing in full military dress as if he were Brezhnev or the veritable Generalissimo; the artist had reworked Nadze's personal proportions so that he appeared sixty kilos lighter and half a meter taller than he actually was. The rugs were antique Persians, the furniture—a divan, five chairs, two tables—new and made of fine materials: golden oak, gleaming walnut, maroon leather soft as a glove. In clearing room for the seven boxes now stacked upon his desk, Nadze had pushed aside a collection of clear plastic snow globes, each housing an architectural icon of the West: the Statue of Liberty, the Eiffel Tower, the Parthenon. Price tags were still glued to their scratched acrylic curves. Heating pipes and radiators brought warmth to the room; the fireplace was sealed, its mantel stripped away. Instead of a welcoming hearth there was a television so large that, had it been hollow, several members of the formerly cultivated classes could have found shelter within. The set was on, tuned to 2times2, but the sound was off. An afternoon magazine program showed scenes of the ongoing tragedy in Chechnya. These stark visuals were shortly superseded by a commercial for RossiyaFund, which, until the recent murder of its president, guaranteed all investors a ten thousand percent return on their money.

"Excellent, Max," Nadze said, after he and Bok checked the contents of each box, slicing open every bag. "I knew you were a man of your word."

"This should solve our problems, insofar as our late ac-

quaintance is concerned," I said. "Now if we can move on and
discuss the situation of my wife—"

"It's admirable to see a widow take time from her period
of mourning to help sweep up the mess her husband left behind,"
Nadze said, smiling as he looked at Sonya. "We should be inspired
by your example."

"Thank you," she replied, lowering her head as if showing respect.

"A beautiful widow too, if I may tell you."

As much as my koshka adored flattery, I don't believe this
compliment, paid by one at least partially responsible for her becoming a widow (however advantageous that might prove to her),
evoked the response he imagined it would. "Thank you."

"If everything is as it should be, I ask that my wife be
released."

"You're anxious to see her, aren't you?" Bok asked.

"I see no need for her to be held prisoner any longer."

"Tell me, Max," Nadze said, "why do you express such
concern for your wife's well-being when you so obviously prefer
your mistress?"

"We are discussing business," I said, "or at least I think
that is what we should be discussing. Why should aspects of my
personal life concern you?"

"I find it odd," he said. "Interesting, but odd."

Bok turned toward Sonya and opened his mouth wide,
revealing double rows of gold. Evidently, he intended to smile but
looked instead as if he planned to swallow her like an oyster. "It
is too bad more women in Brighton Beach do not look like you,"
he said to her. "You would be queen of the boardwalk, if you were
there. Do you own a bikini?" Sonya shook her head; I listened,
not liking what he said. "String bikinis such as Brazilians wear
look best, in my opinion. A string bikini, high heels, a thin gold
chain around the waist. Beautiful."

"Can I not have profound feelings for more than one person?" I asked Nadze, still uncomfortable that he had shown this
interest in my private concerns. I kept an eye on Bok, uncertain
of what he intended by his monologue. "Is that so unusual?"

"But surely you have a preference."

"My wife and I are bound by marriage, and her safety comes

uppermost in my mind," I said. "It's a matter of principle. We should discuss this situation, I think—"

"What a good Communist you must have been, Max," Nadze said. "Principles, they come before everything, yes? Even at the cost of the love of the people. I hadn't realized that you and Mrs. Gubina here were so close. I thought at first it was only a question of milking the cow once in a while. But clearly, there is a closeness between you that transcends animal passion. That is good to know."

Bok eased a long, rubbery arm around Sonya, fastening his claw on her waist. Her expression showed nothing of either fear or shock, but I could perceive her disgust—wisely, however, she did not try to pull away.

"Gentlemen, let us attend to matters at hand," I said. "I'm only a businessman."

"As are we," said Bok.

"An excellent businessman," Nadze said. "I think you must have Caucasian blood somewhere in your veins, Max. We rarely meet a native Russian blessed with genuine entrepreneurial sense."

"You overstate our similarities," I said. "Obviously we have different economic goals. I am happy working on a much smaller scale."

"Are you really? There is one thing we have in common, I'm sure. We want more money. Yes?"

I couldn't deny such a truth. "Of course. But I think we should discuss this property of my wife's—"

"What is there to discuss?" Bok asked.

"Exactly," I said, at once understanding that their decision had been already made. "The property is yours, in total. There'll be no problem with Tanya's partners; I can take care of them. So—"

"Today we've been thinking more about *your* property, Max," Nadze said. "Look at the situation from a godlike perspective. We have mutual desires, mutual needs. Why should we not join our forces? Let us together plan for the future."

I didn't like this suggestion in the slightest but thought it best to understate my demurrals, at least until my wife was released and we were somewhere other than inside the Georgian's house. Bok still held on to Sonya, neither taking further liberties nor easing his grip. "What kind of plan?"

"We should form an alliance."

"An alliance of equals?" I asked.

Nadze grinned. "Max, Max. Let's be realistic."

"Your banks are extremely profitable," Bok said, peering above his glasses; why one so beady-eyed would have chosen spectacles which only enhanced his physical failings puzzled me. "An ideal situation would be for us to build upon the sturdy foundation you've laid down."

It pleased me to see him take his arm away from Sonya; it frightened me when I watched him walk to Nadze's desk, extract a hearty pinch of white powder from an open bag of fred with his fingers, and stick it into his mouth as if it were sweet candy. He grimaced, however; fred has a bitter taste. My koshka moved closer to me, and I took her in my own embrace. "I wish you wouldn't do that, Valentin," said Nadze. "It's not cocaine." Bok shrugged and said nothing.

"What do I get in return?" I asked.

"The opportunity to run the banks for us," he said. "People would kill for such a chance. Your Universal Manufacturing Company interests us as well. An operation with real growth potential. So many times, an entrepreneur, alone, is unable to bring business concepts to fruition."

"Gentlemen, I'm very happy working for myself."

Nadze shrugged. "Who among us stays happy for long?"

"I've done everything I was asked to do," I said. "There on your desk is the material Dmitry tried to steal from you, brought here as requested. You are welcome to take every share of the columbarium held by my wife's firm. Now, please, would you release her?"

Bok scratched the back of his neck as if to loosen a hangman's rope. He sneezed, sneezed again, and withdrew a pair of handcuffs from his black suit's jacket. For a moment or so he stood there, wobbling slightly, as if he were being thrown off balance by the flow of blood rushing through his veins. "God damn you," he said, and then turned around and shoved Sonya toward the nearest wall, where she landed against a heating pipe that ran from floor to ceiling. Moving with speed which was without question artificially enhanced by fred, he fastened one cuff around her left wrist, drew the chain behind the pipe, and clicked the other cuff on her right wrist, trapping her arms. He had her imprisoned before she, or I, knew what was happening.

"Stop it!" I shouted. "That isn't necessary—"

As quickly, Bok had his hand affixed on my throat, holding it there long enough to make me believe he intended to snap my neck. For someone who appeared so sickly he was preternaturally strong. How much strength was his own, and how much came from fred, was of course an unanswered question. Sonya struggled, trying to break the handcuffs' chain against the pipe, to no avail.

"You kidnapped the wrong woman, Lavra," Bok said, shoving me down onto the floor. Nothing of mine broke when I landed, but I can't say I should ever want to repeat the experience. He drew back his right foot as if hallucinating that I was a soccer ball. Before he could go for point, however, Nadze reminded his colleague that it wasn't yet necessary to injure me.

"Enough!" he shouted. "Step away." Bok did, half walking, half stumbling toward Sonya. Sweat poured from his forehead down the sides of his face, rolling into the craters beneath his high cheekbones. I pulled myself into a sitting position. "Max, look at your options," Nadze continued, not taking his eyes off Bok. "The benefits are plain, if you objectively examine the situation."

"Tell them about the room, Max," Sonya said. "Tell them. They can have it all if they want it."

"What room?" Nadze asked, seeming only mildly curious.

"Where he kept the boxes," I said. "You knew Dmitry was a collector of art objects. He held a vast collection, we discovered. Hundreds of pieces. Jewelry, icons, precious metals. Inconceivably more valuable than any of my businesses will ever be. You can't imagine what he has. Take it all, it's yours. But let us go, let my wife go. We should all get on with our lives."

"I agree, no question," Nadze said. "You know, we actually have some idea of his holdings."

Bok came up behind Sonya and lifted a length of her hair, as if unfolding tissue. "No gold could be pure as this," he said, enunciating each word carefully, lovingly, as if hearing for the first time the sound of his voice. She tried shifting her head. He grasped the hank he held as if preparing to rip it out of her scalp. "This is your greatest treasure, I think."

She looked at me; what could I do? I was not in chains, but I was as much a prisoner of these lunatics. "Don't hurt her," I said. Bok stared in my direction, and let go of her hair, and began stroking her back with the care he might stroke a kitten. I had a suspicion his good mood would not last—it didn't. Seizing her hair once more, he tore loose a handful of tresses. My angel screamed. Bok folded the hair in his hand as if it were a skein of wool and shoved it into his pocket.

"Collectors nowadays have so little concern for provenance," Nadze said. "The art you see here in my office—look around you—every piece was obtained from reliable, trustworthy sources. But Dima, really. As you can imagine, he consorted with low characters of unsavory heritage. Of course, sometimes we find ourselves dealing with their ilk as well. Long before we entered into this arrangement with Dima, we prompted several middlemen who came our way to tell us about certain of his recent purchases; we were curious as to who might be foolish enough to buy them. These crooks informed us of the special qualities of the objects they sold him, and where they had obtained them. It was as I'd guessed. They were pleased to have a client who asked so few questions."

"You're trying to poison us, aren't you?" Bok asked, reaching out and seizing me by the collar, almost pulling me off the floor. "Assassins! *Toads!*" The look in his eyes resembled the one that was there when he began shooting everyone, the day before, save for the fact that now there were no perceivable human emotions in his unfocused gaze. Plainly, at least, Bok had come into the room unarmed, or else he'd have already put us all out of our misery.

"Stop it, Valentin!" Nadze shouted, and Bok released me. "Remember where you are."

"Look, when we tested your boxes we detected only the lowest levels of radiation," I swore to them. "Safe levels, an expert assured me. All I can say is, check for yourself."

"Not a bad idea," Nadze said, strolling behind his desk and opening a drawer. He took out what I recognized to be his own dosimeter. "I'm not worried, Max. You're not the sort to play nasty tricks on us, I don't think." He turned on his machine and examined the dials. "They're safe enough, Valentin."

"Good," Bok said, slapping his hands against his arms as if killing flies.

"So what do you say, Max?" Nadze asked. "Partners?"

"Let me pose a hypothetical question," I said.

"The safest kind."

"What if I say no?"

"Hard to imagine."

"A hypothetical question," I reminded him. "The hypothetical answer?"

"You say no, we kill you," Bok said. "This one, we keep." As if he were whipping a blanket off a bed, he yanked Sonya's wool dress above her waist. She broke off her fingernails as she scratched at the wall. He tore open the seam of her tights, exposing her backside.

"You're a lucky man, Max," Nadze said, staring at her exposed skin, pale as parchment. Bok brushed his fingers over her behind, smiling as he watched the flesh quiver. "Honestly, Valentin, can you imagine *Dima* with her?"

The hyenas laughed. Sonya stomped her foot down, grinding her boot heel into Bok's shoe, an admirable if foolish act, under the circumstances. He screamed in pain; I didn't find the sound as cheering as I ordinarily should have. "She broke my toe!" he shouted. "Pig-fucking whore." Throwing his full weight into the blow, he punched her in the head. She groaned and fell to her knees. The handcuff chain rattled as it, and she, slid down the pole. Even as he swung, I was on him; within an instant of his hitting her I had brought down both of my fists on his neck. Were I a younger, stronger man, I doubtless would have killed him with that initial strike—as it was, I managed to knock him face forward onto the floor. Had Nadze not fixed me so quickly in his revolver's sights, I would have carried through my attack until the swine lay dead.

"No, Max," he said, his finger on the trigger. Bok pulled himself up, blood dripping from his nose. "Valentin, don't do anything rash." Bok leaned against the wall and took out his handkerchief, stanching the flow of blood as best he could. With his free hand he gingerly rubbed the top of his shoe. "Both of you, listen to me," Nadze continued. "My office is no place for this mindless carousing. Do you understand?"

We signified that we did. Bok and I stared at each other, neither of us willing to be the first to turn away; after a moment, he looked as if he forgot why he was staring. My poor koshka groaned as she knelt on the floor, her hands still locked in place around the pipe. Blood trickled through her golden hair. Nadze slipped his gun back into his pocket, picked up one of his snow globes and shook it, watched white flakes descend slowly, gently, over Big Ben. "Valentin, you're like a pimp who can't keep his prick out of his whores. Stay out of the material."

"Okay!" Bok shouted, speaking to the wall, pounding it with his fist. "Okay! Okay!"

Nadze shook his head and walked across the room, tossing the globe up and down in his hand, never failing to catch it. "Max, do you know who I think you're acting like? Do I have to say his name? You know better than this." He stopped behind Sonya and with gentlemanly actions helped her to stand. She supported herself against the pipe, so as to keep from collapsing once more to the floor. Although she kept her face hidden, I could tell from the way her shoulders shook that she was crying. Now Nadze was the one who lifted her dress, examining her body as if she were a flawless statue. "A natural blonde," he noted, looking down and peering through her legs. "How rare." He pressed the snow globe between my koshka's buttocks, as if to shove it into her. "Did you know the human body can hold five of these?"

"God help me, I'll do anything you say," I told him. "But don't hurt her. Please. Leave her alone."

"We are not monsters, Max," he said, setting aside the globe and lowering her dress so that she was again decently covered. "Now, before we do anything else I think you and Valentin should settle your differences in an appropriate way."

"Appropriate to whom?" I asked.

"Who do you think?" Bok asked, taking his handkerchief from his nose. He braced himself against the wall, extended his leg—it was vibrating like a tuning fork—and glared at the smudge on his shoe. "Your bitch ruined my shine," he said. "Get to work."

I looked at Nadze, and he nodded. You may be disappointed in me, reader; you may marvel that I did not refuse but instead accepted the noble if idiotic death that would surely have been mine for having refused. But I would have licked his whole stinking carcass before I would choose such a method of suicide and leave Sonya to their absence of mercy. When Bok held his shoe out before me, I fell to my knees; when he thrust it into my face, I extended my tongue and polished the leather as effectively as I could polish it in such an untraditional manner. "When I was outside this morning, I think I stepped in shit," Bok said, shoving the sole of his shoe against my cheek. "Lick it off."

Well, what would you have done? You will not be surprised to hear I would have preferred coypu, any day of the week.

"You missed a spot," he said. "There."

After I spent unforgettable minutes wetting the bottom of his shoe, laving it clean, he at last appeared to be outwardly content—I could tell that he in fact enjoyed an even more profound and unnerving satisfaction. Had I been him (and not taken such pleasure), I might have given me a solid kick in the teeth; he did nothing more except to push me backward with his foot before lowering it to the floor. He limped over to Nadze's desk and placed another heaping pinch of fred in his mouth. I wanted to be out of that house before he could feel its recharging surge. "The cunt still broke my toe," he muttered.

Taking out a key, Nadze unlatched the handcuffs that bound my koshka. She pushed him away as he removed them from her wrists and rushed to me, finding some solace in my arms. Her wet eyes sparkled bright as a deer's, and her lips trembled with the ghosts of words. As I held her, unable to prevent her from shivering, I vowed that these Georgians would have no opportunity to torture her again. Nadze threw his handcuffs and the globe on his desk and took a bottle of vodka from the shelves behind him. "We should drink to our new partnership."

"No," I said. Sonya trembled all the more violently. "When do you want the necessary documents of ownership transferred to you?"

"Tomorrow," Nadze said.

"Here?"

Bok shook his head. "The pet market first. Our appointment is at three."

"Very well," Nadze said. What would they be doing at the pet market? "Max, we'll meet you at your bank near the Telegraph Office at four. Make sure any explosive devices on the premises are disconnected before our arrival, of course."

"Of course."

"Max, you don't look happy."

"We'd like to go now," I said, swallowing with difficulty, as if my throat were swelling shut with rage. "What about my wife?"

"Valentin has been overseeing her," he said, and directed his next question at his associate. "What about it?"

Bok nodded and spoke without looking at me. "Go to Patriarch's Ponds at eight this evening," he said. "She'll be standing by a tree in the southeast corner of the park. Stay in your car until you see a light flash three times. That will give those who bring her time enough to leave."

"For everyone's security, of course," Nadze said. "We have treated her with all the respect you yourself have showed her."

After leaving the Georgians we drove at once to our trysting place, wanting nothing except to be left alone. During those hours before we went to the park we said very little, or I would here report it to you; most of the time we spent lying together on the bed, fully clothed, ensnared in our separate thoughts. Almost overnight, my world had been upended: my income was to be stolen from me, the businesses I'd built taken over; my lover had been degraded; and my personal freedom sacrificed to satisfy the whims of those who would have me indentured to them hereafter. As for my poor koshka, in the interim between event and recollection her mind honed the memories of what had been done to her to an unbearable sharpness, and for the moment, at least, she wanted nothing to do with my touch.

"I'm sorry, Max," she said, and I told her I understood. "You *can't*," she replied. "You can't understand."

At a quarter to eight we left our small flat and drove to the park, arriving shortly before we were expected to get there. I pulled the car alongside the curb and we sat there, saying nothing, staring into impenetrable gloom. No more than three or four lamps were on in the nearby streets or in the park, and, notwithstanding municipal maintenance of late, I suspected this was not coincidental. Even before we saw the three flashing lights I had a foreshadowing of the condition in which I would find my wife; I felt no conscious apprehension, but something else—I think even at that moment, when nothing yet seemed amiss, I was already considering what my reaction and my response would be when the moment came.

"Do you want to stay here?"

"No," Sonya said, getting out of the car. "I don't want to be alone."

She put her arm around me and I held her close, not worrying about what my wife would think. Together we entered the empty park, walking over the muddy snow, and after a few minutes I glimpsed my wife leaning against a tree. She was wrapped in a long Georgian robe.

"Tanya!" I shouted. There was no response, even when I stood no more than a meter away. "Tanya?"

My dear wife's stillness was not wholly natural—or rather it was, but of a naturalness that is not to be preferred. The robe in which they cloaked her body prevented me from seeing that she was not in fact leaning but was instead propped against the tree's ice-frosted trunk. With some difficulty I carried her onto the nearest path, beneath a functioning lamp. Sonya said nothing but walked closely behind us. In the sickly yellow light I detected unusual reflections in my wife's wide-open eyes. They were coated with thin layers of ice. Fine strands, spun as if by spiders, married her eyelids to her eyebrows. The stitching was of a quality bespeaking experienced fingers.

Sonya cried. I cradled my wife in my arms and carried her back to where we found her. Bok must now have felt he'd fully assuaged the pain of his broken toe. He and Nadze must have believed they'd left me with a choice of evils: to do nothing and accept my loss, or to deny them their wants and wait for them to kill me. Those stupid, stupid bastards. Those *motherfuckers*. I had no difficulty making this decision. Between two evils, I chose the third.

9

"This is a grave tragedy for you, without question," the militiaman charged with overseeing the investigation told me the next morning, at the central bureau. "Let me express profound sympathies."

He said his name was Viktor, and that much was believable. (Dealing with the Moscow militia necessitates that you be at least cautious, and preferably paranoiac.) Although I was sure to receive no satisfaction here, I had to report the murder of my wife, and there was a chance I would be lucky enough to speak with one of the militia's few honest representatives. After paying a series of exorbitant bribes, I was taken directly to this supervisory office. But when I saw Viktor perched behind his boat-sized desk, bulwarked by black telephones, I nearly turned and walked out. He didn't remember me, but I recognized him at a glance. You will not be shocked to hear that Viktor was one of the many who visited the Georgians' house to pay off their respects in full. He and Nadze had exchanged comradely embraces and perfunctory kisses. He offered me a brisk handshake and the use of a hard chair.

"The kidnappers told me she was alive," I said, inflamed with thoughts of their bald-faced lies.

"You expect gangsters to tell the truth?" Viktor asked, leaning back in his chair. "These monsters think they can do as they please. Rest assured, Borodin, my men will not sleep until we bring these criminals to justice."

Before deciding if it would be wise to tell what I actually knew, I thought it best to ascertain how sleepless they'd been. "Were you able to find any clues at the scene?" I asked. Simply from my layman's observations I could tally a few: the robe in which she'd been wrapped, the thread that held open her eyes, the method of needlework employed, the bullet wound in the back of her skull, the bullet still at rest within her head, tracks in the snow around the tree—surely, you would think, the department's forensic experts would easily have noticed these.

"Nothing. They may as well have been ghosts," Viktor claimed, keeping the straightest of faces. "If you hadn't moved the body, possibly we—"

"Not a clue?"

He shook his head. "These killers were professional, if perverse," he said. "So perverse that we are investigating the possibility of serial killer involvement." My expression must not have been the one he expected to see on my face, and he elaborated. "Mind you, there are several such fiends presently operating in Moscow. This is not information we disseminate at will. I think your wife fell prey to one."

"Haven't I made it clear she was kidnapped? I spoke to the kidnappers. I spoke to my wife while they held her."

"And how do these beasts obtain their victims except by kidnapping them? I see no flaws in this theory, but possibly I am missing something. Tell me, was ransom demanded? Rarely do serial killers ask for ransom."

"The kidnappers wished to take possession of valuable property to which they believed I had access."

"That doesn't sound like a ransom demand to me," he said. "Do you think the killer was trying to make you think it was a business-related kidnapping?"

"That's exactly what it was, I'm telling you," I said. "Serial killers had nothing to do with this."

"You seem remarkably certain," he said. "Perhaps, by whatever means, you possess more information than we do. Tell me, who do you think may be responsible?"

I could have told him; and what might this Viktor do with such useful information? He could do nothing; he could tell Nadze I was spreading scurrilous rumors and allow the Georgian to deal personally with the problem; he could have his men haul in some hapless numbskull, charge him with the crime, and arrange a jailhouse suicide; he could produce evidence that proved me to be my wife's murderer. I would have leaned toward the last possibility, myself, and I thought I perceived him tilting in that direction. Our country's investigatory justice system can be called many things—awesome will suffice.

"I don't know," I said. He barely contained his smile. "Mafia, possibly, wishing to take over my business."

"That word comes so freely to everyone's lips these days. Somebody does something you don't like, call them mafia, yes? May as well blame it on the Jews." Undoubtedly, they were second on his list of suspects, just ahead of Mormons or the Amish. "Citizen Borodin, every businessman has enemies."

"It's not possible to narrow the list of suspects?"

"It would be difficult," he said. "Can you tell me anything else?"

We gazed into each other's eyes until I imagined I could see into the space that lay beyond them. "No."

"We'll do everything we can," he said. "More, possibly."

Hearing Pavlov's bell ring at his subtle hint, I handed over three hundred-dollar bills. His forlorn expression as he thrust them into his wallet made it clear to me that for so small an amount he would continue to perform his duties with a certain reserve.

"We'll look into it," he muttered. "I have a sea of work awaiting, if you'll excuse me."

"When will you be finished with my wife? I must make arrangements."

"Monday," he said. That wouldn't do; I passed him two additional hundreds. "Friday." From a pile of papers on his desk he withdrew a blank form, scratched arcane symbols across it, and initialed his handiwork. From an assortment of impressive stamps, he selected three and illuminated the text. "Present this to the

morgue attendants. Your funerary hirelings will be allowed to retrieve her."

"I can't thank you enough."

He waved a pen in the air as if it were a gun and reached
for one of his eight telephones. "Sleepless nights, rest assured. We'll
call you."

Knowing I would never hear his voice again, I left his office. Before I continue with my narrative, I want you to be well
aware that not until I attempted to deal with this crime by way of
legal channels, and learned almost at once the degree of satisfaction I would receive thereby, did I proceed with the plan I knew I
would follow all along.

Sonya waited for me in the hallway, swaddled in her gray
fox coat. "Let's go," I said. "No one is in danger of being arrested."

"He gave you no assistance?"

"He's an acquaintance of the criminals. The case will remain officially unsolved."

"What now?"

"I must get busy. Come on."

To a degree my angel had recovered from her appalling
experience of the previous afternoon, but neither she nor I were
yet wholly ourselves again. She could bear little more than my
lightest touch, and when we climbed into my car she slumped in
her seat, pressing her back against the passenger door as if to prevent anyone from sneaking up behind her, drawing far enough
away from me that, had you seen us together, you might have supposed we were married.

Nevertheless it was Sonya who had possessed the emotional
distance necessary to deal quickly with the horrific situation
of the night before; possibly I am being cynical, but I imagine
that on the animal level of reaction the sight of her rival, dead,
did not greatly displease her. She called the militia after we found
Tanya's body and spoke to them when they arrived, lulling them
into a sedate mood, so that they did not arrest us for having disturbed their peaceful evening. And when, after they finished their
interrogations and loaded my poor wife into the body wagon, we
went to my apartment, Sonya called Arteim for me, so I could tell
him what happened and, more important, what he should plan
to do.

"Where are we going, Max?" she asked as we drove off.

"My office. I have to be ready for them when they go to the pet market. Telman is keeping an eye on them for me."

"When who goes to the pet market?"

"Bok and Nadze. I heard them talking yesterday, before we left. Before meeting me, they're going to the pet market."

"Why?"

"I don't know, but it doesn't matter."

"What are you planning to do?" she asked, but I knew better than to tell her everything I had told Arteim. Still, I don't have to tell you that she was too intelligent not to make the correct deduction. "Max, no, are you crazy? Let the militia handle this."

"I may as well ask the Georgians to arrest and sentence themselves," I said. "If anyone takes care of these bastards, it'll have to be me."

"They'll kill you."

"If I do what they tell me, they'll kill me. This way, maybe not."

She turned away from me and stared out the window at the Kremlin Wall's dried-blood bricks. Whatever her qualms, for whatever reason, she could not prevent me from taking revenge on these Georgians. "Whatever you're going to do, I won't let you do it alone."

"No," I said. "You could also be badly hurt or killed. See what happened yesterday when you insisted upon coming along?"

"If I hadn't been there to distract them, you don't think they'd have hurt you instead?"

"Maybe. But I don't want them anywhere near you again."

"I'm going with you, Max," she said. This was not the best moment to get into such a pointless debate, and I said nothing else. Before I left to confront the Georgians, I'd simply make sure she stayed with Arteim. "Don't think I'm not."

I pulled the car into the lot behind the Universal Manufacturing building. Two of my guards stood at the street entrance, shooting admirably cruel looks at each passing stranger. When we reached my floor I was pleased to see another brace of guards, carrying army-issue submachine guns, stationed between the elevator and the office suite. Most of my staff was not in the office, in accordance with my directions; but Ludmilla was there, as was Tomas, hunched over his desk, hard at work on his assignment.

"Everything's secure?" I asked my now-sober assistant.

"The documents you requested are in this valise," Ludmilla said, handing over a heavy aluminum briefcase which, as per my instructions, contained nothing except worthless records detailing the failure of the Turkmen corn harvest in 1961, a fair substitute for my valuable business documents; all I needed were papers enough to give an instant's false impression that what I brought them was what they'd requested I bring. "Tomas has nearly finished the job, but he needs a new photo of you. My God, Mr. Borodin, what have you done to your forehead?"

"They did it," I told her, touching my scabbed-over brand. Ludmilla eyed Sonya, wordlessly expressing profound if expected disapproval—I hadn't yet told her what had happened to Tanya; she didn't yet need to know. "There's not enough time to take and print a new one. Give him this." I picked up the framed picture of myself she kept on her desk for daily inspiration and handed it to her. She looked as if I had asked her to cut off her own feet. "Don't worry, I'll bring you a new one. It's essential he finish as quickly as he can. Tomas! Here you go."

Ludmilla frowned and shook her head, but took the photo from me and handed it to him. Slipping it out of its frame, he picked up a pair of scissors and cut out a small square in which my face was exactly centered. "I need to make a couple of phone calls," I said to Sonya as I took a seat at my desk.

"Tell me what you are planning, so I won't be surprised," she said, lying down on the couch. "I'm going with you, so don't say otherwise." She shut her eyes and folded her hands across her breasts as if practicing to lie in state. It was as stupid as it was endearing that my koshka wished to be with me when I went to face these Georgians for the last time. Still, I was heartened to see that she was supplanting her interior rage with healthy anger at the world without—even if, for now, she chose me to represent that world.

"Hello?" Alla asked, answering the phone. I didn't tell her of Tanya's death; it would serve no purpose to trouble her with tragic news while she needed to supply me with a clearheaded report.

"It's me," I said. "Did Iosif return?"

"No. I've called his apartment several times, and no one answers."

Undoubtedly the pathetic rat had panicked when he saw me the other day at the Georgians' house. He could hide in any hole he wanted; we'd have him by the tail soon enough. "All right. If he does show up, do what I told you last night. Listen—"

"What about Tanya? Have they let her go?"

If I were to tell her now, we would be on the phone for half an hour, and I couldn't spare that much time. "Not yet," I told her, and she did not further interrogate me. "Tell me something, if you know. What was Iosif doing before he started working at your firm?"

"Tanya told me." Several interminable seconds passed before she recalled what my wife had said. "He was a bookkeeper for a crematorium."

"Which?"

"The Glow of Life, at Nicholas Archangel," she said. "In Reutov."

At once I grasped his plan. After taking the position at my wife's firm, he had proposed that they invest in the company for which he had been working; even then, I was sure, he was conspiring with Nadze. Probably he thought he was working for himself, as much as the Georgians; once they had control, he would doubtless find himself in an overseeing position. When Tanya asked him to serve as her spy, she unwittingly assisted him in his nefarious plans; once he better understood our personal situation, he could use our secrets to further his own purposes.

There was still an aspect to this which I could not understand. What, precisely, was he doing with these Bruneians? Was Sovietland in danger of being captured by these gangsters? Worse, could my imbecile brother be going along, *willingly*, with Iosif's secret plans, whatever they were, and not telling me? That thought, however, stopped me short; I was deeply bothered to realize that with frightening ease I had made myself as suspicious of my brother as I was of those who actively, and provably, plotted against me. I must tell you, it is not difficult in our country to work oneself into a state of highest paranoia in a matter of minutes (rational paranoia, by and large). There is no point wondering if Russians can ever trust the rest of the world's citizens and vice versa. The truer question is, Can a Russian ever trust another Russian?

"Max?" I heard Alla ask.

"I'm here," I said. "Listen, there should be guards arriving at your office this morning, if they're not already there. If any takeover attempts are made today, they will serve as your line of defense."

"Are we safe?"

"Completely," I said, having no idea. "A precaution, nothing more. With luck this crisis will be over by evening. I'll keep you informed. All right?"

"Be careful."

Sonya lifted her head from the sofa cushions as I hung up. "That was Tanya's friend?" she asked, as I called Telman.

"Her co-worker, Alla," I said. "You've met."

"Why didn't you tell her what happened?"

"Later, I promise."

"You don't think she'll be upset with you when she finds out?"

"Koshka, if she is, she'll forgive me."

"You're not infinitely forgivable, Max."

Telman answered on the first ring. "Any movement?" I asked.

"Not yet."

"The moment they depart, call me. The men are ready?"

"I've assembled twelve of the most dependable. They're prepared to act at an instant's notice, Max. Say when."

"I'll check in again in an hour if I don't hear from you in the meantime. These Georgians aren't supposed to be going to the pet market before three, but they may leave early. Keep me informed."

"Don't worry."

As I hung up, Tomas knocked on my office door. Only while he was working at his table did he move with evident coordination; as he made his journey across the room to where I sat he struck his foot or knee, in turn, against the couch, a chair, and my desk. With shaking hands he presented me with the document he'd prepared. "Will this do?"

I examined the folded paper closely, making sure the format was correct. Once more, he had come through: the color of the document, the typeface, the watermark, and the stamp impressed into the photograph were all exactly right. "Beautiful," I said. "Perfect." Even the highest officials in the SVRR would not have been able to tell that this was not one of their properly issued identification documents. Not a militiaman in Russia would trouble me for long, once he saw this. "Let me give you a bonus for your good work." From my wallet I drew three hundred-dollar bills and handed them to him. "I'll not forget you at New Year's, either. Thank you, Tomas."

"Any time," he said, grinning, turning, and stumbling out of the office.

"What do you need such documentation for?" Sonya asked, coming over and looking at the paper before I slipped it into my inside jacket pocket. "Is this part of your plan, whatever it is? Aren't you liable for arrest simply by carrying such fraudulent papers?"

"If you didn't know better, could you tell they were fraudulent?" I asked, and then called to my workers through the door. "Ludmilla, we're leaving now. You and Tomas go home. I'll have one of the guards accompany you."

"I got here fine by myself," she said. "Who bothers old women? The young ones hold their interest," she added, turning eyes as black as a sturgeon's toward Sonya. "You have your briefcase?"

"Right here," I said, taking my bulletproof vest from the closet and removing my shirt, tie, and jacket. "Give me a moment to change."

She shook her head and walked out, closing the door behind her. I took care that neither she nor Sonya saw me sliding my revolver into my coat pocket. "Now where are we going?" my koshka asked.

"Evgeny's. Arteim'll be there. He'll wait with you till my business is done."

"Will you tell me what your business is?"

"I shouldn't."

"Why is subterfuge so beneficial when you're the one employing it?" she asked. "All you do is complain about people never telling you the truth, and how easily does truth slip through your lips?"

"Sonya, this is no time to argue," I said, angered by her remarks. "In situations such as this, you do what's necessary."

"I'm coming with you, Max."

"No," I told her again. "It'll be too dangerous."

I hadn't yet convinced her; so be it, I thought, and we went downstairs, to head to our next stop. Before we left I watched to make certain the guard walked Tomas and Ludmilla in the right direction, for I did not feel I could fully trust even my guards—but for the moment I still had to depend upon them. It disconcerted me to know that these unwanted encounters with our society's more unsavory members illuminated the darkest crannies of my soul, the ones in which I deliberately, long ago, left off the lights. Never before had I needed to traffic so directly with mafias; always I ran my industries in an admirably legal manner (I grant that *legal*, in the Western sense, is a word that should rarely, if ever, be used in the same sentence as the word *Russia*), but now, through the entanglements in which Dmitry had snared me and through my late wife's secretive pacts, I found myself circling in orbit around the world of thieves, endlessly whirling with all other citizens of our nation.

But what else could I do? I glanced in the rearview mirror as we drove away, checking to see if we were being followed; checking, too, that it was my face I still saw reflected in its surface. Was it me? Could I still recognize myself? For years I'd reveled in my successes as they came, never thinking of what the ultimate cost might be, once the bill came. Since boyhood I understood that rising to the top of any organization, be it company or state, requires the assumption of a pathological mind-set; though everyone may be born sane, by the time positions of power are gainsafed, those who attain the summit have invariably been driven mad by the struggle—history proves this to be inherent, even necessary, to the nature of systems. As for me, make your own inferences.

When we arrived at Evgeny's I discovered that my brother was, of course, nowhere to be found. "Where is he?" I asked Arteim.

"He drove out to his park of frolic," my associate told me. "He took his girlfriend with him. What an adorable young woman she is, Max."

"Is she Circe? One of the Sirens?"

"I don't understand."

"She seems to have put you into a coma of entrancement," I said. "What did I tell you? Keep him here at all times! Were they alone?"

"Of course not, I sent one of our best guards with them," he said. "A big fellow, with experience."

"You still should have kept him here," I said. "Tied him up if you had to. It's dangerous for my brother to be wandering freely in the best of times."

"I tried," Arteim said. "But his builders called this morning, they told him the first ride was ready. The tunnel of love. He couldn't wait to have a look."

"How could I be related to such a fool?" I asked, speaking more to my late parents in heaven above than to anyone in the room; I wondered, too, if it had truly been his builders who called. "He's made his own bed, it can't concern me now. Nothing else unexpected has happened?"

"No. You're sure the danger is as great as you told me last night?"

"You have to ask?"

He shrugged. "You seem tense, but—"

"I find my wife murdered in the park and I'm tense? Killers tell me to hand over my business to them and I'm tense? This shocks you? How would you feel?"

He turned pale, as if I scared the blood out of him. "I would shake with fear."

"Exactly," I said. "If my apartment's secured, let's go. You and Sonya will stay there until I return."

"Now?" he asked. "Give me a moment."

"Max, I'm not—" she started to say, but I was already handing over her coat and slipping on my shoes. Arteim shrugged and zipped up his own boots. My trusty associate is always prepared to handle the tasks I assign him, but unlike Telman, Arteim prefers to carry them out at his own pace, in the relaxed southern manner (some call it dilatory—lazy is the word they mean); if forced to respond with haste, he begins to suffer an almost debilitating nervousness which, however, never culminates in collapse until the task is done. That morning, not only my brusque actions and speech but my very metabolism seemed to affect him; possibly he is allergic to adrenaline, and I was so charged I think my body was emitting the very scent of the natural chemical, choking him as pollen chokes the asthmatic—I shall have to read up on this subject in the scientific literature.

For as my moment of decision approached, I became ever more mentally sharp, feeling as if I had drunk a liter of strong coffee, almost believing myself able to know my thoughts before I thought them—the sign of a more personal paranoia, you could possibly say. Often, in combat memoirs, you read of how the processes of life are most highly charged by death's proximity, and in such moments of crisis you are one hundred percent aware of knowing what it means to be alive—that was how I felt, that day. Even as I write this, I can approximate a semblance of that remarkable state as easily as I can call to mind, and fingertip, the texture of my late wife's skin.

"We have accompaniment en route?" I asked Arteim as we got in my car. He pointed to our left, where two of our stalwarts sat in an unwashed black Volga. Feeling more secure, I fastened my belt and looked in the rearview mirror at my koshka, as she took her place in the back seat—I'd decided it would be too dangerous for her to sit in the front.

"I called Ivan Ivan and gave him your message," my associate said.

"He's willing?"

"Freelancers are always looking for work," he said. I pulled the car into a side street, thinking it wise to take a roundabout route to my apartment. "He's more dependable than he looks, Max. We've seen for ourselves, Ivan has the cold eye of the serpent."

"Which serpent is going to do what?" Sonya asked.

"A subcontractor, a job," I told her, unwilling to detail what I had in store for Iosif, once—if—I survived the afternoon. "Nothing, pay it no mind."

"Max is sending someone to the camps without the right of correspondence." Leave it to Arteim—of course!—to boast of my prowess (admirable, but not always wise), his voice piping with excitement, like a child's. He was shocked but not surprised when I struck him on the arm. I hadn't realized he would be so elated by this particular plan of mine, but I should have expected him to be pleased that, at long last, I had decided to work in a more time-honored métier.

"Who are you having killed?"

Where had she gained such familiarity with subtle expressions of prison cant? We would not kill him until we found him, but there was no need to note this. "Arteim's exaggerating. Don't listen to—"

"Max," he said, "you'd better pull over." Glancing in the mirror, I saw the lights of a militia vehicle coming up behind our car, drawing ahead of our guards' Volga. I stopped at the curb and switched off the engine.

"Of all mornings, why are they stopping me now?" I asked. "What is the problem?"

"You'll be the problem if you don't calm down," Arteim said. "Act like nothing is wrong. He'll go as soon as we give him money. If you have to, show him that special document."

"That's the first thing he'll see."

The officer took precious time, emerging from his car. He stretched and yawned, as if he hadn't been awake long; he carefully adjusted his sideview mirror and closely examined his front fenders for dents. Something about his uniform didn't look right. Finally, he chose to wander over to where we waited for him. He was young, weighed down by no more than twenty-odd years, and wore his single-starred hat on his head at an angle, apparently thinking it gave him an insouciant air. At first I believed his walrus mustache was natural, that he'd grown it to look older, but when he peered down into the car I realized that his furze had been pasted on with careless hands; a yellow glob of mucilage clung to the tip of his red nose. This made me even more suspicious. Keeping his hand on his gun, he signaled that I should roll down the window and give him my identification. I passed over my license and my SVRR document. He looked them over for several minutes, as if wonderstruck by the intricacies of the Cyrillic alphabet.

"Problem?" I asked.

"Your right tire," he said, still staring at my license and papers. "It looked as if it could start wobbling. Accidents could occur."

Something was plainly wrong; the moment he saw those SVRR papers he should have admitted his terrible error and allowed us to go on our way. "But it wasn't wobbling?"

"Not yet," he said. "But it's a dangerous possibility. You should be more careful."

"How much?" Arteim asked.

"Are you the driver?" the militiaman replied. "No, I didn't think so. You should keep quiet." He handed back my documents and tapped his fingers on the side of the car as he examined the wheels. "This is very serious, worse than I thought. Tires such as these could blow out and cause fatal accidents. You need to take care of this problem immediately."

That bastard militiaman Viktor must have taken it upon himself to do a favor for his friends from the South and sent one of his sleepless worthies to make certain I caused no further difficulties for anyone—certainly Nadze would not liquidate me before I delivered the documents he wanted. But if this young fool were an assassin, he should already have killed us. What was his game? Did he even know what he was doing? The militia has not been able to retain the most capable workers of late. "What do you think I should do?" I asked.

"You're a lucky man. I happen to have with me some excellent Michelin tires. They will fit your car, I'm sure."

"Probably these aren't free tires you're offering."

"They are worth two hundred dollars each," he said. Could he be *real*? No, it wasn't conceivable. "If you were to buy them from me at one hundred, you would be saving money and that would take care of this problem, I think. Why don't you get out and help me roll them over to you? You can change them later at your convenience."

"Max, his car has a light but otherwise it's unmarked," Arteim whispered to me in Armenian. He adjusted the mirror on his side so I could see that the officer's car bore no distinguishing insignia. This imbecile was acting on Viktor's orders, no question. "Don't get out."

Our guards were double-parked some short distance behind the official vehicle, letting their engine idle, ready to spring into action with a moment's notice. Would that be time enough?

"Get out of the car," said the militiaman.

"Didn't you see my identification papers?" I asked. "Don't you know who you're dealing with?"

"I know exactly," he said, drawing his gun as he pulled open the door. "Get out."

As soon as my guards saw his weapon come into play, they responded, although with more alacrity than I should have preferred. Our highwayman had not been too bashful to threaten gunplay in the midst of a busy side street, but the citizens passing were as familiar with the more hallucinatory aspects of our reality as anyone and accordingly acted as if they weren't seeing anything, if they happened to take notice at all. So my guards believed it quite within their rights to floor the accelerator of their car and run down the officer before he even saw them coming. He fluttered into the air as if he were a pigeon, but landed like a thrown brick. In their mad rush my guards also managed to tear off the driver's door of my car, although it did not fly so far. We were badly shaken by the near collision, but none of us was hurt; several minutes did pass before Sonya and Arteim stopped screaming. Their howls alone would have captured the attention of the most blasé, but what excited unavoidable comment in the crowd was when our guards, noticing the militiaman struggling to crawl away, threw their car into reverse and finished the job they'd begun with a stomach-turning crunch.

"We should leave, Max," Arteim said. I agreed, and wasted no time starting the ignition and speeding away from the curb. Our guards took their place behind us again. No one in the crowd did anything after we left, I saw; the militiaman lay alone in the street in the place where he had been flattened. The wind blowing through my now-open door froze my arm as if I had plunged it into icy water.

"Is everyone okay?" I asked when we stopped for a traffic light, several blocks from the scene of our unpleasant encounter. Glancing back, I saw no cars more threatening than our guards' black Volga, its metallic smile now smashed inward as if it had been in a brawl. No one answered, but I saw my koshka nodding silently when I looked in the rearview mirror. Her face was the color of a dead fish. When the light changed, I turned left, heading toward Tverskaya Street, leaning to the right to keep from tumbling through the open door; my seat belt, luckily, helped keep me in place. "Would someone please say something?"

"We could have been killed," Sonya said.

"I told you this would be dangerous." She looked even angrier with me at that moment than she had earlier. So many times my koshka allowed emotions to overwhelm her good sense, and this was rarely advantageous. Pedestrians stopped to stare at our open-air transportation as we passed, and I hoped no authorities, real or otherwise, would stop us to ask why we so evidently enjoyed the alluring scents of exhaust and burning oil. I was infuriated that my fine car had been so senselessly damaged, but there was nothing I could do now except try not to fall out. My beeper went off. Arteim and I leapt up in our seats as if we were being strafed. Telman's number surfaced in the gray field of the read-out, and I handed my phone over to my associate. "See what's up. Call him."

The light at the Manège turned red and we stopped. A man in a cab next to us rolled down his window and shouted over to me, "Your door!" As if I might not have noticed! I brusquely waved him away, and he nodded, pleased to have been of assistance.

"Telman," Arteim said, speaking into the receiver. "What is it? What are they doing?"

"What?" I asked. My teeth chattered with cold. The light changed, and I drove up Mokhovaya. Ahead of us was the Hotel Moskva, Red Square to our right; if I had consciously tried, I could not have selected a busier route through which to maneuver my all-too memorable vehicle. However, I thought, once we got to my building I could store this car in the garage and take Tanya's when the time came to depart. A moment later, I discovered that the time was here.

"They're leaving, Max," Arteim said. "All of them, he thinks."

"Who all?"

He gave attentive ear to what Telman was saying. "The leaders, their guards, some of the Kazakhs, including that Mels you described. Twenty altogether."

"They're already leaving?" I asked; it was not yet one, earlier than I'd expected them to depart. "Which direction are they heading? Can he tell?"

"Telman, where are they going?" he asked; then, to me: "Southeast. To the pet market, he's guessing. He says you'd better head over there now to meet up with him if you want the plan to proceed."

"I told you I'd be coming with you, Max," Sonya said, speaking up. She was right; I had no choice. If the Georgians were already going to the pet market, I had to be there to confront them, I'd have no second chance.

"You'll wait in the car," I said. Without hesitation I turned left, preparing to circle the block before heading southeast.

"What do I tell him?" Arteim asked.

"Say we'll be there shortly. Keep him on the line in case they change directions."

"We're on the way," he told Telman, speaking into the receiver.

"Max," Sonya asked, "what exactly is your plan?"

I gritted my teeth, tightened the grip of my hands on the wheel, and made another hard left. "Telman and twelve of our guards will meet me at the pet market, where Bok and Nadze are going. They won't expect to see me there. We'll catch them by surprise, talk to them shortly, and then kill them."

"But there are at least twenty of them," Sonya was thoughtful enough to note. "Have you and your men ever been involved in anything like this before?"

"Not exactly."

"What's going to happen, then?"

"Exactly what I say is going to happen," I said, speaking purely out of bravado; common sense told me otherwise. But the only other thing I could do was run—and I would get no farther, running from these mobsters, than Iosif could run from me. As we crossed the river, the wind coming off its ice-free surface lowered the air temperature in the car perhaps fifteen degrees; I was sure I'd be frostbitten before we reached the market. Arteim patted his coat, making sure he had his gun—this was not a sight that comforted me. My associate had many skills, but a familiarity with weapons was not one of them. Considering his incompetence with small arms, I wanted him to be far from the scene of unpleasantness. He would stay with Sonya in the car; perhaps I could even convince him to take her to the Metro and return with her to my apartment. Sonya was as scared as she was infuriated by my prediction, I believed, but how could I lighten her troubles when I was so overwhelmed by my own?

"Good," she said, seeming vastly—surprisingly—pleased.

Before I tell you what happened there, let me describe Moscow's open-air pet market for you, because unless I give you an eyewitness account you will not easily believe that such a medieval spectacle still exists in this most modern of all world cities. The Zayauze, an old neighborhood of immense charm, is located to the southeast of the central district, where the Yauza empties into the Moskva. At the junction of these rivers stands one of the Master Builder's seven skyscrapers, a twenty-four-story apartment block whose soaring needle is still topped with a Communist star. Close by are six magnificent churches, the eighteenth-century Yauzskaya Medical Clinic, and streets lined with mansions of the same period. Many times these vintage structures have been threatened with demolition, but the neighborhood's only new building is a miracle of modern architecture, the Taganka Theater, on Taganka Square: there the first dramatization of *The Master and Margarita* was presented; there my favorite balladeer Vysotsky worked, and from there his funeral procession began its solemn march. Even the Taganskaya Metro station is one of the most attractive in the system, with blue and white ceramic decor throughout—picture a subway station designed by Wedgwood, had Stalin captured Wedgwood and moved its workers to Moscow. The square itself is broad, dirty, and difficult to cross, typical of all city squares save for Red Square. A short distance away, on the far side of a tramline, is a large plot of vacant land, a choking desert in summer, a frosty Siberia in winter, a treacherous swamp in fall and spring, where, for as long as I can remember, you find the animal fair.

Moscow's pet market, our oldest capitalist institution, has never known the grimy touch of state fingers. Emerge from the Metro and walk toward the market; you see at first only an anarchic mass of thousands of disagreeable people, and overhanging all a permeating barnyard smell, but once you blend into their assembly you discern the time-perfected structure. Ramshackle wooden stalls, easily moved kiosks, and open flatbed trucks demarcate the sides of wide, crooked aisles; each passageway is given over to the trade of a different species, and their sellers expound at length upon the unsurpassable merits of their beasts. "Stop! Look here!" they shout. "No finer companion! The children's nursemaid! The friend of the family! A comfort to the old and feeble! A joy to the lame and sick! My prices can't be matched!" In the dog aisles you find intelligent mongrels and choice specimens of every breed: poodle, terrier, mastiff, dachshund, spaniel, or retriever. In cats, take your pick of Siamese, Burmese, Persians, or Abyssinians. If you come looking for birds you find cages of budgerigars, finches, mynahs, parrots, and cockatiels stacked six or seven high. There are glass tanks and bowls containing schools

of iridescent fish; tubs piled deep with turtles; terrariums full of
frogs, snakes, and lizards; crates stuffed with straw and sleeping
rodents therein—hamsters, guinea pigs, mice, rats. Ferrets and
skunks are paraded along on leashes, trained pigs on ropes. Many
times, like all Muscovites, I have spent blessedly wasted time here
in the authentic heart of Russia. I loved the pet market.

We got there without further interference, which improved
my mood, even if I was frozen half to death. I parked on a street
near the market; our guards pulled up twenty meters ahead of us.
As I climbed out of the car I noticed five or six motorcycles, in
alignment, halfway down the block from where we had parked,
and three swarthy men stuffed into black leather standing nearby.
I took my phone back from Arteim. "You're in place?" I asked
Telman.

"You?" he replied.

"Ready."

I handed the phone back to Arteim and took my briefcase
from the back seat. Sonya got out, and I didn't try to stop her. The
motorcycle gangsters hadn't yet appeared to have seen us—or if
they had, they gave no indication that our presence concerned
them. I didn't see any of my other guards in the midst of the citizens making their way to the market, animals in hand; for a moment I wondered if Telman was telling me the truth and they were
truly there. There were countless numbers of Southerners in the
crowd, and I had no way of distinguishing those who were harmless from those who were members of Nadze's party.

My koshka extended her hand, and I took it. "Let's go."

"Shouldn't you secure your car?" Arteim asked, unbutton-
ing his coat to allow access to his weapon. I stared at the missing
driver's door until he saw what I was looking at and realized why
I did not trouble myself with removing the wipers and side-view
mirrors.

"Pay attention to everything I tell you," I said. "Stay close
by me. My men will have joined us by the time we find them. Hang
back as I approach them, and continue to keep your distance. If
all goes as it should, I'll talk to them briefly and offer to give them
my briefcase; I'll say my important documents are inside. I'll kneel
and open it. The instant I open it, fall to the ground. That's the
signal for the men to start firing."

The sky was cloudless; the wind had settled, and the air was not as cold as it had felt in the car. Ordinarily on a day such as this I would have been happy to have gone for a long stroll along Tverskaya, enjoying the sight of the faces in the crowd around me, looking up at the crumbling buildings, taking in the smells and sights and sounds of our world in beauty such as we rarely find it. Sonya took my arm in hers and kissed me lightly on the lips. Then we stepped into the crowd's stream, flowing with them into the marketplace proper, our shoes slipping on mud and snow and shit. Arteim spoke softly into my phone, as he kept us apprised of Telman's observations.

"Where do you think they'll be?" Sonya asked. "Dogs? Cats?"

"They're not here to buy a canary, let me tell you," I said, finding it hard to hear her over the barks and yelps around us. "Arteim, where to?"

"Go to the left, Max," he said. We turned down one of several dog aisles. Ahead of us a group of young men examined the teeth of a brown retriever, judging its health; a fat woman tried to stop us so we could look over her Pomeranians. The yapping nearly deafened me as we pushed our way along. Nothing is as overpowering as the smell of the dog aisles on a rainy day, but it is powerful enough in clear weather to make you dizzy, after a while. When we crept by an especially malevolent-looking Doberman, trying not to disturb its rest, the monster roused itself enough to snap at my leg as if it belonged to a tender chicken. "Watch your feet, imbecile," its owner shouted at me, but I ignored the peasant and stepped out of biting range. More than one mongrel barked at Sonya as we walked by, and had I not been so preoccupied I would have teased her and asked if she thought the dogs, seeing her fox coat, might recognize their brothers.

"Big-animal row," Arteim told us, and we headed off to the right. Once we took leave of the dog aisles the crowd thinned, and I could better size up the people in our immediate area. On the far sides of the aisle, striding in unision with us, were four of our guards, spaced accordingly for full coverage. They sauntered like musicians, moving their heads in time with their steps, not missing anything going on around them. We passed a pair of cows, and a flock of filthy sheep that resembled a clutch of maggots, but the first truly big animal we saw was a muzzled bear. Its battered uni-

cycle lay in a nearby puddle of mud. His owner, a mustachioed
lout wearing an embroidered vest, proclaimed his creature's un-
paralleled merits. "What a noble face," he shouted. "Belshazar can
ride anything on wheels, see for yourself. Talk to me and I'll make
a good deal." The pathetic beast resembled a rug sewn together
from old hats; probably it could not have walked without crutches.
Grunting feebly, Belshazar tugged at the heavy chain that bound
it to a metal stanchion driven into the earth.

"You!" the owner shouted, pointing at me. "You're a man
who needs a bear, I can see. Let's talk."

He not only startled me into a near-seizure but then ges-
ticulated so wildly, walking over, that everyone in the immediate
area turned to see his victim."Give it to the circus," I shouted back,
striding forward, trying to ignore him.

"My name is Filipp. I am happy to meet you," he said,
grasping my hand as if in friendship. Arteim motioned to the guards
nearest us that they should not yet move in but be ready. "Come
examine its fur. I guarantee you, Belshazar is free of parasites."

The bear was not as unhealthy as he looked; as Filipp tried
pulling me closer to his stall, the animal raised up on its haunches
and swung wildly at us, its blood-encrusted claws narrowly missing me. "I don't want your fucking bear," I told him, jerking away
before either of them might catch me.

"Don't insult the merchandise, you prick," he said, using
all the subtle arts of salesmanship he possessed as we got away.
"Fool! Years from now you'll regret your decision. Idiot bastard!
Durak!"

"Max, a little to the right," Arteim said, keeping his ear to
the phone. "Behind those trucks."

Filipp continued shouting after us, but we ignored his
taunts. Thirty meters away were several military vehicles converted
to civilian use; the largest, a platoon carrier, still possessed its
canvas-covered flatbed but had been painted a medicinal orange.
Behind the truck, staring into its storage space, was a gang of dark
men. The closer we came, the faster my heart beat, but I was in
no danger of suffering a coronary attack—rather, I felt supernatu-
rally calm, as if I were floating through a dream.

"There they are."

Bok and Nadze wore dark suits and stood out in the crowd
like crows in snow. Mels was also there; he looked cheerful and

threatening in his layers of leather wraps. They were speaking to a barrel-shaped man wearing a long green army coat. Behind their small group stood a dozen men, other Georgians and Kazakh guards.

"Now what?" Sonya asked.

"We're more evenly matched than we thought," Arteim noted.

"Don't believe what you see."

I watched as more of my men turned up, seeming as idle browsers whiling away an afternoon, awaiting our signal. Then I finally glimpsed Telman; he brushed past me as if we were strangers, but I heard his whisper as our paths crossed. "Ready," he said.

"Stay here," I said, taking my phone back from Arteim.

"No," said Sonya, holding tight to my arm, stepping forward as if to drag me along. Mels saw us; he flashed a smile and tapped Nadze on the shoulder.

"That's it," I said, accepting the fact that I would not be alone when I met them. "All right, then. Let us go meet the hydra."

We'd plainly surprised them, if nothing else. Mels stepped away from his superiors, moving closer to the other Georgians. Bok did not look at all cheered to see us. Nadze chose to welcome us as if we were friends and directed his guards to stand at ease. Nothing in his face revealed untoward emotion of any kind. "Max," he said, shaking my hand. "This is the last place we expected to see you today."

"A remarkable coincidence, isn't it?" I asked. He gave Arteim a particularly long look, as if ascertaining how many weapons might be concealed on his person.

"Listen, there's something I should tell you—" he started to say, but Bok interrupted him.

"You found your wife?" the monster asked, giving me his skull's grin.

"Of course. I wasn't surprised, I have to tell you."

"She put up an unfortunate struggle," Nadze said. "It couldn't be helped."

"Thank you for sewing her eyes open," I said. "She'd have appreciated that."

Bok surveyed our surroundings; I hoped he could not spot every one of my men. "What are you doing here, Max?" Nadze asked.

"Well, my niece's birthday is tomorrow," I said. "I thought I'd come to buy some white mice, perhaps."

Neither one of them looked as if they believed me for a moment. "In this part of the market?" Bok asked.

"I had no trouble finding them."

If I acted too rashly, I would increase the likelihood of failure, but I could not give them time enough to formulate a defensive plan. I'm sure Sonya's presence confused the Georgians; why should I have brought a woman to an ambush? For that reason alone I was grateful she was with me.

"Mrs. Gubina, I hope you are feeling well," Nadze said. "You appeared upset when you left us yesterday."

She didn't even look at him. "What are you doing here?" I asked.

"Come see what we have bought," Nadze said, and with Bok and the man in the green coat he stepped around to the rear of the truck. Arteim and Sonya stayed close to me as we followed him; possibly it was a trick, but I didn't think so. I saw several of my men falling into place, some five meters behind the Georgian guards. As we walked past him Mels smiled at us again and then, unexpectedly, winked. Had he guessed why we were here? Was he pleased? Nadze pointed at a large steel cage on the flatbed of the truck, beneath the canopy. "What do you think of our beauties?"

Inside the cage were a pair of tigers. Their thick orange fur was a darker shade than that of the canopy above them; the black stripes gave an impression—justified, doubtless—of powerful muscles. Each tiger was perhaps a meter high at the shoulder; their paws were the size of dinner plates. They stared at us with eyes more disdainful than even those of Bok's. The man in the long coat was evidently their seller.

"Siberian," he said, extending his arm, speaking in an incomprehensibly thick Kamchatkan accent. "Rare and costly. Forest kings."

"I am donating these to the New York Bronx Zoo in the name of Georgian-American friendship," Bok said.

"Tigers are forbidden to be exported, aren't they?" I asked, keeping a sharper eye on the uncaged beasts surrounding me.

"We have all necessary documents and exemptions," Nadze said, clapping me on the shoulder. "You know how easy it is to obtain such papers." The smile he offered was unencumbered by happiness. "So we will see you at your bank at four, as planned?"

"I have my materials with me," I said, patting the side of my briefcase. "As long as we are all here, why don't we get this over with?"

"This isn't the best place for such an exchange. We should follow our original plan, don't you think?"

"But the sooner you have my papers, the sooner you have official control."

"We have control now," Nadze said. "Why are you so willing to give us your property? If I were you, I think I'd do everything I could to keep it out of our hands."

"It's not as if I have much of a choice," I said. Sonya and Arteim looked nervous; I knew I could control my own emotions, but how much longer could they? "So why don't we—"

"He said we should not do it here," Bok said, leaning forward so that I could look deep into his dead eyes as he spoke. "Are you deaf?"

"On second thought, perhaps we should take you up on your offer," Nadze said, seizing the briefcase and pulling it out of my hands. "Who knows what else you may have in here of interest?"

As he toyed with the latches, seeming ready to look at what I'd brought him, I prepared to seize my companions and dive for safety. Blood beat so loudly through my veins that I thought I could barely hear him. The directions I'd given Telman were to start firing if either Nadze or I opened the case. But the Georgian refrained, and instead handed it to Mels. "It'll be interesting to see what you've brought us," Nadze said. "Do you know, an idea occurs to me. Possibly it would be a good thing if Mrs. Gubina came with us, back to our house. Not that I doubt you, Max, but simply to be sure. You understand, I'm sure."

Mels moved forward, as if intending to take my angel from me. She held on to my arm as if she were glued to it. The moment was here, I believed; better we should be killed where we stood, rather than let them drag her away. I glanced over to Telman; he and the guards closest to him were already drawing their weapons. But before either of us could shout the command to commence shooting, I heard an all-too-familiar cry.

"Max!"

Petrenko was not alone: Debalov was with him, clutching something large, brown, and wriggling. My old pal waved his arms at me as if to bring me in for a landing.

"Where is your stall, you capitalist bastard?" he shouted, coming closer. "What will you try to sell me?"

"You know him?" Nadze asked, gripping my shoulder as if planning to use me as a shield. "You know fucking *Petrenko*?"

Never have I been gladder to see a lunatic approach me in such a spirit of warm camaraderie. He and Debalov were followed by a sizable band of broken-faced supporters, the Hawks. Each of the louts, including Petrenko, wore a black and yellow leatherette jacket; each broad back bore the crossed-T insignia of the People's Party of Hammer and Steel. Evidently they were coming from, or going to, a rally or congress. They looked like a provincial hockey team come to spend a playoff weekend in the city, drinking, fucking, and bashing heads.

"We're not long acquainted, ourselves, but he and Dmitry were business partners." Nadze and Bok stared at one another in dismay; I encircled Sonya's waist as Mels, sensibly, stepped backward until he stood with his fellow Kazakhs. "You didn't know?"

"*Pizdastradatil!*" Petrenko said (*cuntsufferer* is as close a translation as is possible), hugging me and planting a sticky kiss on my neck. "My partner in crime. What a happy accident, our seeing you again so soon." Nadze's expression didn't change, but Bok's did; he began to look as if he had just come in on a thirty-hour flight, having sustained himself on fred the entire way. "Men, this is a good Russian man," Petrenko said, nearly lifting me into the air as he introduced me to his brigands. "Max Borodin. A strong supporter of our party."

"What are you doing here, Pavel?" I asked.

"Buying a bulldog," he said. "Gyorgi! Show Max."

Debalov lugged over the writhing hound. It struggled in the grip of its bearer, snapping its jaws like a prehistoric turtle, chewing at the chain attached to its spiked collar. The thing panted incessantly; strands of drool streamed from its tongue to the ground. Foul gases escaped constantly from its nonbiting end. The sight and odor of this canine atrocity sickened me; if, as some believe, Satan made the world, then such a creature was his first creation.

"Man's best friend," I noted.

"Yes, yes. Masculine men need masculine dogs," Petrenko explained. "His name is Minetchik, but I will change that."

"Of course," I said (in American English, I believe the beast's name could be best translated as Pussy Eater). The Georgians hadn't moved; apparently they were so taken aback by Petrenko and his band they didn't know what to do. Mels and his Kazakhs, on the other hand, were subtly moving toward the edges of the encompassing crowd, as if to be able to leave quickly when the time came. "Pavel, do you like Siberian tigers?"

He nodded. "All native Russian fauna are unequaled in splendor."

"May we?" I asked Bok and Nadze, walking past them, keeping a firm hold on Sonya. Petrenko, Debalov, and Arteim followed me to the back of the truck. The tigers roared, seeing him—Petrenko roared back.

"Beautiful!" he exclaimed, turning to me and slapping me on the chest—I don't know why. "Gyorgy, allow my dog to have a good look at these cats. I do not want him to become too swollen with pride." Debalov put a choke hold around Pussy Eater's neck before lifting him in front of the bars. The tigers drew back into the corners of the cage and made pitiful, anguished screams. Obviously they were as horrified as I had been by the sight of this slobbering, flatulent hellhound. "Where are they going, the zoo?"

"Yes," I told him. "The New York Zoo."

"*What?* Who says?"

"They do." I pointed behind me, toward Bok and Nadze.

"Who are these black bastards, Max?"

We moved back into the open, where the Georgians and the Petrenkovites stood exchanging baleful stares. Beyond them, I could see my men on all sides. Mels and his Kazakhs had neatly shifted their position, taking control of a distant area of the field, remaining close enough so as not to disconcert their employers. My briefcase still rested at Nadze's feet. Bok watched us carefully as we walked toward them. Arteim positioned himself to my right; Sonya bound herself to me as if with ropes—she knew she would be safe as long as I was close by. "These are Dmitry's business partners, Pavel," I explained. "At least they were until they killed him."

"Killed him? When? Why?" Petrenko asked; but when what I told him finally sank into his brain, the change of expression on his face could only have been called lycanthropic. "Partners? Are you telling me he was in league with these parasites? These corrupters of our people?" he asked, spraying Bok and Nadze with a rain of spittle.

"Lavrenty, who is this pig-ugly devil?"

"Pavel Petrenko," Nadze informed his partner as he wiped off his face with his handkerchief. "One of our many little Hitlers. He serves the secret police at his leisure, or so we have heard." He unbuttoned his coat, as if he wished to better relish the feel of freezing wind. "What is this shit, Max?"

"Dmitry double-crossed us all," I said. "Pavel, he was taking money from both you and these Georgians." Debalov placed his flea-ridden cargo on the muddy ground, handing the end of its chain to one of their attendant youths. "When they found him out, they murdered him." Then, in further explaining Dmitry's scheme, I chose to effect a subtle reinterpretation of historical event, estimating that I needed to do what I could to bring this crop to harvest. "Only yesterday, I discovered he gave them the money you lent him."

"*Chort!*" Petrenko said. His comrades, spoiling for battle, started unsnapping their party jackets, facilitating easy access to personal hardware. "Shit-brained weasel! Blood-sucking crab louse! He gave our party's money to these felons? These bastards, these Turks?"

"Georgians!" Bok shouted; amazingly, that was all he did. As I hoped, Petrenko was too infuriated to remember that, as far as he'd known, I'd been hard at work turning out counterfeit currency for him—later (if I was lucky, and I was now almost positive I would be) I could think of justification to explain my failings.

"We gave *him* money," Nadze said; for the first time since I met him, I discerned fear in his voice—it sounded as sweet music in my ears. "He gave us nothing! He tried to steal from us. We took nothing from you fascist morons."

"Do you know what else they did, Pavel?" He turned avenger's eyes toward me as he listened, keen to hear every accusation I might have to offer. "They kidnapped my wife and murdered her. In cold blood."

"Traitor," Nadze said to me. "So you're also serving these schoolboy Nazis?"

"Your wife, Max?" Petrenko asked, clearly shocked. "Why did they kill her?"

"For the hell of it," I said.

"I've had enough of these fucking fascists," said Bok, waving his arm as if signaling their forces. The other Georgians seemed oddly reluctant to respond and the Kazakhs only grinned.

"Who the fucking hell are you calling fascists, you fucking vermin?" Petrenko shouted back, screaming with such vehemence that Sonya turned to hide her face—more likely, her ears—against my chest. "Murderers of Russian women! Believe me, I will piss in your faces until you go blind."

"*Pizda!*" Bok said, which unerringly steered this exchange ever faster toward its explosive conclusion. *Pizda* cannot be translated and should never be spoken, not even in Russian (although it often is). The term, in English, approximates *bastard*, but that word is but a lover's kiss in comparison to the Russian epithet.

"Hey, you!" I heard someone shout, somewhere to my right. "Hey!"

"Asian trash!" Debalov cried, responding for his speechless, infuriated master. "Ass-licking mongrels! We'll burn you for firewood!"

"Split your ass on a horse prick," Bok yelled back.

"We'll fuck your mouths!" replied Petrenko. "Devils! Abominators!"

"Hey! You!" called out Filipp the vendor, stomping through the crowded aisle, walking his bear alongside him; I supposed he had been preparing to leave when he had the good fortune to see me. It was a tragedy that I could not warn him away in time. "So you're still here. If you hadn't been such a bastard—"

"Subhumans!" Petrenko screamed.

"*Zhopnik!*" Bok answered. "Homosexual!"

So much went on in the next few seconds that I can only recount events as if they had happened at a more measured pace, rather than simultaneously. Taking advantage of the momentary distraction afforded by the appearance of Filipp and his mangy bear, Nadze drew his revolver. "Sorry, Max," he said, shoving the barrel against my temple. For an instant I prepared myself to be shot into the afterlife but I hadn't counted on the bravery of my sweet koshka. While huddling against me, seeming to suffer a re-

currence of her catatonic state of the afternoon past, she had slyly
taken from her purse a long metal nail file. As Nadze prepared to
fire, she brought up her arm and stabbed the file into his neck at
the junction of chin and ear; a thin stream of blood spewed forth
as if from one of his fountain maenads. His gun slipped out of his
fingers as he clasped his hand to his neck, trying to stem the arte-
rial flow.

Meanwhile, my worthy associate Arteim bravely flung himself at the ground, and in so doing he accidentally assured my
survival. "Enough! Enough! Enough!" Bok shouted, pulling out
his pistol as Nadze staggered off, but Arteim crashed into his legs
on his way down, knocking him against Filipp the bear seller.
Holding tight to Sonya, I dragged her to earth with me. As we
descended I saw Petrenko's gang taking out their guns—Debalov
wielded two, one in each hand—and the Georgian ancillaries, who
were already aiming at them. The Caucasians, of course, didn't
realize that my guards had them fixed in their own sights. My
koshka and I hit the ground hard; reaching into my coat pocket,
thinking I'd found my own gun, I whipped out something small
and hard, only to discover that I was pointing my telephone at Bok.

"Fire!" Telman shouted, and everyone did.

"Max!" Sonya screamed, and without thinking I threw
myself atop her, hoping to shield her from injury. Half the citizens, and every animal in the market capable of voice, cried in
alarm at the sound of dozens of guns going off at once. The noise
split my eardrums, but that didn't concern me much at the moment. Bullets ricocheted off the trucks and struck the ground like
rain, throwing up clouds of earth and water. An inordinately heavy
load collapsed upon me; I choked, unable to take a single breath.
My own weight, combined with this undesired blanket, served to
press my koshka's face into the wet mud, and I feared she would
suffocate. With unnatural effort, I pushed away the tonnage that
was crushing us. Sonya lifted her head, gasping for air; when I
looked to see what had almost killed us I saw the bear, Belshazar,
who—happily, I suspect—had now cycled into the great sky circus.

The barrage lasted no more than a minute or two; then, as
suddenly as it began, it ended. Everywhere I heard screaming.
"You're all right?" Sonya asked.

"I'm not dead."

Nor was she. We waited a minute more before hauling

ourselves up. As we got to our feet I was struck anew by her supernal loveliness, even though she did not look her best, at that moment; her face was blackened with mud, as if for one of her beauty treatments. I looked to see who, and what, still stood. Bok was the first victim I recognized. His black suit gleamed with blood; he'd taken not less than thirty hits. Beyond him, scattered haphazardly across the field as if they'd been tossed out of heaven, were additional casualties. Most, thankfully, looked to be Georgian. Filipp and the Kamchatkan were dead; several of the younger corpses wore Hammer and Steel jackets. I was saddened to see that a few of the dead appeared to be members of my own honored guard. There were also a number of people who must have been doing nothing more than passing by—you should always be careful where you choose to stand, in Russia.

"Max!" Telman shouted, leaping over bodies as he ran toward us. "Max, are you all right?"

"We seem to be," I said. "You?"

He nodded and stopped long enough to drag Arteim from beneath a pair of Georgians; he, too, was unharmed. Hearing a groan, we looked to our left and saw Nadze, crawling through a pool of dark water; he still held his reddened hand against his wet neck. "Max," Sonya said. "Give me your gun."

Now, under calmer conditions, I found it quickly and handed it to her. She unclicked the safety and strolled over to our former oppressor. She turned him over with her foot, kicking him in the side. He opened his eyes to see who was there. My koshka knelt down and leveled the barrel of my gun just above his right eye. "You like what you see, this time?" she asked, and fired before he could answer. Then—an understandable if superfluous act—she aimed and fired again, taking out his left. With slim fingers she extracted her nail file and wiped it off on her sleeve before returning it to her purse, stood up, and handed back my gun. Then she took a few short steps away and began to vomit. Being a considerate man, I decided to wait until she finished before I attempted to comfort her.

"Are they all dead?" I asked, picking up my much-punctured briefcase.

"Yes, praise God," said Telman.

"How many did we lose?"

"Only two," he told me. "Pyotr and Raschid, poor fellows.

But they didn't suffer and have no relatives. The fucking Kazakhs got away, though."

"They ran away," I said. "Their hearts weren't in this, I don't think."

My surviving guards and those of Petrenko's company, including their leader and his aide, emerged from their battle stations, shambling over the field as if shell-shocked. My ears still rang from the bombardment, but I could hear sirens in the near distance. "Militia on the way, Max," said Arteim.

"I'm ready," I said, taking from my pocket my forged SVRR documents. "Pavel! How are you doing?"

"What the fucking hell, Max," Petrenko said. He was so covered with mud as to appear dipped in chocolate. "It is always exciting around you, no question." Debalov strutted over, his outfit unblemished by even a smudge of dirt.

"The militia is coming," I said. "Everything will be under control, but you must let me handle it. All right?"

"Max, you are the master of masters," he said, trying to catch his breath. His hands shook violently, and I think only a rush of adrenaline was keeping him upright. "What a massacre! Those bastards killed three of my fine men. Who were these Georgians anyway?"

"As soon as the authorities are taken care of, I'll explain," I told him. "Ultimately this was all Dmitry's fault, but it's too complex to go into here. Don't worry, just do as I do until the authorities are satisfied."

"Why would the militia trouble me?" he asked, seeming not to expect an answer. The sight of hundreds of market-goers racing in our direction, the better to see the leavings of our conflict, did not hearten me, but I thought there was enough blood to keep them content. I had started counting the bodies, and got as far as eleven, when I felt something tug violently at the cuffs of my trousers; I looked down, startled and afraid, only to see Petrenko's noxious animal gnawing on the fine if filthy wool, washing the mud off my handmade shoes with his maw's acidic saliva. Like Debalov, Pussy Eater had also somehow survived the attack unscathed. "He likes you," Petrenko said, grinning.

Nine militia vehicles, including an armored personnel carrier and a pair of black crows, stopped on the far side of the tramline. Two score armed militiamen emerged and rushed across the field, led by a captain who wore a vest of service medals across his chest. He had out his gun, and his aides kept close to his side, notebooks in hand. "What the hell is going on here?" he shouted, waving his weapon at us as if it were a water pistol, carelessly crushing the hands of corpses beneath his boots. "Who are you? What has happened?" In the aftermath of violent situations such as this, our appointed upholders of disorder most often arrested everyone and selected the guilty at their ease, but I knew I carried myself with enough of an official air to seize his attention and gain his respect.

"This has been a government action," I said to him, in tones as commanding as his own, as I gave him my papers.

"On whose authority?" he said, not looking at them. "Speak, you bastard."

"Mine," Petrenko said, employing the baritone voice he used only when screeching his public rants. "What of it?"

The captain looked over, to see who dismissed him so perfunctorily. "A simple inquiry," he said, wasting no time once he realized it was Petrenko. At once, he called to his men, telling them to cease rounding up suspects. "What do you need us to do?" he asked, practically clicking his heels. His immediate obeisance pleased me more than I can say, but I could not help but believe that his response would not have been so satisfying had Petrenko not been there.

I did not question my luck. "Take care of the wounded, and go about the business of removing the corpses as if it were nothing more than a tragic accident," I told him. "Investigations are under way. Send the dead to First City."

"At once," he said, and then turned toward Petrenko for confirmation. "Everything else will be under your control?"

"Everything, eventually."

"Excellent," said the captain, and he turned to leave. As he walked across the field he gave directions to his militia underlings, and his men began to break up the crowds. With a brisk kick I shook off the grip Petrenko's beast retained on my leg.

"So, Max," he said, watching me put away my fraudulent papers. "It's good to see you are vouched for. I have suspected you might be."

His suspicions didn't seem a problem. "That was very impressive, Pavel. I didn't realize you commanded such respect."

He grinned and embraced me so that I might be more thickly layered with mud. "They know who will one day have the butter."

Sonya walked over, cleaning mud and vomit from her face. She looked as relieved, and as drained of energy, as I must have looked—I must tell you, I've had easier days. "Pavel, how are the tigers?" I asked, disturbed by the appalling sight of the obese rug, the one-time bear lying nearby. "They weren't shot?"

"No," he said. "What proud animals. You hear them roaring?"

I did. "Tell the militia captain to have them sent to the zoo, the Moscow zoo," I said, and gave him my business card. "We should be on our way, I think. Call me tonight, there is much I need to explain to you."

Whether I would tell him the exact truth, of course, remained to be seen; it might not be necessary. "Fine, Max. Gyorgy, where is my proud fighter?"

"There," said Debalov. Petrenko's animate gargoyle had perched itself atop one of the fallen. Had it been any other breed of dog, the sight would have been bad enough, but the sight of this satanic imp lapping up the blood of the dead with gusto was too much—I was reminded of the grisly tableaux found in Bosch's more hallucinatory efforts.

"*Bad* dog!" said Petrenko, seizing the end of Pussy Eater's chain and yanking him off the carcass. "We will be doing much talking, Max."

Telman and Arteim accompanied us as we returned to my car. When we reached it, of course, there was little left of my beautiful Mercedes save for the chassis and windshield wipers. Attached to the latter I noticed a brief hand-scrawled note and read the nearly illegible writing. *We have business to discuss.* It was signed *Mels*.

Did we? "Not everyone should take their opportunities when they see them," I told Telman. "See what they want. If it's not what we want—"

He understood perfectly. "Of course, Max."

Arm in arm with Sonya, I strolled with her to the Metro, enjoying what remained of a lovely afternoon. Not until we reached my apartment did I start throwing up, but not for any longer than I should have expected; I was much better by four that morning and then slept the sleep of the saints.

10

Our skies are full of two-headed eagles. Bats have been loosed from their caves, worms crawl out of the earth, wolves prowl the land at will. All the rocks that for years weighed upon our country have been overturned, and we will be beset by the long-hidden horrors that lay beneath them for the rest of our days. But we must nevertheless do more; we must overturn the rocks that lie yet within each of us and stare without flinching at the vermin that tunnel through our souls.

When I woke the next morning, my eyes were wide open. For a half-conscious instant I imagined that I was sleeping with my wife again and prepared to draw away before she could notice that my body was touching hers; then memory shook me by the neck, and with delight I recalled who lay naked alongside me. I kissed Sonya awake; she returned my affections, for my deliciously wicked angel, having avenged herself upon her molester, was her own self again.

"Koshka."

We got out of bed an hour later. My faculties had also returned to me, and at first I believed I suffered no lingering after-

effects from the week's demanding events. As I dressed, I looked
out the window to offer a silent good morning to my tired goddesses, who were always there to comfort me—as was Khrushchev;
I almost expected him to wave as he walked past his window,
scratching his hog's ass.

I gathered up the newspapers from outside the door; young
Sashenka brought them by for me every morning. It pleased me
to see almost nothing in them regarding the pet market massacre
of the day before, save for inchoate remarks in *Arguments and Facts*
suggesting the likelihood of possible mafia involvement. There
were more casualties than I'd realized: thirty-six in all, including
nineteen innocent bystanders, but the poor folk of Russia are continually at the mercy of criminal brigands, and the authorities did
not seem too troubled; the militia captain explained to reporters
that most of the unaffiliated deceased were low-use segments of
the population.

"Max," Sonya said, emerging from the bathroom, wearing
black wool slacks and nothing else. "Do you want me to stay here
with you?"

"Of course, angel," I replied, embracing her. I wanted my
koshka just as much now as when I'd awakened, but as I'd not
recovered from our morning exercise, I restrained myself. "Why
else would I have brought you over?"

"No, I mean do you want me to move in?" she asked, part-
ing my hair with her fingers. "I have to get out of our old apartment and away from that treasure room. Do you want me here with
you all the time?"

"Of course."

"Then will you be doing something with Tanya's belongings? I feel as if she'll be walking in on us at any minute."

"That's impossible, koshka. You know that won't happen."

"I'm only describing my emotions, Max. These things of
hers make me uncomfortable. They make me feel like I shouldn't
be here."

As I looked around I realized the degree to which my poor
wife's presence in the bedroom far exceeded my own. The doors
of her closet were wide open, revealing racks of expensive clothing, hats, belts, bags; on her dressing table were her grooming
implements, perfume bottles, decorative boxes, cloisonné figurines,
and Chanel scarves. On the walls were photographs of Tanya as a

child, as a student, and as a newlywed, standing with me on the Sparrow Hills and looking out at the view over Moscow. There were photographs of her parents, of her sister, of our son.

"All her possessions?"

"Certainly not, but you weren't thinking of leaving things exactly as they are, were you? Do you want to live in a museum?"

"No," I said. "I'll sort it out, my angel. I may not be able to get everything put away by tonight, or tomorrow—"

"Of course." She kissed me and headed back to the bathroom. "It was something I needed to tell you."

The reason we Russians so treasure our *poshlaia*, I think, is that we have no other guides by which to tell if reality correlates with our memories. When I looked again at those photographs, I knew I'd once had a son, that he'd not been a fantasy; when I glanced at the dressing table and saw my wife's brush, matted with gray-russet hair, I was reminded that while she had been here only days ago—hours, really—she would not be back again. Ultimately, I think, *poshlaia* is neither good nor bad in itself; like fred, it reflects the emotions and mood of its user. And like many drugs, *poshlaia* keeps you from sleeping but allows you to dream.

Did it sadden me to lose my wife before I could leave her? Would I be human if it did not? I cannot deny that the emotion my wife and I felt toward each other was love, true love—but married love, the kind that attains maturity only through years of shared trauma, becoming the love that forgets why it should remember its name. And, hear me, the problem with such love is that each partner comes to comprehend the troubles of the other so well and so constantly as to sweep from the soul all traces of passion (the emotion most dependent upon mystery and unavailability and, when sustained, capable of heightening the earthier aspects of existence into the spiritual plane) and, with passion, life. The marriage bond is no different from a dental plate: it can't be ignored, but you get used to it; it causes discomfort, but rarely enough to ruin your life; it usually looks good from the outside, depending on the angle of the viewer; and when it is gone, the unfillable space strangely feels so much better.

Some of the photographs I would rehang elsewhere in the apartment; the figurines and boxes could be placed on the shelves in our parlor, along with *matryoshkas* and banners and hand-

painted thimbles. Finding an envelope in a dresser drawer, I pulled
out the hair that clung to my wife's brush and slipped the tangle
inside; then I dropped the envelope in the wastebasket.

When I looked up and out, I felt sick. Evidently Khrushchev had undertaken a calisthenics program. He stood near but
faced away from his window, bending over repeatedly as if imagining himself able to touch or even see his toes. I don't have to
tell you he had not purchased special exercise apparel. As if this
hellish sight did not make me suffer enough, I watched, appalled,
as the young woman I had seen earlier reappeared. She'd not yet
found her clothing, but this did not appear to concern her. My jaw
dropped as I watched the girl throw herself physically onto
Khrushchev, seeming unable to effectively fight off the attraction
of his overpowering personal magnetism.

"My God," I said. "This is reprehensible."

"What?" Sonya asked, coming to the window, peering out
at what I saw. The girl was dragging Khrushchev to the floor, perhaps to assist him in doing push-ups. My koshka laughed, but not
out of malice; she plainly sympathized, which I could not help but
find mind-boggling. "What a happy couple they are. Do you often
spy on their love nest?"

"What is that poor girl doing with that fat old bastard?" I
asked as they disappeared from view. "He must have drugged her.
Why else would she be there?"

"Because she wants to be," Sonya said, pinching my arm.
"What, you think he's imprisoning her as his sexual slave?"

"He must be. Didn't you get a good look at him? Have you
ever seen anything like it?"

"I thought he looked a little like you," she said, smiling
and returning to the bathroom to complete her ablutions. For a
moment (longer, perhaps) I feared I was having a stroke. Faint
hope; once more, my astonishing powers of recovery preserved me.

"Ten minutes for final farewells. Hurry, hurry."

I asked Alla to give the eulogy at Tanya's funeral the next
afternoon, for I did not know what I could say about my late wife,
or about my love for her and my hatred of our long-fought struggles,
that would not somehow offend most of those in attendance. No,

better to let another speak well of the dead; on that day if no other, if I could not speak truth I would say nothing.

"We all miss Tatiana Sergeyevna," Alla began. "Our sorrow would please her."

There were not as many in attendance as my wife would have liked; it was a long drive to Nicholas Archangel and the Glow of Life Columbarium, after all. None of Tanya's relatives were still alive, save her sister Olga, and she had moved to Paris in 1991. When I called her to commiserate and tell her when the memorial would be held, she told me she had neither the time nor the desire to set foot in Russia ever again—she'd managed to almost forget that the country, and her sister, existed.

All workers of her firm were at hand save one—we hadn't yet found Iosif, but his trail was burning hot. Anatoly and Roman sat with Sonya and myself in the front row, dabbing at tears with pocket squares soft as skin, while the office staff sat in the general congregation. Arteim and Evgeny were there, and Tanya's lawyer Zhukov, with whom I had already exchanged unpleasant words; but he would do my bidding soon enough. Although I recognized everyone by face, if not by name, I could no longer be certain there were no representatives of the criminal classes present—excepting, of course, the crematory hooligans themselves.

"A woman of strength," I heard Alla say. "Possessed of unwavering opinions. An inspirational figure in whom we can all take pride."

I had made sure no disco organist would despoil the ceremony; Alla's words alone echoed through the chamber as she spoke. Her eulogy was touching but unmemorable, and no one was surprised or disappointed—few people in our country have either the ability or desire to actually say anything of meaning when making a public address. It isn't that our brains have been polished smooth by the constant rush of lies pouring over them, or our tongues numbed by the ceaseless flow of drink; only that anyone who has grown up in Russia is long-conditioned to bury the most innocuous beliefs beneath mountains of scenic rhetoric. How could the noblest words retain meaning, used by people trained since birth to say nothing that might offend someone, somewhere, sometime?

"—unlimited devotion to her work and to her husband, Maxim—"

Sonya took my hand and squeezed it, expressing love; save for such tender and welcome gestures, my koshka behaved herself admirably during the funeral. She was well aware that mortuary etiquette demands that rituals for a deceased spouse should proceed uninterrupted by the lubricious behavior of the chief mourner's lover.

"Before we go," Alla said, "I should like to remember our happiest—"

The columbarium's female attendant flung open the doors and strode in, waving her arms as she stepped in front of Alla. Two apes followed in her wake and began taking away the bouquets surrounding the bier, so that the coffin could descend unhindered into the hungry flames. "Final farewells must be concluded at this time!"

Alla, with good reason, glared at the woman as if she were a barefooted peasant. "I'm not finished."

"So what? Your time is up and there are people waiting. Hurry, hurry! Be off with you."

"Max!" Alla shouted across the room. I stood and moved quickly to the front of the room. The attendant turned her back to me as I approached, plainly thinking that nothing I could say to her would be of any importance.

"This funeral is for an owner of this very facility."

She shrugged. "We are equal in death."

"This woman"—I pointed to Alla—"and I are also owners. I demand that she be given time to finish her eulogy."

"I know who you are," she said. "It's still impossible."

"Will you tell me why?" I asked, seizing her shoulder and shaking her. She nodded once to her thugs, who pressed a button on the wall. As we watched, Tanya's coffin disappeared through the floor into the hungry oven. The attendant jerked away from me and signaled that her assistants should step forward, to be ready to act in the event I continued to offend her.

"What you think doesn't matter to me," she said. "We run a tight schedule. Many people are dying and need to use our facilities." She directed her tattooed thugs to let in the next group. "Now listen to me, you people must get out of here," she shouted to Tanya's mourners, who were already walking away. "Go! Go! We join you in your sorrow! Good-bye!"

There was nothing else to do, considering that my wife had now been stolen from me for a second time. It was evident why the attendant had treated us the way she did, ignoring the accepted folkways of nonobtrusive service so blatantly, but she would pay for her crimes. I placed my arm around Alla's waist, and our party left the room.

"I'm sorry," I said as we reached the entrance lobby and I helped Alla on with her coat. "We should have expected that. What did your agents tell you?"

"We'll have full control of the facility by the end of next week," she said. "Max, when they give you Tanya's ashes, will you make sure they are hers?"

"They will be. Several of my men are downstairs, watching them and seeing to it that the hooligans do as they're supposed to."

Upon gaining access to the property through right of ownership, we had quickly discovered why the Georgians so desired to take possession of the Glow of Life. Not only could such a facility and its experienced workers serve—and had been serving—as a convenient disposal operation for those hundreds who each month fell astray of gangsters, but bone ash has many profitable uses: to spread over icy streets in winter, to adulterate flour exported to the near abroad, as an industrial abrasive, and as an additive to cut the purity of drugs.

"That's good." Alla might have been a stove, she glowed so red-hot with anger. "I could strangle that bitch. How soon can we be rid of her?"

"We can be rid of all these employees once they are no longer owners," I reminded her. "Don't hound yourself sick with worry, I'll take care of these minor details. Do you have a ride back to Moscow?"

"With Anatoly," she said. "Good-bye, Max. Thank you." She kissed me on the cheek, and we briefly embraced. "I'll call."

As she walked out of the building, Sonya lifted her arms so I might slip them into her own coat's sleeves. "Will you have the woman fired?"

I shook my head. "Killed."

Sonya said little to me on the way back; the events of the week appeared to have caught up with her, and she peacefully

slept, her head on my shoulder. On our return to Moscow we joined
the caravan of reconditioned army trucks barreling into the city,
hauling goods legal and illegal to market. One open carrier had a
blackened-bronze statue of Lenin strapped securely onto its
wooden bed. All ten meters of this representation had been molded
in a standard pose; however, as Vladimir Ilyich lay on his back
rather than standing atop a pedestal in a miserable township beyond the Urals, his outstretched arm pointed toward the sky instead of the luminous if ill-perceived horizon. In his other hand
Lenin held his cap over his heart; thanks to the inventiveness of
the sculptor, he wore a second cap rakishly tilted on his head. So
many consumers outside our country, especially in America, find
these icons of the Age of Small-brained Lizards so inexplicably
attractive that I think, if demand continues to increase, it would
be smart to reopen one or two shuttered statuary factories so that
fresh-cast icons of our ham-headed egoists may be produced as
desired to satisfy market needs. Glory ever be to the profit-making
people! As we have always done, we shall offer the West a choice
of monsters; but this time they shall be happy with the return on
their investment.

During the next few days Sonya and I made several trips,
tranferring her belongings into our apartment. The furniture and
Dmitry's possessions—including those isotope-tainted valuables in
his treasure room—would be left in their old flat until I ascertained
a suitable method of disposal. Once we emptied the place of everything she wanted to keep, I had the building's cooperative seal
the apartment tight for the duration.

"Did you see what happened to the little coma girl's father?" she asked me as I helped fold another dozen of her dresses
before packing them away. Not until the last night of moving did
we attempt to order her storehouse of clothing.

"Coma girl?"

"In Ekaterinburg," she said. "He was on trial for murder."

"Oh, the dog-killer," I said, at last remembering what she
was talking about; recalling, too, Tanya's inordinate interest in the
case. "What happened? Is the trial over?"

She opened another suitcase. "Not guilty. That's not the end of it."

"Why?"

"The mother and her family were so traumatized by the miscarriage of justice that, when everyone left the courtroom and went outside, they killed the father and his lawyer with axes."

"They overreacted, clearly," I opined. "They've been charged?"

"Their trial should begin in several months," she said. Then, entirely without warning, she brought up a subject that was so unlikely I at first did not know how to respond. "Are you tired of Russia, Max?"

"What kind of question is that?"

"Do you think we have a future here? Do you think anybody does?"

"Of course we do. It only depends on what we do with it."

"I've been thinking," she said. "Maybe we should go to America."

"We could use a vacation. Is that where you'd like to go?"

"In truth I thought we could move there one day."

This was a possibility I'd never remotely considered. "You've never been out of Russia before," I said. "Why not visit first and then decide? How do you know you wouldn't hate America, once you see it in real life?"

"How do you know I wouldn't love it?"

"Moving to another country is not like moving across town," I said. "And something happens to American Russians. They change."

"They become Americans. Is that a bad thing?"

"I don't know that it's good," I said. "Something in the soul transforms, I think. It's clear to me from talking to my friend Lev that he's greatly changed since he went there."

"I'm not Lev," she said. "Maybe he believes you're the one who's changed."

"Maybe he'd be wrong."

"You've never been there either, so what are you doing, telling me all about America? People I know who have been told me about what they saw with their own eyes. New York, Miami,

San Francisco. What magical names. I have heard Las Vegas is beautiful, Max. The lights at night make night disappear."

"I think you are imagining dream America, angel," I said. "I have no objections to visiting, so we may see it through our eyes and not someone else's. But why should we leave our country when all is finally beginning to go well?"

"Because it can go wrong very quickly," she said, opening a fifth suitcase and packing away more stacks of frocks, slacks, and skirts. "How can we predict what will happen here next year, or even next month? Look at what has happened just this past week. It's only luck we're still alive, you know."

"I can't believe my luck," I said, embracing her, hoping to distract her from giving continued attention to these incomprehensible desires.

"You're scared to move to America," she said, taking my ear between her teeth. "Aren't you?"

Nostalgia may be the preferred opium of our people, but America has always been the favored drug of a certain percentage of the intelligentsia, of the cultivated classes; even of the *nomenklatura*, though none of its members would ever admit it. Understand, in the Russian mind America is the Anti-Russia, the earthly heaven that has never existed: an enormous, welcoming utopia with golden cities, green pastures, fields of grain, dark forests, rivers of wine, and candy mountains. But this land of fantasy must surely bear no greater resemblance to the real America than the perfect Soviet Union did to this magnificent, tormented country in which we live, have lived, and will ever continue to live. Who wants to live in utopia, ultimately? Only those who cannot or will not adapt to the sometimes soul-crushing stresses and strains of existence. For me, emigration was an impossible possibility. Leaving Russia would be as inconceivable as leaving Sonya, losing my country as painful as losing my wife.

"I have unbreakable personal ties here," I reminded her. "My businesses, my heritage, my many associates."

She laughed and eased out of my grip. "You're an intelligent man. You could do well anywhere, you know that."

"America drives people crazy; even their poets say so."

"And what do Russian poets say?" she retorted. "You're scared."

"All right, I am," I said, almost losing my temper. "I'm scared seeing the West might affect you as it affected my son. How can I be sure it wouldn't?"

You may laugh and think I am being sentimental, but that was honestly how I felt and what I feared. I must have turned koshka-like eyes upon my angel, for the expression on her face suggested that she herself was set to melt. "There's no danger of that," she said, speaking very softly. "Oh, my hard one."

"But you aren't sure," I said. "Besides, what if one day my son was to come back and I'm no longer here?"

She stared at me without saying anything for what seemed a very long time; as if I had expressed the belief that if we flapped our arms long enough we could fly. "Do you really think that could happen?" she asked, and I nodded. Why should I not believe it possible, even if I cannot think it probable? I am not so different from my countryfolk, after all; only I would prefer to live in a familial, rather than a societal, utopia. If that is as foolish a dream, so be it.

"We'll go to America this fall for a visit, if you'd like," I told her. "I promise you. Then we'll see what we think. All right?"

"All right." My koshka smiled but did not look happy; perhaps she believed that by the time September came, I would have forgotten I'd ever made such an assurance and even deny that I had. I cannot pretend I had not given such avowals to Tanya, more than once, and afterward denied them; but believe me, I am no longer a person who could tell such outrageous lies to one I loved. "Max, there are still some sweaters of mine in the dresser in our bedroom. Would you get them? I have to attend to myself." She headed toward the water closet.

"Do you need help?"

"Devil," she said, and skipped back across the room to kiss me, nipping my lower lip as she drew away. "Oh, Max, wherever we wind up, what a future we have ahead of us!"

After she shut the door behind her I entered their bedroom and slid open the top drawer of her dresser. Before my eyes lay an astonishing collection of lingerie. "What about these intimate items?" I shouted.

"Keep your filthy hands off those," she cried out. "My sweaters are in the second drawer from the bottom."

Poor Tanya never wore anything beneath her street clothing that was not outsized, white, and cotton, but Sonya's tiny
underthings came in every color, in silk, satin, and lace. I couldn't
resist passing my hands through their fragrant softness. The enticing feel of her most personal articles, combined with indelible
visions of the body upon which this lingerie so charmingly fitted,
stimulated me to such an extent that I could no longer contain
myself. Fishing up a handful of her lace pants, I pressed them
against my face and deeply inhaled her lingering perfume. Teen
Spirit; I smiled and shivered with anticipation of lovemaking. The
toilet flushed; as I quickly thrust her delights back into the drawer,
preparing to close it, I saw something I hadn't expected to see,
tucked beneath pairs of black silk stockings. It was an airline ticket
folder from Swissair; even as I lifted it out of the drawer I could
tell that it had not been slipped away and forgotten, months or
years ago; by the feel of its crisp envelope, I judged it might have
been issued as recently as the past weekend.

I held the ticket in my hand, studying the design of the
airline's corporate logo. Had Dmitry gotten away, would there have
been no one waiting to meet him?

"Max?"

Even in Russia you can sometimes be too cynical. Perhaps
I shouldn't have, but I trusted my koshka enough not to look at
the ticket itself and ascertain the destination and time of departure. Still, I thought it wise to open the *fortochka* in the bedroom
window and leave my lingering curiosity forever unsatisfied. I
watched the ticket float out and then down into the night's darkness until I could see it no longer.

"I'm here, angel." Romance will be the death of me yet.

The following weekend, we paid our first visit to the site
of Sovietland, fifteen kilometers south of Moscow's Outer Ring,
on forty thousand hectares of land running along the Moskva River.
I took Sonya, Evgeny, and Irina there in my late wife's BMW. Spring
had at last returned unhindered to our land; the sky was swept
clear of clouds, fields sprouted green with new grass, gentle winds
shook the branches of budding trees. "The site may look a little
rough to you," Evgeny warned us while trying, and failing, to ward

off the devoted attentions of his youthful charge. "Probably it will
help if you use your imagination."

"What did the Bruneians say when you brought them out
here?" I said, as we turned onto the rutted gravel road leading into
the site. Nothing of the park could be seen from the highway.

"They were speechless, Max. I wish you could have seen
their faces."

"If you had told me you were bringing them out, I would
have." Even before we reached the site I was suspecting that we
would never see the Bruneians or their vast wealth again.

"It was a spur-of-the-moment decision," he said. "They
needed to return to their native land and insisted on seeing how
the project was coming along. I called, but you weren't in your
office."

"You could have called my cellular number."

"These advanced technologies are very complex, Max. It's
not as if I didn't try." He pointed out the window at the magnificent stands of birch forest that surrounded us. "These woods
will of course be chopped down to provide plenty of room for
parking."

After another five minutes the blue river came into view.
Not far from the banks of the river were several antiquated
earthmovers, a crane, two or three trucks, and four high mountains of excavated dirt. Twenty or so workmen wandered about
aimlessly, as if they'd been struck on the head, seeming to believe
they were giving an impression of frenetic energy.

"Pull over there, Max." My brother directed me to a barren flat several hundred meters from the construction area. I
parked in an area that looked not quite as sodden as most of the
ground, but I erred; the instant we stepped out we sank ankle-deep
in mud. I estimated it would take two hours for an earthmover to
extract my car from the fen, unless the ground entirely swallowed
it in our absence. "It's the wet season," Evgeny reminded us, as
sucking mud coated my once-fine shoes. We were but a short distance from grass when my poor koshka screamed, sinking up to
her waist in a bog; I had her out in no time.

"I can barely control my excitement," Evgeny said. "This
is wonderful, Max. You will not believe what I have to show you."

"Where is this ride?" I asked.

"Over there," he said as he ducked, pointing to another expanse of rubbish-strewn acreage upon which nothing stood save an unpainted wooden shed, some hundred meters or so in length, which I fancied to be a temporary construction used to store easily replaceable equipment.

"Where?"

"There, Max. Right there."

"That shack?"

"The exterior needs work," he admitted. "The contractors thought it wise to first complete the interior, and the ride itself, before tackling the outer decor. Now that the weather is improving, the essential framework can be covered with appropriate plaster decorations. Soon it'll look like a big lump of sugar."

"My mouth's watering," I mumbled, realizing I would have to start spending less of my money and more of my valuable time, keeping a keen eye on the actions of these contractors. I saw a concrete-lined canal running entirely through the shed.

"Everything we build will contribute to the aura of a magic Communist fairy kingdom," my brother noted, trying desperately to interpret all we saw. Six small rowboats without oars floated in the canal's inky water. A workman who looked to be blind drunk— granted, it was long past noon—leaned against the rough wall of a small outbuilding housing an assemblage of outdated electrical equipment.

"How do we get aboard?" I asked.

"A pier is in the planning stages," said Evgeny, picking up a long grappling hook and drawing a boat toward us.

"What kind of ride is this?" Sonya asked, peering into the dark cavern that confronted us as I took my seat alongside her.

"This is the Progress of the Proletariat Tunnel of Love," Evgeny said, helping Irina into our boat, giving her a good feel as he lent his assistance. "Bone-chilling but educational. The dioramas detail the course of world history in accordance with unbreakable laws of dialectical materialism." My brother turned to shout at the ride's bibulous operator. "Andrei! Start us up."

I listened to the hum of a generator warming up. Our boat shuddered violently and then started to glide into the tunnel. Evidently a moving track was set in the floor of the canal, and each boat was hooked on with chains.

"Are you all right?" I asked Sonya; she shivered and pressed herself against me.

"I have mud in my undergarments," she whispered, offering me (for later inspiration, as necessary) a vision deserving of my imaginative powers. "I'm freezing cold. I'm filthy as a pig. I'm *furious*. Is this damned thing safe?"

"Don't touch the water while the boats are moving, whatever you do," Evgeny said. "There may be unfortunate leakage of electricity."

"Are you serious?" He nodded. "What, are you trying to kill us?"

"I think it has been repaired but be careful, in case."

The moment we floated into the shed an overpowering scent of mildew filled my nostrils, the smell of a ill-tended bathhouse. An unearthly voice blared over unseen speakers, startling us so that Sonya and I lunged forward, almost falling out of the boat into the lethal waters. I knew I had heard the voice before, but static prevented me from sure recognition. "Who is that speaking?"

"Igor Kirillov. I hired him to read historically appropriate narration, as part of the multimedia experience."

Kirillov worked for twenty years as the news reader for *Vremya* and in that post served as the ex-officio voice of the state. Everyone takes what work they can find in these difficult days; I was sure he hadn't come cheap. "He's barely understandable," I said, my ears ringing with the amplified squawk. "The feedback is deafening. How do you expect people to put up with this?"

"By the time the park is open to the public, we will have wireless headphones installed for the benefit of riders. The narration will be simultaneously translated into every language in the world. Don't worry, Max, I've thought of everything."

Our craft bumped against the side of the canal but continued on without sinking. We sat, not moving, as we floated past the first illuminated diorama on our right. On the cracked surface of the concrete was a communal group of papier-mâché ape-men, encompassed by primeval plastic jungle undergrowth, warming themselves as they huddled around a red lightbulb that, I suppose, represented fire. Not one of the cave hominids exceeded half a meter in height, and some were smaller; the ape-women, in truth, looked like Barbies that had also fallen prey to the site's hungry mud. The display in its entirety might have been made by children—unintelligent children—for a school art project.

The speakers worked as they should have, the farther we penetrated into the tunnel's blackness, and I better understood what Kirillov was saying; *understood*, however, is not the most accurate word. "Time passes quickly," he intoned. "Things which only yesterday or today or the day before yesterday happened seem to have happened in the past even before they happen. Tomorrow we may tire of what has happened, and the day after tomorrow not even remember what these things that happened were."

"Who wrote his narration?" I asked.

"I did," said my brother.

"Were you drunk?"

"Only on the music of language," he swore to me. "You know I abstain from spirits when I am creating."

Next we saw Egyptian pyramids—both of them, neither of which would have come up to my knees—and teams of slaves hauling matchboxes over a scattering of sand under the guidance of pharaonic oppressors. Papier-mâché mannequins, some already missing limbs, were again employed to instill in the willing audience a mind-shattering semblance of reality.

Great drops of water fell onto my head from new-forming stalactites as history progressed. There appeared, in turn, Spartacus leading the Roman slaves into revolt against their conquerors, mitered popes gleefully overseeing the torture of heretics, crowned kings commanding troops to rape and murder the honest working people of defeated lands, and Czar Ivan the Awe-Inspiring relishing the sight of a long line of patriots undergoing sanctifying decapitation at the Place of Skulls in Red Square. The level of workmanship glimpsed in the first diorama was equaled in every instance.

As we entered the nineteenth century, where capitalists wearing top hats and smoking cigars cracked whips at hapless workers in satanic mills, Sonya pressed her lips against my neck; plainly, she was seized by the desire to be held fast in the yoke of capitalist slavery; so that the time spent within this miserable hole would not go entirely to waste, I responded by lovingly caressing my dirty girl.

"Max, Max!" my brother shouted, with impeccable timing, and we looked up. "The thrilling conclusion. This is best of all."

We floated through a gauzy, blood-red curtain illuminated from behind. "The International" began playing over the speakers, the boat cleared the curtain, and I saw ahead of us Moscow as I had seen it in my dream: the nexus of the Socialist utopia, the capital of the Soviet Union of the mind. "Great is our admiration of this heaven-worthy place," Kirillov began to shout above the anthemic music. "We look on in breathless wonder at its beautiful main streets, splendid new buildings, reconstructed and well-paved suburbs lined with workers' palaces, gleaming factories whose chimneys egust snowy smoke, all witnessing to the persistent and devoted efforts of the Party."

What the narrator now proclaimed was coherent, if still nonsensical. Probably my brother had lifted this text directly from one of our many literary masterworks of the late era. As we floated past the perfect society, I saw that it was presented in a most accurate manner: the Workers' Paradise was made of flaking plaster, rusting chicken wire, warped scrap metal, and badly painted plywood. Each smokestack had tacked onto its free end a puff of ash-smudged cotton. The tiny figures scattered throughout the display had been amateurishly carved out of clothespins.

"Go forth in pride, workers of the world! Salute as you go the Father of Us All, the Coryphaeus of Socialist Forward-looking Thinking! Be happy here in the happiest land on earth!"

Above the exit was a glass globe; as we approached, its inner light blinked on, and we saw that the gleaming sphere was blown in the shape of Stalin's head. No sooner did we start passing under it than the bulb within exploded, raining sharp-edged fragments onto us. No one was cut badly; sunlight blinded us as the boat emerged from the dark, and we shut our eyes against the glare of day.

As I felt the vessel bump to a halt, I looked up and saw the murky tarn into which the canal flowed. Malaria would be an especially memorable souvenir for our guests to take back from Sovietland. Evgeny patted my shoulder. Rarely have I seen my brother so ebullient.

"What do you think?" he asked, helping Irina out of the boat. Once they were on shore I lifted Sonya to safety.

"How much money was spent in preparing this marvelous exhibit?" I asked.

My brother counted on his fingers while he made his tally. "Seven hundred and fifty thousand dollars."

"Dollars, not rubles."

"That's right."

"You idiot," I said, not yet raising my voice. "You cow-headed imbecile. You brain-addled fool."

"What is it, Max?" he asked. "What's wrong?"

"What's right?" I replied. "I've never seen such a pathetic display. You've sunk vast amounts of money into this thing, and this is the result?"

"I warned you to use your imagination."

"Tolstoy wouldn't have enough imagination," I shouted. "Small wonder the Bruneians went back home."

"You're seeing only the initial phase, remember—"

"The last phase, I call it. Count yourself lucky they didn't kill you when they saw what you'd done with their money. Not to mention what you've done with *my* money. Do you honestly believe you have something here that anyone will pay to see?"

"But Max, there's—"

"Father was wrong about me," I blurted out; had we not been interrupted, I would have gone on to say, *He was right about you.* Naturally, I would have forever afterward regretted saying that aloud, but it did not come to that. An unexpected cry caught our attention, and we turned to see who was calling us.

"Borodin!" A workman was coming across the field, holding something wrapped in a rag in his hand. He stopped, halfway over, and again shouted. "Something here you need to see!"

"What?"

"This way," he said, returning in the direction whence he came. The four of us caught up with him in a matter of minutes.

"What is it?" Evgeny asked.

"You need to see."

We silently walked a short distance over the waste toward a house-sized excavation one hundred meters from the riverbank. Two earthmovers were parked at the rim of the pit; a group of workers stood on a dirt ramp that descended into the black ground, staring at whatever lay at the bottom.

"We discovered bones," the workman told us.

"You mean fossils?" Evgeny asked. "Mammoths? Antediluvian beasts?"

The workman unwrapped the object he held in his hand, revealing a small browned skull. Turning it over, he pointed at the bullet hole in the back of the cranium. "Not as prehistoric."

"An old cemetery?" Even my brother knew better than that.

"No headstones," the workman said. "Many bones, stacked four to five meters deep. All ages, I would say."

The day was as beautiful as it had been minutes earlier, but now all had been cast in different light: shadows were darker, the blue of the sky appeared to be a more disconcerting hue, the caw of carrion crows sounded harshly in the ears. It was as if we had been awakened to be told we'd been sleeping with corpses—and that was precisely what we *had* been told.

"What was going to be built here?"

"The disco," Evgeny told me. "It would have a clear plastic floor, with colorful lights shining up from underneath." He held a hand to his mouth; Sonya and Irina looked as if they could not contain their tears for long.

"That's obviously ruled out," I said. "The rest of the area should be dug up as well. Likely as not, there will be many more underneath us."

"What about Sovietland, Max?" my brother asked. "What are we going to do?"

The workman looked at us and looked back at the pit; he spat on the ground. For several minutes I stared at the small skull in his hand and listened to the women crying. "I have an idea."

"Good evening, friends!" Mels proclaimed to all who ascended the broad granite steps and knocked at the high oaken doors. His midnight-blue tuxedo fitted him perfectly, his tremendous size notwithstanding; as he had insisted on wearing both his black leather jacket and black leather trench coat over his formal garb, however, the fine workmanship of its tailoring was not readily evident. "Welcome to Sovietland."

His assistant Baiken, a fellow Kazakh of even greater size, asked each arrival a follow-up question. "You on the list?"

"Of course," said the gentlemen awaiting entry, handing over gold-edged engraved invitations as they thrust stubby fingers between neck and wing collar, struggling to loosen their clothes enough to take a free breath. "Oleg Lavreich Gertsenzon of Menatep." "Valera Arkadich Kovalev, Ministry of the Interior."

Baiken looked over his documents until he found their names. "Enter, friends. Do as you will within reason."

The Petrovsky house, restored to its full splendor, was the ideal setting for such an exclusive private club as Sovietland. I smiled, reassured that my trusty gatekeepers were admirably performing their duties on this opening night, and so went back inside, glad to be out of the chill October air. Thus far, over a thousand representatives of Moscow's elite had paid their ten-thousand-dollar annual dues, and I knew everyone here on this memorable evening would go out the next day and sign up two more. They would be welcome: we employ no elitist standards to deny entry to anyone; while you have money, Sovietland is yours to enjoy.

(High government officials, of course, are favored with honorary dues-free membership, as befits their useful placement in society.)

In the entrance hall, after handing in weapons, our guests paused to check their thick chesterfields and fur wraps with the coat girls, five lithe brunettes dressed as French maids. Male guests clearly appreciated the way their short starched skirts flipped up to reveal lace-frilled lingerie, and more often than not—as I'd predicted—our female guests would prompt their companions to go at once to the gift counter and purchase comparable sets of expensive intimate wear.

"Maxim Alexeich," I heard many times that evening, "this is the finest club in Moscow."

I stopped in the antechamber long enough to adjust the sleeve cuffs and smooth the satin lapels of my dinner jacket. Our guests paused to gaze in wonder at the golden fountain's mythic figures. The speakers in the base now played Frank Sinatra at low volume, rather than ear-splitting disco, and instead of unnaturally hued water the fountain now recirculated vintage Armenian brandy. Racks of glasses were attached to the wall so that our guests, if they desired, might select and dip stemware into the amber nectar and savor a delectable refreshment before deciding which of the many activities provided by our club seemed most attractive. At all times, I had two guards in formal wear stationed in the room, so they could prevent our less cultured guests from urinating in the fountain.

"Maxim Alexeich," I heard, more than once, "tomorrow I will call you. We have business to discuss."

Upon leaving the antechamber, guests could proceed to different rooms offering something for every taste. In one chamber there was a churning Jacuzzi capable of holding twenty people; in another, a karaoke stage; in a third, a library environment with comfortable leather chairs, dark wood paneling, green-shaded lamps, and naked female dancers (for looking, not touching). In the former dining room we installed a bar/restaurant and small casino. If you wanted to see a film, we had a screening chamber in which prints of upcoming Western movies were projected (director's or even editor's cuts). In the ballroom that evening, and for the next two weeks, we provided live entertainment twice nightly for a small cover charge of fifty dollars: Elvistroika and the Happy Guys. The former claimed to have obtained his gem-studded white jumpsuit from the American rock king himself; the latter were sons of the originals and no less talented.

"Maxim Alexeich," I heard, repeatedly, "may we honor you in some way?"

Stepping past the antechamber's guards, I climbed the curving staircase to the second floor, trailing my hand along the balustrade's cold stone waves. I strolled down the hallway, nodding to each of my upstairs guards until I reached my office, which had once been Nadze's. When I unlocked the door I saw Telman and Ivan Ivan waiting for me inside. Their long search had at last paid off.

"What has he told you?" I asked.

"He hurts."

Heavy chains secured the weasel; Iosif dangled from a ceiling fixture, his wrists bruised black by the pressure of his fetters, uttering a series of high-pitched vowel sounds. He substituted nicely for the room's chandelier. The toes of his shoes just scraped the floor. As I walked by I gave him a push, so as to increase the momentum of the arc he described. My associates had stripped off his shirt. Needled permanently into his chest, back, and arms were a multitude of remarkable tattoos.

"He must have been imprisoned with a Rembrandt of the art," Telman noted. "Very attractive designs."

"Are either of you familiar with the symbolism?" I asked.

"Sure," said Ivan Ivan, stepping up and pointing at a blue knife covered with red blood stenciled into the right shoulderblade. "This signifies that he told tales on people while in custody." Our consultant redirected my attention to Iosif's waist, where there was an apparent representation of a bloody carcass. "The skinned rabbit lets us know he raped and killed a child molester. Very commendable." Ivan Ivan's fingers moved to a pair of azure skulls on the lower left deltoid. "Two other murders. No one important." In the center of Iosif's back was a breathtaking illustration of a woman copulating with a black stallion. "This is a new one on me. Homage to Catherine the Great, maybe." Ivan Ivan stepped around to look at Iosif's chest and laughed at what he saw on the right pectoral, a black tomb encircled with black words: *Sleep Mother and Wait for Me.* "She won't be waiting long."

Iosif started to groan more loudly, but I didn't worry that our guests would be disturbed. Nadze was farseeing enough to have had his office thickly insulated for soundproofing purposes, and nothing could be heard by anyone outside the room, even in the adjoining hall. Our prisoner opened his eyes; seeing me, he miraculously recovered the power of speech.

"Take me down!" he shouted. "God help me."

"Who are you to give orders to either of us?"

"My arms," he said, gasping for breath. "Pulling out of their sockets."

"That must be very painful," I said. Keeping the arms fixed overhead in such a position for very long eventually results in death by suffocation—the chest muscles slowly lose their operative power; this principle explains the efficacy of crucifixion, as I understand it. "I wonder how painful it was for my wife, before they killed her."

"I didn't know what they'd do," he said, trying to speak and breathe at the same time. "I didn't know, I didn't."

"If they sewed open her eyes while she was still alive, I should think that would have been very painful."

"Please—"

"My wife's eyes."

"Mother of God, they forced me to do what I did."

"You had no free will?" I asked.

"I'll tell you anything you want to know," he pleaded, his breath seeming to fail. The chains holding him rattled as he shivered. "I confess. I confess."

I shrugged. "*Nichevo.*"

He made a choked strangle and then howled all the more. I felt confirmed in my belief that I could never have worked for the competent organs in an interrogative capacity. To treat this bastard in such a fashion satisfied without stimulating; at no time did I feel the profound cosmic intensity which it seems professionals in these arts often experience, far exceeding (or so I have been told) the mere emotions stirred in man by love of woman, food, or country. To be assured that this particular felon was paying for his particular crime gratified me, but I knew no apotheosis, however momentary, into godly realms through the instrumentality of torture. I am sorry to tell you, in fact, that the longer I watched him hanging there the more bored I became.

"Finish him off, Ivan," I said. "Pick up the dolls down the hall as agreed. Telman will show you."

"Barbies?"

"Three hundred, in boxes."

"Excellent, Mr. Borodin."

"Come downstairs when you're done, you'll need a drink."

He reached behind the divan and lifted up a meter-length scimitar that possessed a jeweled handle and a blade of shining steel; it appeared to be a museum piece of highest quality, worthy of display in the Kremlin Armory. "A magnificent weapon," said Telman.

"It's been in the family for years," Ivan Ivan claimed.

I helped Telman unroll plastic sheeting beneath Iosif before leaving. "Mind the furniture."

As I closed the door behind me, I stepped directly into Sonya's arms—she'd finished dressing in our flat on the floor above and waited in the hall until I emerged. Before I could express appreciative surprise, she'd fastened her mouth onto mine, and I happily allowed her to suck out my air. For this special evening she had worked herself into her red leather jumpsuit and tall black boots, making me for a time unable to think of anything but carnal pleasures to come.

"I hope it will not be too great a struggle to get this off, Mrs. Boroda."

She shook her head. "You'll have no trouble skinning your cat."

As we kissed once more and I held her close against me, I realized that not even my own eyes told me utter truth—although her suit appeared to be nothing more than an extra layer of epidermis, the material had been cunningly cut in order to artificially lift, separate, and emphasize her provocative features. I sighed; not even Sonya could be as ageless as she appeared to be. But what right did I have to complain? Were I to look too closely and too honestly at myself in a mirror, who would I have seen glaring back? Khrushchev? Beria?

I knew the answer and so tried never to look.

"Tickles," she said, touching her fingers to the mustache I'd grown. It had come in white, but what should I have expected? So I was aging—I would be a good vintage. I was pleased to imagine that my koshka and I might grow old together. "What were you doing in there?"

"Going over the books. Let's go downstairs. The evening is quite a success."

We descended the rear staircase and went into the bar, which was filled to overflowing. I think that two of the many reasons this room proved especially popular were our waiters and waitresses. All were black graduates of Lumumba University, who had not had luck finding jobs in Moscow until I afforded them the opportunity. The waiters wore American marine dress uniforms; the waitresses, gorgeous native African costume. They were far more intelligent and trustworthy than most of our fellow Russians, especially those who work in the service sector (nonobtrusive or otherwise), and possessed an exotic appearance that incited our clientele, male and female, in ways that would cause them to spend more money as they attempted to sublimate socially problematic desires.

Indirect lighting shining through blue filters lent subaqueous ambience to the room. Arteim stood at the long bar, observ-

ing the crowd, talking to Evgeny and Irina. My stylish associate
wore an expensive tuxedo like mine, but I was not surprised to
see that my dear brother had been more inventive in selecting
evening wear. His suit was a glistening gray-green, reminiscent of
polluted sea water. Irina had fitted herself into a strapless silver
lamé gown, which showed to great advantage her powerful back
and shoulder muscles. Most of our male guests wore subdued if
expensive clothing; their women, however, outfitted themselves
in spectacular ensembles: black sheaths that hid the torso and little
else, tall suede boots with spurs, sequined gowns cut to the pubis
in front and the coccyx in back. I wasn't sure how Ivan Ivan would
react, walking into such a gathering, and I hoped he'd remember
his place.

"How is everything?" I asked Arteim. The barmen, seeing
me, stopped juggling bottles long enough to offer bows of respect;
I leaned against the bar and directed them to get back to work.
Sound vibrations shook the counter's wood. The beat of the songs,
so-called, blasting through the room (jungle, according to my beloved music consultant), was so stimulative and so unceasing I
briefly worried that our older guests might suffer cardiac seizures
from mere exposure—but, after due consideration, judged their
escorts to be more hazardous to their health.

"A complete success," Arteim replied, shouting back.

"We should have thought of this years ago," Evgeny said
to me, raising his glass in salute. My koshka smiled at her brother-
in-law as she coyly rubbed her leg against mine; I trembled. "There
are no brothers as smart as mine," he reminded his youthful
protégé.

"No incidents?" There was no danger of our being assaulted
from without; the Kazakhs had long experience in securing the
perimeters of the house and its grounds, and the mines we'd set
into the lawn along the length of the encompassing wall further
assured peace of mind. However, no one can foresee how people
will behave in a sybaritic atmosphere, and so I took further steps
beyond simple disarmament to ensure that no untoward events
would occur inside the club.

"None," Arteim said. "These people are the most of the
most, Max. But our undercover men are scattered throughout, to
be sure." He stood on tiptoe in order to whisper an additional

comment in my ear. "As directed, they are also keeping notes on shameful behavior."

"Excellent." Such irrefutable records could prove useful, later on, when and if we wished to make business arrangements with otherwise hesitant club members—certainly the records could be edited, if need be, by my reliable workers at Universal Manufacturing.

"Look who's here," my koshka said, placing her hand on my chest, deftly prompting me to glance up and over.

"Max!"

I embraced my associate, allowing him to crush me in his usual hearty fashion. It pleased me to see that Petrenko had taken my advice and refrained from bringing either his two-footed or his four-footed dog to this gala occasion.

"What a grotesque saturnalia!" he shouted. "It sickens me. *Bartenders!* Lemon vodka!"

"A bottle," I told them, and they provided. Petrenko pulled off the cap and poured a full glass. He lifted the brim of his fedora to better take in the sight of my koshka, studying her more intently than I would have expected him to do.

"What kind of uniform is this?"

"Private army," she replied. "Would you like to join?"

He blushed, as if his mother had caught him enjoying himself in his room with pornographic pictures. "I'm astonished, Max," he said, turning from her. "This will serve me as the exemplar for all that is wrong in our society."

"Villains wallowing in soul-sapping decadence," I offered, and his eyes glistened with joy—or alcohol; he drained half the glass with his first swallow. "A good investment, Pavel, wouldn't you say?"

"I couldn't be happier," my silent partner said. "Max, I have brought along someone for you to meet. Allow me to introduce you." He snapped his fingers, and an older man wearing a gray suit stepped up to shake my hand. I recognized him at once.

"It is a pleasure to meet the Vice-President," I said, before he could speak. We stared into one another's eyes until he finally turned away and grinned.

"A mutual pleasure," he said. "Allow me to thank you for your remarkable donation to the Armory. Our spirit of appreciation exceeds anything that could be put into mere words."

"What else could a Russian do, finding himself in possession of an irreplaceable exemplar of our noble heritage? Such a treasure belongs where it can be seen and appreciated by the multitudes," I said, knowing full well the Fabergé egg had already been hidden deep within the very bowels of the Kremlin, where it would never be exposed to harmful light again—unless, of course, one of our captains of government had stolen it. "I am sure you will find a way to best express your satisfaction."

"The President looks forward to meeting you next week."

"My heart leaps at the prospect." Petrenko and I glanced at each other and smiled. "Bartender," I commanded. "A toast." Rounds were poured for the Vice-President and myself, and we lifted our glasses. "To Russia." I swallowed my mineral water as he downed his vodka. "Another, please. Tell me, how do you like our club? Have we provided a comfortable environment?"

"I know of nothing better," said the Vice-President, taking in the vision of Sonya. "My God," he whispered, "Oktobriana." She smiled in return and ran her tongue along her lips. I quickly placed my arm around her waist, so that he would not start feeling too comfortable. "A much better idea than that theme park we heard about," he said. "Have you entirely discarded that notion?"

"Not at all. We've had to move up the proposed completion date," I explained. "The property required additional preparation. Sovietland the park will be built one day, as long as we can obtain necessary funding, which is difficult. It is in fact terribly complex."

"Let me speak to the Minister of Finance," he said, sidling over in order to speak quietly into my ear. "I can tell you, Mr. Borodin–"

"Call me Max."

"Max, let me tell you in confidence that the Minister is very pleased with your background and business record. I don't have to tell you, it is not often we see entrepreneurs who attain such rarefied levels of success without mafia assistance."

"We do what we can."

"Undoubtedly he will have suggestions, some advice," the Vice-President said. "I will recommend he consider setting aside funds for assistance."

Ivan Ivan and Telman came into the room, gaping at the

women as if they never before had seen such creatures. It heartened me to see that my associate had convinced Ivan Ivan to change clothes and put on a suit. Even though my conversation with this high official was proving as useful as I had hoped it would be, I thought it best to continue our discussion elsewhere, at a later date. "Splendid," I said, grasping his hand. "When I come to see the President next week, may I drop by your office? There is another matter I should like to talk over with you. A question of finding someone for whom I've been looking for a long time."

"I will set aside a free hour. I'll give you all the help I can."

"And I will leave you with happy memories in return," I said. "Tell me, have you had a chance yet to see all of our club?"

The Vice-President frowned. "Pavel refused to enter the room with the naked hostesses."

"Shameful hoydens," Petrenko said, refilling his glass. Sonya and Irina laughed.

"Arteim," I said. "Would you accompany our guest to the library?"

"I would be honored," he said, and they walked off, the Vice-President's security retinue in tow. Ivan Ivan and Telman made their way to the bar, moments later. Our consultant held tight to the handles of a plastic carrier bag.

"Finished?" He opened the bag and I looked in, careful not to let anyone around me (Sonya, in particular) see what I saw: two pink Barbie boxes. "What is this?"

"Souvenirs." Ivan Ivan reached in and shifted the boxes, giving me a better view. Through the clear cellophane windows I glimpsed two tattooed hands. I looked over at my associate—he shrugged—but I demurred. Had I wanted to keep any part of Iosif, I should have asked for the head.

"Good job," I said to Ivan Ivan. "Telman will tell you where they should be left when he shows you out."

"Keep me in mind, whenever you need assistance. My skills are many."

As Telman led Ivan Ivan away through the crowd, Petrenko leaned over and tapped me on the shoulder. "I thought you and the Vice-President would get along. We've known each other for years; he's a good man. Listen, Max, when does the sport begin?"

"Five minutes," I said, glancing at my watch. "Let's go take our seats. Evgeny, will you be joining us?"

"I think we will go home," my brother said, idly (unconsciously) fiddling with Irina's sequin-hidden nipples as if they were radio knobs. "It's getting late."

"Yes, you should obviously get to bed," I told him. "Good night."

Sonya and I linked arms and followed Petrenko as he elbowed his way through the crowd, past the games of chance, toward the room we called the Betting Circle. Not even the Petrovsky house had space enough for a gymnasium, but sport on a smaller scale could be readily provided for our guests. The door of the Betting Circle was outlined in pink and blue neon; two Kazakhs stood guard, making certain that all who entered had money enough to wager. Murat and Nursultan were formerly the outside gatekeepers, but I judged them deserving of promotion—they at least possessed greater fashion sense than their staff overseer and had had their tuxedos made of black leather, so the superb tailoring could be appreciated.

We stepped inside, evidently the last to arrive. The walls of the Betting Circle were hospital white; in the center of the ceiling was a high-powered halogen lamp, which cast intense light onto the round dirt-floored pit directly below. A dry moat through which the animal handlers moved separated the pit from ten rings of bleachers. A small section at the front was roped off, reserved for my personal guests and myself; the fat asses of our nation's rulers filled the other seats. There were in attendance financial manipulators and stock market officials, military officers and ministry heads, SVRR kingpins and masters of the wholesale trade—the golden youth gone gray—each one accompanied by his own personal Moscow Barbie. They were the elite, truly, but the collective stench in the crowded room may as well have been that of a beer hall's. A swirling blue-gray haze of cigarette smoke fogged the air.

The attendants moved quickly through the narrow aisles, noting and collecting bets. "Fifty!" said one gambler, the new owner of the October chocolate factory. "Eighty," an army general cried out. "Sixty-five!" "Ninety." *"One hundred and twenty!"* The winner would be the one who accurately guessed the final count in advance; he (or she—the women bet as well) would receive all the money wagered. In the case of more than one winner, the pot would be divided equally; if the precise number had not been picked, the money went to the house. As the club's animal handlers tallied the official count, you can probably guess whom the odds favored.

"How good is this first dog, Max?" Petrenko asked me as an attendant came by to take our bets.

"I don't know," I said, speaking honestly. "They are all supposed to be masters in their field, I'm told."

"One hundred and ten," he said, handing the attendant a hundred dollars.

"I say seventy-four," said Sonya, extracting a ten-dollar bill from her *poitrine*. "You're not betting, Max?"

"Gambling holds no charm for me," I said. "I'd rather watch."

The attendants rushed off to count the take, in the company of two of my more trustworthy guards—a certain amount of skimming is to be expected, of course. As they stepped out of the room, two dwarfs waddled in. The little trolls wore cut-down versions of a Cossack's splendid garb, complete with tall fur hats, and leaned long valveless trumpets against their shoulders as if they were rifles. "Ladies and gentlemen," they screeched. "Presenting Champion Rex." Lifting the horns to their mouths, they loudly blew the first call; you would not have imagined they had so much air. One of the animal handlers lifted a shit-brown bull terrier over the shiny glazed walls of the pit, dropping him inside; he sprang up and off the sides, racing back and forth, barking as maniacally as a politician. The audience applauded and cheered wildly, shouting and waving their fists in the air.

"You should bring Pussy Eater here sometime and see how he does," I suggested to Petrenko.

"Not Pussy Eater!" he shouted. "Stormbreeder is my dog's new name. I have told you more than once: Stormbreeder!"

"I forgot."

"He is too valuable and beloved a possession to risk, Max. I couldn't consider it." That saddened me, but as long as I didn't have to see the beast too often, I would live with it. "There is something I want to tell you," he continued. "I am not adept at expressing appreciation, you know. A hard man finds it hard to relate his private emotions to others."

"I understand, Pavel," I said, my suspicions aroused.

"I want to—" He grunted, and then began again. "Listen, thank you for the help you have given me and my party." I relaxed. "Do you know, we have been able to triple our funding through the sale of that bastard's treasures?"

"I thought they would be more readily disposable than that egg."

"By far," he said. "So many of our business and governmental supporters delight in possessing rare items of our national heritage; I would not have guessed. And the prices they pay! You have made them very happy."

"They'll enjoy them as long as they live," I said accurately. Sonya jabbed her elbow into my side. "Thank you for reinvesting some of the money in what will clearly be a thriving concern."

"But a hive of decadence, however profitable. In public, I will have to continue speaking my public mind. I must not go easy on you, Max."

He winked; we smiled. "What are friends for?" I replied.

"*Match!*" the dwarfs cried out and raised their trumpets again; in unison, they issued another ringing blast. Doors in the sides of the pit slid open; the audience shouted in delight and the doomed rodents rushed out, trying and failing to scramble up the walls. Champion Rex snatched them off their scratching feet, sometimes two at a time, snapping their necks and hurling them to the ground. A few of the rats made brave attempts to fight back, leaping onto the terrier's back, trying to fasten their teeth in the dog's short hair or clipped ears—to no avail; the instant they slid off, they were broken.

The crowd stood up to cheer all the more lustily. "More! More!" some shouted. "Stop! Stop!" others cried. Their eyes shone with pleasure and fear as they watched the dog mow through the squirming pile. A number of times Champion Rex shook loose a rat with too much fervor, sending the bloodied corpse into the midst of the bettors. Women screamed each time a rat landed on or near them; their gentlemen, tempers hot as the terrier's, stomped on one another as they fought to be first to flatten the carcasses.

"*Pizdyetz!*" Pavel shouted, shaking his fists in the air as

Champion Rex disposed of the last few rats, scattering the dead as he went for the survivors, adding their blood to that which ran streaming down the walls of the pit. Arteim entered the room, and walked over to where we were sitting, taking a place next to me, while Petrenko continued to stand, waiting with everyone to hear the final tally once the handlers swept up and counted the rats.

"The Vice-President is happy?" I asked.

"He is well satisfied, I'll tell you," my associate said, subtly uncapping a vial and palming a small mirror. I glimpsed my face in the mirror and quickly looked back, into the pit. One of the handlers passed a slip of paper to the shorter of the two dwarfs, and he held up a small fist to gain the crowd's attention.

"One hundred and eighty-three," he cried, and a moan of disappointment rose from the crowd. The attendants began taking the second round of bets while the handlers hosed off the walls of the pit. Petrenko fumbled through his wallet, pulling out another hundred before waving frantically to our attendant.

"Take my bet! One hundred seventy-two!"

"This just came in?" I asked, whispering to Arteim. He nodded and poured a thread of powder onto the mirror he held; inserting a golden straw in his nose, he speedily inhaled the drug. Had it been snowy white, I would have known it was cocaine, intended for the domestic market; but since it was a rich brownish-beige, I knew it was fred—fred as our operatives prepared it—and therefore destined for export to the biggest market of them all. "How is it?"

"Bony," he noted, rubbing his nose. By lifting an eyebrow, I evidently changed my expression just enough to fill his heart with fear. "Gritty, I mean. Gritty." I stroked my mustache as I watched him sitting there silently for a moment or two; then his eyes went out of focus, his breath came faster, and he wordlessly nodded his approval—this latest shipment could be delivered to an anxious world. I whispered a word into my koshka's ear.

"Angel."

She embraced me, revealing a multitude of sharp teeth as she smiled. "Devil."

Where else could I know such bliss? O Russia! Capitalist utopia! Magisterial society! Heaven on earth! *Land of opportunity!* Nothing can be proven, so my conscience is clear.

Afterword

When I first saw Moscow in March 1992, I knew I was finally seeing the world as it is and the world as I perceive it in congruence.

Thanks to Vladimir and Tanya Trofimenko, and to Max Maslakov, for making sure I did not get into much trouble while I was there, and for showing me around their remarkable city. Thanks to Valera, Olga, Ira, and Roman, who also made me feel at home.

Thanks to Alla Verlotskaya and Karen Robson, who arranged the details of my trip and put me in touch with the right people.

Thanks to Nancy Ramsey, my link to America while I was there, who every day was able to tell me what ghastly things I had done the evening before.

Thanks to Edward Pressman and Cotty Chubb, who sent me over.

Many thanks to Rachid Nugmanov, who has helped me better understand both Russians and Kazakhs. There is no *durak* with whom I would rather sit up all night, at a kitchen table in Moscow, thinking about life.

Many thanks to William Gibson, for constant and unwavering support and in particular for originating the idea of radioactive icons, for reminding me of tales told of fred, and for prompting me to think about grit.

Many thanks to Morgan Entrekin and Colin Dickerman, and to everyone at Atlantic Monthly Press.

Many, many thanks and much love to my U.S. agent, John Ware; my British agent, Vivienne Schuster; and my longtime British editor, Jane Johnson, for always believing in what I do and making sure others know it.

Much love, again, to my companion, Carrie Fox.